KISSING A SCOUNDREL

He pulled her away from the wall suddenly and then brought his ankle to her heels, sweeping her feet from beneath her. In a blink, he had lowered her with one arm to the ground, the stones somewhat softened by a thin carpet of old leaves and moss.

"I could scream," she said, but her tone was not at all sincere. She had never felt as alive as she did just then.

"I fully intend for you to," he confided as he leaned more fully onto his left side and reached down with his right arm to snag the hem of her skirts.

"Oliver," she whispered. She had to stop this while she still had some shred of sanity left. "We can't do this."

He went still against her, but she could feel his breaths against her skin, swirling in the hollow behind her ear.

"Yes, we can," he whispered as he began kissing her once again . . .

Books by Heather Grothaus

THE WARRIOR

THE CHAMPION

THE HIGHLANDER

TAMING THE BEAST

NEVER KISS A STRANGER

NEVER SEDUCE A SCOUNDREL

HIGHLAND BEAST
(with Hannah Howell and Victoria Dahl)

Published by Kensington Publishing Corporation

NEVER SEDUCE A SCOUNDREL

Heather Grothaus

ZEBRA BOOKS
KENSINGTON PUBLISHING CORP.
http://www.kensingtonbooks.com

ZEBRA BOOKS are published by

Kensington Publishing Corp.
119 West 40th Street
New York, NY 10018

All Kensington titles, imprints, and distributed lines are available at special quantity discounts for bulk purchases for sales promotion, premiums, fund-raising, educational, or institutional use.

Special book excerpts or customized printings can also be created to fit specific needs. For details, write or phone the office of the Kensington Special Sales Manager: Attn. Special Sales Department. Kensington Publishing Corp., 119 West 40th Street, New York, NY 10018. Phone: 1-800-221-2647.

Zebra and the Z logo Reg. U.S. Pat. & TM Off.

ISBN-13: 978-1-4201-1243-6
ISBN-10: 1-4201-1243-0

First Printing: March 2012

10 9 8 7 6 5 4 3 2 1

Printed in the United States of America

For Brandi Clopein.
Mushy!

Chapter 1

February 2, 1277
Fallstowe Castle, England

Cecily Foxe was fairly certain she was going to hell.

She had been standing alone for the better part of two hours following the lavish supper, struggling to maintain a serene expression while she watched the revelers and their atrocious behavior. It was proving increasingly difficult. Men drank so heartily and hastily that the fronts of their tunics were dark with wine, and most women recklessly attempted to keep pace with them. Unmarried couples danced, although the lewd displays of bodies touching so intimately could hardly be defined as a supposedly innocent activity.

Cecily bristled as she watched even the least of the nobility, the humble, the homely, the meek, carry on with members of the opposite sex. Even poor Lady Angelica, who had a lazy eye and spat upon anyone unfortunate enough to be engaged in conversation with her, was being twirled about Fallstowe's great hall with sordid abandon. Cecily had clearly seen the young man currently in possession of Lady Angelica unabashedly grasp the woman's breast.

Only Cecily stood alone.

No one had asked her to dance. No young lord dared come near and whisper lurid suggestions to her, proposing they steal away from the hall for an hour of private sin. She was a lady of Fallstowe, wealthy beyond comprehension, powerful by her connection to Sybilla, perhaps even wanted as a criminal by the Crown. Unmarried. Both her eyes pointed in the same direction and she kept her saliva properly in her mouth when speaking.

And yet they all simply pretended she wasn't there.

To everyone who knew her—nay, even knew *of* her—she was Saint Cecily. Middle daughter of Amicia and Morys Foxe. Slated for a life of quiet, gentle sacrifice. Although she had yet to formally commit to the convent, Cecily already fulfilled many of the obligations put upon one under holy orders. Up to even the wee hours of that very morn, she had assisted Father Perry in the countless and tedious preparations for the Candlemas feast; and in general, she looked over Fallstowe's charitable responsibilities, tended the ill and dying, duteously prayed the liturgy of the hours.

Most of them, any matter.

She seldom raised her voice in a passion of any nature. She did not lie, nor indulge in gossip. She was obedient to her older sister, Sybilla, the head of the family now that both of their parents were dead. She was not ostentatious in either dress or temperament, preferring to wear costumes so closely akin to the habits of the committed that strangers to the hold often greeted her with a deferential incline of their heads and a murmured, "God's blessing upon you, Sister."

Cecily knew she was admired and even revered for her restraint and decorum. She was not outwardly bold, like young Alys, seen now dancing gaily with her new husband in the middle of the crush of guests. She was not obviously ambitious like the eldest, Sybilla, who ruled Fallstowe with a delicate iron fist. Cecily had spent the greater part of her score and two years carefully cultivating her gentle qualities. Molding herself to them.

And yet, at that very moment, her supposedly meek heart was so full of discord, she was quite surprised that she had not already burst into flames where she stood.

The dancers continued to whirl past, little carousels of gaiety and color around massive iron cauldrons that blazed with fires fed by the brown and brittle swags of evergreen and holly that had festooned Fallstowe's great hall since Christmas. Although the blessed candles burned in their posts, the remainder of the celebration was largely pagan, bidding farewell to the barren winter while at once beckoning to the fertile light of spring. Cecily knew that her elder sister had purposefully sought to emphasize the heathen aspect of the celebration—unfortunately, Sybilla seemed to thrive on wicked rumor.

The Foxe matriarch herself weaved through the crowd now, both adoration and jealousy following close at her heels as she made her way toward Cecily. The men hungered for Sybilla—those few who'd once held her let their eyes blatantly show the aching memories of their hearts, and the many who had not been honored with the privilege of her bed pursued her without a care for their pride. Sybilla was powerful, desirable; Cecily was not.

As if to emphasize this point, Cecily again caught a glimpse of the primary object of her bitterness.

Oliver Bellecote.

He could have been your husband, a wicked little voice whispered in her ear.

"Hello, darling." Sybilla had at last fought her way through the pulsating throng to stand at Cecily's side, her slender arm pulling the two sisters together at the hip. "I would have thought you to be abed an hour ago."

Cecily was careful to keep her tone light. "This may well be my last feast at Fallstowe, Sybilla. I would remember it."

Sybilla gave her sister's waist a gentle squeeze, but did not comment on Cecily's reference to Hallowshire Abbey. The two women observed the debauchery that ruled the supposedly holy day feast in silence for several moments. Then Oliver Bellecote whirled past once more, causing Cecily to lose control of her suddenly wicked tongue.

"I am quite surprised to see him," she said, thankful that, at least, her tone was casual.

"Who? Oliver?" Cecily felt more than saw Sybilla's shrug. After a moment, she said quietly, "I suppose I must call him Lord Bellecote now."

Cecily's heart thudded faster in her chest, and her indignation made pulling in her next breath difficult. "August has not been dead a month, and yet he is here—still behaving as if he hasn't a care in the world or one whit of responsibility. It's indecent and disrespectful. To his brother and to you."

Sybilla drew away slightly, and Cecily could feel her sister's frosty blue gaze light the side of her face. Cecily's ear practically tingled. She hadn't meant for her comment to come out that way at all.

"I am not offended by Oliver's presence, Cee, nor by him enjoying himself at Fallstowe. Although 'tis no secret that Oliver oft exasperated him, August loved his younger brother. And Oliver loved August."

Cecily turned to look at Sybilla, the question out before she could restrain herself. "Did *you* love August?"

For the briefest instant, Sybilla's lips thinned and a fleeting fire came into her eyes. But then it was gone, replaced by a washed-out melancholy that wrenched at Cecily's heart.

"No, Cee. I did not," she admitted as she turned her attention back to the crowd, now dispersing from the center of the hall as the music came to an end. The guests seemed only able to communicate in shouts and shrill laughter that sounded to Cecily like tortured screams. Yet she heard her sister's low murmurs as if the two women stood alone in a cupboard. "I'm certain you pity me now."

"No, not pity," Cecily insisted. "I only worry for you. I was with the two of you the last time August was at Fallstowe, Sybilla—I remember."

"As do I." Sybilla's eyes scanned the crowd disinterestedly. "I told him not to come back."

"You didn't mean it, though."

"Oh, but I did," Sybilla argued, quickly but with

her signature coolness. "And now he never *will* come back. Now Oliver is Lord of Bellemont, a position I know from his brother that he never wanted, and is perhaps ill-equipped to fill. Oliver deserves a final farewell to his carefree existence before he truly dons the mantle of responsibility over such a large hold. Perhaps he'll marry Lady Joan Barleg now— Bellemont needs heirs." She paused as if thinking, and when she again spoke her voice was low. "It gladdens me to see him at Fallstowe."

"It wasn't your fault, Sybilla." Cecily had forgotten her selfish pity at the thought that she had caused her sister to relive such sad memories. "You did nothing to cause August's death. 'Twas a terrible accident, and that is all."

"Hmm. Well, perhaps you should pray for my soul, any matter."

Cecily tore her gaze away from her sister's pale, enigmatic profile as the dancers reformed at the opening notes of the next piece. "I do hope he *does* marry Lady Joan," she said abruptly. "He's been toying about with the poor girl for the past two years. She must be completely humiliated. Are they already betrothed?"

Sybilla chuckled. "Oliver took nothing from Joan Barleg that she didn't freely offer him, and now that he's Lord of Bellemont, she has the chance to better her station immensely. Had Oliver been first-born instead of August, Lady Joan would have had little chance of winning him." A faint smile remained on her lips. "You likely don't remember, but there was talk of a betrothal between you and Oliver when you were children."

Cecily indeed remembered, but she gripped her tongue between her teeth painfully. Should Sybilla continue to goad her so, Cecily would end up as Lady Angelica, spitting her words rather than speaking them.

Sybilla continued in a bored tone when Cecily gave no comment. "It would be quite the coup d'état for Joan. But I have heard no formal announcement from either of them as of yet, so who can know?"

As if their talk had summoned him, Oliver Bellecote himself slid between a pair of dancers, becoming momentarily entangled in their arms. The three shared a raucous laugh as he extracted himself with a lewd pinch to the woman's buttock, his chalice held high above his head to preserve the wine contained within. Cecily felt her diaphragm shrivel up uncomfortably at his approach.

Then he was before them both, bowing drunkenly, his lips crooked in a cocky grin beneath the close shadow on his face. His brown eyes were like muddy pools powdered with gold dust—dark and dirty and deep, the bright sparkle hiding what lay beneath. His thick black lashes clustered like reedy sentries, both beckoning and guarding at once.

"Lady Sybilla," he sighed, drawing up Sybilla's hand beneath his face and kissing the back of her palm loudly three times.

Cecily rolled her eyes and sighed.

Sybilla only laughed. "Lord Bellecote, you flatter me."

He should have risen then. Instead, he dropped to one knee, pulling Sybilla's hand to his bosom and then lowering his chin awkwardly to kiss her fingers once more before raising his slender, strikingly handsome face to gaze adoringly at Cecily's sister.

"Lady Sybilla Foxe, my most gorgeous, tempting hostess! Won't you marry me?"

Cecily gasped.

Sybilla threw back her head and laughed even louder, and although it was likely only the candlelight and smoke, Cecily thought she saw a glistening of tears in Sybilla's eyes.

"Is that a no?" Oliver asked, feigning shock.

"Guard your honor well, Lady Sybilla!" a female's gay shout rang out, and Cecily looked up in time to see the comely Joan Barleg skip past them in the arms of her dance partner, her golden curls spilling recklessly from her simple crispinette. She looked so carefree and . . . at ease. Cecily's spine stiffened further.

Sybilla gave the woman a wink and raised a palm in acknowledgment. She then looked back down at the still-kneeling Oliver Bellecote.

"It is a no," she affirmed.

To Cecily's horror, Oliver Bellecote gave a horrendous wail—as if he'd been shot with an arrow—and then collapsed fully onto his back, the drink inside his chalice still miraculously maintaining the level.

"I am crushed! *Defeated!*" he shouted in mock agony. Several guests were now pointing and laughing at the display he presented on the stones. He raised his head abruptly, took a noisy swallow, and then looked at Sybilla. "Will you at least sleep with me then? Completely inappropriate, I know, considering our very slight degree of separation, but I fear I am now considered quite eligible."

"Oh, this is truly too much," Cecily gritted out from between her teeth. Her cheeks felt as if they were on fire.

Sybilla cocked her head and gave him a sympathetic smile. "Sorry, Oliver."

His forehead wrinkled, giving him the appearance of a chastised pup. "Damn my slothly feet—you're already spoken for."

"I'm afraid so," Sybilla answered.

"Sybilla!" Cecily hissed, outraged that her sister would have such an inappropriate conversation—even in jest—with this man where any could overhear their lewd banter. This man *in particular.*

"Forgive me, Cee," Sybilla conceded, turning amused eyes to her sister while Lord Bellecote staggered to his feet.

Cecily squared her shoulders, somewhat placated that Sybilla had at last remembered both her station and her very public venue.

"How thoughtless of me," Sybilla continued. "Lord Bellecote, I *am* engaged with other business this night, but I believe Lady Cecily, however, is thus far unattended."

Cecily's entire body went ice cold. She was unsure whether she would cry or throw up.

Oliver Bellecote had tardily gained his feet, brushing at his pants with his free hand. Sybilla's flip invitation caused his movements to freeze. He slowly raised his face until his eyes met Cecily's.

She would have gasped had she been able to draw breath. His direct gaze was like witnessing lightning striking the ocean. The first thought that

came into her mind was, *Why, he's as lonely as I am.*
Her stomach hardened into a pained little stone.
She wanted to scream at him to stop looking at her,
wanted to turn and berate Sybilla for drawing her
into such an indecent exhibition—

—she wanted Oliver Bellecote to suggest something inappropriate to her so that she might agree.

Oliver's eyes flicked to Sybilla's and in that next
instant, both the notorious nobleman and Cecily's
sister burst out in peals of laughter.

"I am sorry to tease you so, Oliver," Sybilla chuckled, drawing her arm back around Cecily's middle,
and Cecily hung a brittle, fragile smile on her numb
lips. "My dearest sister would not have the likes of
you wrapped up in the holy shroud itself."

"Nor should she," Oliver agreed with a naughty
grin and deep bow in Cecily's direction, although
his eyes did not look at her directly again. "Alas, I
am not worthy of such a gentle lady's attention, as
our wise parents decided so long ago."

Sybilla quirked an eyebrow. "Yet you are worthy
of my attention?"

The rogue winked at Cecily's sister. "One must
never cease to aspire to the heights of one's potential." He bowed again. "Ladies." And then he slipped
back into the writhing crowd with all the grace of a
serpent in the garden.

Cecily felt her eyes swelling with tears, and she
swallowed hard.

Sybilla sighed. "Perhaps he— Cee? Cee, are you
all right?"

"Of course, Sybilla. I'm fine."

Sybilla's expression turned uncharacteristically sympathetic. "I'm sorry. You appeared so forlorn standing there, I only wanted you to join in a bit of merrymaking."

How would you have me join in? Cecily screamed in her head. *No one will so much as speak to me, and I've just been rejected by the most notorious womanizer outside of London!*

But she pulled together every last scrap of her dignity to give Sybilla a smile. "I'm fine, Sybilla. Don't apologize. It was . . . it was amusing." She tried to laugh but it came out a weak, stuttering breath. Cecily pulled away from her sister slowly, deliberately. "It *is* late. I am off to Compline and then my own bed."

Sybilla's fine brow creased, and Cecily leaned in and pressed her cheek to her sister's. "Don't worry so. Would that you ask Alys and Piers to wait for me in the morn so that I might bid them farewell. I fear 'twould take me an hour to find them tonight in the crush."

"Of course," Sybilla promised. "Good night, Cee."

Cecily could not return the sentiment, as it had been anything but for her, and so she simply smiled again and walked away.

She made her way around the perimeter of the hall beneath the musicians' arched balcony, excusing herself quietly around little clusters of people oblivious to her passing, until she at last came to the lord's dais—Sybilla's dais now. The stacks of tables and benches cleared away from the great hall floor to give the dancers room felt like a haven, a fortress, shielding Cecily from the cruel celebration as she ducked through the hidden door set in the rear wall.

The stone corridor was cool and blessedly unoccupied, a welcome relief from the humid cacophony of the feast. Cecily's footsteps were quick and quiet as she made her way to her rooms to fetch her cloak for the walk across the bailey to the chapel.

He hadn't considered her for one instant, even in jest.

She reached her chamber and stepped inside, forcing herself to close the door gently, when what she wanted to do was slam it loose from its hinges. She crossed the floor to the wardrobe.

She didn't understand why she was so completely and suddenly enraged. She had decided her path long ago, even if she had dragged her feet in formally committing. She loved the peace of a prayerful life, found meaning in service. The beauty and wonder of the world—and its wickedness too— explained and supported by faith. In pledging herself to the religious, her life would forever be simple, predictable. Peaceful.

Cecily found her cloak easily among her few gowns and pulled it out. She held the worn material in her hands and looked down at it, musing suddenly that the old cloak was not unlike her life in the present— the weave coming slowly apart, rubbed thin and transparent in places, the hem ragged and uneven. In truth, the garment was much too short for her now. She hadn't noticed before that moment how shabby it had become, although when her mother had sewn the final stitches, it had been quite enviable.

She realized that had been ten years ago. Had any at Fallstowe known peace since then?

Her parents had seen little peace while they'd lived. Morys Foxe had held Fallstowe against the Barons and with King Henry III, and then after that weak monarch's death, as well as Morys's own, Amicia had seized the reins of Fallstowe in bitter defiance of the king's son, who thought her a spy against the Crown. And now that Amicia was gone, Sybilla had taken up their mother's dangerous banner, rebelling against Edward I so that Cecily was certain the consequences would be most dire.

Alys was safe now that she was married with the king's own blessing, yes. But what of Sybilla? Her pride would never allow for surrender to Edward's demands, no matter how rich and well-tended the monarch promised to leave her. Cecily did not often dwell on the possibilities that lay in store for her older sister, although she knew they were quite real, and more pressing now than ever. Alys and Piers had carried rumors from London of a siege only two months ago. Sybilla could be imprisoned.

She could be put to death.

One of her sisters was a solitary warrior, the other now a simple farmer's wife. Cecily was truly in the middle, and not just because of the order of her birth. She could not choose either path—to fight or to surrender. And so she had chosen the only other option that was likely to bring her peace—

She had become invisible. And for years, her inconspicuousness had served her well.

Then why was she, this night, so very unhappy? So atypically discontented, and even envious of the carefree and pretty Joan Barleg, of all people? And why was she so put out at the thought that a man who would lie naked with a donkey paid her no mind?

Cecily wondered for the hundredth time this evening how her life would have been different if she and Oliver Bellecote had married. Would they be happy? In all likelihood, she would still be known by the hated moniker of Saint Cecily, if only because people would surely look upon her with pity at being married to such a scoundrel as Oliver Bellecote.

The terribly handsome, lonely scoundrel.

She sniffed loudly and then wiped at her face with the hem of her cloak before swirling it around her shoulders. She turned to the little plain clay dish on the table near her bed to retrieve her prayer beads.

This will all have passed away by the morn, she reasoned with herself. After all, Alys had been in the very depths of despair when she thought she was to marry against her will, and Alys had gone on to meet her husband at the F—

Cecily's head came up. Her chamber was as silent as the bottom of a well.

"The Foxe Ring," she whispered aloud, and brought her fingers to her mouth, the smooth, round beads in her hand pressing against her lips, as if trying too late to stifle her words.

The old ring of standing stones at the crumbling Foxe ruin was rumored to be a magic place. Men and women throughout the land had used the mysterious circle for generations in order to find a mate. The legend was unlikely, yes, but Alys had gone, and Piers had found her in the midst of a very unlikely set of circumstances.

Perhaps . . . perhaps Hallowshire *wasn't* Cecily's true vocation, which might explain her sudden, fierce reluctance. Perhaps she, too, should visit the Foxe Ring. Perhaps—

Cecily dropped her hands and her gaze went to the floor while she shook her head. "Superstitious nonsense," she said sternly, quietly. "Likely a sin, as well." Hadn't she herself warned Alys of such on the very night her younger sister set out for the ring?

But weren't you also wrong then? a little voice whispered in her ear.

She tried to ignore it.

Besides, the moon wasn't even full presently, as the legend commanded. It wouldn't be full again for a fortnight, and by that time, her letter of intent would be firmly in the hands of the kindly and elderly abbess, and this indecisive madness that had suddenly seized her would be naught but a faint and unpleasant memory.

Cecily took a deep breath and blew it out with rounded cheeks. Then she walked determinedly to the door and quit her chamber, her feet carrying her purposefully toward the wing of the castle that would allow her to exit in the bailey closest to the chapel. The sounds of the feast behind her—

the shouts and laughter—chased her from her home in diminishing whispers until she was running, and she burst through the stubborn wooden door with a gasp, as if coming up from the bottom of a lake.

The bailey was empty, the sky above black and pin-pricked with a hundred million stars. Her panting breaths clouded around her head as she recalled her mother telling her that the night sky was a protective blanket between the earth and heaven's blinding glory. Starlight were angels peeking through the cloth.

The thought led Cecily's mind to another faded, bittersweet memory—herself and her two sisters, as girls, playing at the abandoned keep. It was spring-time, and Cecily, Alys—she could have been no more than four—and even Sybilla collected long, spindly wildflowers, yellow and white, while Amicia watched benevolently from the shade of a nearby tree.

The girls weaved in and out of the tall, standing stones, singing a song Amicia had taught them, their arms full of ragged blooms.

> *One, two, me and you,*
> *Tre, four, forever more,*
> *Five, six, the stones do pick,*
> *Seven, eight, 'tis my fate,*
> *Nine, ten, now I ken.*

Cecily stared up at the sky for a long time.

When her heart beat slowly once more, she began walking determinedly toward the chapel—the exact opposite direction of the Foxe Ring, which seemed to be sending out ghostly echoes of that almost forgotten childhood song. As penance for her sinful thoughts and desires, Cecily decided then that she would specifically pray for Oliver Bellecote. Surely that would be akin to wearing a hair shirt.

Any matter, she would *not* be going to the Foxe Ring.

She stopped at the doors to the chapel, the night still around her, as if the angels above the blanket of sky held their breath and watched her to see what she would do. Her hand gripped the latch.

Cecily looked slowly, hesitantly, over her shoulder.

Chapter 2

She prayed Compline (the seventh canonical hour). And she felt somewhat better afterward, although by the time she whispered the final *amen,* her skin was numb from the chill wind that had persistently breathed through her thin, worn cloak, and an ache had crept into her legs from the clammy circles made by her knees pressing into the damp ground. She sensed the solid mass of the Foxe Ring's center stone at her back, although she wasn't touching it, and she certainly wasn't facing it as if it were a proper altar—God forbid the very idea. The slab of rock was nothing more than a convenient place to set the small oil lamp she'd borrowed from the hook outside the chapel doors, the tiny light as effective as a single candle flame in the vastness of an inky ocean.

She looked up from her beads to the rock summits of the rectangular standing stones, carved into a midnight sky black with a new moon. What a contradiction she was, praying in a location full of superstitious magic, looking for a miracle in the midst of a legend, hoping for wisdom in a place of blind divining. What would Father Perry think if he could see her in this moment?

But Amicia Foxe had taught that God was everywhere, and Cecily still believed her mother. And she couldn't help but think that there was a reason for her to come to the Foxe Ring, even if it was only to clear her head. Cecily certainly did not expect to be happened upon by an eligible nobleman. Even if she was, the man would likely only ask Cecily the way to the nearest town.

Which would be quite ironic, she thought, as it was she who so desperately needed direction.

"Where is my place?" she asked the sky, directing her question well above the taint of the stones. "Who am I to be, and where do I belong?"

The night air answered her with only the quiet sigh of a sleeping babe.

Cecily dropped her gaze back to her hands upon her thighs, still clutching her beads in cold fingers. Her knees and legs throbbed now from the damp cold. She blew out a short breath through her nose and then gained her feet. Looping her string of beads around her palm, she backed up against the fallen down slab of rock in the center of the ring and heaved herself up to sit atop it, her slippered feet swinging idly beneath its edge. The glowing oil lamp scattered uneasy flickers of light over the cold, gray stone.

"Still waiting," she called out pointedly to no one in particular. "Very patiently, I might add. It's quite cold." She whistled a short trill of merry notes, rubbed her palms across her thighs briskly. "Waiting, waiting . . . oh, come on! A lightning bolt? Earth tremble? I would settle for a plague of frogs at this point!"

She'd not had time for another properly dramatic sigh when she heard faint hoofbeats.

Her brow crinkled and she frowned as she looked through the standing stones opposite her, but the blackness revealed no rider. Only the distant whispering of a horse at full gallop, somewhere beyond the ring. Distant now, but drawing quickly nearer.

She looked up at the night sky warily. "Really?"

Perhaps it was a soldier come to fetch her home. Perhaps there was some emergency at Fallstowe and Sybilla needed her.

No. No one knew where she was, and even should someone be searching for her, the Foxe Ring would be the very last location any who knew her would think to look. Besides, when was the last time Sybilla—or anyone else, for that matter—had ever really needed her?

Cecily's heart beat faster, keeping time, it seemed, with the furious pounding of hooves. She could hear the ragged breaths of the horse, so close was she to at last seeing her visitor.

The muzzle pushed between two stones as the horse penetrated the circle, flared nostrils, deep brown mane flying wildly over the reins behind its elongated neck. The cloaked figure astride pulled up hard on the tethers, causing the mount to rear slightly before stamping and dancing to a halt before Cecily.

Although Cecily recognized the beast as one of

Fallstowe's own, it was not Octavian, Sybilla's mount, nor was it one of the soldiers' geldings. Cecily raised her eyes to the shadowed triangle of hood belonging to the slender rider. In the next instant, a cloaked arm raised and threw back the hood.

"Lady Cecily!" the rider gasped, and in that moment, Cecily wanted to lie down atop the pagan monument on which she sat and die.

Joan Barleg smiled down. "You are the last person I would ever imagine to happen upon at the Foxe Ring! Are you all right?"

"Good evening, Lady Joan," Cecily said lightly, as if the two women were meeting over a meal in Fallstowe's great hall. "Yes, I'm quite fine, thank you. Only taking some air." She tried to return the young woman's smile.

Lady Joan's eyes narrowed as she turned her head to look sideways at Cecily, and then she leaned slightly over the horse's neck. "You do know that the moon is not full this night, do you not?"

Cecily felt as though Joan Barleg had just informed her that Cecily was out of doors in only her underclothes. "I fail to see what that has to do with anything," Cecily choked out, striving to keep her voice level. "Why would I have a care for what phase the moon was in, Lady Joan?"

Joan's eyes widened and then she gave a tinkling laugh to the black sky. "*Of course* you don't! How silly of me," she chuckled again, and then gave Cecily a mischievous grin. "I only thought about the old legend and that perhaps—but no." Her blond curls bounced on her shoulders and Cecily noticed that the woman's simple headpiece was now completely missing from her artfully mussed hair. "I apologize if I have offended you."

Cecily gave a silent sigh of relief. "Don't trouble your—" she began.

"Oliver has always said that you are too good for any mortal man, so the idea that you would come to the Foxe Ring looking for a husband is completely ridiculous, of course. Coolish like your sister, and isn't it fitting for the pair of you?" The woman laughed again. "To think that— Oh, my! I've had too much to drink and it is affecting my judgment!"

Cecily could not even swallow, let alone think of a single reply to the woman's statements.

People thought her to be like Sybilla?

At that moment, the faint sound of hoofbeats once more wound their way through the stones, and Lady Joan's face swung away from Cecily to look over her mount's rear. When she looked to Cecily again, her eyes were merry.

"I must be back to Fallstowe before he catches me. He's so drunk, I don't know how he is still sitting his horse," she confided with an indulgent grin. And then her innocent-looking eyes caught a shade of devilment. "Although he has been much drunker and managed to stay erect before."

Cecily's stomach lurched.

Joan wheeled her horse around. "Good night, Lady Cecily, and good luck in your many holy endeavorations. Pray for Oliver and me if you think of it— We'll get married, you know."

"Joan!" The hoarse male cry sounded faint and far.

"You certainly were made for each other," Cecily quipped before she could think better of it.

"Why, thank you, Lady Cecily," the woman said softly and with a surprised smile. "Your blessing is almost as good as a priest's."

"*Joan!* Where are you, blasted woman?"

The blond woman shouted into the blackness. "This way! If you catch me you can keep me—forever!" She turned her head, gave Cecily a saucy wink, and then kicked at her horse's sides. The mount sprang into a run, kicking up clods of soft, damp dirt before bolting past the center stone and out of the Foxe Ring.

Cecily could have been carved out of the same stone upon which she sat, so still was she. Her whole body was numb, and not entirely from the cold wind that played the standing stones like a pipe. But her heart still pounded in her chest.

He would ride right past her. He would disappear into the night, chasing Joan Barleg, having never known she was there. And that was the very best thing, in Cecily's opinion. Let him tell his drunken mates that she was too good for a man's attentions. Cecily understood now—she was but a caricature to make fun of, mock. Ha-ha, frigid Cecily, isn't she odd?

She would send her letter of intent to the abbess at Hallowshire with the rising sun.

She could feel the reverberations of the approaching horse through the stone. Surely he would gain the top of the small rise and then swerve around the ring to chase after his betrothed.

She heard the horse's scream in the same moment the beast's head and forelegs came into view just inside the standing ring. Cecily saw its knees lock, its legs elongating, deep furrows of dirt ploughed up and over its hooves like soft, short boots. The horse stopped.

Its rider did not.

A black, tentacled mass flew through the air in a high arc, and although Cecily expected some sort of cry of dismay, the rider's flight was silent, if supremely energetic. Perhaps he thought to sprout wings at the last moment and float safely to the ground.

Cecily let her head turn and follow the human projectile. She flinched as the body collided with the center stone on which she sat, mayhap only two feet away from her. She heard a sick, solid snap, and then the body rebounded to the dirt beneath her slippers, motionless.

She leaned forward slightly to look down upon Oliver Bellecote, his slender, handsome face pale as milk, his full lips slack, his reedy lashes resting on his cheeks. His cloak was spread out on the ground behind him, like the wings he was woefully lacking, his shirt pulled open in a deep V, revealing one sculpted pectoral muscle and shoulder.

"Are you dead?" she inquired.

The body did not move.

Cecily leaned back into her upright position and then stretched out her foot and ankle, nudging Oliver Bellecote's hip with the toe of her slipper. His torso rocked, and he gave a ghostly moan.

"I suppose not," she said grimly.

His eyelids fluttered open, and his eyes rolled back in his skull as if attempting to ascertain the damage sustained with his pitifully small brain. He blinked his gaze aright with effort and then seemed to try to focus on her.

"Lady Cecily?" he whispered incredulously, then he squeezed his eyes shut again slowly as if in great pain. Cecily supposed that he was. *"Fuck me!"* he gasped, bringing his left hand across his chest to grab at his right bicep.

One of Cecily's eyebrows lifted.

Oliver's head swam a bit. His arm hurt. He felt a pinching of sorts on the right side of his ribs with every breath. He looked up at the serene woman still looking down at him from her perch upon the wide slab of rock.

Saint Cecily Foxe.

In that moment, Oliver had never seen the woman look quite so . . . unconcerned. Considering that he had just been thrown from his horse and now lay sprawled on the ground in pain, he was surprised at her lack of empathy. Wasn't she honor-bound to aid those in need? Yet she only looked down upon him as if he were little more than an interesting breed of dog that had wandered over and flopped down at her feet.

"Aren't you going to help me up?" he asked.

Her brow creased slightly, perhaps tardy concern at last, and Oliver couldn't help but notice again how much she resembled her older sister, Sybilla. They shared the same ivory face, the same thick, mahogany hair. But where Sybilla Foxe's eyes were eerie, blue ice chips, Cecily's face boasted big, warm pools of chocolate. Sybilla was charming, bold, seductive, powerful; Cecily was meek, dutiful, chaste. Even his older brother, August, had sung Cecily's praises while head over heels in love with the Ice Queen, and so Oliver could not understand the chill coming from the woman now.

She gave a little sniff, and her forehead smoothed as she turned her face up to the sky. "I do think it's beginning to rain."

In the next instant, he felt a cold splash on his cheek. *Perfect.*

He levered himself onto his left elbow and then struggled to pull his knees beneath him. The right side of his chest seared. Keeping his right arm close to his side, he pushed off from the ground with his left hand and rose slowly, his whole body swaying and his head spinning sickly while two more drops plopped onto his scalp through his hair. His cloak seemed to be attempting to choke him, topple him, and so he reached up with his left hand and jerked the clasp loose, letting the heavy garment fall to the ground.

"Where's my horse?" he muttered, looking around him, and wondering how he had managed to be found inside an old ring of stones alone with Cecily Foxe, who continued to eye him coolly.

"It wasn't actually your horse though, was it?" she parried. "Any matter, he ran off the instant he had unseated you. He's likely halfway back to Fallstowe by now."

"Perfect," he said, aloud this time. Then he turned his head back gingerly to look at the supposedly godly woman seated on the stone slab. "What about your mount? Or did you come on your broom?"

She shook her head and then smiled serenely. "I walked. Human legs work in nearly the same capacity in moving one from place to place as horses', in case you didn't know."

He shot her what he hoped was a sarcastic smile. "Helpful. Thank you."

"You're quite welcome." She nodded toward his upper body. "It's broken."

"It isn't," he argued curtly. "Only sprained. Fuck!" The rain now made little pitter-patters on the stones and ground at his feet. The flame in the oil lamp sputtered. She was sliding off the stone now to her feet, and so he took a step toward her. "I seem to have lost my bearings. Which way to Fallstowe?"

She casually picked up the oil lamp and then turned to face him. After a moment, she extended her free arm to point generally behind her.

"And it *is* broken," she insisted. "I've tended many injuries like it, and so I can tell you with a fair amount of certainty that, combined with the bump you took on your empty skull, you are in shock. If you attempt to walk back to Fallstowe in the cold rain, you'll likely die." She blinked, gave him that serene smile again. "Please, be my guest, though."

Oliver frowned. "I know I'm drunk, but what's come over you, Lady Cecily? On every other occasion of our meeting, you have only been sincere and accommodating. What have I done to offend you so besides getting thrown from my horse?"

Cecily shrugged. "Oh, I am quite sincere, I promise you. Perhaps I simply have run through my stores of hospitality for Sybilla's addlepated and selfish guests. And as for you getting thrown from your horse, what kind of sympathy do you expect from me? Apparently you yourself have no regard for the possible outcomes of such an accident. That is the way in which your brother only very recently died, and yet you cavort about Fallstowe in the dead of night, soaked in drink, and on an unfamiliar horse."

Oliver's blood, until very recently heated by drink and pain, ran cold. He shook his head, hoping the motion and the cold rain would clear it, but it only brought a sickening ache.

"What did you just say to me?"

"Why? Did you find it *cold*?" She gave a little chuckle, but her eyes were hard. "You heard me correctly, *Lord Bellecote*."

"What a right bitch you have turned out to be, when away from your den," Oliver said hoarsely, more than a little nonplussed.

"Then that shall be yet another trait Sybilla and I have in common, no?" She turned and began to walk in the direction opposite from where she had indicated Fallstowe Castle lay.

"You've had everyone fooled, haven't you?" he called to her retreating back, even though he still felt that he was in the grip of some nonsensical nightmare. "Pure, sweet, innocent Saint Cecily—so far removed from her sisters and the rumors of witchcraft! And where do I happen upon you?" he demanded, looking around him and recognizing at last where they were. "The magical Foxe Ring, with your prayer beads clasped in your hand! I can see

the damp patches on your skirts, Lady Cecily—
giving the Devil his due, were you?"

Cecily Foxe stopped, and for a moment she was
absolutely still. Then she slowly turned to face him,
holding the lamp in one hand, the flame revealing
her face in an almost ethereal glow. The rain came
down in a steady shower now, and yet her hair, her
shoulders, did not appear the least bit damp.

"Jealous?" she asked, and then gave him a slow
smile.

Oliver felt his head draw back as if she had
reached out the twenty or so feet that separated
them and slapped him. A strange sensation tingled
in his spine, and perhaps it was only the drink and
the pain that was affecting him, but the front of his
breeches felt uncomfortably tight. He had the odd
compulsion to march up to her and insult her
again, so that she might truly strike him.

He suddenly craved a very physical altercation
with Cecily Foxe.

She turned once more and began walking away.

"Where are you going?" he demanded.

She didn't answer him. The light of the oil lamp
bobbed, dimmed, and then seemed to disappear altogether.

Oliver was left in the cold rain, the darkness pressing against him like an invisible, malevolent entity.

"Cecily!" he shouted, and then winced and
brought his left hand to his head briefly.

The only reply he received was the shush of the
rain on the stones of the Foxe Ring, as if they were
warning him to be quiet, be still.

Oliver felt as though his world had been poured into a sack, shaken enthusiastically, and then dumped out on the wet ground. He had left Fallstowe pleasantly inebriated, able-bodied, on horseback, and chasing after Joan Barleg—the very reason he had drank so much in the first place. But the blasted woman had taken his pursuit as nothing more than another game.

Now, he was injured, afoot in the rain, and was fairly certain he had just revealed Cecily Foxe to be an evil, black-hearted succubus.

His arm wasn't broken—he wouldn't allow it. He thought he could find his way back to Fallstowe with only marginal effort, although he would return quite wet and cold. No matter, he would simply delay speaking to Joan Barleg until he had warmed up—and sobered up—properly.

He looked back to the darkness into which Lady Cecily had disappeared.

Jealous?

Her parting word to him seemed to echo in the cold wind that blasted through the stones, and Oliver shivered. Lewd and heated images of the middle Foxe sister sprang into his mind as if planted there by the Devil himself—images that even an hour ago, Oliver would have forced himself to the confessional for.

His arm no longer hurt at all.

He walked into the darkness after her.

Chapter 3

Cecily practically dove through the old stone doorway of the ruined keep, then spun and flattened her back against the wall. Her chest heaved as though she had just run the entire way from Fallstowe, the oil lamp rattling in her shaking grip. She squeezed her eyes shut and tried to breathe through her nose. Her cheeks were afire and even her teeth clicked together as her jaw trembled.

What on earth had come over her just now, speaking to Oliver Bellecote in such a manner? Never in her life had such cold, hateful, and even lascivious words fallen from her lips. The man was a wastrel, yes, and perhaps a bit of an insensitive dandy, true, but he had just lost his brother in a terrible accident, and had only moments ago nearly been killed in the same manner himself. He had spoken rudely to her, but only after Cecily had baited him.

And now he was alone, injured, and quite drunk, in the cold rain. She had spoken the truth when she'd said he was in shock, and now he could wander off from the ruin and die, and it would be Cecily's fault.

What was *wrong* with her tonight?

She opened her eyes and listened, but could hear nothing beyond the rain now falling in a roar beyond the jagged bones of the old keep. The oil lamp illuminated the inside of the dubious shelter only to the point that it was not pitch black, and Cecily could barely make out the ghostly shadow of the old stone stairs clinging to the wall on the far side of the doorway. The short flight went nowhere now, of course, the old wooden floor that was once the great hall above having rotted away years ago. She reminded herself to keep her wits about her— only four or six paces straight ahead was the stone-lined pit of the keep's foundation—the dungeon. She could hear the rain running into it like a water-fall, hidden away in the night.

At least standing against the curved exterior wall she was sheltered from the downpour. Over the decades, half of the old conical roof that topped the keep had fallen in, but the other half had merely sagged against the ancient, massive center cross support, collecting a variety of leaves and seed that had colonized the rotting wood and, in the spring and summer, appeared from afar to be a jaunty, grassy green cap. Now it contained enough dead vegetation to keep Cecily dry.

In other circumstances, Cecily would have breathed a prayer of thanks for the little miracle of the ancient ruin sheltering her, but tonight she felt as though she were trapped here. Outside was the rain, and Oliver Bellecote. Outside was the Foxe Ring, which Cecily fancied was still whispering echoes of the scandalous words she'd spoken. Far beyond was Fallstowe, and the ghost of the Cecily she had obviously abandoned at the Candlemas feast.

She felt as though during those few moments in the Foxe Ring between being happened upon by Joan Barleg and then Oliver Bellecote she had changed in some fantastic, supernatural way. Who was she now? Was that woman brave enough and humble enough to go into the storm and search for a wounded man? Or would she crouch in the ruin like a vain coward and wait for the rain to stop so that she could hurry home to her rooms, pretending that this night had never happened?

She was afraid of Oliver Bellecote. Afraid of what he stood for, who he was, and the shameful way she had reacted to him only moments ago. According to Joan Barleg, he mocked Cecily to his friends, thought her cold like Sybilla. He did not even view her as a woman, only a joke, or perhaps a useful piece of furniture.

"'Aren't you going to help me up?'" she sneered into the dark. "'Which way to Fallstowe?' Pig." Cecily gasped and then clapped her free hand over her mouth.

Definitely, *definitely* going to hell.

She would visit Father Perry at sunrise, her letter of intent in hand. Obviously she had been possessed by a demon while praying inside the pagan Foxe Ring, and it would be quite necessary to have the evil cast out of her before cloistering herself at Hallowshire. She hoped the process wouldn't be very painful.

Before she could contemplate further on the mysteries of her impending exorcism, Oliver Bellecote lurched through the doorway of the ruin to her right, charging straight toward the center of the keep, and the subterranean pool below.

"Cecily!" he called drunkenly.

Cecily didn't think, she only reacted. She dropped the oil lamp and with a crash the ruin was pitch black, but Oliver was still clear in her mind's eye. She shouted his name as she rushed forward, reaching out with both hands to grasp his tunic from behind. Her feet stumbled across the oil lamp, and it rolled into the pit with a rattle and a tinkling of glass as she jerked Oliver back with all her strength. She could feel the seemingly magnetic draw of the cavernous opening below pulling at them both, and Oliver gave a surprised yell as he spun round to face her. His left arm wrapped about her waist in a blink, and locked together, he ran her backward into the stone wall once more.

His full weight pressed against her, his breath—perfumed with wine and danger—blasted down into her face. She noticed her hands rested on his chest. It was quite an intimate pose, and so she was taken aback by his next words, panted near her mouth.

"Did you just try to kill me?"

"Yes, that's why I pulled you instead of pushing you, you miserable wretch." Cecily squeezed her eyes shut, and she wished she could afford her mouth the same command. "One more step and what few brains you possess would have been spilt like porridge."

He pulled her closer, his breathing shallow and ragged. "What's possessed you so, Saint Cecily?" he demanded. "Something in the stones, perhaps? Is this place infested with the ghosts of those you've already sacrificed?"

"Perhaps," she shot back, and she was shocked to hear her voice coming from her in a seductive purr. "Are you frightened?" She could feel the heat of his face, his nose hovering over her cheek, then by her ear, her jawline, and then back to her mouth as if he was exploring the scent of her.

"Do I seem frightened?" he demanded in a low voice, and pushed his groin into her belly.

Cecily gasped and turned her face away from him. But then she arched her hips forward.

"A man with a broken arm should not make threats he is unable to carry out," she challenged him, her face heating, stinging, tears swelling behind her eyelids. It was all so sordid, so base, so—

Delicious. He wanted her. This was madness.

"Arm's fine," he half slurred. "And so is another part of me, you deceiving witch."

Cecily slid her hands up his chest and when he brought his mouth to her neck, she raised her face and gave a throaty laugh, sounding so unlike herself that she almost wondered if they were being watched.

With the Foxe Ring just beyond the open doorway, perhaps they were.

"Wasn't it said only recently that I would not have you wrapped in the holy shroud?" Cecily taunted.

"Mmm," he acquiesced into her neck, and then

nipped at it roughly. Cecily felt her skin snap back against her throat and she whimpered as he continued. "We shall see if you'll have me or not as I slide into you."

He pulled her away from the wall suddenly and then brought his ankle to her heels, sweeping her feet from beneath her. In a blink he had lowered her with one arm to the ground, the stones somewhat softened by a thin carpet of old leaves and moss. He lay atop her, his right arm held to his side, his left elbow supporting him.

"I could scream," she said, but her tone was not at all sincere. She had never felt as alive as she did just then.

"I fully intend for you to," he confided. He hissed softly as he leaned more fully onto his left side and reached down with his right arm to snag the hem of her skirts. Cecily felt the material sliding up her legs until her thighs were bare to the bite of the cold air.

What am I doing? she screamed inside her head. This was not how a woman intended for the convent behaved—mating like an animal in an abandoned, cursed ruin with a man not only known as a careless womanizer, but who was also drunk, with a broken arm, and betrothed to another woman!

"Oliver," she whispered, as he ran his face up between her breasts and then suckled at her neck again. He was nudging her legs apart with his knees, and Cecily was aghast at the fact that she did not resist.

"What?" he mumbled.

She had to stop this while she still had some shred of sanity left. "We can't do this."

He went still against her, but she could feel his breaths against her skin, swirling in the hollow behind her ear.

"Yes, we can," he whispered as he began kissing her once again, beneath the clasp of her cloak across her collarbone to the base of her throat, then down between her breasts. He paused. "You lure me out here in the middle of the night—"

"I did no such thing!"

"—tempting me with your old family magic, your angelic face, offering me your body—"

"No!"

His mouth was at her breast now, wetting the fabric of her gown over her nipple. He pressed his groin into the juncture of her legs as he raised his head once more, and Cecily gasped as she felt the hot contact of his hardened flesh.

"You cast a spell over me with your body, your luscious mouth."

"I'm not a witch, Oliver," she said, her words rough little pants. "You're only drunk. You're not thinking clearly."

"I'm drunk, yes," he admitted, moving his hips in a way that breached her slightly and Cecily gave a little cry. "But I've seen a side of you tonight that has at last made me understand my brother's obsession with your sister—cold, heartless, brazen temptresses! Think you can say such hurtful things to me without consequence?"

"I'm sorry," she moaned, realizing that the

sentiment could apply to so many areas of her life. But what she was most sorry for at that moment was that Oliver Bellecote was taking so very long to have her.

"It's too late for that now," Oliver growled. "I mean to have my revenge on you. Would you deny me?"

Cecily's pulse thudded wetly in her ears as the most intimate parts of her body throbbed. The night swirled around her head, muddling her thoughts. All she could feel was his heat, his arm around her, the wanton display of her flesh to the blackness of the inside of the ruin.

"Cecily," he demanded sharply, bringing her back from the brink of her ecstatic self-absorption. He nudged further into her and Cecily hissed. "I'm going to punish you. Are you ready?"

And then it was as if the night went multicolored around her, blinding her, deafening her to the meek words of restraint spoken by the girl she had been for so many years, and once more she became the woman of the old stone ring.

She pushed back against him and leaned up to whisper opposite his mouth, "Do your worst."

He took her mouth then, pushing her head back to the ground so swiftly that her skull knocked against the stones, and he kissed her deeply. His tongue swirled in her mouth, his lips pulling at hers. She could feel the scratching of his slight beard, smell the masculine scent of his sweat and faint cologne, taste his desire for her body in his own mouth. She was the one who felt drunk now.

He broke away, leaving both of them gasping. "You mock me?" he challenged down into her face.

"I simply don't feel very punished as of yet," she panted. "You talk and talk and—"

Oliver Bellecote growled and then took Cecily's virginity with a single, hard thrust, and she in fact did scream. It did not slow him though.

Cecily cried out with each thrust—the pain was very real. But there was something beneath it, a hunger for him that was not yet sated, and she welcomed each intrusion. "Oliver!"

"Feeling it now?" he asked in a low, hard voice, never slowing his pace.

"Yes!" she cried.

"Good. I want you to remember this the next time you think to speak to me so coldly, Cecily Foxe." He turned his head away for a moment and groaned in his throat. He drove into her deeply and paused. Again, and then paused. He was breathing through his nose now, as if attempting to restrain himself.

The sharpest pain was gone from Cecily now, replaced by an uncomfortable but compelling throbbing of her flesh, an opening of her body to him. She arched up into him, whimpering at his lack of attention.

"Oliver," she said again, hearing the keening want in her voice.

"What is it, Cecily?" he asked hoarsely, taking up maddeningly deep, slow strokes. "Tell me what it is you desire."

"More," she whined.

"More?" he taunted, and she could feel the shuddering of his thighs against hers, the shaking of his left forearm as it pressed against her shoulder.

She turned her forehead into his arm and nodded.

"Ah-ah," he chastised darkly. "You must say it again. This is your punishment and you will accept it as I command."

"More," she moaned, arching her neck and her back.

He drove into her swiftly twice and then slowed once more. "Is that what you want?" he teased.

"Yes!"

"Tell me," he pressed.

"More," she repeated. "Faster."

He increased his pace, but did not enter her fully. "Like that?" he taunted.

"Nooo," she moaned.

He leaned down near her ear, licked it. "Tell me," he ordered darkly.

"Hard," she panted.

Oliver obliged her with her next breath, driving into her until Cecily cried out.

"Is that it?" he demanded. "Is that what you wanted?"

"Yes!" she cried out. "Yes!"

"I've watched you for years," he said at her ear. "Wondered what lay beneath those drab gowns, fantasized about having the pure, sweet Cecily beneath me."

With his every scandalous word, Cecily could feel

herself drawing nearer release, as if his voice was pushing her toward the edge.

"Don't stop," she pleaded.

"Oh, I won't," he said in a pained voice, and drove into her even harder. "You dirty little liar." He claimed her mouth again, pushing his tongue inside.

Her climax came over her like falling from the top of Fallstowe's tallest tower. Her entire body tensed, seized, her breathing stopped. Oliver pulled his mouth away from hers suddenly, and Cecily gave voice to her deep, forbidden pleasure, her cry echoing off the stone ruin in waves.

"Oh, Cecily," Oliver panted. "Perfect, so—" And then his hoarse yell chased the fading chorus of her cry as he drove into her a final time, so deeply that Cecily screamed.

Oliver gripped her throat with his weak right hand and moaned over and over as he pulsed inside her. Cecily realized she was weeping with the power of what they had just done.

After a moment, Oliver leaned down and kissed her mouth, deeply again, but so slowly, gently. Then he pulled out of her and rolled to his back at her side. Cecily's chest was hitching, and she raised one hand to swipe at her cheeks with the back of her wrist.

She felt positively *reborn*.

"Jesus," Oliver gasped.

Cecily turned her head to try to see him in the humid pitch black, scented with their recent passions. His profile was a darker shadow against shadow.

"My fucking arm hurts," he wheezed. "Ribs, too."

"It shall be tended properly when we return to Fallstowe in the morn," Cecily said timidly. She was unsure how to take him now. "Perhaps your horse will still be about after all, and we won't be forced to walk." She pushed her skirts down awkwardly and then rolled over on her side to face him. "Can you feel your hand at all?"

Silence pressed between them.

"Oliver?" she queried softly, leaning toward him.

He snored loudly.

Chapter 4

Great pain woke Oliver.

He gasped, and the sudden, deep motion of his lungs brought another hellacious wash of torture upon him, so that his breath was stolen away. He lay still, his jaw clenched, his eyes squeezed shut, his mouth pulled into a wide grimace. He tried to bring his left hand across his chest to reach the wellspring of the most intense pain, but the motion of his bicep pressing so slightly into his chest bit into his breath again, and even though his left hand was still more than six inches away from his right arm, the pain increased, as if warning him not to touch it.

"Gah!" he shouted, and opened his eyes as his left arm fell back to his side, against a hard, rough, cold surface.

A roof was above his head, or at least, it had at one time been a roof. Now a semicircle of low, gray clouds mated with a corresponding arc of sky-shot black. The stone walls supporting the decaying shelter were also curved, gaping holes letting in the day where many of the squares had tumbled away as if at the insistence of prying years.

Where was he?

God, his head hurt. He tried to recall the events of the previous night—the feast of Candlemas at Fallstowe Castle. He remembered drinking—heavily—and then trying to no avail to get Joan Barleg alone. But the damnable woman had run off, thinking to engage him in another one of their old games, and Oliver had given chase on a horse stolen from the Foxe stables. He'd tracked her for hours, it had seemed, and then—

Then what? He couldn't remember.

Oliver gingerly turned his head to the right to look at his arm—the slim-fitting sleeve over his bicep looked as though it was ready to burst. He tried to clench his hand into a fist and felt a queer mix of nothing and stinging tingling. He was certain that at least a pair of his ribs were broken on his right side— Jesus! Even his knees felt butchered.

He heard muffled footsteps approaching.

"Hello!" he called out, and his head threatened to split open from the bridge of his nose up and over to the very base of his skull. A black outline appeared over him a moment later, and he squinted as his eyes tried to adjust. A gorgeous, pale, solemn face coalesced within the darkened hood of a cloak.

"Good morning, Lord Bellecote," she said. "How is your arm feeling?"

"Lady Cecily?" Oliver frowned. And then in an instant he remembered flying through the air, landing against something very stationary.

She returned his frown, only hers was tinged

with a wariness that Oliver could not explain. "Yes?"

As her brown eyes skittered over his face, Oliver's mind was muddling together pieces of nonsense, Lady Cecily naked—an old fantasy, but this time, there was detail, nearly the caliber of an actual remembered event. Snippets of a female voice, throatily speaking to him in a manner more befitting a harlot.

Her cheeks began to pinken as he remained silent, and Oliver blinked and glanced away. "I apologize." He knew he had likely embarrassed her, staring at her so boldly. He looked back into her face. "Where are we, and how did I get here?"

Her fine brow crinkled for only an instant, and Oliver wondered if he had imagined her fleeting look of surprise. "We're at the old Foxe ruin," she said evenly. "You . . . you were thrown from your horse into one of the stones in the Foxe Ring."

That explained his memory of flying through the air. Perfect! August had only been put in the ground a month ago from the very same accident. Oliver noticed that he was trembling.

"I think my arm is broken," he said to the lady as she sank to her knees at his side and pushed back the hood of her cloak. She folded her hands primly in her lap over her drab skirts, and Oliver's eyes followed her face as she glanced down the length of his body and then back to his face. "My ribs, as well."

She nodded. "Yes, I do believe it is. I would have cut your sleeve to examine it, but I have no blade, and I was afraid of exposing your skin to further chill lest we remain here for any length of time. I'm afraid you left your cloak in the ring, and it has been rendered useless by the rain."

"Have you been caring for me since last night?" he asked incredulously.

After only a breath of hesitation, she nodded a single time.

God, the woman was truly a saint! Alone the whole of the night in what had to be for a woman a frightening location. And he had been so drunk that he could not remember one whit of what had transpired after his accident. He prayed silently that he had not been his usual, crass self.

"I owe you a great debt," he said solemnly, and he meant it. He realized then that, alone after an accident like that and so very inebriated, he might have died. "Surely you did not drag me here?" She was so slight, so fragile looking, she could not possess such strength.

"I . . . I washed you up a bit," she confessed, her face going a wild shade of scarlet. "You came into the ruin on your own though." Cecily gave him a little smile and a nervous huff of a laugh, but her eyes remained wary. "You nearly fell into the pit. You don't remember it at all?"

"No. No, I—" He broke off, looked away as again a sordid fantasy of the chaste woman bloomed in his mind, begging him to take her, over and over. He forced himself to look back at her. "Did I hit my head as well?"

"Yes," she said. "But you also seemed quite . . . ah, well."

"Drunk?" he offered with a grin that increased the ache in his head. She nodded and her eyes darted away toward his knees. This conversation must be torturous for her. "Yes, I believe I was. Again, my most sincere apologies." He paused, and then although he knew it might cause her some discomfort, he had to ask, "Lady Cecily, did I . . . I didn't say anything untoward last night, did I?"

She looked back at him, and her face took on an expression Oliver could not decipher. "Not at all, Lord Bellecote."

"Are you certain?" he pressed. "Don't feel as though you need to spare my feelings. I am fully aware how boorish I can be when into my cups and I would never wish to offen—"

"No," she cut him off abruptly, and then softened her tone somewhat. "I was not offended by you in the least." She cocked her head and her gaze was curious, as if there was a question she wished to ask him but didn't dare.

Oliver was struck once more by how very lovely Cecily Foxe was. So much softer, warmer, more human than her older sister. He had the sudden notion that she would smell sweet, like honey on warm bread, were he to lean close enough to her to place his nose just beneath her ear.

"It's just—nothing. I simply must have endured some strange and punishing dreams while I slept."

"Well, you certainly slept deeply. Your back had no sooner met with the ground then you were snoring."

He would have laughed had his head not warned him better of it. "I hope I didn't keep you from your rest."

She shrugged. "I wanted to stay awake to . . . to keep watch over you, and in case anyone happened to search for us in the night. I didn't wish for us to be overlooked."

Oliver knew he did not deserve such compassion and kindness after he had made such a terrible ass out of himself. Fallstowe would be losing its finest resident when Cecily Foxe devoted herself to the religious life. For some reason, the thought of that now brought an odd pang to Oliver's gut.

"Would you like something to drink?" she asked. "The old keep well in the back of the ruin is still sweet."

His mouth felt as though it had been scrubbed with a burnt piece of firewood. She gave him a thin smile as she rose to her feet.

"I'll be back directly," said Lady Cecily.

She turned and began walking away from him and Oliver noticed the back of her cloak—the material seemed to have been nearly shredded. It also came to his attention that Lady Cecily seemed to be moving quite gingerly.

Had she been injured in his accident?

"My lady!" he called out.

Cecily stopped and half turned. "What is it, Lord Bellecote?"

"Your cloak—were you also injured in my accident last night?"

The cold air inside the ruin seemed to go thick and humid. A breeze rushed through, blowing Cecily's hair from over her shoulder to flutter behind her back, and she chuckled. Oliver's breath caught in his chest at the sight of her.

"This old rag? It's a disgrace, I know. My mother made it for me many years ago, and the material is simply giving up its life. Its poor condition and my stiffness are simply the only witnesses of my back against stones last night. Nothing more."

Oliver smiled his relief and Cecily turned to disappear from his line of sight. He stared up at the half ceiling, waiting for her to return, while in his mind the last word she'd spoken to him needled him incessantly.

More. More . . .

Cecily wanted to weep, but she was unsure whether it was from relief or frustration as she struggled to extract the small, folded leather cup in the pouch on her chained belt. Certainly, she had been quite anxious about meeting Oliver Bellecote in the light of day after the night of reckless sin they had shared. Would he think her a harlot? A shameful, sinful woman no better than any tavern wench? Would he tell his friends of his conquest of the meek and chaste Cecily, forever exposing her to painful gossip and damaging her reputation? Those had been some of her worries.

And in the darkest hours of the night, she had also foolishly dreamed. Dreamed that he would awaken and be completely enamored with her for her secret boldness. He would swear to love no other above her. He would rush to Sybilla, broken arm and all, and beg for Cecily's hand in marriage. She would become the lady of Bellemont, her husband the most sought-after bachelor in all the land.

Their sudden love affair would set all of England on its ear.

But he didn't even remember.

She bit her lip as she filled the cone-shaped leather. He remembered nothing beyond being thrown from his horse. Oliver Bellecote had taken her virginity, and the only one who knew it was Cecily.

She drank the water that was in the cup and then refilled it slowly, buying time before she must return and face him once more. Would her reputation still take a lashing? It was completely unseemly for an unmarried woman to spend the night alone with an unmarried man—even one who was so desperately injured.

Especially if that man was Oliver Bellecote. Obviously his reputation was spot on—a broken arm had been little hindrance to him in his conquest of her. Verily, Cecily had all but thrown herself beneath him. She hoped that she would not have to endure the sideways glances cast upon a woman tainted with whispered scandal, but in that same instant, she wondered how it would feel to be thought of for once as reckless, dangerous.

What of poor Joan Barleg, though? How would she withstand the rumors of her betrothed spending the long, dark night alone with an unmarried woman? Speculation would be thick, and ugly, surely.

Shame filled Cecily then. She was an adulteress. A liar. A woman of no moral fortitude whatsoever. Thank God the only mortal who would ever know it was she. Cecily composed her face and then turned to walk back around the pit to Oliver.

He had propped himself up against the stone

wall, and Cecily's heart clenched at how haggard he looked. His dark stubble was more beard than shadow now against his gray skin, and deep purple crescents cupped the undersides of his eyes. He held his right forearm over his stomach, his right knee drawn up and his left one crooked and falling open—his pants over them ruined. Cecily saw a straggling lace trailing along the stones at his hip and it made her stride falter.

She had mistied his breeches in the dark.

Cecily recovered and held out the cup to him before she had even come to his side.

"Here you are," she said lightly, sinking to her knees and placing the cup in his left hand. "No gulping—'twill only aggravate your ribs."

He sipped obediently, pausing often to take shallow breaths, and Cecily realized how much pain he must be enduring. When the cup was empty, she took it, and he looked up at her, his face solemn.

"Forgive me, Lady Cecily," he said.

"Forgive you for what?" she replied, gaining her feet once more to shake the cup dry and then return it to her tiny pouch. She turned her back to him as he spoke.

"I can't imagine your embarrassment."

Cecily froze, but did not turn. "Why, Lord Bellecote, whatever can you mean?"

"You know what I mean," he said in a low voice.

Cecily turned slowly, the blood leaving her face, her heart quickening.

"An innocent, such as yourself." He looked away, as if shamed. "Forced to care for a drunken sot, forever overcome by foolishness. I only hope that I have not damaged you irreparably."

Cecily huffed out a laugh, her heart still pounding in her chest. "We all make mistakes, Lord Bellecote."

"Not you," he argued.

"Yes, even me." She cinched her pouch closed with more force than was necessary, although she kept her slight smile. "I can assure you that any embarrassment I am enduring is of my own making. Had I not ventured from Fallstowe last night, I would not be here now." She let her bag thump against her hip, and then swirled her ruined cloak from around her shoulders and held the fragile material between her hands. It made a weak cry of resistance as she tore the cloth up the back.

"Thank God you were!" Oliver choked. He still directed his gaze to the floor, and Cecily saw the muscles along his jaw bulge.

Cecily frowned and glanced at him, as her hands worked to liberate the faded trim from her cloak. "Lord Bellecote?"

At last he looked at her, and Cecily was taken aback by the raw anger she saw in his face. "My brother, August—he . . . it was the same manner of accident that took his life. Only there was no one there to care for him. Certainly not I." He looked away again.

Cecily could no longer resist. She tossed the scraps of her cloak away and then went to her knees once more, only a large, ragged square of cloth in her hands now. "Lord Bellecote, your brother broke his neck in his fall. There was no help for him."

Oliver shook his head absently. "He didn't die

immediately though, did Sybilla not tell you?" His eyes—piercing, full of pain—went to her face.

Cecily shook her head as she folded the material into a triangle and worked two ends into a knot. "No. How could anyone know that?" She motioned him to lean forward and then slipped the makeshift sling over his head, helping him to seat his injured arm.

"Thank you." Oliver leaned his back against the stones and closed his eyes. "It's too gruesome. You've had enough forced upon you."

"Tell me," Cecily insisted. "I am not made of glass, Lord Bellecote."

His throat convulsed as he swallowed. He did not open his eyes. "The way he landed. Face down in a wide ditch. It was obvious that he had been paralyzed by the way his limbs remained pinned beneath him. But his face—" Oliver broke off as his voice went rough. "His face was turned upward, toward the sky. I will never know the effort that took, to turn his face in such a manner. No one save our mother and I knew, but August was frightened of the dark. He lay there alone, helpless. Staring hungrily toward the daylight even as night fell around him. Then he died."

Cecily swallowed and blinked away the stinging in her eyes. This was a side of Oliver Bellecote that she had never even guessed existed, much less witnessed herself.

She thought instantly of the hateful things she'd said about him, thought about him, only the night before at the feast. Things she'd said to Sybilla, August's lover, who had known the details of the man's death. And then Cecily combined it with the memories she had of the way Oliver had loved her, so fiercely, so passionately.

And she knew a shiver of discontent in her heart.

"I was to meet with him that day," he continued. "I had only just returned from France, and he had wanted to speak to me of family business. I was late for our appointment, and August was already gone from his rooms when I arrived. I was impatient to be reunited with my friends, and did not inquire of him. I didn't care what had transpired at Bellemont in my absence. It mattered not to me, any of it. His man, Argo, fetched me from my bed, still half drunk." He paused and his voice grew wistful. "And now he is gone, and Bellemont is mine. *And I do not want it.*"

Cecily swallowed again. "I am sorry for the loss of your brother, Lord Bellecote."

Oliver chuckled. "Each time someone addresses me as Lord Bellecote, I think that August must be in the room." He opened his eyes, his head still tilted back against the stones, and looked at Cecily down the length of his nose. "Any matter, I thank God for your foolishness, Lady Cecily. I believe it is only through His grace that you were there last night. You saved me."

Cecily shook her head. "I didn't. Don't martyr me, Oliver."

"Saint Cecily," he sighed, and closed his eyes again. "So sweet. So forgiving. Indeed, I should witness at your beatification."

Cecily's cheeks burned. "You're tired, in pain. Rest a while," she suggested.

His eyes snapped open and he frowned slightly.

"What is it?" she asked.

"I believe we are about to be rescued."

Cecily turned her face toward the jagged stone doorway and indeed, heard the sound of riders approaching. She gave a short sigh and a frown that matched Oliver's.

Now, she would know the beginning of the rumors. Perhaps then . . .

"I'll wave them over," Cecily said, and prepared to rise. But before she could gain her feet, Oliver Bellecote seized her wrist.

"Forgive my boldness in touching you," he said. "But I swear to you now, no matter who is without, I will not allow a whisper of scandal to touch you. Any who speaks against you will answer to me."

Cecily tried to smile and gave him a pathetic nod. "I do not fear idle talk, Lord Bellecote."

He released her and chuckled again. "Of course not. Mere words cannot shake you, can they?"

"I'll be right back," she said, and then rose before he could see her cross frown.

She marched to the doorway and swept from the ruin. Did no one think her capable of human error? Not even the man she'd slept with the previous night?

And then all her questions of rumor were laid to rest and her heart shriveled up and fled to her stomach as she saw the riders approaching. Sybilla, racing toward the Foxe Ring, leading the party upon the wild Octavian; Alys and her husband, Piers, each of them leading a riderless horse.

And, almost as a spiteful afterthought, Joan Barleg rode behind them all.

Chapter 5

Sybilla looked like the goddess of the hunt, leading the mounted party up the hillock to the Foxe Ring. She spurred Octavian into the ring and through it, the large gray destrier's wide hooves churning up clods of mud as it swerved tightly around the fallen down center stone. She was in a morning gown of ivory, with sheer, netted overlay that streamed out behind her, defying the wind along with her unbound raven hair and flapping cloak of deep violet.

Cecily did not flinch as Octavian barreled toward her, and Sybilla leapt from the horse before it had even come to a complete stop. Sybilla marched to her, her arms swinging at her sides, and in the moment before Cecily felt her sister's embrace, the tears came.

After a brief moment, Sybilla leaned back to look into Cecily's face, holding her by her upper arms. "I could scarcely believe it when Lady Joan said that she had seen you at the Foxe Ring last night. Are you all right?"

Cecily nodded, unreasonably relieved to have

her older sister there. "I'm fine, Sybilla. I'm sorry to have worried you. But—"

"Lady Cecily!" Joan Barleg was trying to dismount her horse, kicking at the stirrup, which was stuck on her foot. In a moment, she was down and skip-running toward Cecily, her beautiful blond hair plaited neatly into a long rope. It was quite a contrast to her abandoned appearance of the previous night. "Lady Cecily! Have you seen Oliver?"

Cecily looked back to Sybilla, unable to meet the young woman's eyes.

"Lord Bellecote also failed to return to the feast last night," Sybilla explained unnecessarily.

Cecily nodded. "He's in the ruin. He's alive and will recover, but he is injured. He was thrown from his horse last night, Sybilla."

Sybilla's already milk-pale face faded, and it was as if the blood in her lips bloomed. She released Cecily without comment and dashed toward the stone doorway, Joan Barleg following in a swift walk. Cecily was left standing, arms dangling useless at her sides. She watched as Piers helped Alys down from her horse.

As usual, Alys's smile was inappropriately gay. "What an adventure you must have had!" she said mischievously, before embracing Cecily tightly.

"You've no idea," Cecily murmured into Alys's hair before pulling away.

"You look dreadful. Are you truly all right?"

Cecily couldn't help but roll her eyes at her younger sister's appraisal of her appearance. "Yes, Alys, I'm fine." She looked to Piers Mallory, the stocky, solid, quiet man her sister had married. "Good morn, Piers.

Forgive me for bringing you out so early on the day you were to depart Fallstowe."

"Good morn to you, my lady. Do not trouble yourself about the hour," he said with a humble incline of his head.

"In truth," Alys was laughing, "we have been up before the dawn. Life on a farm manor has changed me into quite the morning soul, Cecily. Always so much to do!" Alys raised her eyebrows and glanced toward the ruined keep. "Poor Lord Oliver. And poor Cecily, too. Did you stay with him all the night?"

Cecily nodded and felt her face heat.

"Oh, my darling," Alys cooed, her eyes scanning Cecily's face and head. Cecily knew her sister was reading her, and she hoped that her misery was not so very obvious. "You're concerned about the talk, aren't you?"

"Not very, no," Cecily said shortly, and then looked to her brother-in-law. "I hate to further inconvenience you, Piers, but it is unlikely that Sybilla and Lady Joan will be able to move Lord Bellecote—he's broken his arm and several ribs, and taken a bump on his head."

Before she had completely finished, Piers was nodding and stepping away from Alys's side to stride toward the ruin. Both sisters turned to watch him disappear through the stone opening.

"You have married well, Alys," Cecily said quietly, and she wondered at the little splinter of jealousy that scratched at her words.

"Yes. I have," Alys replied in a matter-of-fact tone. "Perhaps if the talk is very bad, Sybilla will demand that Oliver Bellecote marry you, as repayment for your mercy on him. You know Sybilla will not tolerate slander."

Cecily's heartbeat stuttered at the swift change of subject. "That's a ridiculous notion. Joan Barleg told me only last night that the two of them were to wed."

Alys cocked an eyebrow. "Really?" she said with mild interest. She inclined her head toward the ruin. "Well, we shall know soon enough—here they come."

Piers Mallory came through the doorway first, leaning heavily to his left as he bore Oliver's weight against the length of his right side. Oliver's left arm was stretched across Piers's shoulders, and though he wasn't standing upright, Oliver appeared easily half a head taller than Alys's stocky husband. Oliver's right arm, still cradled securely in the long piece of Cecily's cloak, was held against his ribs. A permanent grimace seemed to have taken up residence on his slender face.

Although Sybilla exited the keep after Piers and Oliver, she swiftly overtook them, striding toward Cecily and Alys. Cecily could tell from her sister's face that Oliver's accident had shaken her, and after hearing the details of August Bellecote's recent death, she better understood the depth of Sybilla's mourning.

What might have been between Sybilla Foxe and August Bellecote would not ever be known. It could never be righted.

"He shall return to Fallstowe." As was her habit, Sybilla began letting her will be known before she had properly come upon her sisters. "I'll send a messenger straightaway to Bellemont, so that Argo might more thoroughly oversee the lord's interests there while he recovers."

Cecily frowned. Then her stomach turned as Joan Barleg came swiftly in Sybilla's wake toward where Piers was leading Oliver to one of the spare mounts. The pretty blond woman appeared distraught.

"He is to recover at Fallstowe?" Cecily asked. "It could take weeks, though. Surely he would be more comfortable in his own home, Sybilla."

Sybilla shook her head. "No. He is in no condition to make the journey to Bellemont—you of all people should know." Sybilla cast a disgusted look toward the Foxe Ring. "And as it is through Fallstowe's ruin that he was injured, Fallstowe shall bear the responsibility. This place is a menace. I should have it razed."

"Oh, Sybilla!" Alys gasped. "You can't!"

Sybilla shot Alys a challenging glance. "I can."

"Wait," Cecily interjected. "Who is to care for Lord Bellecote?"

Sybilla's brows lowered and she looked quizzically into Cecily's face. "Why, you will, of course, Cee."

"Why me?" Cecily demanded. "It isn't at all proper, especially after I have already spent an entire night alone with him."

"It's not as if you slept together, Cee," Alys interjected.

"No one knows that!" Cecily said, shocked at the words that were coming, completely unbidden, from her mouth. "Perhaps we did!"

Sybilla ignored the very suggestion. "You are the most experienced at Fallstowe, Cecily. Nay, even in all the land, you are the most skilled. He will have no better care. It is the very least I can do for August's brother."

"If it's the very least *you* can do, then *you* nurse him, Sybilla!"

Her older sister's frown displayed mild annoyance. "In any other instance you would be begging me to allow you to attend an injured child of God. Are you feeling unwell, Cecily?"

"I'm fine," Cecily ground out. "I simply think that, under the circumstances, *certain persons*"—Cecily glanced pointedly toward Joan Barleg—"might find discomfort in the fact that the same woman who spent an entire unchaperoned night with a man would now attend his every private need! There will be enough talk as it is, Sybilla."

Cecily's dread increased as Joan Barleg herself marched from where Oliver Bellecote had at last gained his seat atop a horse. She stopped directly before Cecily. Now would be the moment the young woman would voice her protest.

"Lady Cecily," Joan began quietly, intently.

Cecily felt her chin lift, although her cheeks were afire. "Yes, Lady Joan?"

The woman then sank into a deep curtsy, bowing her head, and Cecily was so shocked, she wanted to yank Joan Barleg aright. When at last the woman stood once more, her eyes shimmered with pretty, delicate tears.

"I couldn't help but overhear your protestations. It *must* be you who cares for him," she said quietly. "You saved his life last night!"

"I did not," Cecily blurted.

"Oh, so humble!" Joan sighed. "You did, though. How foolish of me to think, when I happened upon you in the Foxe Ring last night, that you were trying the legend, seeking a man of your own." Joan Barleg's chest heaved with another great sigh.

Cecily felt her teeth grinding together.

"God sent you there, to protect *my* Oliver," Joan continued. "Had he been kept company by a monk, he would not have received such courageous and noble care."

A monk? Now she was not even a woman?

Cecily shook her head. "It was only a coincidence."

And then Alys opened her big, big mouth. "But do you not always say, Cee, that there are no coincidences in God's grand plan?"

Cecily tried to kill her younger sister with only her eyes. "I have said that before, yes, but it does not apply in this instance."

"Well, *I* don't think it was a coincidence, and neither does Oliver," Joan Barleg said decisively. "He called you an angel, and I agree with him. You are *our* angel, our own Saint Cecily."

Cecily did not know what to say. She looked at Sybilla, who stared coolly back. Next to Alys, who grinned gamely and then nodded her head in encouragement. Cecily looked back to Joan Barleg, and to her horror, the woman dropped to her knees.

"Must I beg you?" she asked sweetly. "I would trust no other woman."

"*Get up,*" Cecily ground out.

Joan clasped her hands in front of her breasts. "Please?"

Cecily looked around at the faces staring expectantly at her, which quickly grew to include Piers Mallory, who held the reins to Oliver Bellecote's horse. She dared a glance up at Oliver's face, and to her dread, he too, stared at her intently. It was nearly bearable until he spoke.

"You needn't agree to this, Lady Cecily," he said in a low voice. "If you decline, I shall yet sing your praises from here to London. I have no desire to impose upon Fallstowe, and I certainly would not heap punishment upon you, after all you have already done for me."

Punishment.

Her mind went unbidden to the rough way he had taken her in the ruin only hours ago. It seemed a lifetime. He stared down at her, his eyes filled with pain and fatigue, and a hint of perhaps confusion.

And she remembered the sad story he had shared with her about his brother's death. How loath he was to seize the reins of Bellemont, even when she knew just how much fierce passion and daring lay within him.

It was too dangerous. She could not agree to it.

"Very well," she said calmly. "I will simply postpone my departure to Hallowshire."

Sybilla watched Cecily ride off ahead of their little group toward Fallstowe, supposedly to arrange for rooms to be prepared for Lord Bellecote, as well as the supplies needed for his immediate treatment and care. But Sybilla was no fool.

Cecily was immensely, royally, miraculously cross. It didn't happen very often. And so although Sybilla had considered agreeing to Cecily's wish that Oliver be returned to Bellemont or that someone else be put in charge of his care at Fallstowe, all thoughts of acquiescence were cast to the winds once Sybilla had seen the depth of her younger sister's discomfiture and reluctance.

As if reading Sybilla's mind, Alys spoke. "It's almost as if she hates him, although I can't understand the why of it."

The two sisters were bringing up the rear of the party. Ahead of them, where Sybilla could keep close watch, Oliver Bellecote sat his horse, flanked between Piers Mallory on his right and Lady Joan Barleg on his left.

Sybilla nodded. "She was unusually catty toward him last night at the feast, as well."

"So unlike Cecily—she loves absolutely everyone. Do you have any logical explanation?" Alys continued in a whisper.

Sybilla thought to herself for several moments before answering. "Perhaps it is because Oliver is the precise antithesis of everything our dear sister lives for. Where she is holy, he is irreverent. Where she is meek, Oliver is brash. Cecily loves rules and order and courtesy. Oliver . . ." Sybilla broke off with a shrug.

"Oliver does not," Alys supplied with a wry smile. "I think he is wonderful."

Sybilla smiled. "As do I."

"It seems dangerous to me though, Sybilla. The king was quite adamant in the message Piers and I carried to you from London: he is coming for Fallstowe. Would it not be best to see Cecily safely away to Hallowshire rather than be happened upon by Edward's soldiers? He could descend upon you in a fortnight, or on the morrow!"

"I feel we have some time yet," Sybilla said. "I have been summoned to the court at Midsummer with Fallstowe's troops. It is still only February. Any matter, Oliver Bellecote is not the only guest Cecily shall soon be entertaining at Fallstowe."

"Who?" Alys demanded, intrigue high in her voice.

"A member of the religious. He is being sent by the bishop to oversee some of the goings-on at Hallowshire, and wishes to meet our saintly sister."

Alys gave an exasperated sigh. "Then would it not be more convenient—and safer—for him to do so at *Hallowshire*?"

"Yes," Sybilla conceded with a slight smile. "But Cecily could not care for Oliver Bellecote if she were away at Hallowshire."

The hoof-falls of the horses were muffled by the slow pace and cold, wet grass. The wind blew from the Foxe Ring, seeming to push them toward Fallstowe. The party breached a slight rise, and the castle came into sight, small and far away, dark gray and still. Sybilla drew Octavian to an impatient stand to look at it, and Alys stopped alongside her, while the other three riders carried on slowly ahead.

"This isn't entirely about Cecily though, is it? August, then?" Alys asked quietly. "Sybilla? I know the nature of Oliver's accident is a macabre coincidence, but it was truly just a drunken, stupid accident. You are no more responsible for Oliver's spill than you were for August's death, and caring for Oliver will not bring back his brother."

"Are you still leaving today?" Sybilla asked briskly, signaling that the conversation was over. She kicked Octavian into a walk once more.

Alys waited a moment before matching pace with her again. "Yes. Piers's grandfather is watching over things while we are away, but my husband is anxious to return to our home. As am I. This is the first time I've been on a journey without Layla and I miss her."

Sybilla chuckled and rolled her eyes. "You and that damned monkey. You treat her as if she were your child."

"Well," Alys drew out slyly, "perhaps it is good that I had her to practice with."

Sybilla looked quickly to Alys.

Alys nodded happily. "You're the very first to know. I suspected before we departed Gillwick, but I didn't want to say anything to Piers."

"He would have never let you come," Sybilla guessed.

"I'll tell him once we're nearly home, when it's too far from Fallstowe to turn back, and yet too close to Gillwick for him to have a cart fetched for me."

"Will you tell Cecily before you go?"

"I couldn't keep it in any longer while you and I were alone, but I dare not tell another soul before my own husband," Alys said. "Keep my secret for me, Sybilla—I so wish to share the news personally, when Piers deems it is safe for me to travel again."

"He'll never allow you to ride while you carry his child, you know that, surely."

Alys nodded and giggled. "It will give him enough time to have a cart outfitted splendidly for my conveyance."

Sybilla reached across the space separating her and Alys to grasp her hand. "I am happy for you."

"Thank you, Sybilla." Alys squeezed her hand and then gave her arm a gentle tug. "And I *am* sorry about August."

Sybilla pulled away from her sister's grasp and looked ahead to the younger—alive—Bellecote brother, swaying in the saddle ahead of her.

"So am I," she said quietly.

Chapter 6

Oliver had never been formally interred in one of Fallstowe's grand guest chambers before, although he had snuck into one or two of them with a willing female companion at his side during the many feasts held at the castle. In any matter, he'd never been witness to the lavishness in the daylight, and had he not been in so much pain, he might have been more properly impressed by the rich tapestries, plush upholsteries, and towering wardrobe.

But all he could think about outside the searing pain in his arm and the tearing in his chest was Cecily Foxe's lovely, frowning face. Now, his throbbing eyes continuously glanced about him, searching for her presence.

He could not wait to see her again.

His newest mate, Piers Mallory, helped him onto the tall, wide bed and Oliver could not help but cry out as he half collapsed onto his left side. His lung felt as if it would be ripped open with his next breath.

"Easy there, friend," Piers said, as he moved to the end of the bed and began unlacing Oliver's boots.

"My thanks," Oliver wheezed.

"Think nothing of it." Piers dropped the boots to the floor and moved up the side of the bed.

Oliver raised his head at the sounds of the chamber door opening and saw a line of servants, no fewer than six, streaming into the chamber, bearing all manner of trays and baskets and stacks of linen.

Piers attracted Oliver's attention once more. "I wish you a quick recovery," the man said mildly. "And before I leave you in the capable hands of your nurse, I have but one piece of advice for you."

"I am rapt, I assure you," Oliver quipped, closing his eyes. He was so tired.

He felt rather than saw Piers Mallory lean over him, to speak low near his ear.

"Your reputation is known so vastly that it has reached even my ears at humble Gillwick," Mallory began. "And what I have not heard through idle gossip has been relayed to me by my sweet wife, who is never idle."

Oliver's eyes opened, and he was surprised at the scowl on the Mallory man's face. In such a vulnerable position as Oliver was at the moment, the simple farmer seemed quite intimidating.

"Sir?" Oliver queried.

"Alys loves both of her sisters. I had no family until marrying into Fallstowe's rather peculiar trio, and so I am also a bit protective of both Lady Sybilla and Lady Cecily. You are going to be in very intimate proximity to the most vulnerable of the two, you ken my meaning?"

"I do," Oliver said warily. "But I can assure you that—"

"Good," Piers cut him off without apology. "It has been many months since I have pounded a grown man into pulp. I do feel the urge. And Fallstowe is not so very far to satisfy my craving, you ken?" he repeated.

"That I have the utmost respect for Lady Cecily, you can't know how much," Oliver said. "And my own brother, August, was in love with Sybilla."

"Rightly so," Piers growled. "But even as strong as Sybilla is, and as capable as she may be of fashioning your liver into a hassock, I feel I need make you aware that, should you make but one untoward comment to Lady Cecily, I *will not hesitate*"—Piers Mallory brought up one meaty fist beneath Oliver's nose—"to turn your scrawny frame inside out. You k—?"

"*I ken,*" Oliver insisted through clenched teeth.

"Good." Piers thumped Oliver's breastbone twice with the flat of his palm, as if in a show of good faith, and Oliver cried out.

Piers gave him a lopsided grin. "Sorry about that, friend. You get well." He saluted Oliver with a wave of his hand and then turned to quit the room.

Oliver presented his middle finger to Piers Mallory's back.

As soon as the stocky farmer was gone, Oliver was descended upon by three of the maidservants who had entered his chamber. With murmured "milords," and several stifled giggles, they began to efficiently tug at his clothing. In the midst of the fog that seemed to have enveloped his brain, Oliver realized they meant to undress him, and for the first time in his adult life, he felt moved to resist.

"Hello there, yes, now—what's all this?"

A dark-eyed maid replied, although neither she nor the other two women slowed in their tasks. "You're to have a bath, milord."

"A bath?" Oliver cried. "My arm's broken!"

"Oh, not to worry yourself, milord," the youngest-looking maid cooed with a coquettish smile. "You shan't have to lift a finger."

"Well, now," Oliver stuttered as the maid withdrew a slender blade and pulled the front of his shirt from his pants. She gripped the end of the garment in one fist. "I don't see that as necessary at this point. What are you—*I say!*"

The woman drew the knife up the center of his shirt, splitting it cleanly in two.

The maid gave a happy little sigh. "There we are, milord. Can't have you twisting yourself up in knots to get out of this thing, can we?"

"I do think perhaps we should"—he broke off as he caught sight of the other two maids at each of his feet, both wielding identical blades. "What are you two about? No, no, no! That's not called for. I—"

In a blink, his legs felt the cool air of the chamber.

"I've no other clothes!" Oliver cried. "Lady Cecily is to see that—"

"We're acting upon her ladyship's command," the dark eyed maid said, calmly sawing a ragged yoke around his groin. "I would ask that you hold quite still now, milord. I have no desire to . . . nick you in such a manner."

All three maids giggled.

Oliver lay his head back and closed his eyes, praying that Cecily Foxe would not choose that moment to walk into his chamber. The innocent would likely faint dead away at the sight of him so unclothed.

And then the idea of her seeing him naked caused other unbidden fantasies to flood his mind. The feel of her skin on his, the scent of her hair—it would smell like honeysuckle and sandalwood, Oliver thought. A strange combination in reality, likely, but for some reason it seemed to fit.

"For all his protests, I do believe milord is quite anticipating his bath," one of the maids said lightly, followed by a shower of giggles from the other two.

Oliver realized that he was experiencing a dreaded physical manifestation of his bawdy imaginings, and was so atypically mortified that he could not open his eyes.

He felt a breath near his ear.

"We could perhaps take a bit of your pain away if you please, milord," a maid whispered into his ear. "Soothe your aches . . . ?"

Oliver had never had sex with three women at once before. Two, yes. And, before this morning, he had always been of the opinion that one could never have too many enthusiastic participants in such a friendly pursuit. But now, the only thought that filled his mind was of what Cecily Foxe would think of him should she happen upon—nay, even find out about—him having intimate relations with the chambermaids in her home.

"No, thank you," he ground out through his

teeth, his damned manhood nodding as if in agreement. He felt a small, cool hand slide up his thigh. "Very kind of you, but—"

He heard the scrape of the chamber door opening, and his stomach seemed to collapse onto his spine in a quivering knot. His nightmare was about to come into reality. Cecily would see him in such a state and know him truly for the cad he was. She would never speak to him again, let alone deign to tend him. He might not ever see her again.

A woman's merry laugh rang out. "Of course. Word gets 'round that Oliver Bellecote is abed at Fallstowe, and the tarties come out hot and fresh."

Relief flooded Oliver's body at the sound of Joan Barleg's voice, and his erection surrendered at once. But his consolation was short-lived as the reality of the situation dawned on him.

"Joan, no! I'm unclothed!"

She laughed again as she came to stand at the bedside, looking into his face indulgently. "I can very well see that, Oliver." Her attention went to the now sulking maids who were removing his sleeves from his arms. "Off with you now, you shameful wenchlets. I am certain this is not what Lady Cecily had in mind when she bade you to comfort and reinfreshenate Lord Bellecote. I shall take over from here."

The women seemed to dawdle in bundling the rags that had once been Oliver's clothes, but Joan was insistent.

"Shoo!" she cried, flapping her hands at them and chasing them toward the door. "Brazen cows!"

The door slammed shut, and Oliver reached his left hand to snag a wrinkle in the heavy coverlet at his side. With a sharp intake of breath through his teeth, he jerked it toward him, mostly covering his lower half.

"It's your own fault, you know." The screech of wood on wood accompanied Joan's chatter as she pulled a small table laden with a wide shallow bowl, fine-edged cake of soap, and a stack of soft-looking linens near the bedside.

He looked up at her, her blond plait over one shoulder as she efficiently readied a rag by dunking and wringing it in the water and then taking hold of the soap. She was still the same Joan he had known yesterday—pretty, friendly, free with a smile and a laugh.

"What's my own fault?" Oliver muttered crossly.

"The maids." Joan wrapped the rag around the cake of soap and rubbed the wet package between her hands briskly. "You can't expect to tumble about the land in such a gay manner and then not have everyone take you for a circus, Oliver." She opened the rag over the bowl and the cake of soap dropped in with a plop and a splash.

"Joan, no." Oliver held up his left palm when she approached him with the soapy cloth.

"Why ever not?" she demanded. "It's not as if I've never seen you naked before. Your lovely nurse wishes you clean, and you wouldn't want to offend Lady Cecily by demanding she wash you, would you?"

"God, no!" Oliver felt his face glowing.

"Well, then I do not see that you have a choice." Thankfully she began by swiping at his face and neck.

"It's just that—" He sputtered and turned his

face to the side ineffectively as Joan ran the sudsy rag across his mouth.

"Sorry," she chirped.

Oliver spat and blew the soapy film from his lips. "I know that I can be rather . . ."

"Tarty yourself?" Joan offered.

"Friendly," Oliver corrected her with a frown. "And I don't wish to shock Lady Cecily after what she's done for me."

"Oh, I agree completely," Joan said, dunking the rag and then repeating her earlier motions with the soap. "The woman is too innocent to be true. Do you know, even now, as word is spreading about your accident and her rescue of you, not a single person has batted an eye about the two of you being alone together?"

"I should say not!" Oliver growled. "How could anyone even suspect—"

"They don't," Joan said simply. "It's not Lady Cecily's nature, even when thrown together with a *friendly* humor such as your own." She smiled at him indulgently as she began to wipe his chest. "Obviously they feel that she could withstand the most vile onslaught of her dignity and still be untouched. Not that you would seek out a woman such as she, any matter."

"Of course. But—" Oliver broke off. "What do you mean by a woman such as she?"

"Oh, you've said as much yourself." Joan wrung out the rag again. "Quiet, meek. A bit plain. You also said she thought herself too good for a mortal man, and cold like, well"—Joan broke off and looked over her shoulder before continuing in a whisper— *"Sybilla."*

A picture of Cecily Foxe, as he had seen her this morning, bloomed in Oliver's mind. She was anything but plain. She was exquisite. Stunning.

"Wait, I never said I thought her cold," Oliver argued. *"Or* plain."

"If it were me though," Joan continued, unfazed, "I do believe I would be a bit crossed that you *hadn't* tried to seduce me. Even if I were Cecily Foxe, in all her holy sweetness."

"No man in his right mind would even think it," Oliver said decisively.

Joan shrugged, and then laid the wet cloth aside in favor of a small, soft towel, which she pressed to the damp skin of his chest and face and left arm.

"Well, you certainly were into your cups last night. Oh, lover—your arm looks simply dreadful. Does it hurt very much?"

"Yes," Oliver bit off. "Don't touch it." He was beginning to become quite annoyed with Joan Barleg's insistent presence.

"All right, poppet," she said condescendingly. She laid the towel aside and wrung out the rag again, moving to his legs and quickly flipping the coverlet back. "Whatever happened to your knees, though?"

Oliver knew it would be useless to protest her uncovering of him, and he certainly could not win a physical contest with the woman at that moment so he let it go unchallenged, fixing his eyes on the canopy above him. He was spared complete humiliation by the fact that the maids had failed to remove the yoke of his pants by the time Joan arrived, and so he still sported a loincloth of sorts.

"I don't know." He started to bring his left forearm to cover his eyes, but it pulled at his chest and so he lowered it again. "I have no recollection of anything after my fall. I assume I landed on my knees."

"It's a miracle you weren't killed, really. They're not very bruised," Joan observed as she dabbed at the abrasions carefully. "Just terribly sputtered."

Oliver gave a wordless shrug. *Sputtered?*

Joan finished washing his legs and then dried them gently. She covered him once more with the coverlet—"We shall wait until Lady Cecily treats you before seeing you in bed properly."—and then began collecting the soiled linens.

Oliver pulled the weighty blanket the short distance remaining to his chin, chills overtaking him, and watched her. He had known Joan Barleg for nearly her entire life, and had known her in an intimate—if casual—manner for the past two years. She was quite attractive, her hair a rich blond, long and thick, like a mane. Her brown eyes had a slight lilt at the outside corners, perhaps a nod to Turkish ancestry. Her skin was clear and bright, but with a peachy undertone rather unlike the typical English milky complexion.

She was easy for a man to talk to, if not exactly sharp witted. Her peculiar habit of butchering and then reassembling words for her own use hadn't ever really annoyed Oliver before. Most thought her charming. She loved a joke or a juicy rumor. Her family was not well connected, which made Joan ambitious, and not afraid of a challenge. One score in age, junior to Oliver by seven years. Loyal—she had never, not in a single instance that Oliver could recall, displayed jealousy over his numerous women.

In theory, she would make the perfect wife.

"Joan," he said to her after she had finished setting his bedside to rights, "there is something I would speak with you about."

"Yes, you said that last night." She gave him a smile and a wink before perching on the side of the bed below his feet. "I didn't dare hope that you would bring it up now that you are in so much pain. But I suppose a cozy with death does call for a change in one's priorities."

Oliver was quiet for a moment. It would be easier for him to wait until he was feeling more himself, not so broken and agonized physically, and mentally tormented with ludicrous thoughts of Cecily Foxe of all people dancing circles in his brain. But it was unfair to continue to allow Joan to believe that he would be part of her future. He could ease into the news, he supposed. Break it to her gently. But he had no patience for that right now. Chivalry had parted ways with his intentions in much the same manner as the bones in his arm were broken. Better for them both to treat the matter as a thick thorn stuck in the bottom of one's foot.

Yank it out, and staunch the blood.

"We'll not get married, Joan."

The only change in her expression—smiling eyes, curved lips—was the slight downward flinching of her eyebrows.

"Whatever are you talking about, Oliver?" she asked with a wider, if mildly perplexed, smile. "You're going to be fine. I've no fear that I'll be made a widow by a broken arm."

"I mean, I have no *wish* to marry."

She gave him a true frown then, but was calm where Oliver had expected an explosion of emotion.

"That's a silly thing to say. Why not?"

"I've a lot of responsibility, now that August is gone. I am Lord of Bellemont, a position I never thought to hold. It will take much adjusting on my part, and a woman to care for is the last thing I need at the moment."

"The very idea is stressful, of course," Joan said easily. "Oliver, I know how you feel about taking August's place—how you dread it. But don't you see? That is prexactly why you need a wife right now. And not just any wife—you need *me*."

"Sorry," Oliver said. "I'm not following you."

Joan rose to her feet and moved around the end of the bed, to climb upon it and stretch out so that her head was near his.

"I know you, lover," she said, and raised a hand to rake her fingers lightly through the top of his hair. "I know you, how you think. I have not pro-tested your conquests outside my bed. I do not resent them, or you. *I know you,* and so therefore I know that these dalliances are just a trait of your character. Something you need to entertain you. A hobby, if you will."

"You think I sleep with other women as a hobby?" he asked incredulously.

"Why wouldn't I?" she challenged logically. "Have you been in love with any of them?"

"No," he answered right away.

She raised her eyebrows and tilted her face slightly, as if to say, *So there you have it.*

"Some men drink. Some men hunt. Some men tournament. You"—she trailed a finger down his forehead, along his nose, and then tapped him lightly over his lips—"make love. Would I rather that it was exclusively with me? Of course. But a starving man does not discard the entire apple for a single bruise."

"Wait a moment," Oliver said, immensely flustered. This was not going at all how he had imagined. "Are you saying that you would not expect me to remain faithful if we were to marry?"

"Could you?" she asked.

"I don't know," he replied.

Joan smiled again. "Well, I do. Certainly, I could demand that you be loyal to me, and you do have a wonderful sense of honor, so I think that you would do your very best to accommodate my wishes. But I know there would come a day when you would stumble. And if I forbade it, well . . . that would make you a cad and me a very unhappy wife. However, if I enter into our marriage with realistic expectances of our relationship and indulgify your occasional dalliance, then I fail to see how we would both not win."

"Win," Oliver repeated.

"Yes, of course." She paused, looking at him expectantly. When he said nothing more, she sighed and continued. "Oliver, you must marry, eventually. Bellemont commands it. Your parents are long dead. Your brother. You are the last remaining Bellecote. You must have an heir."

"Perhaps I will marry one day," Oliver conceded. "But not now."

Joan's brows did lower then, in an expression of annoyance. "Yes? One day? And who do you think to marry 'one day'?"

The question made Oliver quite uncomfortable, and had he been able to move more freely, he would have likely squirmed.

"I don't know exactly," he said defensively. "Any number of women, I suppose."

"Oh, really," Joan said flatly. "Granted, Oliver, you are the most sought after man north of Oxford. But don't you find it odd that none of the women whom you've *known,* for lack of a less rudimentary term, have tried to convince you to marry them thus far?"

"Not really," he replied testily. "Some of them were already married."

Joan laughed then, and her smile was back. "That's exactly it, though, lover. You are known far and wide. Women love you, but only with their bodies. They don't dare trust you with their hearts. They don't want the humiliation of trying to tame you once they have you, to try and curb your appetites for other women. No woman in possession of good sense would want a husband who has slept with half the female population of not only England, but most of Europe, too."

"You do," he tossed at her.

She smiled. "I am realityistic. There is no fairy tale in my dreams of the future. I would trust you, because I would accept that part of you. No other woman will."

"You don't know that," Oliver said, becoming

quite offended. Was he truly that bad? "But in any case, I will simply have to take my chances. We're not getting married, Joan. And I'm sorry if you feel that I have strung you along these two years."

"You never promised me anything," Joan admitted. "And I don't believe that you don't want to get married. You have been through a series of terrible shocks lately, and I know that it is only the strain of them that has you spouting such nonsense."

"It's not nonsense. I'm very serious."

There was a knock at his chamber door, and then it creaked open the smallest inch.

"Lord Bellecote? Are you prepared for me?"

It was Cecily Foxe, and at the smooth, husky melody of her voice, the hairs on Oliver's neck bristled. He wanted Joan Barleg out of his room, now, and especially off his bed in her relaxed, intimate position.

He was more than prepared for Cecily Foxe. In fact, he felt as if he had been waiting on her for *years*.

Before he could reply, Joan answered for him. "He's quite covered, Lady Cecily. Do come in." Joan turned her face back to Oliver as he heard the door open fully and quiet footsteps approach. "Now, I must return home to gather some things. I will be back in a pair of days. In the meantime, you rest and get well. Do everything that Lady Cecily asks of you, and we will talk of the wedding when I return." She leaned forward, and although Oliver tried to turn his head at the last moment, her lips still landed on the side of his mouth.

"I can come back if you'd rather," Cecily said from the end of the bed. "I didn't mean to interrupt,

I just thought you would be in want of the draught I have for your pain."

"No," Oliver began, trying to crane his neck around Joan's head to see the woman just out of his sight.

Once again, Joan usurped him. "It's all right, my lady. I was just leaving." She rolled over on the mattress and gained her feet, and while she was straightening her skirts and hair, Oliver looked at Cecily.

She was staring back at him, gripping a small tray in her hands so that the fine skin over her delicate knuckles was white. Their eyes locked. Her face was framed with little damp tendrils of dark hair, her gown fresh. But there were little lavender crescents under her eyes, and two bright pink spots on her cheeks.

Oliver felt his erection returning beneath the coverlet.

"Thank you again, Lady Cecily," Joan said, breaking the spell weaved around Oliver. Both he and Cecily turned to look at the blond woman. "I do hope he doesn't give you too much trouble."

"Good day, Lady Joan," Cecily said quietly. "Godspeed you on your journey, with hope for a safe return."

Joan blew Oliver a kiss from her fingertips and then left the room. He looked back to Lady Cecily, and found that she was staring at him again. He didn't want to be rude, but he couldn't help but return her appraisal. It was as if his eyes were drinking in the sight of her, as if he had been lying in that very bed for months upon months, only waiting for her to appear.

"Hello, Lord Bellecote," she finally said, and her voice was a bit raspy. She cleared her throat delicately. "How are you feeling?"

"Wonderful," Oliver said.

Cecily frowned.

"Not really, of course," he said, and muddled together a grin for her. "I actually feel rather dreadful."

She gave him a sympathetic little smile, and then at last—at last!—stepped around the end of the bed toward him. Had Oliver's arm and ribs not pained him so very much in that moment, he would have risen up on an elbow, anticipating her approach. He could feel his nostrils flaring with his shallow breaths, trying as he might to catch her scent.

Good God! Were his brains truly addled?

She stood there a moment, seeming nonplussed when she noticed the small table near his bedside already occupied by the wash water and linens. She looked around and behind her for a place to set down the tray, laden with items that Oliver did not recognize. Her forehead had creased into a lovely frown once again.

"Shall I shove over a bit?" he suggested, letting his eyes flick to the sliver of mattress along his right side when she turned toward him.

"Absolutely not," she said, shaking her head. "I would not have you move before you have your draught unless it is unavoidable. I'll just"—she stepped toward him, lifted the tray, then hesitated. "If you'll forgive me reaching across you." She gestured with the tray to the opposite side of him.

"Of course," he said as casually as he could.

She gave him a tentative smile and then leaned over his stomach to place the tray on the sheet near his hip, and as she did, her movements stirred the air, filling Oliver's nostrils with a scent—honeysuckle and sandalwood. It hit his brain like a large, spiked hammer, and all around him seemed to slow down infinitely as wild images and sounds collected in his head.

I'm not a witch, Oliver.

He drove himself into the darkness, over and over, a woman's passionate, pleading whimpers below him.

More . . .

Faster . . .

And then time regained its sanity with a loud whooshing in Oliver's ears as Cecily Foxe stood aright once more, a small metal cup in her hand.

"This will taste quite awful, I'm sorry. But it will ease your pain while I bind your arm." She tentatively held the cup toward his left hand. "Can you, um . . . ? Or shall I . . . ?"

"Yes, I think you'd better," Oliver said quickly, trying to force some remorse into his voice. "I don't trust the steadiness of my hand at the moment." Which was actually true.

She came closer to him, slowly, as if dragging her feet each inch along the floorboards at his bedside, her eyes trained on his mouth. She reached out with her left palm and slid it behind his head, her fingers parting his hair like cool little marble pins. Her small palm cupped the back of his skull, and she urged his head up gently.

"Small sips," she advised, bringing the cup to his

lips. "A little at a time. 'Tis a potent brew. Too much too quickly and you will wish yourself dead in only a moment." The cool metal touched his lower lip and Oliver opened his mouth.

The liquid was lukewarm, and although it carried the familiar hint of strong spirits, it was indeed a vile concoction. Oliver forced himself to swallow when Cecily withdrew the cup slightly, then he gasped.

"Gah!" he muttered, and stuck out his tongue.

She actually giggled a bit. "I warned you. It will be worth it though, in a few moments. Here we go, once more." She brought the cup to his mouth again.

He took in a large mouthful.

"Can you feel your hand at all?"

Water dripping in the darkness.

Can you feel your hand at all?

The liquid halfway down Oliver's throat did an abrupt retreat, and with an exploding breath, it exited from his mouth.

Chapter 7

"Oh!" Cecily shouted and stepped back quickly as Oliver Bellecote spat the majority of the draught she'd worked so hard on all over the bed.

The man then fell into a queer sort of spasm, his breaths snorting out of his nose intermittently, his body bowing to the right, his eyes squeezed shut. He finally succumbed to several barking coughs—each followed by a shout—before letting his head fall back to the pillow. He looked immediately to her.

"Sorry. Sorry," he wheezed.

"Are you all right?" Cecily asked, and tentatively stepped toward him again.

"Yes, yes. Quite fine. Sorry about the mess." His eyes flicked to the liquid-splattered coverlet.

"It's no matter." She raised the cup, trying to slow her pounding heart. It was nerve wracking enough simply being in such close proximity to Oliver Bellecote himself, his naked chest. Then to have him nearly scare the daylights out of her by choking. Cecily had almost wet herself. "Shall we try again with what's left?"

"Yes, but—" His eyes narrowed and he looked at her intently. "Lady Cecily, did you ask me if I could feel my hand when we were at the ruin last night?"

Cecily swallowed, and it felt as though she was trying to force a chicken—feathers, feet, and all—down her throat.

"Um . . . I may have. I'm not certain."

"I think I remember," he said slowly, still staring at her.

She leaned toward him without actually realizing she was doing it. "You do?" Her voice came out a tiny squeak.

"Yes. I was . . . I was lying down."

"And?" Cecily prompted, then held her breath.

"And," Oliver said slowly, "that's all."

She stood upright once more, her stomach feeling quivery and sick. "Well, that's . . . that's good, I suppose."

Oliver frowned and looked away from her. "No, it's not. I can't help but feel that I'm missing something important."

"You're missing the use of your right arm, certainly," Cecily said desperately.

"No, something that needs remembering." His face turned toward her again, and it held a faint grin. "Although that was quite funny."

"Was it?" Cecily asked, taken aback. No one had ever said she was funny before.

Oliver waved his left hand. "Never mind. It will come to me soon enough. Let's carry on with the poisoning."

"It's likely nothing, any matter." Cecily smiled and fit the rim of the cup against Oliver's mouth once more, trying with every shred of her will not to remember the feel of those same lips on her own, and on her neck and breasts. It was impossible, though, as she was forced to keep her eyes trained on his lips as he finished the draught.

How many women had he kissed, made love to, that he could not even remember what had transpired between them last night?

And did Cecily truly want him to remember?

He had shown less than any interest in her before his accident at the Foxe Ring. He'd never even glanced her way. And when he had been forced to acknowledge her at the feast, it had been only in jest. He was going to marry Joan Barleg. Should their affair come out, it would hurt Joan terribly and ruin Cecily's reputation. It might even damage her standing at the convent. She would lose the respect of Fallstowe's folk, and perhaps even of kind Father Perry, her mentor and dear friend.

And what would Sybilla—Alys—say should they find out? Would they think ill of her? Call her out for the liar that she was? Cecily knew her role in the family—she had known it since she was a young girl, and its duties did not include sleeping with a notorious womanizer who just happened to be betrothed.

If he never remembered, though . . . well, then it would be as if it never happened. That was better for everyone involved.

Wasn't it?

"Thank you," Oliver rasped as she withdrew the empty cup and set it aside. "I think."

Cecily smiled as she wiped her hands on a small

towel. "You will feel the benefits of it soon. I'll start binding your arm in a few moments." She began walking away from the bedside, toward the door.

"Where are you going?" Oliver demanded.

She glanced over her shoulder at him as her stomach did a little flip. It was as if he was concerned that she was leaving him. "Only retrieving a chair." She grasped the back of a wooden chair and swung it up in front of her, turning back to face him. "I must confess that I'm a bit fatigued from our shared misadventure, and would rather sit than stand while I wait for your draught to take effect."

"Oh," he said as she neared him, seeming nonplussed, then regretful. "I do apologize for keeping you from your rest. I'm certain you are weary."

Cecily sat down, knees together, hands folded in her lap. She composed her face. "After your arm is bound, we will both sleep."

Oliver nodded.

The chamber filled with silence, hairy and tickling. Cecily wanted to squirm in her chair. The moments ticked by, pacing slow, tapping circles on the floorboards.

"Are you hungry?" Cecily asked abruptly.

"Yes, famished," Oliver answered practically before Cecily had finished speaking.

"I'll have a tray sent up straightaway."

"Thank you."

"You're welcome."

Several moments slithered by before Oliver spoke again. "Half *you* eaten?"

"No," she said, looking at him intently now. "I'll take a tray when I retire."

"I shee," he said, and Cecily realized she was hearing the slight slurring of his words.

"Feeling anything yet?" she asked. His eyelids seemed to have acquired a gentle droop.

He pulled a face and shook his head. "Nary a think, milady. Per'aps I am shimply too used to shrong drink for it to affect me properly."

Cecily tried to hide her smile as she stood. "Well, let's see if you can tolerate it. If the pain is too much, we shall stop and I will have another potion made."

He dropped his chin to his chest as if bowing courteously in his invalid state. "Ash my lady wishes."

Cecily folded the coverlet further away from his right arm, and then turned to walk around the end of the bed, her heart pounding.

"I'll need you to sit up a bit more if you're able," she said, crawling onto the mattress with as much decorum as possible. "This would be easier had the maids left your arm in the sling I fashioned, but I will help you as much as I can."

"Hussies tried to shtrip me bare," he muttered as Cecily slid her right forearm behind and under Oliver's left shoulder.

"I beg your pardon?" Cecily asked.

"Nothing," Oliver said dismissively.

"All right then—hold on to your wrist and try to keep your arm as still as you can while I lift you. There you are. Ready? On three. One, two, *three.*"

Oliver's breath shushed out through his teeth as he dug into the mattress with his heels and Cecily pulled. She said a small prayer of thanksgiving that they were able to move him into a suitably upright

position on the first try. She was unsure how composed she could remain with her hands on his hot,
bare skin.

"Very good," she praised quietly, and skittered
backward off the bed, noticing his pallor and
clenched jaw. "Arm?"

"Ribs," he whispered.

"I'll go as quickly as I can." She returned to the
side of the bed nearest him and leaned across
Oliver Bellecote's lap to lift the lid from a silver serving tray, where a mound of slimy, steaming dressings
lay atop a hot stone. She picked at an edge with her
fingernails until she could grasp a single piece, and
then pulled a length from the pile.

True to her word, Cecily worked quickly, drawing on her years of experience in treating the ill
and injured. To his credit—and perhaps that of
Cecily's fine draught—he did not cry out as she
firmly wrapped the first course of linen soaked in
plantain-infused lard high up on his bicep. In moments, his upper arm was covered with the treatment from shoulder to elbow, and Cecily finished
the dressing by winding long strips of clean bandages over the poultice.

She dared a look at his face as she made the final
knot, and to her surprise, his expression seemed
more relaxed.

"Lord Bellecote?" she whispered, wondering if
he had fallen asleep.

His eyes cracked open and he turned his head
minutely to look at her. "Hmm?"

"I've brought a proper sling with me—we'll need
to get you into it before you sleep. I was going to

wrap your ribs to give you a bit more comfort, but if you are feeling well enough to rest now, we can always do it later."

"Later," he whispered with a slight nod, and his eyes drifted shut again.

Cecily looked at his handsome face for a long moment, wondering about the position she now found herself in. She had slept with this man, handsome, wild, notorious Oliver Bellecote. Even if *he* never remembered it, *she* would remember him and their night together for the rest of her life. And so Cecily told herself that it was only nostalgia that caused her heart to smile a little bit at the sight of him lying so still and weary before her.

She fashioned the sling with the required knots without a whisper of sound, and when she slipped it over Oliver's head—urging his back away from the headboard slightly—he leaned his forehead against her breast.

"You smell lovely. Like a dream I had once."

The words were so quiet, had she been breathing properly, Cecily might have missed them.

She eased him back against the headboard and brought the sling down over his arm, cocking it slightly at the elbow and slipping the linen down toward his wrist. His eyes were still shut.

"You can move down a bit more now, if it's more comfortable for you, Lord Bellecote," she said quietly.

Oliver slid down with a grimace, and Cecily fetched a pair of pillows to bolster his arm. She lingered over him. He had not opened his eyes, and she thought he might already be lost to sleep.

Her left hand rose hesitantly, and after only an

instant of thought, Cecily smoothed her palm over Oliver's forehead.

He sighed and then his lips barely moved as he spoke. "Best dream I've ever had."

Cecily froze, her hand still in his hair. His breathing was measured now, and she was certain that he had finally surrendered to slumber.

"Me, too," she whispered. "Sleep well, Oliver."

She rose, gathered the tray and the domed lid and lifted it from the bed. She looked at him a final time before turning away, knowing that once she left the room, all thoughts of reminding him of the evening they had shared would be gone from her mind. Her opportunity was lost. It would be over, and no one would ever, ever know.

She gave a deep, soundless sigh, and then, walking so carefully that her slippers made not a whisper, she left the chamber, and the man who was once her lover, behind.

Chapter 8

After leaving Oliver Bellecote, Cecily first went to the kitchens, where she returned the tray and then spoke briefly with a maid regarding the preparation of a hearty meal for the lord when he awoke, as well as the manner of inquiring as to the discomfort of his broken ribs. Oliver likely expected Cecily to return to his chamber this evening, and should she receive word that his ribs needed binding, she would see to it as she had promised. The very thought of seeing him again caused her heart to pound with anticipation.

She didn't seem to know who she was when she was in his presence.

After quitting the humid and smoky kitchens through the open double doors in the back of the annex, Cecily crossed to the nearby chapel. She glanced up at the sky, remembering for an instant the last time she'd had intentions of visiting this place of prayer and had instead wound up at the Foxe Ring. No starry blanket crowded the sky now, only low clouds, appearing disgruntled and as if they were contemplating a shower out of spite. Or perhaps boredom. Cecily loosened the scarf from around her waist and tied it over her hair before pushing one side of the heavy doors open just far enough to slip through as thunder stirred from far away.

The chapel was empty, save for the fleeting and nearly invisible appearance of the old, stooped maid who tended the church and Father Perry's quarters. The servant bobbed her head and raised a gnarled old hand within the gloomy shadows at Cecily's arrival, and then disappeared through a black doorway with a hitching shuffle, her small brush broom riding her back like an emaciated child.

Cecily took a deep breath, feeling a slight release in the tension between her shoulder blades. The smell of old incense permeated every surface inside the chapel, and the subtle, leftover perfume of it was truly a comfort. She stood just inside the doors for several moments, her eyes fixed on the altar ahead, and felt a foreign bloom of hesitation. The chapel was her home, the place she felt the most comfortable, even more so than Fallstowe. And yet she knew the sins she had committed—they shouted inside her head to make their presence known: lust, acedia, wrath, envy, pride. She dared not reveal these particular failings to her most trusted counsel. He would know it was she, certainly—what other unmarried young lady at Fallstowe was contemplating the religious life, and had also rescued Oliver Bellecote after his accident?

And then slept with him?

She knew that she could be forgiven outside confession by being in a state of perfect contrition; the problem was, Cecily was unsure whether she was contrite at all, let alone perfectly.

She took a deep breath of the perfumed air and let it out before clasping her hands at her chest and walking down the aisle.

She knelt at the altar railing and made the sign of the cross.

She raised her face to gaze upon the crucifix above the altar.

Her mind went completely blank.

Cecily's brows knitted downward into a frown. *All right,* she told herself. *I shall just start simply.*

She recited six different prayers from memory, hoping they would purge her mind of the block that was preventing the easing of her conscience, her knees already singing from the hardness of the stone beneath them. But even after the last *amen,* she could not force an original phrase from her mouth.

"Do you not want *my confession?"* she whispered crossly. *"What is it, then? I* am *sorry that I'm not sorry about the proper things. I don't know what else to do— this has always worked before!"* She laid her forehead atop her folded hands with a sigh.

Her head rose abruptly at the familiar scraping of the chapel door behind her, and then Father Perry's mellow voice in midsentence.

"—you see that we are outfitted quite splendidly despite our isolated location, and—" He broke off abruptly, and Cecily surmised that he was not expecting the chapel to be occupied at that particular time of day.

Cecily made the sign of the cross once more and rose, prepared to greet Father Perry and his guest. She turned and watched the two men walking toward her, one short and slight and clothed in the familiar uniform of Fallstowe's priest, the other of slightly taller height and clothed in the garb of a wealthy nobleman. The stranger had dark blond hair that fell in one length to just above his shoulders where the hood of his fine cloak lay in soft folds. The front-most lock of his hair was caught behind his ear thoughtlessly, as if in a habit to keep it from hindering his vision. His face was lean and square, and even in the shadows of the dim chapel, his blue eyes shone like chips of aquamarine.

"Lady Cecily," Father Perry said, his voice rich with obvious delight. "I'd hoped we'd find you, although I would not begrudge you a day's rest after the trying evening I've heard tell of."

"Good day, Father," Cecily said, forcing her eyes from the handsome stranger. Funny, but she could not recall ever having taken marked notice of members of the opposite sex before. "Prayer is a balm for many things, and I have found my need of it to be far greater than rest of late."

"Of course, of course!" Father Perry beamed at her and then looked up at the man next to him. "Vicar John, *this* is Lady Cecily Foxe." Father Perry looked to Cecily once more. "Lady Cecily, the Most Reverend John Grey, of Hallowshire Abbey."

Cecily's stomach did a little flip. *Hallowshire.* Beyond the thick walls of the chapel, the thunder rumbled more ominously now.

The striking man gave a bow, but his eyes never left Cecily's face. "Lady Cecily Foxe," he said, rising. "Just the woman I was looking for."

Father Perry had dismissed Cecily and John Grey with a smile and a wave, refusing each's offer to assist the priest with the preparations for the next hour. The vicar had led the way back down the aisle to the chapel doors, but once outside, he'd extended a long arm, indicating that Cecily should precede him.

"We could talk in the stables if you like," Cecily offered, untying her scarf and slipping it from her head now, and noticing John Grey's eyes flitting admiringly over her hair. She felt her cheeks tingle. "It will give us a bit of privacy, and Fallstowe does boast of an obnoxious number of fine specimens."

"As you wish." The vicar inclined his head. "I must confess a love of good breeding, in the realm of animals. My father keeps a stable also of the obnoxious caliber, and I find myself pining for the old smell."

"This way, then." Cecily started to walk toward the long, large structure that housed Fallstowe's mounts. She glanced up at the sky, which seemed ready to burst at any moment. Her heart pounded in her chest, her breathing was shallow.

Why was someone—especially a man—from Hallowshire looking for Cecily? They walked through the wide doorway of the stables just as fat, cold raindrops began to splatter noisily on the packed dirt of the yard.

"I reckon you're wondering why I've come,"

John Grey said, and the coincidence of it caused Cecily to frown.

She stopped and turned toward him, her hands clasped tightly in front of her. "I was unaware that Hallowshire had gained a new priest," was her only reply.

"Oh, I'm not a priest," John Grey said with a slightly embarrassed grin. "Not yet, any matter."

"But Father Perry referred to you as a vicar."

"It's more of a courtesy title than anything, really." John Grey walked leisurely to a nearby stall and grasped the muzzle of one of Sybilla's hunting horses. The bay snorted and blew and pushed into the man's hand. "Hello there, big boy. I've been studying the last two years at Coddington. My father and the bishop are old friends, and as there seems to be a shortage of priests in the area, well, he sent me to ascertain the health of Hallowshire."

"That's quite an honor," Cecily said lightly. "How are you finding the abbey?"

"Not well, I'm afraid." John Grey patted the bay soundly on its neck and then turned to face Cecily once more. "Mother is in poor health, as are the abbey's coffers. The sisters there have grown unruly, with no strong female leadership. They've begun taking in paying travelers for board. The ministry is suffering."

Cecily frowned. "That's . . . that's terrible! Surely it cannot have changed so much since last I visited." Cecily's mind went briefly to the small, happy stone abbey, filled with peaceful women whose days consisted of prayer and crops and industry. She remembered vividly the small inner courtyard, the fountain, the beautiful flowers planted around the statues. Cecily had spoken at length in that garden with Mother, and it had been then that she had decided to one day make Hallowshire her home.

One day . . .

John Grey's eyebrows raised. "Really? How long has it been since you were at the abbey, Lady Cecily?"

Cecily frowned, and then felt her face heating. Had it really been that long? "Well, I guess it must be nearly three years."

John Grey said nothing, but the small smile still played about his lips.

"You said you came here specifically to see me," Cecily prompted, feeling slightly unnerved by the way the handsome man regarded her. Not lewdly, but intently, as if he could look into her eyes long enough to catch a glimpse of her soul.

"Yes." He moved to the stall across the aisle, where Sybilla's pet, a small black mare, stamped impatiently in a bid for John Grey's attention. "Mother spoke longingly of you. She has begun to wonder if you have changed your mind about Hallowshire. Perhaps she has sound reason?"

"I have been thinking on it very deeply of late," Cecily admitted. "Fallstowe has a guest in my care at the moment. A noble friend of my sister's. He was injured only last night, and it is my responsibility to tend him."

"Fortunate man," John Grey said, glancing over his shoulder briefly, his grin widening. "But perhaps

I might be so bold as to suggest that Hallowshire needs you more, Lady Cecily. Not only the purse you would bring, but your dedication, your leadership."

"Leadership? Vicar, I would never presume— I am not yet even a oblate!"

"One need not take vows to be an example," John Grey said, almost musingly. "I have been mulling that idea 'round in my own head while on my mission from the bishop. Laypeople have been at the heart of many a religious institution for hundreds of years. Everyone in the land knows of your dedication and good works, Lady Cecily. Even the bishop himself waits with bated breath for your decision. Should Hallowshire not receive the help it needs, and very soon, it will likely be dissolved."

Cecily's heart fluttered with dread. The *bishop* knew of her? This was much worse than she feared. "So you have come to collect me?" Cecily challenged him.

"Not at all, not at all," John Grey said mildly. "Only to inquire as to your intentions."

Cecily swallowed. For some insane reason, the image of Oliver Bellecote, lying abed in the castle beyond the stable walls, rose up through the murky confusion in her mind. "As I said before, I am under obligation at this time, Vicar. I—"

"I've not come in an attempt to sway you, either way, Lady Cecily." John Grey stepped away from the little black mare and came to stand facing her, perhaps only three paces away. He looked into her eyes again. "Although an alliance with the bishop may also benefit your sister."

He was speaking of the king's stalking of Fall-stowe, Cecily knew.

John Grey cocked his head slightly. "You're unsure yet, are you not?" he asked gently.

"Very," Cecily admitted honestly, although she hadn't intended to be so quick about it.

"I understand," the vicar said. "More than you could likely know." He stepped toward her and held out his hand.

Cecily looked down at it for a moment, and then placed her fingers in his palm. It was cool and smooth. She looked up at him.

"I will be at Hallowshire for the next several weeks, assisting Mother and trying as I might to bring the sisters back to heel. I would be honored if you would allow me to be your counsel during that time."

"Counsel?" Cecily asked.

John Grey looked at her again, his teeth flashing white in the shadows of the stable. It seemed very quiet around them. "Perhaps you might confide in me about your misgivings concerning devoting yourself to Hallowshire. I promise you, I will not try to sway you one way or the other. If, by the time I am through with my obligations at the abbey, you discern your vocation is at Hallowshire, I will escort you there with a glad heart. If not . . . ?" He shrugged.

Cecily's eyebrows rose. "You will simply let it alone?"

He squeezed her fingers and then released them, speaking as he walked to the stable doors. "Well, I *may* be pressed to ask your sister for a small donation." He crossed his arms over his chest and looked up through the doorway at the sky. It had stopped raining.

Cecily smiled at his back. "Small donation" in the bishop's mind usually meant a very large donation. She walked to stand next to him, looking up at the sky in much the same manner. The clouds were no longer thoroughly gray, only at their bottoms now, and the edges of them were fluffy and white like snow, parting sporadically to reveal the lightest shade of blue afternoon sky beyond. A trio of golden beams played over the rain-darkened dirt of the yard, and the bailey was unusually still.

Cecily turned her face to look at John Grey. His profile was sharp against the frame of the stable doorway, and his eyes skittered over the clouds, as if searching for something hidden there.

"Will you stay at Fallstowe?" she found herself asking.

"No. Very kind of you, and your sister as well, to offer," he said, and Cecily was surprised that he had already spoken to Sybilla. What a strange pair of days she'd had. "I will enjoy Father Perry's hospitality for tonight and then return to Hallowshire in the morn. My hope is to come to Fallstowe for a pair of days each week."

Cecily looked back to the sky. "I understand."

"Will you see me when I come?" he asked quietly. "I confess that it will make my time at Hallowshire more bearable, knowing that I have your presence to look forward to."

She turned her face toward him once more,

quickly, and found that he was searching her face much as he had searched the clouds in the sky.

"Will you be taking your own vows when you return to the bishop, Vicar John?" Cecily asked boldly.

He stared at her for a pair of moments. "It is a season of discernment for many, Lady Cecily," was all that he would say.

"Of course I will see you," Cecily answered at last. "You may lecture me on the many reasons why I should commit to the abbey, and I in turn will try to convince you to take your vows as a priest."

John Grey grinned. "Or not."

"Or not," Cecily agreed with a smile.

"Perhaps—" John Grey began, but whatever he planned to suggest was lost beneath the sound of a woman frantically calling Cecily's name from across the stable yard.

"Lady Cecily! My lady!"

Both Cecily and John Grey turned to behold the kitchen maid trotting across the bailey toward them, waving at Cecily with an old rag.

"What is it, Marga?" Cecily stepped from the door frame tentatively.

"Beggin' yer pardon, Lady Cecily, but you must come. Good day to you, sir." The maid curtsied perfunctorily in the vicar's general direction. "Lord Bellecote is near to tearin' the bed apart, milady. I believe the draught you give him is wore off. He's carryin' on dreadful for you, and won't let anyone else in the chamber!"

"I'll come, Marga," Cecily assured the maid calmly. "Keep everyone else away from him until I arrive, and have a tray of cool, wet towels ready for me in the kitchen. Lord Bellecote is likely feeling a superior ache in his skull from the sedative."

"Yes, milady." Marga curtsied again and then turned on her heel and scurried back across the bailey.

Cecily began walking away from John Grey, backward so that she might still bid him farewell. The man was enigmatic, and although Cecily longed to spend more time with him, peeling back the layers of this non-vicar, this not-a-priest, Oliver was calling for her, he was in pain, and she must go.

"Will you stay for chapel in the morn, Vicar?" she asked.

"Yes," John Grey called, and then threw out the challenge of, "Will you be in attendance?" as he bowed, keeping his eyes on her face.

Cecily's smile was her only answer. She waved to him before spinning and proceeding toward the castle in a more proper manner.

Though her bearing was appropriate as she opened the door of the annex, she was still smiling.

Chapter 9

Oliver's head felt as though it would split right 'round the circumference of his skull. His temples ached sickly, his stomach roiled; each shallow breath introduced an onslaught of burning knives into his right lung. His arm throbbed, throbbed deep into the center of each half of his splintered bone. His bicep felt tight, hot, swollen, and an agonizing drone of pain slithered through the tiny spaces of his shoulder joint, his elbow, his wrist. His fingers were fat, numb sausages, his nail beds discolored and cold to the touch.

But even the maelstrom of physical anguish he was experiencing felt placid when compared to the maddening riddle in his head.

Something had happened between him and Cecily Foxe last night.

But what? How far had he gone? The little slips of her he could sift from his shattered memory—burning, bawdy images—could not be the whole truth. Cecily Foxe would never stoop to a man of his reputation. Never.

But why now did he recognize so readily the smell of her, the feel of her hands on his face? He'd asked her of his behavior, and she had absolved him of any wrongdoing, but wasn't that her reputation? To forgive, to absolve?

The idea caused a cold sweat to break out over Oliver's body, drenching him as surely as a fall from a great cliff into the February sea.

He clenched his eyes shut. He had to know, he had to know the why of this maddening desire of her.

Where was she?

There was a soft rap at his door before it cracked open, and her voice called to him. "Lord Belle-cote? 'Tis Lady Cecily. Might I come in?"

"Yes," he said hoarsely. He hoped she had brought another cup of the disgusting draught—enough to kill him this time. It would be the only thing that might put him out of his misery.

The door opened fully, and Cecily Foxe stepped inside, carrying a turned, handled mug. She was followed by Fallstowe's quizzical old steward, Graves, who bore another dome-covered tray.

"Feeling poorly?" Cecily asked as she came around the end of the bed.

She must have been sleeping, Oliver surmised, by the freshened look of her skin and the peace around her eyes once more. The shadows had faded since last she'd left him, and her lips were gentled into a kind of smile. Oliver felt guilty all over again for stirring her from her rest.

"I do apologize for my abruptness," he began,

searching her eyes for some hint of wariness that he had told himself was there before, but he saw nothing of the sort now. "Did someone wake you?"

"Oh, heavens no," Cecily said with a smile as she wordlessly directed the old steward in placing the tray on the now emptied side table. Graves was so steeped in the Foxe nobility that he didn't bother to acknowledge Oliver's presence. It was often joked about that the ancient servant held more sway than the king, being the only man in the land with intimate and reliable access to Sybilla Foxe *and* Fallstowe Castle.

"Shall I stay to help you lift him, Lady Cee?"

Oliver frowned. Was he a downed horse?

"No, that won't be necessary. Thank you, Graves."

The old steward nodded in Cecily's direction and then turned to go. Oliver did not miss the man's look of disdain and rolling of his rheumy eyes in his direction.

Cecily was at his side then, sliding her small cool hand behind his back again. "Let's see if you can sit up a bit."

"Why does Graves suddenly . . . agh!"—Oliver paused once he was upright, his eyes shut, waiting for the searing pain in his side to ebb—"hate me?"

"Oh, I do doubt that he hates you—he admired your brother greatly," Cecily said mildly, and then turned to pick up the handled mug from the table and present it to Oliver. "Here you are. This should help ease your head."

"More of the same?" Oliver asked, sniffing at the light-colored brew warily.

"No, the last draught is what likely caused your headache."

He glanced up at her, knowing his expression was full of accusation.

She shrugged. "Sorry. A distasteful side effect, I'm afraid. This however is naught but strong willow tea. It will help with your pain as well as the swelling."

Oliver took a sip. It was desperately bitter, but not nearly as noxious as the last concoction. Feeling better by simply being in her presence again, Oliver drained the mug in two goes.

"It *will* eat at your stomach, however."

Oliver looked at her, aghast. "Perfect! Are you *trying* to kill me?"

"Not anymore," she said, and actually grinned at him in a way that made Oliver's dormant erection stir. "It's not poison, Lord Bellecote. And it only has that effect on a full stomach, so after your ribs are tended to, you must only have a bit to eat to stave off any unpleasant reaction."

He handed her the mug as best he could with the limited range of motion his broken ribs allowed his left arm. She took the cup, leaning over him gracefully, and again Oliver was struck by the smell of her. The same clean yet musky perfume, blended with the warm scent of fresh hay.

"Where were you?" he asked. When she looked at him, nonplussed, he elaborated. "When I called for you."

"I don't see how that is any of your concern, Lord Bellecote," she chastised lightly. "I was showing a visitor to Fallstowe the stables."

So his sense of smell was not mad, at least. But he couldn't help the stab of jealousy that rivaled his ribs when the gentle smile returned to her lips at the mention of this mysterious visitor.

"Who was it?" he demanded.

"I beg your pardon?" Her hands paused in removing the domed lid from the tray.

"It was a man, wasn't it?" he said, hearing the completely ridiculous nature of his accusation, and absolutely not caring.

"Lord Bellecote," she said with a deep frown, but her cheeks reddened as if she had been slapped. "You are a guest here, under my care. I owe you no explanation of who I entertain in my own home."

He swallowed with some difficulty. "I'm sorry. You're right. I simply— Well, it must be another side effect from that nasty draught."

"Hmph," she sniffed, her nose in the air as she turned and set the silvered lid aside. She fussed with the dressings on the tray for a moment, and when she next spoke, her back was to him. "But if you must know, yes, it was a man."

Oliver felt his jaw clench, but he would be damned if he would further incur her wrath.

She turned to him, a long length of linen similar to that which was wrapped about his arm between her two hands. "Well?" she asked pointedly.

"Well what?" he grumbled, letting his eyes go to the coverlet.

"Your curiosity as to my whereabouts has been insatiable thus far. Aren't you going to ask the identity of the man?"

He looked to her. "Would you tell me if I did? Or

would you simply tell me it was none of my concern? Which it's not, I do understand."

She smiled at him indulgently. "It was the vicar of Hallowshire Abbey. Now, if your interrogation is satisfied, please hold your left arm away from your side so that I might start this first course of wrapping."

Oliver wanted to close his eyes and sigh with relief. She hadn't been conversing intimately with some young nobleman, who perhaps possessed ambitious ideas of securing the middle Foxe sister as a match. She'd been with some stooped, gray, impotent old priest! Of course! Why would he even imagine that Cecily Foxe would be entertaining potential suitors when no man dared insult her goodness?

Well, no man save Oliver himself, perhaps. But that was as of yet unconfirmed.

The bandage was ice cold against his skin, and he involuntarily drew in a sharp breath as she slid the length carefully under his slinged arm and across his nipples. "Argh! *Christ Jesus!*"

"Lord Bellecote!" Cecily chastised.

"S'fucking *cold!*"

"Yes, it is," she said lightly. "Soaked in the same tea as you've just drunk. Cooled now, though, of course." She tied a loose slipknot in the bandage, leaving one long end, and then turned to pick up another length from the pile.

He told himself he was prepared for the shock of the clammy linen, but he clearly was not.

"God *dammit!*"

She tied the knot quickly and then took a step back from the bedside, her hands on her hips.

"Sorry, sorry!" he grumbled. "Wrap it 'round

your belly though, and see if even you don't call down God's curses upon it."

She continued to stare at him, a thoughtful expression on her face.

"What?" he demanded, feeling his face heat. Oliver could not recall another time in his life when a fully clothed woman had disconcerted him so.

"No one has ever dared speak like that in my presence before," she said.

"I've apologized. What else do you want from me, blasted torturer?"

She simply shook her head wonderingly and then turned to retrieve another bandage.

Oliver managed to somewhat curb his tongue while Cecily wound exactly ten of the slimy, frigid wet strips loosely around his middle, the knots and straggling ends roughly center to his chest. Then she walked around the end of the bed and climbed gingerly onto the other side of the mattress. She sat on her heels and reached for one of the long pieces of linen.

"Ready?" she asked politely.

"No," he grunted out.

"All right then." She pulled on the bandage and it tightened around Oliver's chest.

"Good God!" he gasped, and his legs went rigid.

"Is that tight enough?" she inquired sweetly.

"I-think-so-yes." His words were a breathy stream of air.

"Hmm. Perhaps a bit more." Cecily pulled again.

His only response was a terrible wheeze, and Oliver thought for a moment that he might faint.

"Yes, that should do it." He cracked one eye open

to see her nodding to herself. She turned a sunny smile toward him. "You'll thank me when it's over. Only nine more."

The pain was dizzying for a while, but by the time Cecily Foxe had cinched and knotted the last strip of bandage around his chest, he actually was feeling a great deal of relief.

"Thank you," he sighed, and gingerly leaned back against the headboard of the bed.

"You're welcome." She backed off the mattress and came 'round the side of the bed once more. His eyes followed her, her hips, the curve of her breasts. It was as if he knew the size of one would fit perfectly in his palm.

"Lady Cecily," he began, feeling a terrible pained spiral in his stomach. That he wished he could attribute to the willow tea. "May I ask you another quite forward question?"

She was gathering up the supplies, and glanced at him with a wry smile. "Well, I don't see how it could be any more forward than the ones you've already posed, so yes. What is it, Lord Bellecote?" She turned to face him, the tray between her two hands.

"Did we make love last night?"

The terrible crashing of silver on wood filled the chamber with ringing, clanging echoes, as the tray, domed lid, and all the contents between fell from Cecily's hands. She was staring at him as if . . . well, as if he had asked to see her without her clothes. Which, in an after-the-fact manner, he had. Her face lost all color, her lips rolled in on themselves, and her eyes widened with something akin to fear.

It was then that Oliver Bellecote decided that he was a complete, narcissistic imbecile.

Where, a moment ago, her cheeks had been the purest snow, now they flamed with color. *"What?"* she choked. "How—why would you—"

"I know, I know," he rushed, going so far as to lean up slightly against the screaming protest in his arm, holding his left hand toward her. "It's ridiculous, I know. I do apologize for insulting you so, it's simply that—" He broke off, swallowed. "I keep seeing these . . . these *images* of you, in my head. Like dreams, or . . . or very vague memories, perhaps. Of . . . of the two of us, and—"

"Images?" she whispered. "Of the two of . . . *us?* You and I?"

He grimaced. "Yes."

"What sort of images?" she demanded.

He waggled his head back and forth, glanced at the ceiling. God, he felt like a fool. He may as well have asked the Virgin Mary if she danced for coin. "Improper ones, I'm afraid."

She audibly drew in a sharp breath.

"Lady Cecily, please, I beg of you, forgive me." Now he turned his palm upward, beseeching her patience. "I have been under much duress even before this foolish accident, and it seems that my fall has only further damaged any good sense I once possessed. I know that it is completely inappropriate and disrespectful to even broach such a subject with you, but I simply cannot stop thinking of you in . . . in a way that is, well—inappropriate! Whenever you're near to me I . . ." He stopped, shook his head, unable to find the words.

"Whenever I'm near to you, you what?" she prompted warily.

"I'm not quite sane," he gritted out through his teeth. She drew another deep breath, and Oliver forged on. "This has never happened to me before, with any other . . . woman. Well, women that I have known, ah, *intimately* and so I— *Shit!*" He shook his head firmly. "Any matter, I only told you these things because a terrible idea has occurred to me and I simply must know: Lady Cecily, did I try to . . . to force myself on you last night?"

She stared at him for several moments, and Oliver held his breath.

"No," she said simply, quietly.

"You're certain?" he pressed, trying to suppress the premature relief he felt.

"Quite certain," she said with a slight tilt of her head. She was looking at him curiously now.

Oliver gradually relaxed back against the headboard. "Well, then. That *is* good news." He winced. "You likely will refuse to see to my care after this though, won't you? Not that I blame you—horrible, horrible patient I've been. The worst sort."

She stared at him curiously for another moment. "Good day, Lord Bellecote. I shall see you in the morning."

Then she simply turned and slowly, calmly quit his chamber, leaving the spilled tray forgotten on the floor.

Oliver leaned his head back and closed his eyes. No answers. After a moment, he banged the back of his skull on the headboard. Twice.

Hard.

Chapter 10

"Good morning, Lord Bellecote." Cecily walked briskly across the chamber floor, keeping her eyes carefully averted from the bed when the answering groan floated through the murky shadows. She grasped the inner seams of the draperies and flung them wide, and then stood at the window, looking out on the fringe of hills visible in the distance beyond the wall walk.

Hallowshire seemed so far away this morning. Distant, like an old dream. John Grey seemed so much closer, and in truth, he was—just below her, at Fallstowe's chapel.

Of course, the currently dangerous proximity of Oliver Bellecote trumped them both. But she had refused to dwell on his shocking questions and statements from the previous afternoon and chosen instead to fall immediately into a welcome and exhausted slumber upon reaching her chamber. When she had awoken this morning, she told herself that she would simply pretend the conversation had never happened. The end. Carry on.

A hissed curse and then a grumbling came from the bed. Cecily thought that perhaps the latter was an attempt at a proper greeting.

"Are you decent?" she asked brightly, not wishing to turn and happen upon him without the bedclothes. Although she had done her best to convince herself that she had put the fantasy of Oliver Bellecote from her mind, if he were completely uncovered, Cecily feared she would be unable to look away.

She wasn't a saint, after all.

"Depends on who you ask, I s'pose," Oliver muttered. "But I am properly covered, if that's what you mean."

She turned, and immediately noticed his ashen and grizzled face. His hair was matted on the back of his head, and sticking up in great spikes at the crown. He looked decidedly prickly and not at all comfortable.

"How are you feeling this morn?"

"Bollocks."

Cecily pressed her lips together in an attempt to tame the smile that tickled at her mouth. "I'm sorry to hear that. But you might take heart in the fact that you will begin to see an improvement each day forward."

He scrubbed his left hand over his face roughly and made a noise that Cecily could only liken to a growl. Then he turned his reddened eyes to her.

"I dreamed of you again last night."

Her heart skipped a beat, and she had to force herself to approach the bedside, her fingers following her gaze to his exposed and slinged arm. She touched him lightly, turning her face this way and that to examine the swelling and bruising visible above his bandages.

"I'm sorry," she said evenly.

"Sorry? What have you to be sorry about? God, you smell delicious."

"It must be quite bothersome, is all I meant." She glanced at his face for only an instant. "And thank you, although that is a rather inappropriate compliment. How are your ribs?"

"They're grand. Why do you think that is?"

Then she did look at him fully, still bent at the waist over his arm. "It's the wrapping. The tightness keeps—"

"No," Oliver said crossly. "Why do you think I keep dreaming of you?"

Cecily swallowed. "Ah . . . well. I don't really know." She stood abruptly and turned to the small table at her back. "I've brought you some more tea." She tried to keep the spout from rattling against the edge of the cup. Cecily set the teapot down, grasped the cup in both trembling hands, and closed her eyes for a moment to compose herself. Then she hung a friendly smile on her lips and turned.

He was staring at her, and the sight of him looking so disheveled, so rugged and fresh from sleep, caused a funny hitch in her breathing.

"You," he said.

"Beg your pardon?" Cecily said, troubled to hear the words come out of her mouth in a whisper.

"You," he repeated, his lips pausing, widening slightly, as if struggling to form the words. "You have a mole. On your left side. Just below your collarbone." His words were quiet, easy.

Matter-of-fact.

All the air streamed out of her lungs in a wheeze and she couldn't help but glance down at her chest dumbly.

"You must have me confused with someone else," she said, and then thrust the cup at him. "Here is your tea. I'm late for chapel and Vicar John is waiting."

He blew on the surface of the tea, then took a sip, his eyes never leaving hers over the rim of the cup. "If you think the compliment I paid you was inappropriate, linger a bit. I've been thinking a lot. All night, actually. I should like to share with you my theories on how the back of your cloak was ruined, as well as how my knees were turned into ground meat."

Cecily felt her body go ice-cold. "I'm certain it would be a very interesting conversation, Lord Bellecote, but as I've only just relayed to you, I have other responsibilities to attend to this morn. Perhaps I should have Cook reduce the amount of willow in your tea—it seems to be having a strange effect on your logic and sense of propriety. Good day." She turned calmly and began to walk to the door.

"I was drunk, Cecily. Not unconscious," he called out from behind her. "You may as well confess."

She paused, her hand on the door latch. So much for carrying on. "I fully intend to," she said. And then she opened the door and slipped out.

She did not pause in the corridor—her whirling

thoughts would not allow it. Instead she escaped the castle and walked straight toward the chapel.

John Grey's blond hair was like a golden beacon in the morning sun. A halo. A haven. He was not Father Perry, and yet he was not Oliver Bellecote, either. She had to restrain herself from running to him.

He smiled at her and raised a hand in greeting, speaking before she had fully reached him.

"Good morning to you, my lady," he said, and Cecily did not miss the way his eyes swept her from crown to slippers. He took her hand when she came to a breathless stop before him, squeezed her fingers lightly and then released them. "Father Perry commented on your absence. I do hope it was not on my account."

"No, Vicar. No, of course not." She felt on the verge of hysterical tears, but she tried to smile at him nonetheless. "My charge kept me occupied this morning, more so than I had planned."

A look of concern shadowed his face. "Nothing too dire, I hope."

"No," Cecily said quickly, and then drew up short. "Actually, yes. Yes, it is quite dire, I'm afraid."

"My lady?"

Cecily bit her lip briefly. "Vicar, I need your help."

"Anything, of course. Only put name to it and I shall see it accomplished."

"My charge did not keep me from chapel this morn," she admitted.

John Grey's noble brow dropped. "You were deliberately absent?"

"Yes. I—" She stopped and looked around the

bailey. "Would you mind if we went somewhere to speak privately?"

"Well, I was going to suggest that we have a ride about the countryside today since the weather is so unusually fair."

"Perfect," Cecily said, noting wryly her use of Oliver Bellecote's favorite word. "I mean, yes, that would be fine."

"Shall I have our mounts readied and then wait for you in the stables while you change?"

"Let's both go now. I fear that if I put it off any longer, I will lose my courage."

Although Cecily had been barely able to contain the miserable tangle of words trying to claw their way up her throat upon meeting John Grey near the chapel, once they were astride and through the gates, the knot had frozen into a lump of ice that was loath to be dislodged.

John Grey was not ordained. He could not offer her absolution, Cecily well knew. But perhaps he would have some words of wisdom to impart to her. She wondered if, once she had told him her dilemma, he would think her unworthy for Hallowshire.

She wondered if, somewhere deep inside her heart, that was her secret hope.

He did not pressure her into speaking as they made their way into a long, shallow valley, but seemed content to enjoy the sunlight on his up-turned face. Cecily glanced at him often. His profile was rugged, craggy almost, in contrast to Oliver Bellecote's noble, Romanesque features. The vicar's hair was smooth and straight, the color of rich brass. Oliver's was dark, like melted carob, and unruly as a squire's. John Grey sat a horse easily, but she could not imagine him on a merry chase through the countryside at midnight, in pursuit of a woman.

She could not imagine him following her into an abandoned ruin to make love to her, either.

"I didn't attend chapel this morn because I cannot partake of the sacrament," she blurted.

He looked over at her easily for a moment, and then straight ahead once more.

Cecily continued. "I have mortal sin on my heart, Vicar. Sins that I cannot confess to Father Perry."

"You cannot confess to Father Perry for fear of his recriminations? Or because you are not sorry for what you have done?"

His words were so gentle, so matter-of-fact, and so accurate, Cecily was struck dumb for several moments. Was she so transparent?

"Perhaps both," she said quietly at last.

"Father Perry is a good priest," John Grey offered. "He strikes me as a competent confessor— one who would never broach a subject introduced in the confessional."

A pair of birds swooped before the path of the horses and Cecily followed them with her eyes until they were lost in the sunlight. She blinked away the wetness induced by the bright glare. "Indeed."

"You fear the loss of his love, then? The love he holds for you above his flock?" He led them toward a cluster of three trees, their thick, naked gray arms raised to the heavens.

"Yes." John Grey seemed to be pulling Cecily's

feelings from her heart as a mummer would scarves from inside his vest. Precisely, vividly.

He drew his horse up to a stand, turned his face toward Cecily. "What would you have me do to aid you? Shall I secure you another confessor? Perhaps at the abbey . . . ?"

"No," Cecily said. "I want you to hear my confession, Vicar."

He stared at her, but his face held no shock. "I cannot absolve you, Lady Cecily. Surely you know that."

"I do," Cecily said with a nod. "But I cannot tell these things to anyone who knows me, and I cannot bear the weight of them any longer. Perhaps after hearing my dilemma, you might be able to advise me, for in truth, what I would tell you is the reason for my hesitation for Hallowshire. The bishop would not have granted you the mission of the abbey were you not a capable director."

"Lady Cecily, I—" He broke off and looked up at the sky through the netting of branches above their heads. When he met her eyes again, there was a smile about the corners of his mouth. "I must be honest with you—I am very fond of you already. I'm not certain that—"

"Stop," Cecily said. "I'm sorry, Vicar. But if we are to have any sort of true friendship, then it is best that you know this about me now, lest we go on and you be disappointed later. I would not have you think me someone I am not. That seems to be one of my crosses in life."

"All right," he said with a courteous nod of his

head. He kicked the stirrup free and lighted from his horse, crossing over to help Cecily dismount. "Shall we sit?"

Despite the rare warmth of the sun, the mud and dormant grass at the base of the trees were frozen and solid. John Grey went to his saddle and untied the bundled blanket to spread on the ground. Cecily took his hand as she sank to her hip, crooking her legs to the side and leaning on one arm. John Grey chose to sit away from the blanket, a respectable distance, his back against a tree trunk, one knee raised. He rested his elbow on his knee and looked at her, waiting.

"Two nights ago, I went to the Foxe Ring," she began simply. "Have you heard of it?"

John Grey nodded. "I have. If I remember correctly, unmarried persons visit there upon the fullness of the moon in order to divine their future spouse. Is that correct?"

"Yes. Although that's not the reason I went. Actually, that's not true—I don't really know the reason. In other circumstances, my intentions would seem suspect—my younger sister, Alys, met her husband there. And my parents met there, as well."

"Is that the nature of your sin?" the vicar asked, a delightfully indulgent smile on his face. "Surely you do not think it a slight to God that you would simply visit your old family keep? You didn't make a sacrifice of any sort, did you?" he teased.

"No," Cecily said, and returned his smile. "As a matter of fact, I prayed Compline." She dropped her eyes to the blanket beneath her and scratched at the fabric with a fingernail. "I hoped God would show me what I should do with my life. Where I should go."

"Still not seeing any occasion for you to abstain from chapel," John Grey said in a gentle nudge.

"The injured man that I am caring for now— Lord Oliver Bellecote?"

"Yes, I am familiar with the house of Bellemont. As well as the tales of the younger Bellecote brother's adventures." John Grey's smile caused a twinkle in his eye.

"It was at the Foxe Ring that he sustained his accident."

"So I've heard," the vicar said patiently. "Father Perry said it was a miracle that you were nearby when Lord Bellecote was thrown from his horse. The rumor is that he was quite into his cups, as usual. He could have easily been killed. You cared for him through the night."

"He was indeed very drunk," Cecily admitted. She raised her eyes to John Grey's, and she felt heat rippling from her cheeks. In that moment, she wished that she had confessed to Father Perry. It was so much easier to whisper your wrongs in a dark little cupboard, with no blue eyes looking at you expectantly in the bright light of day.

She took a deep breath. "Some . . . inappropriate things happened between us."

John Grey's face froze, the patient smile still on his face, but now without any life behind it. He cocked his head after a moment, his brows drawing down in a confused frown. "By inappropriate, do you mean—"

"*Inappropriate,*" Cecily said emphatically.

"I see," John Grey said slowly.

"And I believe Oliver Bellecote is betrothed to be married."

Now the vicar's eyebrows rose. "Did you find out after . . . ?"

"His intended told me herself, only moments before Lord Bellecote arrived at the ring."

John Grey frowned, displaying clearly his concern.

"Lord Bellecote didn't immediately remember our . . . indiscretion. And once he started to think clearly, I lied to him about it. And I've told no one else." It seemed that once she had started, Cecily could not stop. "No man has ever dared pursue me, and I think perhaps I only wished to feel how other women feel. And what better man to accomplish that feat than the most notorious scoundrel in all of England? I thought perhaps after spending the night with him, people would begin to see me differently."

"I see," John Grey said, his posture now slightly stiffened. "But no one has accused you of anything, have they? I believe I would have heard of the rumors from Father Perry."

"They suspect nothing," Cecily admitted bitterly. "In fact, I do believe I am in danger of being nominated for canonization because of my selflessness."

"And Lord Bellecote now recalls your . . . encounter?"

"He is beginning to, I think," Cecily said, and at last let her eyes retreat to the blanket once more. "I do not know how to respond to him. I don't know how I want him to respond to me."

"He could ruin your reputation," John Grey said matter-of-factly, and Cecily was relieved that the vicar no longer seemed quite so uncomfortable. She was shamed that she had put him in such an awkward and personal position so early into their friendship.

"He could, yes. But I don't know if I care about my reputation at this point," she said honestly. "And I have done naught but deny any little memory he has mentioned, thus far."

"Are you in love with him?" he asked, his tone incredulous.

"I don't know." She looked into his face once more, the heat of the most embarrassing details having thankfully fled. She took a deep breath. "But I think that perhaps he is the reason I cannot go to Hallowshire. Is it possible to fall in love with someone in only a pair of days?"

"I think so, yes." The look he gave her caused a strange sensation in her stomach. "Lady Cecily, he is not worthy of you."

"Worthy of me!" Cecily laughed. "Vicar, did you not hear my confession? 'Twas I who was the seducer!"

"We all stumble," John Grey said easily. "Especially in those areas where we are not well traveled. And although you are called Saint Cecily, no human is without sin. And this little fall of yours should not keep you from Hallowshire, if that's where you truly feel God is leading you."

"I don't know," she admitted miserably. "I don't think I'm being led anywhere, actually. I feel very . . . lost. And like I don't know who I am, or even who I want to be anymore! It's as if my entire life thus far has been naught but an act!" She sighed, letting the heat of her emotions pass. "Do you think me a farce?"

"Not in the least," he answered immediately, emphatically. "You are actually quite noble for tempting Father Perry's curiosity. A lesser woman would have gone ahead, even while under such a heavy heart. You are purer than you realize, Lady Cecily. There is nothing at all wrong with a woman choosing marriage over the convent, even if it is not the path she always thought her life would take. And a simple kiss . . . well, most girls have that out of the way before their years number a dozen."

Cecily was still for a moment, and then threw back her head and laughed, tears coming into her eyes. The vicar thought that she and Oliver Bellecote had done nothing more than kiss.

"I'm sorry," she said, pressing her fingertips to her eyes. For some reason she felt like weeping now more than ever. "I'm not laughing at you, only at the notion you suggested."

He smiled at her. "Don't be so hard on yourself."

"What shall I do, Vicar?" she asked, her smile fading.

"You should spend an inordinate amount of time with me, I do think."

She raised her eyebrows.

"I will tell Father Perry that I am counseling you intensely. When you feel you are able, you may decide on a confessor and put the whole lot behind you, once and for all."

"What about Oliver Bellecote, though?"

"If he remembers, there is little you can do about it save for lie, and that I do fear would only buy you a small amount of time, and perhaps an even larger consequence to bear. If he is not heartless or stupid, perhaps the pair of you can come to an agreement that your transgressions will not be mentioned outside your shared history. I'm certain you have no wish to hurt his betrothed."

"No."

"And he is well known for his dalliances, so I do feel that he will adapt to discretion more readily than you."

Cecily winced inwardly at the reminder of Oliver's prolificacy as John Grey continued.

"I do hope that you will be wise enough, though, to make the time you must spend with him as brief and impersonal as possible. Intimacy with a man of that sort is . . . well, it is dangerous."

"And well I know it," Cecily muttered. She looked up at him sheepishly. "You will make a fine priest, Vicar."

He shrugged. "Perhaps. Perhaps not." He looked into her eyes, and Cecily saw something there, something more than the courteous respect previously apparent. A softening, an intrigue, as he looked at her. "Will you call me John, in private? In truth, I am not actually a vicar, and 'tis my father and older brothers who are titled."

"I will call you John, if you will in turn call me by my given name."

"I would be honored."

Cecily looked at the sun. "He'll be asking for me soon."

"Yes. And I must be on my way back to Hallow-shire." The regret was plain in his voice. "I'll return soon enough, though. Will you see me again . . . Cecily?"

She smiled at him. "Of course. *John.*"

He helped her to her feet, and after he had gathered up the blanket and affixed it to his horse's saddle, Cecily rashly grasped his right hand in both of hers.

"Thank you," she whispered.

His fingers tightened around her own, so lightly that Cecily could barely feel them. Then he pulled away, a strange but pleasant smile on his face.

"Let's get you home."

Chapter 11

He waited for her all day. At every knock on his door, he held his breath, hoping for her gentle voice to inquire as to the state of his decency. But it was only a chambermaid, or a kitchen servant, or old Graves. He wondered if she would ever step foot inside the chamber again.

Oliver remembered.

He and Cecily Foxe had made love—Saint Cecily Foxe!—that night at the old ruin. He now understood why her presence had vexed him so. Each moment she was near him had been like a constant state of déjà vu. But what troubled him now was that, knowing the root of his intimate knowledge of her, his desire to see her had grown exponentially. Every thought in his head was related to her. Every waking moment, every ache in his broken bones whispered her name deep in his core, taunting him, laughing at him.

The scoundrel in him should have been triumphant. He had succeeded in making love to the most beautiful, unavailable woman in all of England. But he did not feel prideful at his half-remembered, drunken pawing of her. And neither was he so chivalric that he feared he had ruined her. He only burned to see her again.

Which was another point of contention within himself. Never had he thought longer of a woman, especially after he had already made the conquest. The chase was enough of a preoccupation for him, the game. Once the prize was tasted, the excitement also fled, leaving him searching for his next prey. He tried telling himself that it was only because he had not been sober enough to savor Cecily Foxe when they had made love, but he knew that was only a rather ineffective balm for his pride. His thoughts were not consumed with seeking out her body again so that he might be fully aware of the treasure of her sexuality.

He simply wanted to look at her, talk to her. Be in her presence. He wanted to ask of her future. Would she go through with her plans to enclose herself at Hallowshire? The old vicar's intentions in visiting with her were blatantly obvious—he was recruiting her. Wearing on her sense of honor. Oliver could just picture the stooped, gray-haired priest kneeling at Cecily's side, the two of them praying fervently for her discernment. Had she been spending such an amount of time with any other man—be he married, single, or eunuch—Oliver was certain that he would have been mad with jealousy.

Oliver didn't have a plan. But then again, he rarely had. His brother, August, had planned out his entire life, and look where that had gotten him, how short that very well-planned life had actually been.

So he didn't want to plan. He just wanted Cecily Foxe, in his room, an hour ago.

His midday meal was cold and mostly untouched by the time she finally arrived, entering his chamber without the benefit of a knock or a greeting. And unlike the other times she had visited him, when she had either been pale and fatigued, or nervous, or quiet, her cheeks were now rosy blooms, and her hair was wild down her back, the sides caught back behind her ears.

It was the first time he had seen her hair both unbound and uncovered, and it mesmerized him as it swung at her waist while she turned to close the door. She was like a fairy creature, clothed in rippling ebony.

His eyebrows rose when she threw the bolt on the door. She stood there a moment, her back to him, as if composing herself.

She turned, and her eyes widened as they landed on him.

"You're dressed," she observed.

"And more properly bathed," he added with a smile. "I could no longer stand myself, much less impose my malodor upon you." He didn't bother to tell her that the freshly laundered shirt he wore was the only clothing he now possessed. Fallstowe's maids had effectively destroyed his only pair of breeches.

She took a handful of hesitant steps toward the bed, her fingers strangling each other at her waist. "Was it very painful?"

He wrinkled his nose and gave a slight shrug of his left shoulder. It had been excruciating.

Her eyes narrowed, but she did not challenge his statement. She took another pair of steps. "How are you feeling now?"

"Much better, now that you're here."

He saw her chest rise in a deep breath, and she looked at the floor, her lips rolling in on themselves. In the next moment, she had claimed the wooden chair at his bedside, and now looked at him directly.

"Let's get it over with then," she said grimly.

He relaxed fully against the headboard and waited. Had he been in possession of two working arms, he would have crossed them over his chest authoritatively. "All right."

"Yes," she said.

"Yes, what?" he encouraged.

"Yes, we did."

Still, he waited.

She sighed and rolled her eyes. "What is it you want from me?"

"Why did you lie to me?" he asked. "You let me believe I was losing my mind!"

"I thought you wouldn't ever remember, since you didn't right away!" she reasoned. "Why would I volunteer information about an incident that I am quite embarrassed about, even if no one else knew it but I?"

"You're embarrassed regarding making love with me?" Oliver asked, wounded more than he would have ever admitted. "I've never thought of myself as hideous."

"Of course I am embarrassed! I am unmarried, discerning the convent, and I had an affair at the Foxe Ring with"—she threw her hands toward him—"*Oliver Bellecote!*"

"Well, of course, I do understand the unmarried scenario and how that would give you pause," he granted. "But I am offended that you would think to even keep it from me, when I would never use such gossip to slander you."

"I don't know that, though, do I?" Cecily challenged him. "You are quite free with tales of your conquests. I have no desire to be added to the list of them."

"Ah, but who conquered whom in our little scenario, Lady Cecily? Or am I not the only one for which the details of our night together remain somewhat blurred?"

"What on earth do you mean?" she demanded, her face going scarlet.

"You lured me into the ruin."

"You *followed* me," she gritted out between her teeth.

"I was drunk, I didn't have my wits about me," he said easily. "I was little match for your wiles."

"My *wiles?*" she choked. "I was a virgin!"

Oliver felt his head draw back as if he'd been slapped. "That's not possible."

"I don't believe I have earned the moniker *saint* as a form of sarcasm," Cecily said with a wry lift of her eyebrow.

"But, a virgin . . ." He felt his own cheeks reddening. Dammit! "There is usually some *evidence* left behind, after . . ." He trailed off, circling his hand in the air as if to encompass the situation.

"There was," she stated. "I took care of it. After you passed out."

His eyes widened, but he could not think of anything else to say. Not only had he slept with Cecily Foxe, he had taken her virginity!

"Thorough, weren't you?" he asked at last.

"I tried to be, yes."

"All right, that was a shock, I admit," Oliver said with what he hoped was a gracious tilt of his head. "But I accept it, and I forgive you completely." He ignored her outraged expression. "So, how would you have us proceed? Shall we call on Sybilla for advice?"

She stared at him for a moment, as if she was unsure whether he was serious or not. "*No*, we should *not* call on *Sybilla.* I would have you recover quickly so that you might leave Fallstowe as soon as possible. Without telling *anyone* of our . . . indiscretion, of course."

"You're worried the vicar will find out, aren't you?" he guessed.

"The vicar already knows," she answered swiftly and calmly, although her eyes darted away as she said it. "He was sent as special counsel to me—as well as an aid to Hallowshire—by the bishop. I told him this morning, straightaway."

"Oh, so *you* can boast of your conquest but not I?"

"I can assure you that there was no boasting involved, and I told you when last I left you that I was going to confess. Unfortunately, Vicar John has returned to his post at Hallowshire Abbey, but if you feel that your actions are weighing on your conscience, I will be more than happy to summon him back for you."

"Oh, *Vicar John,* is he?" Oliver remarked snidely, surprised at the rising of jealousy he now felt. The man was a priest, for God's sake! "I have no need of confession, for the difference between us, my lady, is that I am not at all sorry for what we did."

She paled. "You're not?"

"No. In fact," he said with all the sincerity he could muster, "had I to do it all again, the only thing I would change is that I would be sober, so as to recall it in greater detail."

Her face went from white to red as she stood. "Are we finished?"

"Absolutely not," he said.

"Well, I think we are," she challenged him. "In keeping with the sage counsel I was graced by this morning, the two of us shall have as little contact with each other as possible. We should both soon be able to carry on with our respective lives. Agreed?"

"No," he refused her again.

She stamped her foot, and Oliver wanted to laugh out loud so charmed was he by the uncharacteristic gesture.

"But I will cooperate with your wishes to a reasonable extent, if *you* will agree to but one thing," he conceded.

Her expression grew warily hopeful. "What is the one thing?"

"I want you to kiss me."

* * *

Cecily didn't know whether to laugh or slap Oliver Bellecote's handsome face. He was demanding that she kiss him? She could barely restrain herself while in the same room as him, as it was!

"You can't be serious."

"I am very serious," he affirmed.

"I am not going to . . . *kiss you!*" she stammered.

"All right," he said with a conceding nod. "Then come a bit closer so that I may kiss you. I've never gotten the chance to thank you properly for saving my life."

"I didn't—" She broke off, thinking twice about refuting his claim, not wishing to be drawn into a deeper argument with him. "*You're welcome.* There. Now, may I please examine your arm?"

"No kissy, no looky," Oliver said somberly, belying his childish words. "That is our deal, and I will not allow you to default on it."

"I didn't *make* a deal with you!"

"All right then, we can call it my requirement, if you wish." He looked her up and down while Cecily continued to stammer, her face heating. "Did you know there was talk of a betrothal between the two of us when we were children?"

"Yes. But my mother put an end to it, saying that you were too wild for me, even when you were no more than ten."

"Ah-ah." Oliver waggled a finger at her. "Not so. *My* mother put an end to it, not wishing one of her sons to be married into a family of witches."

Even to Cecily's own ears, the sound that came out of her mouth was an indignant squawk.

He continued nonetheless. "So you see, if things

had worked out differently between our families, we would be married now, and kissing me would be no grand event."

"I'm sorry if it offends you, but I wouldn't consider it a grand event, any matter," she lied.

Oliver threw back his head and laughed. "I have never imagined this side of you, Cecily," he chuckled, his eyes sparkling as he looked at her. "I'm not certain anyone has. I quite like it."

"So glad I can amuse you," she gritted out through her teeth.

"Kiss me," he requested again.

"No."

"Please? There, I've said please. Now you can't refuse me on grounds that it would show poor manners."

"I hardly think that there needs be any facade of courtesy between us at this point."

"All right then," he conceded in a low voice, and it was as if the light in the chamber dimmed in that moment, wrapping them in an evening sunset, hushing and warming the air around them.

"Then kiss me because I cannot stand a moment longer with my lips not touching yours; because whenever you leave, I search the coverlet, the bandages for your scent. When I close my eyes, I see you at the Foxe Ring on the night we met; I hear your voice in my ear, whispering for me to take you harder, faster."

Cecily drew in a sharp breath. His words were having a physical effect on her, as much as if he were stroking her bare flesh. But he was not yet done.

"Kiss me for what might have been those many

years ago, had our families joined us in marriage. Before you became frightened of yourself and went away to hide behind the cross, and before I realized how far short I fell of August's greatness. Kiss me as if we were two new people, only having just met, with our entire future laid before us, free for our making."

Cecily noticed with a soft inhalation that there were tears in her eyes. "If only that could be true," she whispered.

"It can be," Oliver said. "Look at our circumstances, Cecily: I am lord of Bellemont, my family's wealth and power behind me now. You have not yet committed to the abbey, have you?"

She shook her head slightly. "No."

"Then who would tell us that we cannot do as we wish? That the two of us, you and I, cannot be for the other what each of us truly needs. What do you need, Cecily?" he asked earnestly.

She felt mesmerized by his voice, his reasoning. It sounded so simple, the way he put it. So simple and so precisely opposite from what John Grey had advised.

"I—I don't know. Oliver, you are still . . . *you*. And I am still me. We are ill-suited to each other."

"I don't think so," Oliver pressed. "Let us rediscover each other, for who we really are—who we want to be. I am different now, because of you. Perhaps you are different, too?"

Cecily was stunned into silence for several moments while her mind tried to make sense of the outrageous things he was suggesting to her.

"Come here," he commanded softly, patting the mattress with his left hand. Her wary frown must have been quite obvious, for he buffered his order with a little grin. "I shan't attack you."

Cecily walked around the end of the bed as if she was in a dream, not at all certain it was the wise thing to do, but unable to do anything else. She perched her hip on the edge of the mattress.

"Come up here properly." He sighed and rolled his eyes. "Come on, come on—it's not as if the worst hasn't already happened between us. I can't take your virginity twice now, can I?"

Cecily paused in maneuvering herself farther up on the bed to give him a warning look. "Oliver . . ."

Then she was seated next to him, mirroring his position with her back against the ornate head-board. She turned her head to look at him expectantly.

"Why did you make love with me two nights ago?" he asked.

Cecily tried to feel more taken aback, but as she had done little more than mull that very question around in her own head for days, it did not shock her.

"I was very lonely," she said quietly. "And perhaps scared. The time had come for me to make a commitment to Hallowshire or nay, and perhaps I was having a very bad case of nerves." She didn't know why she was telling Oliver this. For all his seductive charms, it wasn't as if he truly cared.

"I don't think you belong there," he offered.

Her eyes widened. "Why not?"

"Because you would have gone long ago, at least shortly after your mother passed," he said gently. "You have been waiting for something. A sign perhaps." He paused, and then his left hand moved so that the backs of his fingers brushed her thigh through her skirts in a soft caress. Cecily's eyes went to his hand. "Perhaps I am that sign."

"Oliver, I do not mean this in jest, or to hurt your feelings in any way. But I think perhaps you were merely a convenient way for me to rebel against my own life that night. I have not decided against Hallowshire, I'm only still undecided. One night with you has not changed anything." *It's changed everything.*

"Give me time, then," he suggested.

Cecily had to remind herself to breathe. What was he proposing?

"Time to what?"

"Time to convince you beyond any doubt that Hallowshire is not where you belong. There is something between us—something deep. How else can you explain a pair such as us, on the surface so very different, experiencing such passion? I have seen a glimpse of the woman you could be, the woman you want to be. You only need someone to help you bring that out."

She couldn't help her wry grin.

But his face remained solemn. "Perhaps one night with me was not enough to convince you, but something has happened to me, Cecily. As I said, I am no longer the same, and in some ways I regret that. But it cannot be changed, nor would I choose to even were I able. I want to pursue you."

"That's madness," Cecily said on a breathless laugh. "Oliver, what would people say?"

"I don't give a damn what anyone would say," he answered fiercely.

"Because I am only a challenge to you," she countered, unable to bring herself to believe he was sincere. "Our affair was a fluke, and now you want a chance to do it on your own terms. Once the novelty of Saint Cecily wears off, you will discard me, as you have so many other women."

She saw him wince slightly as he shook his head. "I don't think so."

He hadn't denied it outright, which gave Cecily pause.

Oliver continued, "Let me become your friend. Perhaps you will feel differently by the time I am well enough to leave Fallstowe."

"I cannot do that in good conscience, Oliver, and you know why," Cecily said, and even to herself, her words were prim, bitter.

"I'm afraid I don't," he said. "Enlighten me."

Cecily gave a short, irritated huff. *"Joan."*

Oliver's eyebrows rose as his gaze rolled over her face. "Joan who?"

"Joan Barleg?" Cecily said pointedly. "The woman you are to marry?"

"I'm not marrying Joan Barleg," he exclaimed. "Who told you I was?"

Cecily felt her lips purse. "Joan Barleg did."

"Cecily, I have not proposed to Joan, and as a matter of fact, I told her when last she was here that I would not. I broke it off with her, even before I recalled what had happened between you and me."

Cecily stared at him for a moment, her stomach doing a funny little tumble. He wasn't marrying Joan?

"Why?" she blurted.

"Why?" Oliver repeated, and gave her a confused look. "Because I don't wish to marry."

Cecily felt her eyebrows raise and she tore her gaze from Oliver's face, looking instead to the coverlet. "I see."

"Wait, that came out wrong," Oliver rushed. "What I meant was—"

"No, don't explain," Cecily interrupted. "If you've no wish to marry, then that is certainly your prerogative. We are simply too different, you and I."

"Cecily."

"Vicar John was right—we must try to avoid each other's company for the remainder of your time at Fallstowe."

"Cecily!"

"For even though you say that you have no wish to marry, Joan Barleg is under the impre—"

"Cecily!"

She stopped with an annoyed sigh and gave him the sparest glance. "What?"

"Cecily," he said again, softly now, his voice low and rough.

The room fell silent around them when he didn't say anything further. After a moment, Cecily could not bear the tension, and she grudgingly turned her head to look into his eyes.

"Just kiss me," he whispered.

Cecily wished what Oliver had said moments ago could be true. That they could be two new people, learning each other as if for the first time. The way he was looking at her was causing an ache in her chest; his gaze seemed to have taken hold of her heart and was squeezing it ever so gently. It was exquisite agony. She wanted him then, perhaps more than she had ever wanted anything in her life. More than when she had let him take her in the Foxe Ring. It was sapping all of her self-control, her mastery of her will, to simply keep from touching him.

"Please," he breathed. "If you don't, I'll simply die."

The words were her undoing. She turned on her hip as if in a trance and leaned into him slowly, closing the distance between their lips in agonizing eternity. She caught his scent, the smell of man, and sweaty sleep, and faint soap, and then she caught her breath as her heart skipped.

He raised his head to meet hers, and their mouths touched lightly, both half opened. Cecily withdrew slightly.

"Again," he commanded in a whisper. "Please."

She leaned forward once more, and this time their lips met fully in a slow, lazy kiss. She tried to once again pull away, but his head followed hers, deepening the kiss and denying her retreat.

Cecily surrendered with a silent sigh. It was so much better this time, so much more tender. . . .

The rapping on the chamber door nearly startled Cecily's spine from her body and she jumped away from Oliver, breaking their kiss abruptly.

"Who in the devil . . . ?" he growled, casting a furious glare at the door.

"Oliver?" a female voice called gaily from the corridor. The latch rattled. "Why is the door bolted?"

Chapter 12

"Oh-my-god, oh-my-god," Cecily stammered in a horrified whisper, fighting her legs in the long tangle of her skirts to disembark from the wide mattress. She was having a terrible go of it. "What am I *doing*?"

Oliver cursed softly. Perfect!

"Calm down, Cecily, I beg you, before you bring injury to yourself—Joan can neither see nor hear us. Your dignity is safe."

Cecily fell off the side of the bed with a little cry and a larger thud.

Well, it *was* safe, until that.

"Oliver?" Joan called through the door again. "Oliver, are you all right? Who's in there with you?"

Cecily appeared abruptly on the side of the bed, her face a startling contrast of red and white. She was wringing her hands.

"She can't see me here like this," she whispered desperately. "Should I hide in the wardrobe?"

"Whatever are you talking about?" he asked, completely confounded.

"No, of course not—the wardrobe is all wrong." Her mouth pinched in a worried frown and her eyes flitted around the room. "Perhaps under the bed, then?"

"Cecily!" he said on the breath of an incredulous laugh. "You are my nurse. Your presence here is more than dignified."

"I would not call what just happened between us dignified," she hissed.

"But Joan doesn't know that, unless you tell her, does she?"

Cecily gave him a strange look, her expression morphing in to one of semidisgust.

"You are exactly the person I thought you to be, Lord I-Don't-Wish-To-Marry," she said in a ferocious whisper. "And I am a fool, in more ways than one."

"What is that supposed to mean?" he demanded.

"I will not be another conquest for you to boast of, and I will have no part in your breaking of Joan Barleg's heart. As of this moment, I am no longer responsible for your care." She stood upright, her shoulders back, her chin tilted. "I hope. . . I hope your arm falls *off!*"

"What the devil?"

But her answer was not for him as she spun on her heel and strode to the door, calling out, "One moment, Lady Joan!" She fumbled with the bolt for longer than was called for, and Oliver reckoned that her hands were less than steady by the outrageous reaction she was having to a simple knock at his door.

"Good day, Lady Joan, come in! I apologize for

the delay," Cecily gushed as she swung the door wide, revealing the blond interruption that turned Oliver's mood to black. "I was only finishing with an examination of Lord Bellecote's arm. I'm quite done now, though. Quite, *quite* done."

Joan gave Cecily a quizzical smile as she stepped into the room, and Bellemont's steward at her heels was a welcome sight to Oliver.

"Good day, Lady Cecily. I do hope Oliver is not giving you too many troubles. Oft times I am convinced that he has no control over his mouth." She flashed him a sweet smile and approached the bed, while Oliver noticed Cecily blanch further. "Good day, my dear. How are you feeling? I've brought Argo, as well as your favorite nightclothes—does that earn me a hello kiss?"

His chamber door slammed, and Oliver knew that Cecily had gone to flight.

Dammit!

"Oliver, aren't you even going to greet me?" Joan demanded piqueishly.

He swung his face toward her and let his irritation come through in his tone. "Hello, Joan. What are you doing here? You said you were going home."

"What am I—? I told you two days ago that I would be coming back, and I *did* go home. To Bellemont. I took much care in gathering the things I thought you'd be in most want of, and this is how you thank me?"

"Bellemont is not your home," Oliver growled.

"Not yet," Joan said with a sly wink.

Oliver clenched his teeth together and then looked to his steward—formerly August's steward—

and he caught the man rolling his eyes behind Joan's back. "Argo."

He gave a curt, shallow bow. "My lord."

Unlike the Foxe family's obvious penchant for tradition if ancient Graves bore any indication, August Bellecote's preference was to only surround himself with the best at Bellemont—the youngest, most virile; the fastest, most cunning, and capable. Even the chambermaids were sharp, swift. Which was perhaps why August was only too happy to have Oliver spend so much time abroad.

Oliver guessed Argo to be in his late thirties, and although the man appeared to be of only average height and build, Oliver knew from personal experience the sculpted and sinewy muscles that lay hidden beneath the man's plain dress, as well as the lightning-like reflexes that could easily restrain a maudlin-drunk younger brother from engaging in a brawl that would have been the neat end of him.

In all of Argo's years at Bellemont, he and Oliver had never quite been fast mates, but since August's death, the steward had become Oliver's anchor. The sight of the man's long, reddish hair and beard— which gave him the appearance of a very angry and very tall troll—brought back some stiffness to Oliver's spine.

"How fares Bellemont in my absence?" he asked.

"All is well in hand, my lord," Argo said, giving a barely noticeable sideways glance toward Joan. One thing Bellemont's and Fallstowe's stewards shared was a distaste for anyone not of their respective holds, and Oliver knew that if there was news of any import to be had about his home, Argo would not share it in Joan Barleg's earshot.

Nor did Oliver want him to.

Oliver looked to Joan, who was now flitting about his chamber as if they were in truth man and wife—straightening the items on his side table, tugging at the coverlets, pouring him a cup of wine, which she brought to his side with a bright smile. He wanted to swat at her as he would a persistent gnat.

He had been kissing Cecily, and she had interrupted them.

"Would you mind, Joan?" he said pointedly, ignoring the chalice. "I'd have a word with my man in private to discuss Bellemont's affairs."

She gave a little huffing sigh and drew the cup to her own bosom. "I don't see why you should be so secretous about such borifying topics as goats and peas." Then she looked at him indulgently, as if to say, You boys and your games.

"Very well." She pulled the coverlet up higher around his waist and bent over to kiss his temple. "I happened to see Lady Sybilla on my way up and she has invited me to sup with her. So, see? You are not the only important guest at Fallstowe, lover." Oliver tried not to wince at her satisfied grin. "Shall I bring you a tray?"

"I shall see to the lord's meal, my lady," Argo offered solicitously, if a bit impatiently. "Don't trouble yourself."

Joan's merry eyes turned frosty. "I don't believe I was addressing you, Argo. It does not trouble me in the least to see to *Lord Bellecote's* sustenance."

Oliver did not miss the steward's clenched jaw. It

was as if Joan was purposefully reminding the man
that his friend and lord was dead, to goad him.

She turned her gaze back to Oliver, her eyebrows
raised expectantly.

"Go, Joan. Enjoy your time with Lady Sybilla. I
will likely be engaged for the remainder of the
evening, so we can say our good-byes now."

When he expected her to move closer, she set
the chalice on the side table and began walking
toward the door with a cheery laugh. "You shan't
miss me so soon, silly! I'm free to stay at Fallstowe
until you've recovered, upon Lady Sybilla's own insistence!" She paused at the door to waggle her fingers at him and then was blessedly gone.

Oliver looked to Argo, his own eyebrows raised
in question now.

The steward nodded grimly and stepped forward.
"She's brought everything she owns, I believe, my
lord. And I was hard pressed to keep her from bringing most of what you own. I needed to set two maids
upon her while she was at Bellemont—it was her intention to peruse each chamber for anything she
deigned necessary to your survival at Fallstowe—
even Lord August's rooms." Argo set a large leather
satchel on the floor and then held up the weapon
he'd been holding—August's sword.

Oliver's sword, now.

Oliver sighed and shook his head before drop-
ping back against the pillow. "My apologies, Argo.
And thank you for protecting the integrity of my
home as well as my brother's personal belongings.
Put the sword atop the wardrobe—I hope I will
have no need of it while at Fallstowe, and I'd not

have it disturbed." In truth, Oliver had no wish to look upon it.

Argo harrumphed as he dragged a chair to the wardrobe. He stepped onto the seat in one fluid motion and slid the weapon carefully along the top edge of the wood, obviously still very much put out by Joan Barleg's antics. "If any at all has leave to go through his lordship's chamber, I daresay it would be you. Or mayhap Lady Sybilla." The sword fell to the top of the wardrobe with a loud, hollow-sounding thud.

Oliver turned his head to look at the steward. "Think you Sybilla would have any care for a memento of him? As I understood it, she broke his heart—threw him out of her bed practically."

"They were not so estranged," Argo said slowly. "I do believe August was advising the lady on her troubles with the king."

"Was the lady listening?" Oliver asked with a wry smile, doubting that Sybilla Foxe would take counsel from any, especially a man she had rebuffed romantically.

"I believe she was," Argo said solemnly. "They had become . . . reconciled before the lord's death."

The corners of Oliver's mouth turned down in surprise. These Foxe women—so many facets. Oliver would never figure them out.

"Now that we are alone, tell me—what news is there from Bellemont?"

Argo's posture straightened, and at once the man went from casual confidant to capable servant. He withdrew a folded parchment from his tunic and handed it to Oliver. "The king has responded to Lord August's death."

Oliver cast a wry eye to the steward when he saw the wax seal on the document was broken.

"I had just received word of your accident and was unsure when you would return, my lord. If the king was not for you, I wanted to prepare our defiance."

Oliver laughed out loud. "You would rally against the king for not recognizing a notoriously lackadaisical and feckless younger sibling's rights to the lordship of Bellemont? Argo, I fear my leadership is not nearly worth such loyalty."

The steward did not crack a smile. "It is what Lord August wanted."

So it was not loyalty to Oliver the man was professing at all, but still August. Of course.

"Perhaps. And so this"—Oliver rattled the parchment in his hand for emphasis—"shall not happen again, ken? I'll have anything of import brought to me—and only me—directly."

"As you wish it, my lord, of course."

Oliver shook the parchment open and read, tossing Bellemont's steward a grateful glance when the man brought a brace of candles near the bedside to bolster the weak evening light against the gloom creeping up the deep stone window seats. After several moments, reading the entire document through twice, Oliver dropped the page to his lap and looked to Argo, who was waiting patiently.

"I have difficulty believing my brother agreed to this," Oliver said, motioning again with the page in his hand.

"He agreed to the mustering at Midsummer, of

course," Argo offered. "And although I am certain the king's other motives were alluded to in the summons sent last year, Lord August never gave mention to it."

"If only our ambitious monarch knew I was reading his directive within the very walls of the treasure he covets. He would be either very, very pleased, or quite put out."

Argo nodded. "Will you respond?"

"Eventually." Oliver crushed the missive in his hand as he grasped the edge of the coverlet. He held his breath and then threw the covers back. "I do hope that satchel contains breeches, Argo." Oliver braced himself again and then pulled in his abdominal muscles and sat up in bed, swinging his leg around in the same motion.

His breath hissed out of him and the blood pulsed, roared in his arm, behind his eyes, in his ears. When the crashing pain at last ebbed to a fog, he opened his eyes. A pair of breeches hung in front of his face, draped over the steward's forearm, and in the man's other hands were Oliver's favorite, worn boots, God bless him.

"If my lord will allow me?" Argo asked solicitously, and then dropped to one knee to begin assisting Oliver to dress.

Oliver found himself very thankful indeed that his brother had only ever employed the very best of men.

Once he was standing and properly clothed—for the first time in days—Oliver took a moment to grasp the bedpost and give his head the opportunity to stop spinning, the blood to stop throwing

itself up against the backs of his eyes. In spite of the
dizziness, the fiery throbbing of his right bicep, it
felt bloody good to be on his feet again.

And the thought did cross his mind that Cecily
would no longer be able to run away from him quite
so easily now that he could give chase. But before he
could track her down and demand a proper explanation for her mad display upon Joan's arrival, he
intended to speak to Sybilla.

Argo followed him to the great hall without a
word of either caution or encouragement when
Oliver was forced to stop several times and lean his
left shoulder against the stone walls of the corridors
for support. His right arm throbbed like black hell,
each beat of his heart sending a shower of fiery
arrows through his veins. Dizziness came and went,
like clouds across the sun, pebbling his skin with
cold sweat. By the time he had descended the final
flight of steps to enter the large, stone-buttressed
room, he felt as though he had walked the entire
way to London.

The great hall was not crowded this evening;
mayhap only two score common folk peppered the
benches snugged up to the long tables on the main
floor. Oliver was uncertain that he had ever been to
the large castle without the benefit of some celebration or another, and the orderly calm in the cavernous room felt strange to him. Hundreds of candles
and bale fires had been replaced with small, plain can-
delabras. Countless huge round iron fixtures hung on
long black chains from a dark, invisible ceiling. Oliver

knew that if each were lit with their own score of candles the hall would be as bright as midday, but the only two presently alight were above the center aisle and over Sybilla Foxe's table.

They cast Cecily Foxe in a soft glow.

Oliver lurched gingerly down that center aisle, noticing grimly and too late the curious stares and whispers he drew from the diners at the tables he passed by. Self-consciously he reached up with his left hand to smooth his hair—an old, prideful habit, he knew—and was dismayed to feel the coarse hedgerows that were sprung up on his scalp. Any matter, she had already seen him at his worst.

Sybilla had caught sight of him as soon as he'd stepped from the stairwell, and the slightest motion of her hand had produced a quartet of servants. By the time Oliver and Argo reached the front of the hall, a place had been neatly laid for him at Joan Barleg's elbow, as well as a trencher for Argo at the front-most common table. As he glanced at Cecily yet again—she who would not meet his eyes—Oliver noticed the strange, seemingly decorative centerpiece of the Foxe matriarch's table: a large, milky, crystal cluster, seeming to sit in its own stone bowl in front of the lady's place.

Oliver bowed. "I beg pardon, my lady, for interrupting your meal."

"Nonsense, Lord Bellecote," Sybilla said with a cool, nearly nonexistent smile. "You are always welcome at my table. I am glad that you are well enough to join us."

"In truth, I had no intention of eating," Oliver began, and he couldn't help his eyes going to

Cecily again. Her gaze was fastened firmly on the tabletop before her face, her hands disappeared somewhere on her lap.

"You missed me so much already?" Joan sighed sweetly. "How romantic, Oliver! I am flattered."

He looked to the blond woman only briefly before finding Sybilla once more. "I need to speak with you, my lady."

"After supper, Oliver," Sybilla said with easy dismissiveness. "Unlike some, I do have an intention of eating."

Oliver doubted as much, as the woman's silver platter clearly displayed a wealth of food completely undisturbed.

Sybilla continued. "And I am very much enjoying the entertaining company of your own Lady Joan. Do sit. We shall discuss later whatever it is you find of enough import to challenge your injuries to be at my side. The stew is quite good tonight, wouldn't you agree, Cee?"

Cecily gave a nearly inaudible clearing of her throat. "Yes, Sybilla. Quite good."

Sybilla raised her eyebrows toward him as if to say *See?*

"I'm certain it's delicious," Oliver said. "But, Lady Sybilla, my man from Bellemont has—"

"Later, Lord Bellecote," Sybilla said.

He shook his head. "Sybilla, hear me—"

Her eyes went to his then, and her gaze was like a sword, cutting off his argument. Oliver thought he saw a kind of odd plea behind her hard facade.

"I already know all about what it is you've come to tell me, and I can assure you that it is not the great concern you think it to be. There are more pressing matters to be attended to first."

"You can't possibly know," Oliver argued. The damned stubborn woman!

She stared at him. "Supper, Lord Bellecote."

"Very well." He bowed stiffly, his jaw clenched, and then made his way slowly down the long table to step onto the dais and take his seat next to Joan.

"I can see that being an invalid does not agree with your humor at all," Joan chirped brightly as he sat down. "Why, I don't believe I've ever been witness to Oliver Bellecote turning away from platter and full cup before! And besides, we were just discussing the fascinating gift Lady Sybilla received today. Look, Oliver—by her ladyship's plate!"

Oliver glanced at the cluster of stones again and growled acknowledgment.

"It's a—a *dream crystal*. Is that right, Lady Sybilla?" At Sybilla's slight nod, Joan continued. "Found right on Fallstowe lands! Isn't it beautiful?"

Oliver could feel Cecily's pull from the other end of the table, as if her physical presence was drawing him to her. He had to steel himself not to lean back in his chair and crane his neck to try to catch a glimpse of her.

"It's lovely," he muttered.

"Oh, don't be so crossed and nasty!" Joan laughed as she swatted playfully at the air near his shoulder. Then she thankfully turned toward Sybilla again. "Please go on, my lady. You were speaking about the legend?"

The screech of wood on stone interrupted the

request, and Oliver saw the top of Cecily's hair appear beyond where Sybilla sat.

"I'm sorry, but do you mind, Sybilla? I still have things to gather if I am to leave at first light."

Oliver's heart stopped, and he could not help himself when he nearly shouted, "Leave? Leave where? Where are you going?"

Two female faces swung around to look at him curiously. Unfortunately, Cecily's was not one of them.

"She's my nurse," he stammered on any matter, feeling his face heat like some green lad's before his first pair of breasts. "And as I fear I'm yet quite unwell, she can't simply leave!"

Cecily did look at him then, but Joan Barleg's merry laugh caused her to turn quickly away.

"Oh, Oliver! So dramatous!" Joan sighed happily. "Although I'm certain it offends your sense of entitlement, Fallstowe's angel has more souls under her care than just yours."

For the first time in his life, Oliver longed to slap a woman. As she was seated on his left, he would be forced to give her the back of his hand, and he would likely have to strike her with some force to gain any sort of accuracy, but one must work with the tools one was given.

"Go on, Cee," Sybilla said. "And have Graves fix a large purse for you—it's been a hard winter."

Cecily smiled at the diners at Sybilla's table, but her eyes did not find Oliver's. "Good night to you, Lady Joan, Lord Bellecote." She turned away.

"*Wait!* Where are you—?" But she was already gone from the dais and disappeared through a little door disguised in the back wall, so that Oliver could only lean forward to demand of Sybilla, "Where is she going?"

"Lady Cecily accompanies our priest on a round through the villages once a moon. She has a knack for healing, as you are already aware, and so she takes medicines and food to the poor and ill. Never fear, Lord Bellecote, your nurse will be returned to you. Most likely. I am certain you will survive in the meantime."

Although her words were matter-of-fact, Oliver clearly heard the undertone of caution in Sybilla Foxe's explanation.

Joan Barleg, however, obviously sensed no such thing. "Such a noble woman of charity!" she exclaimed admiringly, and then leaned closer to Oliver to whisper huskily, "Although I am not as accomplished in the art of healing as dear Lady Cecily, I think I can bring you some relief from your discomfort until her return."

"That won't be necessary, Joan," he began between clenched teeth, but his lecture was cut off by Sybilla Foxe, speaking as if the interruption of Oliver's arrival and her sister's departure had never been.

"Yes, it is known to some as a dream crystal. Supposedly very powerful," she said in a bored tone. She reached out an arm and stroked one of the points with a slender finger. "The dreamer only needs place a piece of the stone under her pillow to see all that she most desires come true."

Joan gasped. "Verily, Lady Sybilla?"

Sybilla withdrew her arm and shrugged, as if she could not have cared less.

"Have you . . . have you ever tried one?" Joan pressed in an anxious whisper.

"Oh, when I was a young girl, I did, I suppose," Sybilla said. She paused, turned her head slowly to look at Joan. "Do you fancy a piece of it?"

Oliver thought Joan Barleg would swallow her tongue, and he was rather disappointed that she did not.

"Truly?"

"Of course," Sybilla said smoothly. She waggled a finger up near her shoulder and Graves was immediately at her side between her and Joan, pulling the large, sparkling rock mass closer to Sybilla.

The eldest Foxe sister picked up her eating knife and looked at the crystal this way and that, seeming to appraise it. She pointed with her knife tip to a long, slender finger of rock that seemed aimed at Joan Barleg. "What of this one?"

"Oh, yes, it's beautiful!" Joan all but squealed.

Sybilla nodded. "Very well, then. Pick up your knife, Lady Joan, and place the backside along the seam, here. There you are." Sybilla spun her own knife in her palm, gripping the hilt in her fist, the blade pointing up. "Very still now—watch yourself."

Joan gave a little shriek as Sybilla Foxe brought the wooden hilt of her knife down upon Joan Barleg's blade with such swiftness that even to Oliver's careful gaze the motion was a blur. A large cracking sound rang out, followed by a muffled little thud. In a blink, the long finger of crystal had wobble-rolled across the table and rocked to a stop before Joan, who stared at it with her mouth in a round O.

Oliver looked back to the large cluster, and saw that the dulled blade of Joan's knife was now buried in the wooden hilt of the utensil still in Sybilla's hand.

"Oh, dear," the Foxe matriarch said smoothly. "Look what I've done." She gently removed Joan's hand from the hilt of the bottom knife and handed both—still joined together—over her shoulder to the ever waiting Graves. "Could you bring us another set, please, Graves? I fear the butler will be much put out with me!" She gave a throaty laugh, and Oliver did not think for a moment that any one of Sybilla Foxe's servants would ever think to reprimand her for anything.

Joan had picked up the stub of crystal with both hands, and was now admiring it close to her face. "Oh, a thousand thank yous, my lady!" she said in an awed voice. "I've never received anything so lovely!"

"Will you use it?" Sybilla asked nonchalantly, picking up her chalice and then taking an easy drink.

"This very night!" Joan promised.

Sybilla smiled. "You must tell me if it works or nay," she said. "Perhaps I might take up the custom as well, should you find it useful."

Joan giggled. "It shall be our little experiment!"

Oliver almost felt sorry for the girl, who obviously thought she was in fast league with the deceptively beautiful woman sitting next to her.

Sybilla then stood abruptly and took two paces to

bring herself to stand in the space separating
Oliver's chair from Joan's. Oliver was shocked to
feel the light touch of her palm on his shoulder,
and he saw that she was making the same gesture
toward Joan. He made to rise from his own chair.

"Don't trouble yourself with courtesy, Lord Bellecote. I am sorry to leave such festive company, but
I have other important matters to attend to before
I retire. I shall leave you two young people to enjoy
the evening on your own."

Oliver snorted and turned his head to look sideways at the woman. "Lady Sybilla, I do believe I am
your elder by at least some months."

She only smiled enigmatically.

"Besides," Oliver began, "I still have need to—"

His words were cut off as Sybilla gasped. "Why,
whatever is Graves doing with a herring on his head?"

"What?" Joan laughed, and turned to look.

Sybilla bent down near Oliver's ear and whispered the words so fast, Oliver scarcely caught them.
"Come to my chamber in the morn. I wake early."
Then she rose. "Oh, my mistake—that's not a herring at all, only his hair. Forgive me, Graves."

Oliver chanced a glance at the ancient servant—
the man did not miss a beat, nor did he crack a
smile. "Would Madam prefer I wear a herring about
my head?"

"I'll certainly think upon it," Sybilla answered.

Chapter 13

The sun had just pulled itself fully over the low eastern hills by the time Cecily and Father Perry approached the farthest of the small villages in the Fallstowe demesne. It had been a cold night, and the dead grass looked like a blanket of crushed diamonds, the horses' steamy snorts like censers before them.

The beloved priest whom Cecily had known since childhood had thankfully made no mention of her absences from chapel the past several days, and indeed, Father Perry had had little at all to say to her since the morning prayers. His eyebrows had risen when she'd walked into the chapel hours before the dawn, but that was all.

It wasn't as if she had roused herself from a comforting slumber.

Wrong atop of wrong. It seemed that she had been incapable of making a correct choice since the Candlemas feast. In truth, she was unsure if she even knew the difference between right and wrong anymore. Her desire to be with Oliver Bellecote, even in the most innocent manner, overwhelmed her body and mind. She longed to talk with him, laugh with him, discover his plans for Bellemont. Like he was a sickness she had caught in the old Foxe Ring, and no remedy existed that could ease her suffering. And that was only the most benign facet of her desire for the scoundrel.

When Cecily was near him, her body reacted. Her good sense, her notions of propriety and purity and honor, fled with a pitiful wail under the onslaught of the pure physical lust that she felt for Oliver Bellecote.

It was bad enough to experience the sin of lust. To have experienced it and acted upon it, not only once, in the old keep, but also in Oliver's room, where she had allowed him to kiss her. And likely would have allowed him much more had he been more able bodied and had they not been interrupted.

By Joan Barleg. The woman who had been his companion for a pair of years, and honestly thought that Oliver was going to marry her.

Yes, bad enough to have given in to lust twice, but the greater humiliation was her inability to stop, when she knew what she was doing was so very wrong. Stop thinking about him. Stop going to his room, even under the guise of caring for him. He was the sort of man who would humiliate the woman who loved him while she waited for him on the other side of his chamber door!

Cecily couldn't know for certain where their kissing yesterday would have led had Joan Barleg not come knocking, and she wondered if she would have had the fortitude to refuse his further advances. Her worry increased when she could not answer yes straightaway.

Well, you hateful little tart, she thought, but to her dismay, she sounded rather pleased with herself.

He was a sickness with no remedy.

She pulled the cowl away from her mouth. "Father?"

"Yes?"

"I am certain you've noticed the . . . the neglect of my duties."

He was quiet for a moment while the horses plodded along. "If you mean the duties you have assumed at the chapel, yes, I have missed you there. But you have many duties at Fallstowe, Lady Cecily. The castle is no abbey, and I am not your superior. You are not beholden to any task. I am only pleased that you accompany me this morning."

She swallowed. Of course, he would be understanding. "I have not been . . . present as much because, well—" She took a deep breath of the teeth-achingly cold air. "What if my heart has been consumed with worldly thoughts and desires? What if . . . what if I'm *possessed*?"

Father Perry laughed. "Although demonic possession is really naught to make sport of, I do highly doubt that your soul is the ideal breeding ground for evil." His chuckles died away, but left a serene smile as a reminder of his mirth. "Are you in love, then?"

Cecily was surprised. "I don't know. Perhaps. Although if this is what being in love is about, what it feels like, I'd really rather not."

"If you'd rather not, then I'd say you *are* in love,"

Father commiserated. "Love doesn't give you a choice. I know him, don't I?"

"Yes," Cecily said hesitantly. "But not well, I don't believe. In truth, I don't know him very well myself."

"A nobleman?"

Cecily nodded. "But, until recently, no one of consequence. He is not his family's firstborn."

Father Perry was looking at her keenly now, a knowing light in his eyes. "Could he commit to you? Is he willing?"

"No." Cecily looked away for a moment, toward the glowing ball of orange in the sky. "I don't know." She shrugged.

"Anything is possible," Father Perry said lightly. "Of course, you would be unable to join Hallowshire as a married woman."

"I'm not worried that he would *want* to marry me, thus making me ineligible for the veil," Cecily said wryly. "I am more afraid that he does not wish to, and that my time with him has ruined me. Ruined the plans I had for my life. That the brief time in which I have known him has given me a glimpse of something both terrible and wonderful at once, and now nothing else will ever fulfill me as he has."

"That is troublesome," Father Perry agreed. "But only because when we look to another human being to fulfill us, they always fall short. They are always a disappointment. Each of us falls short of God's glory. Only He is perfect, and so only He can fulfill us."

"I know," Cecily whispered.

The kindly priest smiled at her. "I know you know." He drew his horse to a stand and Cecily was prompted to follow suit. "Which is why I am not at all concerned for the state of your soul. Don't think that I have not noticed your absence, for I have. Greatly. But I do believe with all my heart that you are being led in the way He has prepared for you, whether that be at Hallowshire, at Fallstowe Castle, or . . ." He shrugged.

"I went to the Foxe Ring," she blurted. It was as close to a confession as she was able to make to the man, like an uncle to her.

"Did you, then? Well." He smiled, nodded, and looked over her shoulder. "I go there often myself. Very peaceful place for meditation, I have found."

"I didn't go to meditate though," Cecily began in frustration. But before she could try to elaborate on her sins, Father Perry turned a widening smile to her.

"It seems as though we will have some company on our mission this day, Lady Cecily. Company I believe will please you." He nodded in the direction that lay behind her.

With a frown Cecily turned in her saddle, wondering who on earth would be game enough to be about the frozen land at sunrise, to minister to the sick and poor with a ruined noblewoman and an old priest.

"A bit tardy this morn, are we, Lord Bellecote?" Graves asked dryly as Oliver neared Sybilla Foxe's chamber door. The dusty, walking corpse was standing watch to the side of the corridor opposite the portal.

"The sun's just come up," Oliver muttered. "Had I been any less tardy, it would still be *night*. Is she awake?"

"Think you I would dare chastise a man of your impeccable manners for his tardiness were Madam not ready to receive you?" Graves countered.

"You are a cheeky one, aren't you, old codger?" Oliver growled, narrowing one eye and looking at the steward sideways.

Graves mirrored exactly Oliver's expression.

Oliver sighed and rolled his eyes.

"If my lord will follow me?" The servant at last moved across the corridor and knocked discreetly on the thick wooden door before engaging the latch and swinging it wide.

Oliver moved past the man, expecting him to remain in the corridor, but Graves was close at his heels, shutting the door with barely a sound and sliding the bolt home.

Sybilla Foxe was completely dressed for the day, including her coif and crispinette, sitting on a tufted chair at a large, plain desk on the far side of the room before a bank of windows. Her mouth was covered by her hand, her elbow resting on the tabletop, and she seemed lost in the misty view before her.

In the center of the desk was the large crystal cluster from her table the night before.

"Sybilla," Oliver said.

She didn't start at the sound of her name, only continued to stare out the window. She slid her hand down to her chin. "Good morrow, Oliver. Did you sleep well? How is your arm?"

"Good morrow. No. And I believe it's still broken."

She raised her slender eyebrows briefly; her mouth turned down, and then she nodded.

Oliver glanced over his shoulder at Graves, who seemed as though he was paying no attention to them whatsoever. In fact, the old man had turned his back toward them and appeared to have a hairbrush in his hand, grooming his thin, gray hair in a small mirror.

"I thought we were to speak in private," Oliver said in a low voice.

Sybilla at last turned her chin away from her hand to look at him. "Graves, you mean? I can assure you that we are more warranted our privacy with his presence than without."

"Very well," Oliver said grudgingly. "So I'll just come out with it then. I received a missive from Edward, mustering Bellemont's due at Midsummer."

She laid her arm along the edge of the desk. "Of course you did."

"Because my brother cared for you so deeply, I would spare you such unpleasantness was it within my power to do so. But there is no gentle way to say this, Sybilla. The king is going to march on Fallstowe."

"I know."

"You know? You seem very calm about it."

"I've had more time than you to become accustomed to the idea." She gave him a faint smile. "The king warned my youngest sister, Alys, himself. And August told me of Edward's plans when Bellemont's service was first summoned, while your brother was still lord."

She hadn't said "when your brother was still alive," or "before he died," and Oliver was unsure whether he should be offended by her lack of empathy or saddened by the idea that she was unable to bring herself to say the words.

"Are you to surrender?" Oliver asked.

Sybilla wrinkled her nose while she shook her head slightly, and behind him, Oliver thought he heard old Graves snort.

"No, I don't think I shall *surrender*," Sybilla said coyly. "August and I had been working on a plan. Obviously, that's gone awry."

Her words put his idea that she might be saddened over losing August to rest. Oliver felt the aching blood in his arm pound harder, until his vision seemed to tremble with each clenching of his heart. Was this woman so cold, so heartless, as to speak of his brother's death as an inconvenience? The roaring in his ears was nearly deafening.

"But I do believe I have come up with a way to partially implement August's ideas, any matter," she continued. "As well as possibly secure you a vast fortune for Bellemont in the process. The king acknowledged your lordship of Bellemont and its holdings, did he not?"

"He did. But why would you care to secure me of anything?" Oliver demanded. "It was August who was in love with you, Sybilla, not I. And I don't think you were ever in love with *him*, so why should *you* give a damn not only about his younger brother, but about pitiful little Bellemont?"

Her blue eyes pierced his, hard, sparkling, and with a seriousness that made Oliver's throbbing blood run sluggish and cold. "Your brother was the best friend not of my own blood that I have ever had," Sybilla said quietly. "Present company excluded, of course, Graves."

"How could I think otherwise, Madam?" the old steward muttered mildly. He came to stand nearby, juxtaposed between Sybilla and Oliver, his hands clasped behind his back and his eyes trained somewhere on the still dark ceiling.

"I care very much about Bellemont's welfare, and your own, for reasons that you will discover as soon as I am able to tell you," Sybilla continued. "In the meantime, I need you to trust me, for I desperately need your help, Oliver."

"You desperately need *my* help?" Oliver sneered. "With what?"

Sybilla's chest rose slightly as she drew a deep, silent breath.

"I need you to propose to Joan Barleg."

Although she had always enjoyed being among the villagers and their simple life, Cecily had never experienced a more gratifying day of service as the one she was spending with Father Perry and Vicar John Grey.

They had passed out sacks of meal and dried fruit,

as well as crumbly little ropes of seaweed. Cecily had brought an enforced arsenal of salves and potions, tinctures and powders, bandages, and herbs for teas. Before the noon meal she had lanced and dressed three wounds, treated an old man for ague, and mixed a special tea for a new mother and her tiny newborn baby, both bedeviled by a nasty case of thrush. Father Perry was kept distant and busy hearing the confessions of the villagers before the celebration, and so Vicar John became Cecily's handsome and merry attendant.

He was the best of assistants, drawing on his experiences at various religious enclosures that often served the ill and dying. He was no stranger to sickness and misery, and yet his training thus far combined with his vocation ensured that he exuded a kind of gentle calm to Cecily's patients. He was not uncomfortable with their poverty or their ignorance, and indeed, he seemed to enjoy conversing with villagers of all ages.

Cecily was particularly touched by the way he held the new babe, she thought perhaps like a father would hold their own child, cradled in his hands, his face bent low over the infant's, a peaceful smile on his mouth and in his eyes as he whispered a happy prayer of blessing near the baby's ear. The sight caused her to pause in stirring the mother's tea.

He looked up at her in just that moment, his smile deepening as their gazes met. Her cheeks tingled as she tore her attention away from the handsome vicar and handed the mug to the woman with a smile, but she could feel the weight of John Grey's lingering gaze on her back.

The mass celebration was simple but beautiful, held in the largest of the cottages. Even then, the overflow of faithful knelt in the dirt beyond the open door. She glanced sideways at John Grey once, from beneath the hem of her long veil that hid most of his profile, but she could glean nothing from his closed eyes and bowed head.

They made their way from the cottage together among the crowd of people, saying their good-byes, and Cecily felt strange when John Grey lightly took her elbow to lead her to where a lad held their mounts at the ready. It was past midday, and the ride would be a long one to gain Fallstowe before dark.

Once at her horse's side, she turned to thank John Grey for his aid and company, but he spoke first.

"I fear our duties this day left us little opportunity for conversation," he said, regret clear in his tone.

"Yes," she agreed. "But your appearance was such a pleasant surprise. I couldn't have treated as many as I did without you."

"How fares your . . . patient at Fallstowe?" he asked in a low voice, glancing around as he said it.

Cecily shrugged and dropped her eyes to her hands, where her fingers were twisting the ends of her veil. "Today has been the first time in a week that I've felt at least marginally sensible," she said on a breathy laugh, but in her heart she feared that she was speaking naught but the truth. She looked up at John Grey, surprised at the intensity with which he was regarding her. "Would that you were closer to Fallstowe, John. Your advice seems so rational, and kind. You have not judged me as I fear others would."

"What have I to judge?" he asked sincerely. "Even I could not enter into the sacrifice today because I was in need of penance."

Cecily frowned. "I would think there to be no shortage of confessors available at Hallowshire."

"Indeed," John acquiesced, and his eyes sparkled. "But I fear my encounter with sin only occurred since my arrival at the village this morn."

Cecily swallowed with a gulp.

"Are you unhappy with your circumstances at Fallstowe, Lady Cecily?" John Grey asked.

"I suppose I am," she answered. "If only he would leave, perhaps I could return to some sense of clarity."

John Grey nodded, as if her answer was exactly what he had expected. "If he will not leave, then come on to Hallowshire with me."

Cecily frowned. "John, I . . . I have yet to decide—"

"Not to take the veil. Only to do what you have here, in this village, today. Mother would delight in a visit with you, and perhaps it would give you the distance you require from your . . . problem."

Cecily turned her face to the south, as if she could see Fallstowe from where she stood, see Oliver Bellecote standing at the window looking for her.

"But I must confess to you that my intentions are not completely noble," John Grey said. "Would that I, too, had you closer at hand. I have been unable to concentrate fully on my duties since the afternoon of our first meeting, Cecily, as I have been contemplating a great number of personal decisions. I . . . I would like very much for us to have time together. In a place—for you, perhaps—not so tainted."

Father Perry came upon them just then, and his presence reminded her that she was to accompany the aging man over the land to their home.

"Thank you, Vicar," she said, smiling weakly. "But my sister will be expecting me, and I would not have Father Perry journey alone."

"What is this about then?" Father Perry inquired with a curious smile.

"I've just asked Lady Cecily for a short visit with Mother," John Grey said easily. "Alas, her devotion to her home is too great to indulge me."

"Nonsense," Father Perry said, his eyes crinkling merrily as they glanced from Cecily to the vicar. "I'm certain Lady Sybilla would not begrudge you a day or two at the abbey where you are contemplating spending the rest of your life. And I am no invalid, young woman—I have trod beside fighting men in many a battle. A simple ride over my homelands will give me much needed time to speak to the Lord about matters on my own heart."

John Grey looked back to Cecily. "I would not press you, my lady. If you have no desire to carry on to the abbey, please feel no obligation to accept my invitation."

Cecily could tell that the vicar meant every syllable of every word he spoke, and she realized suddenly that there was little hope the bishop would win

John Grey for the priesthood. He had made it clear in his own respectable and completely honorable fashion that he wanted her to accept his invitation to Hallowshire. He wanted her company, and she had no fear that John Grey would attempt to further compromise her already secretly battered reputation.

Which brought her thoughts, inexplicably, back to Oliver Bellecote.

Whenever you're near to me . . . I'm not quite sane.

I simply cannot stop thinking of you.

This has never happened to me before.

The greatest scoundrel in all the land, and he was preoccupied with thoughts of Saint Cecily.

Oliver was waiting for her at Fallstowe. As weak as it sounded, she knew she could not withstand his advances. It did not ease her mind that he had disavowed any intention of making Joan Barleg his wife; in truth, that only made things worse. It clearly showed that Oliver Bellecote would go to any length for a conquest. Would stoop to whatever depth necessary to maintain his scoundrel's reputation. He had admitted that he possessed no desire to wed Joan, or Cecily, or any other woman. Cecily could not allow him to make such a fool out of her. Or her to make such a fool of herself.

Perhaps if she did not return to Fallstowe, Oliver Bellecote would then go, taking her shame and weakness with him. Cecily could only hope that he would not also take her heart when he left. It was the only thing she had left that truly belonged to her, now that he had taken her body. The only thing she had left which could still be given away with forethought and intent.

John Grey glowed in the bright afternoon sun, his straight hair glinting with the beams of light that seemed attracted to him. She was reminded suddenly of the tender way in which he had held the newborn peasant babe.

A handsome man.

A titled man.

A man who had himself said that one needn't take vows to be of service to God. He was convincing.

He was *not* betrothed.

The man was as far removed from a scoundrel as could be, and Cecily knew she was safe in his presence. Even from herself.

Cecily looked to Father Perry. "Would you give Lady Sybilla a message for me?"

Chapter 14

Oliver could not recall a time when he had been more cross.

He was seated at Sybilla's table for supper again, but this time he sat to the woman's left, in the chair that Cecily had occupied only last night. Thankfully, Joan Barleg was seated on the other side of the Foxe matriarch, leaving Oliver to concentrate on pretending to eat his food.

Why had she not yet returned?

Oliver had been completely befuddled by Cecily's disgust of him before she'd abruptly left Fallstowe with the old priest, but he was determined that she should have no doubt of his intentions toward her. He wanted her—only her. And he was willing to go to whatever lengths she determined to be necessary to win her. Once that was established, they would go to Sybilla together and Sybilla could detail her insane theories to Cecily herself.

It made little sense still to Oliver. But Sybilla had sworn that the thing she asked of him was somehow tied to the plan his brother had instigated to help

Sybilla Foxe retain Fallstowe, and she had promised to pay him handsomely for his cooperation. Oliver was certain that, once Sybilla explained it all, Cecily would understand. Oliver wanted Cecily . . . he only needed to become betrothed to another woman, first.

Perfectly reasonable.

He shifted uncomfortably in his seat as the women to his right continued to chat about the stupid sliver of rock Sybilla had given Joan last night.

"Think you I placed it too far from my head?" Joan whined.

Sybilla shrugged and swirled the contents of her chalice. "Perhaps, since you slept so very poorly. You may do well to sleep with it."

"You mean hold it in my hand or something of that sort?"

"There's an idea," Sybilla mused, and then took a sip of her wine.

Joan nodded decisively. "I shall try that then tonight. I am certain that it should work. Something so beautiful must be powerful, wouldn't you agree?"

"Completely," Sybilla said mildly.

Oliver was in the process of rolling his eyes when he caught sight of the slender old man dressed in long robes, making his way toward the dais. It could be no other than Father Perry, and if he was back from the mission across the countryside, Cecily could not be far away. Perhaps she was fatigued and had gone straight to her rooms. No matter, Oliver would simply put off Sybilla until the morrow, after he had a chance to talk to Cecily.

"Peace be with you, my lady," the priest said with a broad smile.

"And also with you, Father," Sybilla answered. "How fares the village?"

"Well. We performed the Lord's work today, most surely. Your generosity was appreciated more than you can know. God will reserve a special place for you."

Oliver wasn't certain, but he thought he heard Sybilla Foxe snort daintily.

"I pray that is true, Father," she said. "Where is my sister? I hope not infested with lice again. Cecily always feels she must *cuddle* all the children."

"Not this time," Father Perry chuckled good-naturedly. "But alas she is not here for you to confirm for yourself."

Warning clangs—like crashing cymbals—began sounding in Oliver's already pounding head.

"Not here?" Sybilla thankfully gave voice to the questions banging on the back side of Oliver's teeth. "Where is she?"

"She's gone on to Hallowshire, my lady. With the vicar."

The crashing cymbals in Oliver's ears threaded out into a loud buzz, and it felt as though the bottom had dropped out of his stomach.

Sybilla huffed a little disbelieving laugh and then leaned back in her chair as if she, too, was stumped. "In truth? My, my, Father. Vicar John must be of the persuasive sort."

"That he is, my lady," Perry affirmed with a grin. "I do believe he has taken a special interest in Lady

Cecily, and she values his opinion and regard quite highly."

"That gladdens my heart," Sybilla said in a low, intense voice.

"And mine as well," Father said with a knowing look, and Oliver could not help but feel that, even though the conversation was taking place directly before him, something was being alluded to that he did not understand.

"Did she say how long she will stay before coming home?" Sybilla asked, and then leaned forward slightly. "Is she *coming* home?"

"She did not say," Father Perry confirmed. "She very pointedly did not say."

"I see," Sybilla half sung.

Father Perry nodded sagely.

"What in bloody hell is going on?" Oliver blurted, the pounding in his skull making his vision dance. Everyone turned surprised eyes to him, but he didn't care. "Is she coming back or isn't she?"

Father Perry gave Oliver an amused smile, and Oliver wanted to blaspheme just to spite the meek little messenger.

"Only God knows, my son."

"Only G—" Oliver broke off and clenched his teeth together. But even he could hear the strangled sounds struggling to form into words and burst free from his mouth. His arm throbbed as if a strong little man stood near his elbow, thrashing it with a club. He stood abruptly, the chair legs squealing on the stones beneath his seat.

"If you will excuse me." Oliver turned and gave Sybilla a short bow. "My lady."

"Oliver, what on earth has come over you?" Joan demanded with a puzzled laugh. "I do vow that little blow to your head has completely wuzzled your personability. I'm sure your nurse is quite fine, as you will be with or without her. Don't leave us so soon—we've not even had the pudding yet."

"I don't care for any bloody pudding," Oliver ground out. "Thank you."

Sybilla raised her chalice to her lips again, and although Oliver knew the lady was still waiting on his answer of the offer she'd put forth, she didn't bother to cast her eyes in his direction as she spoke against the rim of her cup.

"The pudding's quite good." She took a sip. "August never missed the pudding."

It was the final straw.

He threw his napkin onto his platter and turned, making his way from the dais and swerving through a right, then a left turn to gain the main aisle. He heard a chair screech from its place just behind him, and then Joan called out.

"Oliver, wait!"

"No!" He threw his left hand over his head but kept walking. "No, Joan. Whatever you do, do not follow me."

"Where are you going?"

"To gather my belongings," he tossed over his shoulder.

"But I don't *want* to leave yet!" she whined.

"Then for the love of sweet Christ in heaven, don't!" he shouted. His steps hesitated for an instant, and he added somewhat more somberly, "Beg pardon, Father."

He stormed through the doorway of the great hall, up the short flight of stairs leading to the entry, and then started toward the main thoroughfare to the upper chambers.

If Cecily Foxe cared so little for him that she could simply take her leave from Fallstowe without so much as a good-bye, then so could Oliver. He hadn't been himself since that damned Foxe Ring, and now he'd had enough. To hell with her. Oliver hoped she was very happy at her blasted nunnery. To hell with heartless Sybilla Foxe and her hare-brained, selfish schemes, as well. To hell with every-one and everything at Fallstowe.

He was going home.

Sybilla glanced over her shoulder at Graves, and in that same instant, the old steward turned from her and disappeared through the narrow doorway set in the wall behind the dais. Then she turned her attention back to the still smiling priest.

"Was there anything else my sister wished to tell me, Father?"

"Only that she is very sorry for any inconvenience her absence might cause you," the man said with a knowing smile.

Sybilla returned it. "Thank you. Won't you join us, Father Perry?"

"Thank you, my lady, but no. I am not as young as I once was, and feel the desire for my own warm bed more insistently than I do a warm meal."

"I bid you good night, then," Sybilla said.

Father Perry bowed, and then made the sign of

the cross in the air over the table before turning and walking away in his swishing robes.

Sybilla turned to Joan Barleg, who was twisting her napkin into a knot on her lap, a worried frown creasing her high, youthful brow.

"Lady Joan, I am not as familiar with Lord Bellecote as you are," Sybilla said mildly, reaching once more for her chalice. "Does he always react in such a manner when offered pudding?"

"The temper you mean?" Joan asked. At Sybilla's half nod, the girl continued. "No. Not at all. It's why I jested with him about the blow to his head. Oliver has always had an easy nature. His behavior of late has been more akin to August's than his own." Then Joan gave a little gasp and turned wide eyes to Sybilla. "Please forgive me, my lady."

"Forgive you what, Lady Joan?" She brought the cup to her lips and drank.

"For mentioning . . . well, so soon after—" She broke off. "Of course, you would be familiar with August's temper. I didn't mean to cause you any undue grief." She leaned forward slightly. "Are you griefish, Lady Sybilla?"

"Intensely," Sybilla answered, and even to her own ears, her tone was full of cynicism. "Why would you think August ever showed me anything but kindness?"

"Oh, I didn't mean to imply that he— I only meant that since you . . . Well, it was said the two of you were very fond of one another."

Sybilla hummed slightly, as if Joan Barleg had said something of high interest. "I am very fond of several people, Lady Joan. Some a bit more than others, though, I suppose. Should any of them happen to die suddenly, I do imagine that I would feel rather put out."

Joan Barleg frowned slightly and then sat back in her chair. After a moment, she sighed. "Well, then. I suppose I should go to my own chamber and gather my things."

Sybilla turned her head slightly to glance at the girl. "Whatever for?"

"Oliver said that he was leaving."

"Oliver also said, in quite a clear if uncharitable manner, that you should stay here if you wish." Now she looked at the young woman fully, studying her. "Now that Lady Cecily has gone on to Hallowshire, I have no female contemporaries to keep me company."

Joan Barleg's eyes brightened. "Truly, Lady Sybilla? You would have me stay only to keep your company?"

"It is my utmost wish at this point, Joan." Sybilla smiled. "It's all right that I call you Joan, isn't it? You may call me Sybilla, if you like."

Joan Barleg appeared ready to either cry or faint. "*Of course* you may call me Joan! *Sybilla*," she added with a simpering smile. Then her face fell. "Oh, but I can't. I really shouldn't. Oliver is still quite injured, and since that disgusting Argo has already departed for Bellemont, I can't let him travel the whole of the way alone." Joan seemed to think hard for a moment, and when she next spoke, her words were whispered on a breath of confession. "Besides, he has yet to propose properly to me, and I do fear I must strive to give him every opportunity."

Sybilla leaned heavily on the right arm of her chair. "Joan." She crooked her left index finger at the girl, prompting her to mirror her pose. "Shall I tell you a little secret?"

Joan Barleg nodded rapidly. "Yes, yes! Do!"

"I think," Sybilla drew out, and then glanced around the hall pointedly before turning her attention to Joan once more, "that Oliver won't go back to Bellemont tonight."

Joan's eyebrows rose.

Sybilla nodded. "I also think that the reason he will stay is . . . you."

"Me?" Joan squeaked.

Again, Sybilla nodded. "Breathe not a word of this conversation to him, you vow?"

"*Of course!*" Joan hissed.

"The two of us, Oliver and I, were speaking of a betrothal between you and him only this morn."

All the color drained out of Lady Joan Barleg's face. "You advised him?"

"I did." Sybilla leaned back in her chair.

"Well, what did he say?"

"He hadn't decided." Sybilla picked up her chalice once more. Empty. Dammit. She rattled its base on the table before setting it back down. In a blink, a kitchen girl appeared with a skin in hand.

"Is there naught I can do to sway him?"

Sybilla shrugged and then took her now-full cup in hand again.

Joan looked confused for a moment. "But he told me not to follow him. I don't think angering him will further my cause." She paused, looking earnestly at Sybilla. "Do you?"

Sybilla gave the girl a slow, solemn wink.

In the next moment, Joan had tossed her napkin atop her own platter and rose from the table, stomping in a dainty manner from the dais and marching down the center aisle.

Sybilla watched her go.

Oliver had not had time to properly put away the things Joan Barleg and Argo had brought him from Bellemont, and so there was precious little to do to prepare for his departure. Everything was still neatly contained in the leather sack save the belt holding his scabbard and sword—August's scabbard and sword—which Argo had hidden atop the tall wardrobe. Oliver stared up at the piece of weighty furniture, easily nine feet tall, considering the ornately carved molding around its crown.

He couldn't reach it, and he couldn't leave it here.

"Damn Cecily Foxe." Oliver turned and looked around the room behind him, flickering in the weak light of only the hearth and a single flame near the bedside. He spied the straight-backed chair at the small table.

"Ah-ha," he growled, and then marched toward the would-be ladder. "Not so much as a farewell," he continued to mutter as he dragged the chair on two legs across the floor. He cursed and jerked on the piece when it caught on the edge of a rug. "Rather spend her time with a moldy old priest, would she? Fine, then. Brilliant. *Perfect!*" He slammed the chair down on all four legs before the wardrobe, shifted its position a bit.

"Should she think that I'll simply wait here for her like some lost pup, well"—he gave a stuttering huff of a laugh—"I think not!" He grasped the back of the chair with his left hand, shook it to check the stability. "I am Oliver Bellecote, Lord of Bellemont! I wait for no woman!" He placed his right foot on the seat of the chair and then pushed off with his left leg.

He was forced to release his hold on the chair back, and now stood atop the chair, swaying slightly, his blood bursting through his right arm as his heart pounded and his head swam. He was surprised at how much his stamina had deteriorated. He waited for the throbbing fire to quiet before carefully reaching up with his left arm, the lintel biting into the middle of his forearm, his stretched ribs screaming for mercy beneath the tight bindings around his chest. He felt for the top of the wardrobe with his hand, but his fingers met only air.

"Perfect!" he bit off, and withdrew his hand. Apparently the ornate carvings atop the wardrobe gave a greater illusion of height than was accurate. Oliver guessed that the proper top to the piece— where his sword lay—was at least twelve inches beyond the reach of his fingers.

He leaned into the piece, and reached up once more, standing on the tips of his boots. He felt ridiculous, like a lad in the larder attempting to sneak a biscuit from the cook's special jar. If only he could reach a bit farther, get his elbow crooked fully over the edge . . .

A rap sounded on his door so suddenly and so loudly, that Oliver cried out and slid to the right against the side of the wardrobe. He gripped the top of the lintel at the last moment, saving himself from falling from the chair directly onto his broken arm. Pain like silver, liquid fire swirled around his ribcage.

Another knock, and then a dusty old voice called out to him from beyond the door, "Lord Bellecote, are you all right?"

It was Graves. That maggoty old servant had nearly killed him!

Oliver righted his stance, but kept a firm hold on the wardrobe's top. "I'm fine, Graves, thank you."

"Did I hear a scream, my lord?"

"It wasn't a scream, it was a shout. A shout of surprise. I'm fine."

"Are you certain?"

"Yes," Oliver ground out.

Oliver heard only the pounding of his own heart and the creaking of his ribs for several moments, until he was convinced that the steward had at last left. He leaned into the wardrobe and was just reaching over the top once more when the scratchy voice sounded again, surprisingly robust.

"May I help you collect your belongings, my lord?"

Oliver shouted again—truly, it was a shout, not a scream—and craned his head around to spy the old man standing in the middle of the chamber floor, his hands clasped behind his back.

"How did you get in here?" Oliver barked.

Graves's sparse eyebrows rose mildly and he

looked over his shoulder at the door. "Did you not hear my knock, my lord?"

"Yes," Oliver ground out. "But I did not bid you to enter."

"Shall I leave?" The old man half turned.

Oliver realized he was still standing on a chair, attempting to gain his most prized personal possession. A chore that his physical injuries were making impossible.

"No," Oliver said suddenly. "Come here and clasp your hands together, like a stirrup. I think if perhaps I get a bit more leverage I could—"

"My lord, whatever are you trying to do?"

"It's my sword, Graves," he said impatiently. "My man placed it atop this damnably high wardrobe, and I cannot reach it with my arm and ribs bound as they are. But if you allow me to place my foot in your—"

"Shall I fetch it for you, Lord Oliver?"

"I can do it myself."

"How could I doubt you?" the old man said with more than a bit of sarcasm in his tone. "But don't you think it would be more prudent for me to retrieve your weapon rather than you risking further injury to yourself?"

"I said I can do it, Graves. Either shut up and come over here or be gone."

The servant stepped to the side of the chair and laced his long, pale fingers together obediently. His face was expressionless and he stared at the wide wall of the wardrobe rather than look at Oliver, although he did give a great sigh.

Oliver placed his right boot into the cradle of

Graves's hands and stepped up, pulling with his left hand until he could hook his elbow over the lip of the wardrobe. His fingers stretched, stretched.

"Dammit! Not high enough! Lift me up, Graves," Oliver panted.

"Does my lord know that he is quite heavy?" the old servant wheezed.

"Fine! Put me down, put me down!" Both Oliver's feet at last connected with the chair seat, and he slapped at the servant's hands at his waist as Graves wasted no time in encouraging Oliver to get down completely from the chair.

He turned to the steward, who had taken a white lace kerchief from some pocket and was now fussily wiping at his palms. "I can't leave here without it, Graves. It's August's sword. You'll have to fetch a ladder, I suppose."

Graves quirked an eyebrow. "If my lord will allow me?"

"I am not responsible to your mistress should you fall and break your old neck," Oliver warned, and went to sit on the edge of the mattress, to slow his breathing and rest his trunk, which ached from his collarbone to his hips.

The steward folded his handkerchief away and then grasped the chair by its back and returned it to its place at the little table. Graves then turned to stare at Oliver, his hands behind his back.

"Unless you can fly—which somehow I don't doubt—I think you'll find that chair to be quite useful in reaching my brother's sword," Oliver said, but Graves made no further move toward the wardrobe.

After several moments, Oliver became more than

a little incensed. "Well, are you going to fetch it or just stand there eyeing me like some old vulture?"

"Does my lord realize how important it is to Madam that he stay at Fallstowe and comply with her request?"

"No, your lord does not. Nor does he care. Lady Sybilla can find someone else to be part of her little game. I have had quite enough of the eccentricities of the Foxe women. It seems money has made them all mad."

"You think this is a game?" Graves said, and for once Oliver thought the man looked genuinely surprised.

"I don't know what it is, Graves. And, again, I don't care. I simply want to go home and forget about—" He'd been about to say Cecily Foxe, but caught himself just in time. "I need to concentrate on Bellemont now. I will not be a replacement for my brother for Lady Sybilla's amusement."

"Why do you think Madam wishes you to align yourself—albeit falsely—with Lady Joan?"

Oliver raised his face to the ceiling and groaned. "Truly, Graves, must I weep?"

"Did you know that Lord August was en route to Fallstowe when he fell from his horse?"

Oliver opened his eyes and looked at the servant. "No. No, I didn't. How do you—"

"*And did you also know,*" the man continued, his voice rising only fractionally, but containing a tremble that betrayed his anger, "that Lord August rode with a companion on that journey?"

"Who?" Oliver frowned. This made no sense. Why would Graves bring up the day of his brother's death in conjunction with Sybilla's request for Oliver to propose to Joan Barleg? If Sybilla was in truth with August when he died, why would she keep that a secret from him? Unless it wasn't Sybilla. And Joan had been in Oliver's bed the morning Argo had brought the news of August's death. Who else knew Bellemont and its lord well enough to be available to him for a journey to Fallstowe?

Oliver blinked. "Anyone who knew August loved him, would have done all in their power to save him. And my brother wouldn't journey with a man unknown to him." Oliver shook his head as if trying to rid himself of a troublesome insect and then looked at the steward. "None of this makes any sense."

Graves continued to stare at him.

Oliver didn't know what to do. "I *thought* you were to fetch my brother's sword. You'll need the chair."

"Are you to stay at Fallstowe, my lord, and assist Madam in her request?" Graves pressed.

"No." Oliver looked pointedly toward the chair. "I'll just call for another servant if you continue to refuse me."

"Care to make a wager, my lord?"

Oliver sighed again, and grasped the bridge of his nose for a moment.

"If I can fetch Lord August's sword for you without my feet leaving the ground, will you do as Madam has asked?"

Oliver couldn't help but laugh aloud. "Graves, that wardrobe is almost twice your height!"

Graves only gave a solemn nod of agreement.

Oliver chuckled. This was beyond absurd. "You

only get one go at it, old crab. One attempt, and even if you should die, I'll not remain at Fallstowe for your wake."

"Is there anything else, my lord?" Graves asked solicitously.

"No, I think that covers everything. Ready, steady, go!" Oliver mocked.

Graves rolled his eyes and then turned to stride in his dignified manner to the front of the wardrobe. The old man opened the doors carefully.

"No standing on the ledge there—remember, feet on the floor!" Oliver stood gingerly from the bed. In moments, he would be forced to call for assistance in retrieving August's sword, and then he would be away from Fallstowe.

He watched, a frown drawing together slowly between his eyebrows, as Graves reached up into a dark corner of the wardrobe with one hand. The steward gave a sharp pull, and the sound of wood scraping on wood was quickly followed by a heavy bang. Graves then reached up onto the topmost shelf with both hands. When his arms reemerged from the blackness, they held at their ends the sheath and belt of the sword.

Oliver couldn't help but shout when he exclaimed, "A false ceiling?"

Graves glided to a stop before Oliver and presented the weapon to him with flat palms, as if in a grand ceremony.

Oliver jerked the sword from the old man's hands just as someone knocked upon the chamber door. "You tricked me," he growled.

"Shall I see to your visitor, my lord?" The old

man bowed and then turned to stride to the door. Oliver did not miss the smug expression tucked into the wrinkles of Graves's face.

Joan Barleg barely let the old man open the door before she burst into Oliver's room, her cheeks flushed scarlet, both hands gripping the ends of her long plait draped over one shoulder.

"Oliver, I know you told me not to follow you, but . . ." Her words trailed away, and Oliver could not help but note her agitated state. She glanced pointedly at the steward. "That will be all, Graves."

The old man stared back at her levelly for a long moment, until Joan had the grace to look away, and then Graves turned his keen eyes on Oliver. "Will you be leaving us tonight, Lord Bellecote?" he asked.

Oliver held the old man's gaze for a long moment, gritting his teeth. "No. I've changed my mind, Graves. I think I shall stay on for a bit."

The old man gave a slight nod and then exited the room easily, as if he had every confidence in the world that Oliver would keep his word. Once the door was shut, Joan began again in earnest.

"I know you told me not to follow you, but I—"

"Joan, shh," Oliver said, gesturing to her with the sword and looped belt in his left hand. "Give me a moment." He walked to the window and looked out.

He felt no real obligation to remain at Fallstowe on his word, since that word had been gained through trickery. But many of the things he'd learned since only last night had driven a splinter of doubt into Oliver's brain. If Sybilla had indeed cared as deeply for August as she claimed—and

Oliver knew for a fact that his brother had been in love with the woman—and if Sybilla was dissatisfied with something about August's death, shouldn't Oliver be as well?

What was this thing Sybilla wanted uncovered, and even more, what was Joan herself hiding from Oliver?

The night through the wavy glass was so black that the portion of the window behind the heavy swag of drapery was a mirror. Oliver could see Joan Barleg's reflection, motionless in the center of the room, save for her hands petting at her hair.

Was Joan somehow involved in August's death?

Somewhere deeper into the black beyond Fallstowe, Cecily Foxe lay—likely in some dank, chilly chamber. Shivering in her fear of him, fear of life itself. Would she stay there, forsaking what they had shared, what they might share again if only she would let go?

It seemed to Oliver that his coming to Fallstowe had opened a Pandora's box. His life would never be the same now, whether he stayed at Fallstowe and assisted Sybilla Foxe, waited for Cecily's return, or if he went back to Bellemont. There were questions he had never before known existed, and which now demanded answers. If he could help solve this mystery Sybilla seemed convinced was real, perhaps it would show everyone who doubted that he was capable, responsible, worthy. Of Bellemont, and of Cecily.

His eyes caught a glimpse of Joan Barleg again,

and the wavy glass showed him only a milky oval where her features would be.

"Joan," he said musingly to the watery reflection that seemed to float in the black.

Her hands stilled on her plait. "Yes, Oliver?"

"Joan," he began again, his stomach clenching on the roiling questions in his guts, his fist gripping his brother's sword.

"Would you marry me, Joan?"

Chapter 15

Cecily had been a bit dismayed at the initial stir caused by her arrival at the abbey, especially among the youngest of the women. It seemed she was something of a celebrity here—the outrageously wealthy noblewoman who was likened already to a saint. It took the vicar's intervention before Cecily could remove herself from the common room and the girls grasping at her sleeve.

But supper had been quiet, simple, and Cecily was very happy to observe the chastised and modest behavior of the oblates and novices that gathered around the tables near her and John Grey. Apparently the bishop had known just the right man to send to Hallowshire to restore order amongst the rebellious young women.

Now John Grey led her away from the dining hall through a narrow, black corridor, the candle in his left hand the only light around him as his right hand grasped her elbow.

"Are we to retire now?" she asked, stifling a yawn. The long journey today combined with her unexpected defection to Hallowshire—and the gaping absence of Oliver Bellecote—had exhausted Cecily to the point that she thought she might drop to the stones at any moment.

John's footsteps slowed. "It's terrible of me, I know. I should take you to your chamber straightaway. But there is something I wish for you to see—or hear, rather—if you would indulge me. It's a small part of the reason I wanted you to come to Hallowshire so desperately. Do you mind? It shan't take long."

Cecily was intrigued. "Of course I don't mind. In fact, the prospect of a secret has given me new life." She smiled at him as he regained his earlier pace. "Where are we going? Can you tell?"

"The prayer chapel," he said. "There is a group of monks who were traveling through the area, and their brotherhood is something you simply must witness. This night will be their last at the abbey."

"Are we to meet them?" she asked.

"No." John winced. "Actually we really aren't supposed to fraternize with them."

"Vicar John!" Cecily laughed in mock scandal.

He smiled his kind, handsome smile at her in the close glow of the candlelight. "If we keep to the shadows and stay quiet, we should be able to escape with only minor penances."

He drew her behind him with one hand, shielding her as they approached a small, arched wooden door braced with black iron across its planks. From beyond, Cecily thought she could hear a queer, low humming. It seemed the soles of her feet tingled with the vibrato.

"What is that?" she whispered.

John stopped at the door and set the candle on a stone jutting from the wall, as if placed there for that very purpose.

"Once through the door, step immediately to your left. Shh," he warned, bringing a finger to his lips. After she nodded, he leaned over and blew out the candle, drenching them both in cool darkness and the smell of spent wick.

Cecily heard the slow, raspy scrape of the door open, and then felt John Grey tug on her hand. He drew her past him and Cecily felt the cavernous space of the chamber even before her eyes adjusted enough to see the faint bank of candles seemingly leagues away at the far end of the chapel. She instinctively crouched down and ducked to the left as John had instructed her, her fingers slipping from his warm grasp.

The humming was more intense here, seeming to vibrate her ribs, her very heart. And when John Grey joined her in the far reaches of the back of the chapel, Cecily felt an expanding of her body.

The humming turned into chanting.

Cecily gasped as the monks, so small in the distance, began to sing in their resonant, guttural voices, so clearly that Cecily felt the tiny hairs in her ears trembling. The Latin words swelled, swirled around her head, tangled in her hair, and she felt tears coming into her eyes.

At her side, John Grey drew closer. His arm was behind her, his left hand braced on the wall. And although he did not touch her, Cecily felt protected. He had brought her here specifically to share this secret with her, knowing somehow that it would move her.

"It's amazing, isn't it?" he whispered into her ear, his words and his breath warm and humid. Gooseflesh layered upon gooseflesh on her arms and back.

She nodded and dragged her eyes from the party of robed men to glance at John's face. His eyes were on her already, and Cecily felt a start of surprise. He was so close—much closer than she'd thought. It struck her as odd, as she had become accustomed to sensing Oliver Bellecote's presence from across the room.

"It is," she breathed. "Thank you, John."

He gave her a smile suddenly. "Would you care to dance?"

Cecily brought her hand up to cover her mouth before a giggle could escape. "That's blasphemy!" she scolded with a wide grin.

To her amazement, John shrugged. "I don't think so. We are celebrating the beautiful gifts given to some rather otherwise homely men. I would think it rather a tribute."

He was serious. The smile slowly slid from Cecily's face.

"I can't," she said.

He gave her a quizzical grin. "Why not?"

"Because I've . . . I've never danced before." His eyebrows rose, and she clarified. "I know how, obviously. I was taught. But I've never danced with . . . with a man before."

"With all the feasts Fallstowe and your sister are

host to?" he asked, as if still unable to believe it was possible.

Cecily felt her face heat, and then shook her head awkwardly.

John stared at her for a long moment, while the monks poured out their praise in low, close notes that sounded as if they were coming from either the depths of the earth or the highest reaches of heaven.

"You're like a fairy tale," John mused.

"Fairy tales are oft sweet exaggerations for the sake of a happy ending," Cecily whispered, and then huffed a weary laugh. "So perhaps I am a fairy tale after all—I don't really exist."

Then John Grey did touch her, grasping both of her shoulders gently and turning her toward him. He took her left elbow, and then the fingers of her right hand, and then he took a step away from her, their joined arms held suspended between them.

"Cecily Foxe," he asked somberly, "will you grant me the honor of a dance?"

For so many reasons, he was the right choice. Cecily knew this just as surely as she knew the way the morning sun fell across the floor of her chamber at Fallstowe each day. And Cecily knew without either of them so much as alluding to it that her answer would grant him permission or nay to pursue her, not for Hallowshire, not for the bishop, but for himself. He could very well be the answer to her many prayers, the solution to her indecision.

But then why did she expect to see dark, unruly hair where golden strands lay? Why did she long for eyes the color of rich, wet earth when such a beautiful shade of sky blue beckoned to her? This earnestness, this blatant sincerity before her seemed to pale before the memory of irreverent passion, reckless sin, demanding desires. A want of something that was most certainly not good for her. She was like a child who cried for too many sweets.

Oliver Bellecote would be the ruination of her. Of her reputation, of what little pride she had left, of her heart. He would lie to her, use her. He would trample her and leave her alone at Fallstowe with only memories and pain. He was the wrong choice. Here, before her now, was the right choice.

Cecily gave John Grey a single, solemn nod.

And then, with the sounds of heaven helping to twirl her along with John Grey, neither one of them smiling and yet both of their eyes locked on each other's, Cecily Foxe, at last, danced.

She had loosely planned on staying at Hallowshire no more than a pair of days. But the company of John Grey and the peace of the abbey worked like a draught on Cecily, and she could often go an entire hour without thinking of Oliver Bellecote. She became somewhat addicted to the hush where once jangling warnings set her to trembling.

And so five days passed, and then five more.

There had been only one truly dangerous moment of weakness, when Cecily had received a message from Sybilla. The missive had reported no emergency, no need for her to return. In truth, her sister had only encouraged Cecily to stay as long as she liked; Fallstowe and Lord Bellecote were managing remarkably well without her.

Cecily's hand had been on the latch of the door

of her borrowed chamber, her small satchel packed
and in her other hand, before she realized what she
was doing.

She had lifted her hand slowly, carefully from
the latch, and crept backward away from the door,
as if fearful that should she make any sound, the
door would open of its own accord and thrust her
from Hallowshire just as surely as if she'd been
launched from a catapult.

He was managing remarkably well without her.

Of course he was. He was Oliver Bellecote. He
had undoubtedly found some other diversion to
entertain him, straightaway. He likely couldn't even
recall what Cecily looked like.

And so Cecily had stayed, and she had learned
that she might have been quite content to make
the abbey her home, had she committed long ago.
There was a schedule, a rhythm to the days and
nights that spoke to her. The novices were a diverse
bunch, some shy and reserved, others jubilant and
full of sweet mischief, but all of them together
made the large, peaceful retreat a tapestry of joyful
service. Yes, Cecily could envision herself at Hallowshire easily, if not for her corruption at Oliver Bellecote's hands.

As well as the abbey's bland, seldom changing
menu, which of late had Cecily longing for one of
Cook's dried apple tarts, drizzled with fresh cream.
She had even dreamed of plates and plates of the
sweet dish, and had woken the next morning with
her stomach growling painfully. She could no longer
abide the taste of any sort of fish, which seemed to
be presented at each meal. Even the smell of it now
was enough to make her want to retch.

Her time at Hallowshire had also allowed her to learn about John Grey. Besides being the youngest child of a rather wealthy and influential northern lord, he was something of an artist, possessing great skill with a small palette of paints and a horsehair brush. He was an accomplished dancer, and possessed of a surprising singing voice that would rival any of the brethren they'd listened to on their first night at Hallowshire together. He had a small land share and house near Oxford—"little more than a large cottage, really," he'd admitted—that was being held by his father in anticipation of his vows.

Vows that he would not be taking, now.

She watched him approaching as she sat atop her horse: Vicar John Grey, striding across the bailey in the unusually robust early morning sun. A cold blast of raw wind swept over the dirt and his cloak flapped behind his knees like the wings of a mighty angel, the hood lying on his shoulders billowing like a dark halo. For an instant, Cecily was reminded of the similar analogy she had applied to Oliver Bellecote when he had fallen through the air from his horse, his cloak flying behind him like wings.

Fallen. Oliver Bellecote perhaps was a fallen angel then.

Cecily shook her head, annoyed with her fanciful and dangerous thoughts, and focused once more on the man approaching her. Such deep-colored vestments might have made another man appear sinister, but not John Grey. His hair fairly gleamed in the cold light, his smile—looking typically pleased and a bit bemused—was only for her, and Cecily could not help but feel a twinge of bittersweet relief.

He reached his own mount and Cecily tossed him the reins she'd been holding. John swung up onto the horse easily and man and beast quickly adjusted to each other.

"Ready?" he asked.

Cecily mustered the best smile she could. "As ready as I shall ever be, I suppose."

She kicked her mount into pace with his across the bailey and then fell back as they clopped across the narrow drawbridge, Hallowshire growing at first tall and bristling behind them, and then shorter and gentler as they gained the rolling valley to the southeast. It would be a long ride to Fallstowe, and only little more than an hour after a breakfast inspired by the sea, Cecily's stomach was grumbling its displeasure. She eyed the horizon of cresting hills with a wrinkle of her nose, expecting unreasonably to see fish jumping over the dried, yellow waves of dead grass. She brought her hand to her lips as she tried to hold back a hot belch.

"How long will we stay at Fallstowe?" she asked, in an effort to distract herself.

"How long do you wish to stay?" John countered solicitously.

Cecily turned her face up to the bright sun and drew a deep breath of the cold air, hoping to cool the sudden flush of her face and neck. She blew it out slowly through her mouth.

"Not long," she said, feeling the perspiration at her hairline and beneath her arms in spite of the frigid wind. The bite of cold felt good on her skin.

"I must confess, it gladdens my heart to hear you say that."

She looked over at him and gave him another smile, knowing he was referring to Oliver Bellecote. A shiver of panic tried to flip her stomach, and she hoped the dark-haired devil would be gone from Fallstowe when they returned.

They headed down yet another slope, and Cecily had to swallow hard before she could continue. "I know you would want to be returned to the bishop as soon as possible so that he might dismiss you properly."

John Grey nodded. "My father will be surprised when we arrive. But pleased."

"Will he?" Cecily glanced at him.

"I think so, yes." His grin deepened. "Are you nervous of him?"

"A bit," she admitted. "My own father died when I was so young; Graves is the closest thing I've had to a male authority figure."

"Besides the king, of course," he said somberly, and then they both chuckled at his little jest. "What of Sybilla? Need I fear for my neck once past Fallstowe's barbican?"

Cecily gave a weak laugh—her stomach was mimicking the rolling gait of her horse. "If your honor and pedigree do not soften her heart, your comeliness and eloquence will have her on her knees."

John laughed again and a blush fell across his face. They gained the next crest and he looked over at her.

"Do you find me comely, my lady?"

Cecily opened her mouth to give a saucy retort, but it did not come forth.

Instead, she leaned to her left and threw up.

Chapter 16

It had been nearly four weeks since the night Oliver had met Cecily Foxe at the old ring, and in many aspects, Oliver was much improved. His arm no longer throbbed with every beat of his heart; now it only hummed a dull ache within the confines of the sling. His ribs were all but healed. He felt no piercing pain in his skull.

But it seemed that every improvement in his physical condition was countered by a deterioration of his mental state. He couldn't sleep. He had no interest in partaking of the fine and lavish meals at Sybilla's table. On nine different occasions, he had come into his chamber to encounter a very willing and very naked female—or two—in his bed, and he'd simply turned around and left. On three of those occasions, the female had been Joan Barleg. He'd not had sex in nearly a month—by far the longest period of abstinence in his adult life. He feared he was doing grave damage to his reputation as a scoundrel.

And he did not care.

Cecily Foxe had abandoned him for the abbey with that decrepit old vicar. For the first time in his life, there was a woman who held his desire and who wanted naught to do with him. Not only that, but after he had made love to her—drunkenly and with extensive injuries, granted—she had retreated to a life of celibacy!

He'd thought hundreds of times of writing to her, of all but begging her to return to Fallstowe and to him. When he couldn't bring himself to do so, he told himself that it was his pride that prevented it, but Oliver suspected that it had more to do with cowardice.

He was in love with Cecily Foxe, there could be no other explanation. Never had a woman—especially a woman whose gifts he had already savored—possessed him so. He longed for the sight of her, the sound of her voice. The greatest pleasure he had found during her absence was when he had discovered the location of her chamber at Fallstowe. He had stood in the center of the stark, cold little room for a long time, and then leisurely touched every piece of furniture, every windowsill, every candleholder, where her hands might have once rested. He had buried his face in large handfuls of the few, plain gowns that hung in the wardrobe. Finally, he had untied the curtains surrounding her bed, and crawled upon the mattress inside the dark, quiet enclosure to stare at the canopy above.

Sybilla Foxe had better hurry with her investigation, for Oliver had vowed to himself that if Cecily ever returned to Fallstowe, he would declare his feelings to her. To hell with what Joan Barleg knew.

August was dead. Bellemont was Oliver's. Nothing Sybilla did or did not discover was going to change those facts.

"Oliver!" Joan said exasperatedly, and when he turned to look at her, he suspected that it was not the first time she had called to him.

"What?" he muttered, lifting his chin from his fist to once more attend disinterestedly to his chalice.

"Have you no care for the discussion of our wedding?" Joan demanded for what must have been the thousandth time in a fortnight. "Lady Sybilla has only just suggested that we be married here, at Fallstowe! Isn't that a marvelous idea? What do you think?"

He shrugged.

"You're uninterestedness wounds me," she whispered bitterly before turning her back to him and engaging Sybilla once more, busy planning their make-believe wedding.

Oliver shrugged again as the cold breeze that was Graves swept behind his chair. Oliver was trying desperately to ignore the chatter between the two women once more, but his ears could not help but pick up the old steward's announcement.

"May I interrupt, Madam, to inform you that your sister and her companion have arrived?"

The chalice Oliver had been holding slipped from his fingers and clanged onto the table, splattering the last inch or so left in its bowl across his platter. Joan cried out in dismay as Oliver tried to awkwardly grab hold of the rolling vessel.

"Sorry, sorry," Oliver muttered as a pair of serving maids appeared at his side to whisk away the mess.

But his heart pounded in rhythm to the song in his head: Cecily was home, at last!

The game was over.

Oliver heard a commotion coming from the large entryway at the rear of the great hall, where beyond lay the steps. He heard a woman's laugh.

He rose from his seat slowly, his wine-stained linen napkin dangling from his hand, his eyes trained on the doorway.

"Oh-ho! What's this? A return of manners, when the lady has not yet entered the hall!" Joan scoffed.

Oliver paid her no heed. There was a shadow lengthening onto the stone floor, the faint clicking of heels. . . .

A blond woman appeared in the doorway, with a monkey on her shoulder.

"Oh, it's Lady Alys!" Joan exclaimed.

Oliver tossed his napkin on the table with a half-hearted flick of his wrist as the youngest Foxe sister came down the aisle, her stocky and ever-frowning husband now close at her side. Oliver gave a shallow, stiff bow toward the pair and then sat down.

"Good evening, Sybilla! Lady Joan, lovely to see you again." Alys looked in Oliver's direction twice before seeming to realize his identity. "Why, Lord Bellecote, I almost didn't recognize you. Healing well, I hope?"

"Perfect health, Lady Alys," Oliver said blithely, and then raised an eyebrow toward her husband. "Mallory."

Mallory gave Oliver a slight nod and then walked toward his end of the table while Joan all but fell over the meal to greet Lady Alys. Oliver heard the youngest Foxe woman gasp.

"Married?"

Piers Mallory now raised his own eyebrows at Oliver as he laid a thick forearm in front of Oliver's platter. "'S that pudding?" He lifted his hand to point at a congealing mass.

Oliver flicked his fingers at the food. "I've no idea. Help yourself, old chap."

The muscular lord swiped a long finger through the center of the plate and stuck it into his mouth. He swallowed, and then looked askance at the women, as Sybilla made her way from the table and exited the hall, Graves like her wrinkly shadow. Alys skirted the table and took her sister's place, chattering with Joan.

"Married, eh," Piers grunted.

Oliver shrugged. "That's the rumor."

Piers gaze was like a physical thing as he helped himself to the plate again. "Wrong woman though. Is that it?"

"What would you know of it?" Oliver looked around, gestured impatiently for the boy with the wine.

"You are clearly miserable. Yes," he said pointedly to the boy, who quickly went off to find another cup. His eyes came back to Oliver. "You look like shit."

"I can see now why Alys married you—verily, the epitome of tact."

Piers laughed and took the chalice he was offered. "I may not possess the refined qualities of one of your *noble reputation,*" Piers said, "but years on a farm have taught me not to mince words for the sake of politeness. If a cow is sick, you heal it or you put it down."

"Reiterating your offer to beat me to death with my only remaining arm?" Oliver snapped.

Piers frowned. "Not at all. Just thought you could use a friend." He raised his chalice in salute. "I can see you're not there yet. Good evening to you, Lord Bellecote." And the large man removed himself to his wife's side.

Oliver sat there for several more moments, drained his chalice, and then he sighed.

He stood, mumbled a good night to the trio to his right, and stepped from the dais. The common tables in the hall were now emptied of diners, the servants swishing along quietly between the benches as he walked slowly down the aisle with his eyes on his boots, feeling utterly useless.

He looked up just as he reached the doorway to the hall, and stopped in his tracks. There she was.

"Hello, Oliver."

"Cecily," he whispered, and even to his own ears, her name sounded like a plea.

She looked radiant. In the same plain gown he was accustomed to seeing her in, but her head was uncovered, her hair twisted back in a long spiral, several curls escaping around her face. Her skin looked like ivory, with the dewy blush of sunrise on her cheeks, her eyes like deep ermine in the shadows of the doorway. He stepped toward her.

She didn't move away. "How is your arm?" she asked, glancing down at his sling.

"Wonderful," he said distractedly. "Why have you

been gone so long? Did you . . . did you commit to Hallowshire?"

She shook her head slightly, still looking into his eyes, and in the dim light they seemed to shimmer. "No. No, I shan't be returning to Hallowshire."

Oliver clenched his left hand into a fist and shook it before him. "Cecily—" He glanced over his shoulder quickly as he heard the exclamations of the women behind him. They would be upon her soon. "Cecily, I need to speak with you. It's quite important."

"Well, I— All right." Her lips thinned and she too glanced over her shoulder, into the dark entryway behind her. "But, Oliver—"

"No, shh. Listen to me," he interrupted. "I have been a complete ass most of my life. I never held love for anything of import, and I have wrecked every opportunity to be a better man. Especially with you. I will not fail you this time, Cecily. I won't. I swear it."

"Oliver, please don't," Cecily whispered.

He shook his head and continued in a low whisper, stepping closer and even leaning forward, trying to convey the depth of his sincerity to her. "Each day that you have been away from me has been like a little hell. I want nothing more right now than to take you into my arms and kiss you, Cecily. I've never wanted anything more in the whole of my life."

"You can't kiss me, Oliver," she said, and the shimmering in her eyes deepened, almost as if she would weep.

The footsteps were near now. Any moment and the women would be upon them.

"I know I can't now. I wouldn't embarrass you so." He smiled. "But soon. I don't think I could bear to be parted from you again."

Her eyes widened. She looked up at him once more, seemed to lean toward him. . . .

"Cee!" Alys squealed as she brushed by Oliver and threw her arms around her sister. The monkey on Alys's shoulder swayed wildly and clung to the blond woman's head. "You look marvelous! And I have the most wonderful news for you. I can't wait any longer!"

"Alys," Cecily gasped, and then gave a little laugh. "I know. I mean, I can guess your news, I think."

Alys stepped back, her hands on her hips, her face set in a frown. "Sybilla wasn't supposed to tell you!"

Cecily smiled. "She didn't. Although I should be offended that you told Sybilla and not me."

"Then how do you know?" Alys demanded.

"I've been so ill!" Cecily laughed, and there were tears in her eyes now, as she looked up to the ceiling and pressed the heels of her hands across her bottom lashes.

"Oh, darling—how dreadful! You felt my morning sickness?" Alys said with a sympathetic frown.

Joan Barleg gasped. "Lady Alys, you've been blessed with a child?"

Alys nodded happily but Oliver frowned. He didn't care. He wished they would all go away. Especially Joan.

"We have our own good news to share, Lady

Cecily," Joan said with a wide grin, and slid her arm through Oliver's.

"Not now, Joan," Oliver ground out beneath a forced smile. "Let the sisters have their moment. Where *is* Sybilla, by the by?"

"Oh no, do go on and tell Cecily," Alys insisted with a stamp of her foot. "Sybilla has already heard all of our news ages ago and would be bored, as only Sybilla can be at the happiest of times."

"Yes," Cecily encouraged, but her words were spoken through a smile that looked to Oliver like it might crack at any moment, and she would not meet his eyes. "Do share, Lady Joan."

"Oliver and I are to be *married!*" Joan sang excitedly. "He proposed the very night you arrived at Hallowshire!"

It was no trick of light; Oliver saw Cecily pale like chalk fields. She revived her smile though, with bright red lips.

"That's . . . wonderful news, indeed." She looked up at him, and Oliver wanted to die. "Congratulations to you both."

No. No more. He could not hurt her like this. He pulled his arm from Joan's roughly, ignoring her squawk. "Cecily . . ."

His confession was interrupted by Sybilla's appearance in the entry, a finely dressed, young blond man at her elbow.

"Lord Bellecote, I think perhaps we should give Lady Cecily the opportunity to share her own good news before we barrage her with requests." She looked to Cecily. "How could you have any doubt of my blessing?"

Cecily glanced behind her at her sister and the blond man and gave them a watery smile. Then she turned her eyes back to Oliver and he felt the intensity of her nameless emotions as surely as a knife. Her chin tilted.

"I am also to be married."

"*Married?*" Oliver exclaimed, and he felt the stone floor beneath him roll like a wave. "What do you mean, *married?* To whom?"

The blond man stepped forward with a polite clearing of his throat. He thrust forth his right hand. "Lord Bellecote, at last we meet. I have heard much about you."

Oliver looked down at the man's hand as if it was a serpent, and then swung his gaze back to Cecily's expectantly, blatantly ignoring the blond man's gesture of good will.

The shimmer in her eyes was gone, replaced with a steely sparkle. "Lord Oliver Bellecote, John Grey."

Oliver's eyes bulged, and a terrible choking sound came from his throat as his head swiveled from Cecily's direction to John's, and then back again.

"J-John Grey?" Oliver stuttered, and Cecily was more than a little surprised at the passion that seemed to have possessed him. "*Vicar* John Grey?" He held out his left arm, pointing directly at the man's face, his forefinger stabbing twice in the air for emphasis. "*This* is the *vicar?*"

Cecily swallowed and managed to nod dumbly. Why did she feel like the guilty party?

"Well, I'm not really a vicar," John amended

humbly, his tone an obvious attempt to rescue her from the awkward display Oliver was presenting. "It's only a courtesy title from the bishop, actually."

"Oh, it's only a courtesy title from the b—" Oliver broke off his snide words and then shook his head abruptly. "You're not even a *priest?*"

"Oliver!" Joan chastised. "How could you be so rudimentary toward Lady Cecily's intended?"

To Cecily's horror, Oliver spun on the pretty blond woman—now his betrothed, she was forced to remind herself.

"Shut. Up. *Joan.* This in no way concerns you." He looked away for a second and then seemed to think better of it, turning back to the slack-mouthed woman. "And that is *not* how the word *rudimentary* is used!"

Joan's face reddened and a breathy squawk came from her rounded lips. She fled past them all and disappeared up the stairs.

"Enough!" Sybilla pushed into the center of the little knot they had created, and for the first time in Cecily's life, she found herself thanking God for her older sister's brazen wielding of power.

"Lord Bellecote, it must have escaped my notice the amount of wine you consumed this night, for certainly you had no intention of insulting not only an honored guest of Fallstowe and my future brother-in-law, but also your own betrothed."

"I was led to believe that this man, with whom your sister was spending so much of her time, was a man of God!" Oliver challenged her, pointing once more at John.

"Aren't we all men of God, Lord Bellecote?" John suggested.

Cecily saw Piers Mallory approach, and he quietly took Alys's arm and led her from the hall against her struggle and whispered protests.

Sybilla stepped into the space separating Cecily and Oliver, her frosty words were meant for Oliver alone, but Cecily heard her sister clearly.

"Control yourself, Lord Bellecote, I beg you," she said, and although the words were a calm request, her tone conveyed the sincerity of her demand. "I must see to Lady Joan before she convinces herself that you are so boorish that she must escape Fallstowe to be rid of you!"

"I most desperately hope that she does!" Oliver shouted.

Sybilla spun on her heel to face John. "Vicar, I apologize for leaving you in such poor company. I do hope Lord Bellecote's atrocious behavior does not reflect too poorly on Fallstowe's charity, as a whole. Please excuse me."

And then it was only Cecily, Oliver, and John left in the hall.

Cecily could not hold her tongue any longer. Although the emotions she was feeling at the moment had turned her logic to the mutterings of a lunatic, she would not allow Oliver to slander John Grey.

"Do you dare insinuate concern for my honor with this man?" she accused him. "I spent more time with you when you first came to Fallstowe, Oliver, and you most certainly are neither chaste nor honorable! Where was your concern for me when you were demanding my presence to serve you?"

Oliver looked at her again, and although he no longer shouted, Cecily sensed that his anger had not diminished. Nay, it had multiplied.

"How could you do this?" he accused her, ignoring her questions.

"How could *I* do this?" Cecily shot back. "Why, I have no idea! Perhaps you could ask *your betrothed!*"

John intervened. "Lord Bellecote, I do understand that you and Lady Cecily had a brief . . . ah, romantic episode, and so this announcement may be somewhat of a shock to you."

"A shock?" Oliver shouted on a laugh. "A shock?" He turned to Cecily again. "You leave Fallstowe with no word to me, without anything between the two of us resolved. You're gone two weeks with a man you led me to believe was an aged old priest."

"I told you no such thing," Cecily argued quietly.

"What else was I to think?" Oliver demanded. "And this entire time that you are away—*supposedly* on the pretense of doing God's holy work," he added snidely, "you have been cozying up to a titleless dandy, soliciting an offer of marriage!"

"Lord Bellecote," John said in a low voice. "I warn you, my sympathy for your state has a threshold."

"I did not solicit anything," Cecily said. She had to stop Oliver immediately, before any more damage was done to any of the three people now gathered together. "John and I developed a friendship. I value him above any other man," she said pointedly, ignoring the way her heart squeezed when Oliver flinched.

Oliver took a step back and his chin thrust forward, tilted. "A friendship, eh?"

John drew closer to Cecily's side, and his hand grasped her elbow. "Lord Bellecote, I am giving up the priesthood in order to marry Cecily. She is an amazing woman, with extraordinary talents unlike any I have ever been privileged to witness."

Oliver nodded pensively and his eyes narrowed, his gaze locked on Cecily's face. "Talents. I see. Yes, yes—I see now." His face swung to look at John. "She gets in your head after you fuck her, doesn't she?"

Cecily gave a gasping cry of horror, but before she could say anything, John Grey took a single step forward and punched Oliver soundly in the mouth, whipping his head around with a nearly audible cracking of his neck.

Oliver brought his left hand up to cradle his chin for a moment. "Come on with you, then, Vicar," he challenged him.

John was not intimidated, and in fact, he took another step forward as he pointed a finger in Oliver's face, while his other hand rested on the hilt of his short sword. "You would do well to remember that I am under no priestly vows, Lord Bellecote, and that you are currently without the use of one of your arms. Should you have anything else to say of a defamatory nature against the woman I am to marry, as God is my faithful witness, I *will* run you through."

Oliver turned his eyes to Cecily as his hand fell away from his mouth. His upper lip was swollen, his lower lip, split.

"I'm sorry. But I was in love with you, too, Cecily. I was in love with you first, actually."

Her knees felt watery, her head swam. Perspiration pricked coolly at her hairline. "You're only saying that now because you can't have me," she said quietly. "You never wanted me in this way."

"I wanted you in whatever way I could have you," he shot back. "Forgive me for making such a misstep—I've never been in love before. Only remember that *you* left *me*." He turned to John Grey and gave a short, mocking bow. "I'm sure you'll understand if I don't attend the ceremony, *Vicar.*"

"You aren't invited," John retorted. "I'm sure *you* understand. Good evening, Lord Bellecote."

Oliver didn't look at her again as he left the hall, and Cecily was glad for such.

Although when John took her into his arms to comfort her, she could not help but gaze fearfully into the darkness where Oliver had gone, searching the grim shadows, listening to his fading footfalls.

Chapter 17

Oliver stormed through the dark upper corridors of Fallstowe Castle, suspecting that Joan Barleg's rooms were in proximity to his own within the guest wing, but unsure as to their exact location.

"Sybilla!" he roared. He zigzagged between the walls, pounding on doors, jerking at the latches, throwing open the barriers that yielded to his attempts and leaving the doors swinging wide.

"*Sybilla!*"

While he raged, Cecily's words circled through his mind like a mill wheel, over and over.

I am also to be married.

You most certainly are neither chaste nor honorable!

I value him above any other man.

Oliver threw himself against a locked door, paused with his forehead resting upon it, his eyes squeezed shut. Then he pushed away with an explosive crash of his fist to continue his rampage down the corridor.

"Sybilla!" He rattled the next door's handle so

soundly that the wood screamed against the iron. How many fucking chambers were there? He backed up and kicked at the door twice with the bottom of his boot.

"Is aught amiss, Lord Oliver?"

Oliver staggered onto both feet once more and swung around, his chest heaving, his hair fallen over one eye.

Graves. Perfect.

The old man stood calmly against the wall opposite Oliver and one door down, as still as if he had been there waiting patiently for Oliver the entirety of his tirade.

"Where is she, Graves?" Oliver demanded.

The old man blinked. "Where is who, my lord?"

Oliver stomped toward him, coming to stand threateningly before the steward. "You know very goddamn well *who!* Where is Sybilla?"

"Madam did not inform you immediately of her intended whereabouts?" Graves pulled an expression of mild shock.

Oliver put his nose level with the old servant's. "I've had enough of your snide insults. As well as your meddling and trickery! Now, you will tell me where Lady Joan has been interred so that I might have a *word* with *Madam,* else I will lay your thousand-year-old corpse across the stones of this corridor!"

Graves nodded sympathetically. "Perhaps my lord will permit me to escort him directly to Madam?"

"Bloody right he will," Oliver growled.

Graves gave him a faint smile while raising his left hand, his forefinger and thumb extended. Before Oliver realized the old man's intention, Graves had latched on to Oliver's right arm through the sling, directly above Oliver's elbow joint.

All the breath went out of him in a rush as blinding pain exploded in his healing humerus. His knees buckled, and Oliver only remained upright through the surprisingly steady grip of the old steward as Graves began to stride down the corridor.

"Let . . . go!" Oliver wheezed.

Graves shook his head mildly. "We wouldn't wish for you to lose your way again now, would we, my lord?"

"Graves, my arm!"

"How *is* your arm, my lord?"

"It's . . . *still broken!*" Oliver choked out.

The old man came to a halt before another featureless door, but he did not yet turn Oliver lose.

"Shall I accompany you inside?"

"No. No, just . . . let go!"

Graves quickly rapped on the door twice and then raised the latch, holding on to Oliver's elbow until the very instant he was over the threshold.

Oliver gave a short cry as his arm was released. He spun to face the old man, but the door was already swinging shut. He turned back to the center of the room to see Joan Barleg curled on her side on the large postered bed, her back to him. Sybilla Foxe perched on her hip at the far end of the mattress.

"Sybilla, I am going to kill that old bastard servant of yours!"

"Were I you, Lord Bellecote," Sybilla replied coolly, "I would be more deferential of Graves in the future. He is aged, but you should look at his many years as a resource of experience and wisdom rather than a liability to his function." She raised her face to appraise Oliver. "Should you challenge him again, a bloodied mouth would be the least of your troubles, and he would need not lift a single finger to bring you to heel."

Oliver realized she was referring to his swollen lip and he raised his left hand to test the cut gingerly. "Graves didn't gift me with this—that deceitful bastard John Grey did."

Sybilla's slender eyebrows rose. "I'm impressed. Though it's less than you actually deserve, I'm certain."

Joan Barleg levered herself from the mattress and turned her head to look over her shoulder at Oliver. "Have you come to apologize, Oliver?"

Oliver let his hand fall away. "No, Joan. I have not. I've only come to inform our most gracious hostess that I will be taking my leave of Fallstowe this night, so you will have to make do with her apologies for whatever slights you feel you have suffered while under her roof. I can assure you they were all, in one way or another, her doing."

Sybilla's brows lowered.

"You're leaving?" Joan whispered, coming to sit fully on her bottom, strangling her long golden plait with both hands.

"Leaving," Oliver reiterated. "I have had my fill of deceit."

"Deceit?" Joan's eyes darted from Sybilla back to him. "What are you talking about? Whose deceit?"

Oliver leveled an arm at Sybilla. "I'm afraid you'll need to ask her, for I am not completely certain what is going on here myself."

"Lord Bellecote," Sybilla emphasized, "you are overreacting. I don't believe you're yet well enough to depart the haven that Fallstowe has been for you."

"Haven?" Oliver shouted incredulously. He pointed at the dark-haired woman again. "All this is on your head, Sybilla—all of it. I hope it drowns you, you conniving bitch. You've cost me the one thing I ever truly wanted in my life."

Sybilla said nothing, only looked at him coolly. But Joan Barleg became immediately alarmed, scooting herself from the edge of the bed and standing, seeming unsure as to whether she should approach him or not. She chose to remain by the bed.

"What do you mean, Oliver? Surely you can't intend for—" She held her hands before her. "Shall I gather my things, as well? I am coming with you, am I not?"

"No. No, you are most certainly not," Oliver said. "I told you when we first arrived at Fallstowe that I had no intention of marrying you, and those intentions have not changed."

"Oliver," Sybilla warned.

"But you . . . you *proposed* to me!" Joan said on a huff of laughter. "We are betrothed."

Oliver turned, intending to quit the chamber. But Joan Barleg's next words halted him in his steps.

"It's Lady Cecily, isn't it?" she called to him. "You're in love with her."

Oliver did not turn.

"It's all right, Oliver," Joan continued in a cajoling, unsure voice. "It's all right if you are. She was . . . she was your nurse. It's common for men to have feelings for those who care for them in an intimate manner, and—"

"That's not why, Joan," Oliver said to the door.

"Not why what?" she pressed, and he knew she was drawing closer to him by the increasing volume of her voice. "Not why you don't want to marry me, or not why you're in love with her?"

"As soon as I've gathered my things from my chamber, I shall depart," Oliver said over his shoulder, his words meant for Sybilla.

"You can't discard me like this, Oliver!" Joan said, her voice growing stronger. "You are mine, by your own vow! You owe me for my faithfulness!"

"I never asked for your fidelity, Joan," he reminded her gently. "In fact, I warned you against it. The only thing I owe you is a good-bye."

Sybilla's words stopped him at the door. "I'd be interested to learn how you plan on returning to Bellemont, Lord Bellecote."

Oliver turned. "How I—? Well, since I can't fly, I reckon I shall be traveling by horse."

Sybilla shook her head slowly, and even from across the room, Oliver could see the icy glint in her blue eyes. "I had hoped to inform you later, when you were in a more receptive mood, but you leave me no choice. Your horse had to be put down. It became quite ill after your accident at the Foxe Ring. I couldn't risk the sickness spreading, you understand."

"You put my horse down?" Oliver asked incredulously. "Without my counsel? When?"

Sybilla's gaze never wavered from his. She blinked. "Just now, I'm afraid."

"Bullshit!" Oliver felt his teeth grinding together. "Even if what you say is true, certainly you will be kind enough to lend me one of—"

"No," Sybilla cut him off. "No, I can't do that. I am quite fond of all of Fallstowe's beasts, and as both you and your brother have proven yourselves less than accomplished horsemen, I cannot in good conscience surrender one of my mounts to you. Especially after this most recent incident."

Even Joan Barleg gasped.

"So I am your prisoner?" Oliver challenged her, taking a step toward Sybilla. She did not flinch.

"Not at all," she replied coolly. "You are free to leave Fallstowe whenever you wish. If you are that determined to quit my hospitality, well, then I suppose you will walk. Or, if you prefer, I will send a messenger to your man at Bellemont, and he may bring you one of your own horses to carry you to your home."

"I will repay you for all you've done for me, Lady Sybilla," Oliver threatened.

"Oh, I think you have done quite enough already."

Oliver felt impotent, faced with two women who held such obvious loathing for him at the moment. He was trapped. He could not leave Fallstowe.

"Send for Argo," he growled.

"Right away," Sybilla promised calmly. "Although I do hope that by the time your man arrives, you might have changed your mind."

"Oh, I am most certainly leaving," Oliver vowed. He jabbed his finger first at Sybilla and then Joan Barleg. "And once I am away, I hope to never again lay eyes upon the likes of either of you. Mad, the whole lot!"

He turned and wrenched open the door, leaving it to swing wide and crash against the wall behind it.

Sybilla heard Oliver's diminishing warning of, "Keep your distance, you evil old cadaver!" She could only assume he spoke to Graves, and she hoped that Graves did not take too much offense. When this was all over, she might kill Oliver herself.

She closed the door deliberately, quietly, and took a moment to compose herself. Things were unraveling now, faster than Sybilla could collect the tangled strands.

"Sybilla?" Joan's timid call roused her from her reverie, although she did not turn away from the door just yet. "What am I to do now?"

What am I to do now? Sybilla wanted to laugh. She was a bold one, Lady Joan Barleg. Very bold.

Sybilla turned. "Don't worry yourself about Oliver's strange behavior, Joan. It will be days before he leaves. Mayhap he will come to his senses."

"He must," Joan said emphatically. "He must. I have worked too hard for this . . . for him, I mean." She flushed.

"It is no mean feat to lead a man to the altar," Sybilla supplied helpfully, and was pleased when Joan visibly relaxed. But now the blond woman regarded her keenly.

"Indeed, it is not," Joan agreed.

"Perhaps a bit of solitude will help Oliver to realize that he must do the right thing," Sybilla said, coming to stand before Joan and steeling herself to take both the young woman's hands in her own.

Joan's blond eyebrows crinkled and she set her lips for a moment before asking, "Lady Sybilla, think you your sister is in love with my Oliver?"

Sybilla did not hesitate. "No. That's ridiculous."

Joan's expression was doubtful. "I understand that perhaps Lady Cecily's honor is more steadfast than the average woman's, but it *is* Oliver. And they were alone together quite a lot."

"Do you wish to know what I think?" Sybilla queried, and at Joan's eager nod, she continued. "I think it likely that your betrothed acted boldly with my sister and she rebuffed him. It is why she left him for Hallowshire with John Grey. And why she has now returned, betrothed to none other. And also why John Grey felt it necessary to strike Oliver for his assumed liberties. You know far better than any the nature of the man."

Joan nodded slowly. "Yes. Yes, that does sound like aught Oliver would do. So perhaps he is only piqued that there is a woman who has refused him."

"Precisely," Sybilla insisted, giving Joan's hands a little squeeze, and wishing her fingers were around the blond woman's neck.

"He's infatuated with the unattainable," Joan suggested. "And the vicar and Lady Cecily are most certainly more well suited to each other."

"I couldn't have selected a better match with my own hand."

Joan nodded again, more surely this time. "So all is not lost. Oliver will come to his senses. He must."

"He must," Sybilla agreed.

"My lady," Joan said hesitantly, "I cannot thank you enough for your assistance these past days. Your generosity and kindness are nearly overwhelming and—I hope I don't offend you by saying so, but—completely at odds with your reputation."

Sybilla gave her a little smile, and Joan took it as encouragement.

"I am glad that we have become friends, because . . . because I think that we shall see each other quite frequently after Oliver and I are wed."

"Verily?" Sybilla feigned pleased surprise. "And why is that, Joan?"

Joan opened her mouth and then closed it again on a smile, but Sybilla could see the glint in her eyes. Did she not know better, she would take Joan Barleg for naught more than a happy innocent.

"I hope to find myself at Fallstowe quite often," was all Joan would say.

Sybilla returned her smile. "It would please me greatly were you never to leave."

Chapter 18

Cecily made her way down the stairs gingerly, touching her temple with the fingers of her hand that was not grasping the stone railing. Her head was pounding, her stomach roiling.

She had stayed in her rooms much later in the morn than was her habit, hoping that the nausea would leave her. After retching unproductively a number of times, she thought that she might at last be safe to emerge. And she thanked God yet again that Alys was the cause of her strange maladies of late.

Cecily was *not* a witch. True, all three of the Foxe sisters possessed some unique and perhaps unexplainable talents. Alys could see a person's colors; Sybilla . . . well, Cecily suspected that Sybilla did quite a number of things that she really had no desire to know the details of. And Cecily had the annoying habit of feeling the sensations of those she loved who were hurt or in danger, much as she had sensed when Alys had been trapped in the forest months ago, cold and in pain. Cecily could at last accept the infrequent feelings, although she would never liken them to something with such sinister connotations as witchcraft. She was simply very close with her sisters. That was all.

Cecily should have known straightaway that Alys was carrying a child. She and Piers had been married for nearly four months now, and from all appearances they seemed quite happy and in love still. A child was the natural progression between them, and Alys was likely still in the early stages of pregnancy, when the sickness and exhaustion lingered for some women. Any day now, the nausea should depart from the youngest—and therefore the middle—Foxe sister.

It could not happen a moment too soon for Cecily. She felt wretched.

John Grey was waiting for her at the bottom of the stairs, his faintly bemused smile doing little to improve Cecily's mood. But she gave him the best impression of happiness that she could as she took his proffered arm and let him lead her into the hall.

To Cecily's unbridled relief there was no sign of Oliver Bellecote or Joan Barleg. Sybilla was also absent, but it was common enough as the eldest Foxe sister rarely had the patience to commune intimately with her household before early afternoon. Only Alys and Piers sat at Sybilla's long table, and Cecily dared to hope for a moment that this morning would mark the transition to her life as the wife of John Grey. A life completely without Oliver Bellecote.

She forced a wider smile to her lips as she and John approached the dais, and Cecily could clearly see Alys enjoying a platter of whatever food she had been served to break her fast. A hearty appetite in early pregnancy was a good sign. Perhaps the nausea would leave now.

John Grey solicitously handed her up the step. As Cecily made her way to the empty chair next to Alys, her heart leapt and she brought a hand to her chest. There, before her flush-faced and smiling younger sister, was a large platter filled edge to edge with—

"Alys! Is that—?"

"Apple tart?" Alys turned her face and mumbled daintily around a mouthful of the heavenly smelling confection. She swallowed and then beamed up at Cecily. "Why, yes, it most certainly is. I have been craving Cook's apple tart for weeks now! I've dreamed about it—I even wrote a sonnet in honor of this fine, fine creation."

Cecily could not take her eyes from Alys's platter as she sightlessly sat down in the chair John Grey pulled away from the table for her. The crags and scallops of fruit and crust ran with thin, white cream.

"Is there"—she swallowed, all traces of nausea and headache gone—"is there any left?"

Alys shoveled another mouthful in and then brought her fingers to her lips while she simultaneously chewed and giggled. She bobbed her head excitedly. After a loud gulp, she said, "It was my express command that there be no fewer than six available at all times while I am visiting."

Alys turned to wave a hand at a serving boy. Once she had his attention, she pantomimed to her platter and then to Cecily.

Cecily shook out her linen napkin as if in a dream,

her eyes on the doorway leading to the kitchens. It took all of her self-control not to push Alys away from the table and attack the tart with her own bare hands.

A pair of servants emerged in what seemed to Cecily like an hour later, each one bearing a tray. The first maid slid a platter of sliced meat and warmed meal before John Grey, and Cecily found herself craning her neck to attempt to see what her own tray held, even as the maid was lowering it onto the table.

A tiny sliver of tart, with a dollop of butter smeared near the rim of the platter.

Alys looked down her nose at the stingy portion and sniffed. "That's a pity."

Cecily's lips thinned and she looked up at the maid with a raised eyebrow. "Bring the rest of it, please," she said in a low voice. "A pitcher of cream, as well."

"A pitcher, milady?"

"Yes, a pitcher," Cecily said in a voice full of forced patience. "It is a receptacle used to contain large quantities of various liquids. I want a *pitcher*. Of *cream*. To go with the *rest of my tart* that you seemed to have forgotten in the kitchen, if it isn't too much trouble!"

Her dining companions to either side of her were silent, and the maid stared at her for a moment in wide-eyed shock before bobbing a quick curtsy and dashing away once more.

"A single bite of tart," Cecily muttered crossly to her plate as she picked up the pastry with her left hand and used the knife in her right to smear the entire glob of butter across the glistening apples.

"With butter, no less." She stuffed half the slice into her mouth. She mumbled around the food as she chewed. "Cream with tart. Always cream."

An abrupt snort of laughter to her left drew Cecily's attention, and she looked sideways at her younger sister. Alys held her napkin over her mouth and her shoulders shook.

"Why, Cecily," she said merrily, "you sounded exactly like Sybilla just then!" She leaned toward her and poked a finger at a rather sizeable piece of crust left on the platter. "You missed a bit—may I?"

Cecily stopped chewing. "I should hate to stab you, Alys."

The youngest Foxe sister collapsed back in her chair, grasping at her stomach she was laughing so hard. A moment later, Cecily joined her.

"I do hope they bring two!" Alys gasped, tears of mirth on her cheeks.

When the maid returned, bearing three whole tarts and two pitchers of cream, the sisters were lost, both collapsing onto the tabletop and shrieking.

Cecily heard Piers Mallory comment to John over their heads, "Sorry, old man. They've gone quite mad."

"Remind me not to have any of the tart," John quipped. "It obviously induces hysteria."

"Stop!" Alys begged. "You're not helping!"

After several moments of hiccupping sighs, the two sisters had managed to regain their composure. Cecily tucked into her proper breakfast, her mouth aching from all the laughter.

Alys wiped at her eyes and scooted her chair closer to the table, attending to refilling her own plate. "I am sorry, Cee, for inflicting this insanity upon you. I had no idea you would be sensitive to my maternal demands."

Cecily chewed, swallowed—oh, it was heavenly! "Don't apologize. I do vow, I much prefer this symptom to the others. Infinitely more delicious."

Alys cut her tart carefully. "True. The sickness was horrid. Thank heavens for the both of us that it was at least brief—come and gone even before Piers and I arrived for the Candlemas feast." She took a bite.

Cecily's utensil stopped halfway to her mouth. She turned her head to look at Alys.

"You're not sick any longer?"

Alys shook her head quickly and shot Cecily a relieved smile. "No. And it lasted scarcely a week, else I'm afraid I would have spent the whole of the feast in the garderobe."

Cecily looked down at the bite of tart still poised between her platter and her mouth. She lay her utensil down carefully, as her stomach began its now familiar, faint roiling. She stood abruptly.

"Excuse me," she choked. "I . . . I seem to have forgotten something in my chamber."

John Grey rushed to his feet, his expression one of mild concern. "Shall I accompany you, my lady?"

"No, no," Cecily rushed, sidestepping awkwardly behind his chair, very aware that three pairs of eyes were trained to her. "I'll return straightaway. But a moment!" She tried to smile at them as she made her way from the dais and then as quickly as possible down the center aisle of the hall without actually breaking into a run.

Her feet flew up the stairs as her face and neck

sprang with perspiration. Her stomach seemed to clench, her throat expanded behind her cavernous-feeling mouth. She gained the top of the entry stairs and stopped.

To the left lay the long flight to the upper corridor; ahead of her, Fallstowe's massive front doors with their ever-present entry guards watchful for any signal from her. Cecily knew she would never make it to the garderobe or her own chamber.

She rushed toward the double doors, an arm stretched out before her, the fingers of her other hand fluttering over her mouth.

"Open," she choked.

The guards threw the doors wide and Cecily burst into the cold March air, stumbling into a man standing with his back to the doors. He wore a white shirt and a long broadsword at his hip, and both arms hung at his sides.

"Excuse me, I'm sorry," Cecily choked, and staggered away without further thought of him.

Dashing along the stones, she squinted against the bright daylight, which seemed to mock her dread. She could go no farther. She fell to her knees, one palm braced against the keep wall. In moments, her stomach was painfully empty once more.

She realized she was crying as she wiped at her face and mouth with the hem of her gown. She'd have to change now, before she returned to the hall to face her sister and brother-in-law. And John Grey.

Alys's sickness had come and gone more than a month ago.

Cecily had been wretchedly ill for only the past

week. Her last cycle was—she counted silently on her fingers—

January?

Oh, no. No, no, no.

"Cecily," a voice called to her. "Cecily, are you all right?"

She lifted her face, knowing who it was—who it could only be—before her eyes could confirm the identity of the concerned party.

The man in the white shirt. The man with the sword, whom she had run into upon her hasty exit from the keep. The man who was the reason she was so dreadfully ill. It was . . .

Oliver had dared not venture to the great hall at such an early hour for dread of encountering any of Fallstowe's inhabitants. So he'd chosen to fritter the time away, making certain yet again that his belongings were properly collected in preparation for his leave of Fallstowe—whenever that might be. He'd taken August's sword from the wardrobe and laid it on the bed next to his leather bag.

As far back as Oliver could recall, he had never seen August without the weapon strapped to his side. He stared at his brother's sword—Oliver's sword now. The wide belt, thick hilt and guard, the blade length proving its intention as a means of death and destruction on a battlefield, but also as a keeper of peace, a mark of a leader, of a lord, of a man.

Besides the usual drunken bravado displayed among mates well into their cups, Oliver had not drawn a sword on anyone in his life. He'd had several drawn on him, of course, and once he'd been chased from a maiden's bedchamber by an ax-wielding father. But he'd fought no great battles. There had been no cause for him to champion. No one challenged him, for he'd never had any significant spoils to award a worthy victor.

He'd never looked farther into the future than his next conquest, the next feast. His needs were met by Bellemont and his very generous older brother. August, who ruled in their father's place with pride and dignity, whose honorable hand was known as widely and as well as Oliver's own scandalous tendencies. August, who'd dared to go after the woman he wanted—the head of the notorious Foxe family, no less—and cared naught for the stir it created amongst his peers, the royal eyebrow it must have raised.

Oliver could imagine the talk about him now, the pity prompted by his recent, careless accident, his unreasonable behavior in regards to Cecily Foxe—the compassionate saint of Fallstowe Castle. Even his confirmation of his inheritance of Bellemont by a merciful and sympathetic king. No one thought him capable of anything, likely. Perhaps even himself.

Oliver suddenly found himself very tired of mercy. Tired of being at the mercy of Fallstowe, at the mercy of his healing body. Tired of being at the mercy of his brother's memory.

He looked down at his right arm and after a moment, he slipped the sling over his head, peeled it away from beneath his elbow. He crumpled the linen into a wadded ball and threw it to the floor.

Then he slowly, gingerly stretched his right arm to its full length.

"Gah!" he cried out, wincing as his muscles, tendons, elbow, creaked and wailed. His fingertips sizzled with invisible lightning. His arm throbbed, but Oliver did not care. It felt good to be free of the sling, to inflict this manner of physical pain upon himself.

He made a slow fist, and a cold ache sank into the bones of his right arm. He held the fist before him and matched it with his left hand.

"My hands," he said to the quiet chamber, clenching and unclenching his fingers, turning his hands before his face. "*My* hands." Then he turned back to the bed, to August's sword.

"*My* sword," he corrected aloud.

He gritted his teeth, and cried out once while working to strap the weighty weapon to his side. His neck was damp with sweat when, for the first time in Oliver's life, he was clothed as Lord Bellecote. He walked to his chamber door and quit the room.

He felt perhaps his fortune had changed for the better when he encountered not a single Foxe en route to the great hall. But that theory was brutally defeated when, stopping in the sheltering shadows of the stairwell, he saw none other than Cecily Foxe, laughing uproariously with her younger sister. John Grey and Piers Mallory flanked the two women and the quartet appeared quite cozy.

Oliver retreated. He would not make a greater fool of himself for Cecily Foxe than he already had. Unlike August, the younger Lord Bellecote knew when he was defeated.

The guards opened the doors for him and Oliver

stepped into the cold, irritatingly cheery sunlight, the wind biting through his thin shirtsleeves and tousling his hair. He had been cradling his right arm out of habit, but now he lowered it slowly to his side, wincing at the sharp bursts of pain the motion caused.

He took a deep breath.

She didn't want him. She didn't need him. And she most certainly did not love him.

The doors behind him burst open and someone stumbled into him, rocking him on his feet. Oliver turned at the strangled apology and saw a whirl of gray skirts, a knot of silky, dark hair.

It was Cecily.

He watched her stagger along the side of the keep wall and fall to her knees in the yellowed weeds, and Oliver's jaw clenched. Her head dropped and he heard the terrible retching. His feet were moving before he could think better of it.

She was standing at the chamber window, contemplating the wisdom of leaving her rooms or not, when she saw the flash of white sleeve close to the wall below. She stepped closer to the window, the cantilevered alcove giving her a ready view of the happenings on the ground. Her brows drew together.

It was Oliver, looking so very much like August from that vantage point—he even had his brother's sword strapped to him now. He was crouching down next to a puddle of woman on the ground. Cecily.

What were they about?

He helped her to her feet, and when it seemed she would have pulled away from him—her face downcast, her head turned aside—he pulled her closer, stepped into her. He seemed to be speaking to her, imploring her to look at him. But she would not. She only shook her head, bringing her fingers to press against her mouth. She nodded briefly, and then shook her head again.

Suddenly, Cecily wrenched her arm free and then turned, walking swiftly around the side of the keep wall toward the doors and disappearing.

Oliver stood alone for several moments, his dark hair a plaything for the breeze. His arm was no longer in its sling. He could have been August then, and she caught her breath as tears came to her eyes. She sniffed and brushed angrily at her cheek. Oliver turned then and she stepped back from the alcove, farther into the shadows of her room.

But he did not glance up. Instead he began to walk across the bailey, toward the chapel. Oliver paused for a moment, and then disappeared into the domed doorway. She saw a glimpse of the heavy wooden door swinging tardily, following after him.

She thought of the finger of crystal, the vivid, frustrating, seemingly meaningless dreams it had induced.

She thought of Cecily's betrothal to the vicar.

Then she thought of the Foxe Ring.

Chapter 19

Oliver departed Fallstowe on the seventh day after Cecily had returned from Hallowshire, his man from Bellemont arriving with an entourage of mounted soldiers and several horses for his lordship. Cecily stood some distance away in the bailey with John Grey, watching as Father Perry bid Oliver a quiet farewell.

Sybilla was absent, but Joan Barleg stood to the side of the great double doors, her eyes red and swollen, her arms across her midsection, her hands gripping her elbows. Oliver thus far had not afforded the obviously brokenhearted woman so much as a glance when he swung onto his horse and adjusted the reins in favor of his weaker arm.

John Grey leaned his head near Cecily's ear. "You must feel relieved to soon have this behind you."

Cecily turned her face to him, looked into his eyes, wanting forever more to be naught but honest with this good man.

"Yes," she lied, and gave him a weak smile.

Wanting something and having it were two very different things, Cecily now knew.

He returned her smile as Father Perry backed away from Oliver's mount, bestowing a blessing in the air before him. Then the priest was striding past Cecily and John, a happy smile on his narrow face.

"It is days such as this that give me more cause than usual to praise God," the man spouted, raising both hands in the air. "Hallelujah! It is a wondrous day for confession!" Both Cecily and John laughed at the man's triumphant-sounding whoop as he disappeared into his chapel.

Cecily could not discern why, when surrounded by men the likes of Father Perry and John Grey, her heart would still be reaching toward the only scoundrel in Fallstowe's midst. The man atop horseback, who was dancing his mount in a circle, its muzzle now pointing toward her.

Cecily raised her face until her eyes met Oliver Bellecote's, but her pensive words were meant only for John Grey's ears.

"It *is* a good day for confession, John."

Cecily felt his eyes on her, sensed his surprise, as she slid her arm from his grasp and turned, walking swiftly toward the chapel.

It seemed a lifetime ago when she had stood at those wooden doors, pausing to gaze over her shoulder toward the Foxe Ring.

This time though, Cecily did not look back.

Oliver watched Cecily's retreat with an ache in his chest. She would not even bid him farewell. His every instinct clawed at him to dismount and follow her, force her to face him. But his instincts, trained on the wrong desires for so many years, had done naught but fail him thus far. Oliver knew that if he ever had the fortune to lay eyes upon Cecily after leaving Fallstowe's bailey, she would be John Grey's wife. He'd had his chance to win her, and he had been judged unworthy. Perhaps, he thought, rightly so.

He looked at the not-a-vicar for a moment, and the blond man looked back mildly, with no obvious trace of resentment on his face. Cecily was likely right—John Grey was a better man than he. The idea of it, of Oliver's failures, burned and twisted in his guts.

But he could overcome his past. He would.

And so, Oliver raised his right hand, even though it felt as though it had been nailed to his ribs. "I wish you well, Grey."

John Grey stood very still for a moment, and then began walking toward him. Oliver opened his mouth as the man drew near, but John Grey turned his eyes to Fallstowe and walked directly past Oliver's horse.

"May God forgive you," John Grey muttered as if it was all he could allow through his clenched teeth. He disappeared through Fallstowe's doors.

"He already has!" Oliver shouted at the thick wooden doors. His frustration was threatening to explode. "So . . . so you can go to hell, Vicar!"

Oliver winced as, at his side, Argo snickered. Not a good start.

He caught sight of Joan, standing against the

keep wall, her face a clear mask of misery. He would fare much better with this attempt.

"Joan," he called.

She pushed her shoulders away from the stones and approached him, her arms locked together across her stomach. She had very recently been crying.

At his horse's side, she stopped, looked up at him. "So now you would call me to you like a dog?" She huffed. "Well, I came, didn't I? What do you want, Oliver?"

"Joan," Oliver began again, "I'm sorry for how things turned out."

She raised her eyebrows apathetically.

"Truly. And I must confess to you before I go, so that I do not leave you with either false hope or ideas that are out of line with what has actually gone on during our time at Fallstowe."

Her eyes narrowed a bit, and she looked slightly more interested.

"I told you upon my arrival here that I had no intention of marrying you, and that was the truth. Even when it seemed that I had made a proposal to you—"

"Seemed?" she asked shrilly. "You asked me to marry you!"

Oliver winced. "Actually, I asked you if you *would* marry me, a question to which I was already informed of the answer. I had no intention of ever going through with it. I only did it at Lady Sybilla's request."

Joan blanched. "What? Why? That makes no sense."

"All she would tell me is that she has some suspicions about August's death, and that she thinks you know something that you aren't telling."

"What?" Joan whispered. "She . . . she thinks I killed August? Oliver, do you think that? Is that why—?"

"No, I don't think you killed August. You were awakened in my bed the morning he was found. But discovering whatever Sybilla thinks you know is why she's been so unnaturally cozy to you the past weeks. Sybilla's reputation isn't false; she is a cold woman. And a dangerous woman, so take care with her. I owe her no loyalty now that August is gone. Telling you was the least I could do after having played a part in deceiving you so."

He saw her swallow, her eyes bulging; even her lips were pale. "Thank you, Oliver. But perhaps . . . might I call on Bellemont? Perhaps we could still—"

Oliver shook his head and cut off her words before she could go any further. "No, Joan. Our time—as friends and otherwise—is over. I bid you no ill-will, but I would rather we not see each other again."

She swallowed again and Oliver could see her tremble.

"I *am* sorry, Joan," he repeated.

Her eyes narrowed. She suddenly spat up at Oliver, and he recoiled from the base attack.

"You will never take August's place," she hissed viciously. "I hope the king strips you of Bellemont and leaves you penniless in the gutter, you filthy, drunken pig!" She spun on her heel to retreat to the keep.

"Joan," Oliver called, shocked at the woman's virulent reaction.

She stopped in front of the doors the guards held for her, turned, and raised her chin.

"He was a better lover than you, as well."

Then Joan was gone and Oliver was left in Fallstowe's bailey, surrounded only by his uneasy entourage. No Sybilla, Graves; no John Grey. No Cecily. Not even the roughest squire of Fallstowe remained to see him through the gates. Only the new knowledge that Joan Barleg had slept with his brother. Had slept with him and then compared them both.

Oliver's face burned. His jaw clenched.

He cleared his throat, and didn't look at Argo as he kicked the sides of his mount. He felt like galloping the whole of the way back to Bellemont.

Perhaps he would.

Chapter 20

It was as if the sun was loath to rise the next morning, perhaps dreading being witness to Cecily's dire missions. But the hearth in Sybilla's sumptuous chamber was roaring, and there were a pair of oil lamps lit in an attempt to pretend the light of day.

Cecily had confessed to Father Perry just as Oliver Bellecote had departed Fallstowe yesterday afternoon. She had begun at the very beginning, with her rebellious and envious thoughts at the Candlemas feast, her journey to the Foxe Ring, her encounter there with Oliver. She had followed each shocking admission with one even more grave, realizing that her words had grown from an anonymous whisper to a somber and very recognizable voice. Father Perry knew everything now. He knew and he had counseled her. And although she knew his advice had been given with the best intentions, Cecily was not at all certain she would follow it.

Cecily had gone straight to her elder sister's room after mass, and after telling John Grey that she would find him again very soon. She had asked

Graves to deliver Lady Alys, sans Lord Mallory—
this would be difficult enough without an intimidating man present.

Sybilla sat at her wide table before the windows,
still in her robe, as was her habit in the mornings.
She did not speak, but Cecily knew that it was not
out of a lack of curiosity, only another of Sybilla's
traits. If she did speak before the noon meal, it was
not pleasantries that typically came from her mouth.
Sybilla's tray of tea and toasted bread sat nearby, as
well as her thick, leather-bound calendar.

Cecily noticed the large crystal was still in residence, as well, although she could not think of a
reason her sister—normally so insistent on fine and
beautiful things—would think to keep it as a deco-
ration of any kind. Cecily thought it looked rather
ugly, and perhaps dangerous.

Cecily herself sat near the hearth in a chair covered in cloth she had embroidered herself. She offered no answers to the questions Sybilla did not
ask. Her hands were in her lap, clammy, her fingers
feeling like sticks wrapped in thin, wet leather. At
least she hadn't vomited.

Sybilla's chamber door swung open, and Alys
burst through, as was her habit, Graves close on her
heels. It never occurred to Cecily to ask Graves to
leave—it would be akin to asking the stones that
comprised Fallstowe's walls for a spot of privacy—
although the old steward only nodded in Sybilla's
direction before ducking back through the doorway and closing the door soundlessly after himself.

"What is it?" Alys demanded, marching to Sybilla's
table and immediately thieving from her tray. She

spoke around the toast in her mouth. "I've not had breakfast yet, and my babe is hungry. Shall I not get below soon, all the tart will be gone."

Tart *did* sound rather good.

Sybilla slid around in her chair to face Cecily at last, while Alys leaned her bottom against the edge of the table and munched. The brunette looked on with cool patience, the blond with spirited curiosity.

Cecily cleared her throat. "Yes. All right. I have something to tell the both of you. I wanted you to know before any others." She paused. "Except Father Perry, of course."

Alys rolled her eyes. *"Of course."*

Sybilla said nothing.

"I . . . well," Cecily stuttered. "I don't want to disappoint you."

"You never want to disappoint anyone, Cee." Alys pulled a face. "Please tell me you have something more salacious than that to share. I *am* starving." She tore off another hunk of bread with her teeth.

Cecily swallowed. "I'm pregnant."

Alys's mouth, still working on a bite of toast, fell open. She dropped the bread in her hand and grasped at the table edge, swallowing with obvious effort. "Oh my God," she gasped, and then lowered her voice even further, her eyes wide. "Is it . . . *immaculate?*"

Cecily frowned. She should have expected that.

Sybilla spoke for the first time since Cecily had entered the chamber. "It's not immaculate, Alys. It's John Grey's."

"Oh my *God!*" Alys shrieked.

Cecily squeezed her eyes closed and shook her

head briefly. "It's not John Grey's." She opened them and looked at her sisters. "It's Oliver Bellecote's."

Both of Alys's hands flew to her mouth to stifle her scream.

Sybilla said nothing. In fact, the only sound that came from her at all was the muffled thud of her body as she slid out of her chair and onto the floor.

The first thought to cross Oliver's mind upon waking that morning was that he had somehow broken his arm again. Although he wasn't at all certain that it was, in fact, morning—even though only half of the heavy draperies that surrounded the bed were drawn, the unfamiliar chamber was dim and somber.

He'd been too drunk to remember to place his arm back in the sling before falling into August's bed last night, and now he was paying for it. He struggled to sit upright in the gloom of the poster bed, groaning and hissing as his forearm and hand felt stung by a thousand needles, his bicep gripped in a cold vice.

His mouth tasted metallic, his head throbbed sickly. His throat felt as if he had drunk a steady river of sawdust the night before rather than Bellemont's fine wine. And what good had that attempt at numbing his mind done him? None. Absolutely none.

He scooted awkwardly from the bed and staggered to his feet, stumbling to the pot in the corner. He was beset by chills as he emptied his screaming bladder.

Oliver didn't know why he had chosen to inter

himself in August's chamber upon arriving at his home the previous evening. Perhaps it had been a subconscious attempt to glean some sort of wisdom from his overly-capable dead brother. But all it had succeeded in doing was to drive Oliver into a deeper state of maudlin. It had not been obvious to him upon casual observation of his brother's room, but upon closer inspection at length with the aid of a wine jug, little traces of Sybilla Foxe seemed to be everywhere.

A length of thin, silk ribbon, likely from a veil or the trim of a dress; a metal cup half full of Fallstowe coins, the scripted F on one side winking in the candlelight amidst little golden discs of the king's profile on the reverse; a pale, dried flower, pressed into the seam of a thin book of bleached vellum. The bound pages were half filled with quite good charcoal sketches, and Oliver had to admit the black and white effect of that particular medium was perfect for capturing the Foxe matriarch.

August had drawn her from memory, obviously, for Oliver had never had occasion to see Sybilla Foxe as smiling and feminine as she appeared on the pages of his brother's tribute to her. Here was her profile, unsmiling, yet wide eyed and sincere; here, as if August stood above her, her black hair falling over the page of white as it would a mattress. Eyes closed in this one, chin tilted back and laughing— he'd even caught the little crinkles where the seam of her lashes lay. When Oliver riffled the pages quickly, showing only blinks of each picture in fast succession, it seemed the woman came to life in jittering starts, and the obvious depth of emotion his brother must have held for this cold, cold woman caused Oliver's heart to pound.

It was the last sketch that twisted Oliver's guts though—a profile again, only this time in silhouette against the stark frame of a chamber window. No detail of face or dress, but hasty, bold lines depicting her figure, her hair tumbling over her shoulder.

And it could have been Cecily.

Oliver had sat down hard in his brother's chair, his thumb holding the pages open in the seam, his other hand bringing his chalice to his lips over and over again as he stared and stared and stared at that inexpert charcoal rendition. He had proceeded to get so drunk that he could no longer properly see the sketch, but that hadn't mattered, for in his dreams his vision had been unhampered by drink.

Now he splashed water on his face, seeking to wash away the last eerie vestiges of the images that had haunted him throughout his drunken slumber. His arm raged at him still, and so he sought the now ragged, stained sling amidst the detritus of his investigation. He was just slipping it over his head with a grimace when a solid rap sounded on the door.

"Come," Oliver called out wearily.

Argo's head appeared around the edge of the door, and after a quick appraisal of Oliver's person, the steward nodded succinctly and swung the door wide before him, admitting two maids bearing trays. They deposited their gifts on the table near the hearth and left silently.

Argo, however, was not so deferential.

"I thought my lord would have want of a bit of sustenance," he said, kicking through empty jugs on the floor. He picked one up and turned it upside down pointedly, raising his eyebrows at Oliver, before setting it on the tabletop with a hollow thunk.

Oliver had no comment, only a glare for the forward steward as he sat down at the table and poured himself a mug of warmed, spiced cider. It scalded his throat and tongue, but he drank it down nonetheless, pouring another immediately.

"Have a clerk sent up to me," he said, lifting each of the small, domed lids as he spoke. "I'd draft a message to the king." Chicken—no. Curds—God, no.

"Very well, my lord," Argo said with a slight bow. "Is it of an urgent nature?"

"Aren't all messages to the king of an urgent nature?" Oliver snapped as he lifted up the last domed lid. Oh ho, this looked promising. "Argo, what's this here?"

The man leaned over and looked down his nose at the steaming pastry and then returned to his previous stance.

"Apple tart, I believe, my lord."

"Perfect," Oliver muttered, and dug into the treat with enthusiasm. He spoke around the food in his mouth. "What does Bellemont's army number?"

Argo's eyebrows rose again, as if in surprise. "Why, I would put us at near three hundred, my lord, including the squires."

Oliver nodded, continued to chew.

"Are we to march on London?" Argo asked sarcastically, and Oliver knew the man was fishing for information.

"No, Westminster is safe," Oliver said smoothly, reaching for the other thin slice of tart. "When

Edward gives the word to march on *Fallstowe*, however, I want our men to lead the siege." He stuck half of the pastry in his mouth.

Argo stood there, blinking. After several moments, he said, "My lord?"

"You heard me, Argo. Sybilla Foxe will get what is coming to her. I did not realize until I had spent time there myself and then come home to this room, to my brother's lonely memories, what effect she had on his manhood."

"Forgive me for saying so, my lord, but your brother was very much in love with the lady. He would have given his life for her, had she required it."

"I am very much aware of that fact, Argo," Oliver said snidely. "And it was obviously the only area in his entire life in which my brother displayed poor judgment. She discarded him once she'd had her sport, made a fool of him."

Argo shook his head vehemently. "No. There was a reconciliation between them. Many letters—"

"What letters?" Oliver demanded, pounding his left fist on the tabletop. Then he stretched out the same arm to indicate the whole of the chamber. "You find them then, and you bring them to me! For I have searched every crevice seeking that which might lead me to believe that Sybilla Foxe is not the heartless witch she is rumored to be. To convince myself that my brother's affections were not misplaced. I have found naught! She may as well have dealt him the death blow with her own hands!"

"He was going to her when he died. *He loved her.*"

"If his love was so pure, then why was he fucking Joan Barleg?" Oliver demanded.

Argo blanched, and Oliver knew then that Joan had spoken the truth.

The man composed his expression with great effort. "It was a solitary incident. If I may be so bold, Lady Joan preyed upon the lord when he was at his most vulnerable. I believe—I believe after the lord and Lady Sybilla had had a row."

"Hmm. I see," Oliver mused, leaning back in his chair.

"The lord was gravely regretful for it. He had hoped no one would ever find out."

Oliver threw up a careless hand. "I could not care less whom Lady Joan chose to spread her legs for. I certainly had no claim to her, nor did I ever intend to have."

"Lord August knew that you would not marry Lady Joan, my lord," Argo said quietly.

Oliver shook his head and stood up. "Regardless, Sybilla Foxe must be held accountable for her actions. Fallstowe will fall, and I want nothing more than to be part of its toppling."

"What of Lady Cecily, my lord?" Argo asked carefully.

Oliver stopped, his back to the steward. "What of her?"

"You would have her home laid siege to, as well? Is she not an innocent in all of this?"

"Fallstowe will soon no longer be Lady Cecily's home. She is betrothed to a man from the north, and it is my understanding that they are to wed quickly."

Now it was Argo's turn to say, "I see."

Oliver swung around. "I'm not at all certain I appreciate your tone, Argo."

The steward only stared at him, and Oliver thought

he saw something akin to sympathy in the red-haired man's eyes.

"I apologize, my lord. I will send the clerk directly. Is there anything else?"

Oliver shook his head and turned away again. "No. That will be all for now." He heard the chamber door slam and scrubbed his left hand over his face.

Oliver told himself that he did not care what Bellemont's steward thought of his motivations. Oliver had been of little use to his brother while August was lord, true, but that didn't mean Oliver had to go on in such a manner now that his brother was dead. If anything, aiding the king would honor the memory of the fine ruler August had been.

Oliver had experienced firsthand how manipulative Sybilla Foxe could be, how she had so easily led him into the machinations of her plan to subvert simple Joan Barleg, who was, if guilty of anything at all, too free with her affections and lacking in self-worth. Oliver had only been at Fallstowe one month—Sybilla had worked on August for *years*.

He walked to his brother's wardrobe and opened the doors, perusing the clothes that hung there— that had hung there since the afternoon August had dressed before leaving Bellemont, never to return. Surely there was something here that would suffice.

What had been Sybilla's ultimate goal? Oliver still could not fathom it. She had said that she thought Joan knew something, but—*Joan*? It wasn't as if the woman had been privy to any of Bellemont's secrets, if even August held any.

He was a better lover than you, as well.

Oliver paused, his hand gripping a long, silk sleeve. Well, yes, there was that. But even so, Oliver doubted August had imparted any great piece of information to the humble lady. Oliver flipped the sleeve aside and continued his search.

Many letters . . .

"Many *missing* letters," Oliver muttered crossly, and then paused again. Against his better judgment, Oliver let his mind dwell on those two pieces of information: Joan had slept with August, and there was correspondence between August and Sybilla that had gone missing, at least since the time of August's death. He recalled Joan's return to Fallstowe with Argo. Hadn't the steward mentioned Joan invading this very chamber?

Could Joan have discovered the letters? And, if so, why would she steal something so trivial and personal, unless . . .

"Unless . . . unless . . ." Oliver turned away from the wardrobe, leaving the door open, and sat down in his brother's chair again.

Sybilla wanted very badly to know what Joan knew, and she had thought by convincing the woman that she was going to marry Oliver that somehow that information would be revealed. If August had in truth been Sybilla Foxe's confidant and coconspirator against the king, perhaps the missing letters detailed some incriminating evidence against her that the Foxe matriarch wanted destroyed.

But Oliver still did not understand his part in the whole deception. What importance did he have to both women, besides being August's brother, and now his heir?

A timid knock sounded at the door and Oliver started, feeling annoyed at the interruption. He wasn't certain, but he thought that perhaps he had been on the verge of discovering how all of the seemingly jumbled pieces of unrelated information were joined together.

"What is it?" he barked.

The door opened, and one of Bellemont's clerks stepped inside. "Argo said you wished to draft a letter to the king, milord?"

"Yes, Clerk." Oliver's brows drew downward, and his brain, still muddled from excess drink, worked with much effort.

"Milord?" the clerk asked.

Oliver stared at the clerk for so long the man turned red and began to fidget with his rolled up leather packet of quills and ink and parchments.

"Yes, I do wish to draft a letter, Clerk. A very urgent one." Oliver stood and walked to the table that still held the trays from his breakfast. He shoved them aside with ringing crashes, clearing a space for the timid man to work, then he slammed both palms on the bare wood.

Nothing made sense! But Oliver would not grant Sybilla Foxe further reprieve. And he told himself that this had nothing to do with spite. Nor jealousy. Nor revenge. Nor the idea that he wanted Fallstowe reduced to rubble because it was the place where he had lost his heart forever to a woman who very much resembled Sybilla Foxe.

Certainly, it had nothing at all to do with that.

Oliver looked up at the clerk. "How quickly can this message find its way into the king's hands?"

* * *

Cecily had never known Sybilla to show any weakness of person, either mentally or physically, and therefore the sight of her strong, older sister unconscious on the floor stunned her so that she was unable to move.

Alys knelt over Sybilla's still form, fanning her face with one hand and making little shrieking sounds. Then she turned her flushed face up to Cecily.

"Would you *mind*, Cee, since it's you who's killed her?"

Cecily bolted from the chair and went to her knees near Sybilla's shoulders, pulling her sister's head gently onto her own thigh.

"She's not dead, she only fainted."

"Why would she faint?" Alys demanded in a hysterical tone. "Sybilla never faints!"

"I suppose"—Cecily swallowed—"I suppose she is shocked."

"No. No, *I'm* shocked. Sybilla is *unconscious!* Cecily, how could you?"

"I didn't do it on purpose, Alys!" Cecily snapped. "How do you suppose I feel?" On her leg, Sybilla's head stirred. "Sybilla? Sybilla, are you all right?"

Sybilla tried to lever herself up.

"Slowly now," Cecily advised. "Slowly. You don't want to go under again."

Sybilla sat on her hip, one long arm braced to the side, her head lowered. She slowly turned her face toward Cecily.

"Are you in love with him?"

Alys's head swiveled back and forth between the

two sisters. "Who are you talking about? *Oliver*? Is Cecily in love with *Oliver Bellecote*? She is to marry the vicar! Of course she isn't in love with Oliver!"

Cecily nodded. "Yes. I am in love with him." She looked to Alys and winced at the innocent disbelief she saw there. "I'm sorry, Alys."

Sybilla turned her face away again. "Oh my God," she whispered. "I'm so sorry. I've made a terrible mistake, Cecily."

"I don't understand, Sybilla—you didn't know. How could you have made a mistake with any of it?"

Sybilla shook her head for a moment and then turned back to look at Cecily. "You're to break it off with the vicar, aren't you?"

"Yes. Of course."

Alys piped up again, regaining some of her lost boldness. "Are you to marry Oliver Bellecote, then?"

"Well, I—that is a difficult question to answer at the moment," Cecily said.

"He doesn't even know," Sybilla mused aloud, and then her lips thinned.

Cecily let her lack of denial be her answer.

"Cecily, you can't not tell him!" Alys nearly shouted. "He's your baby's father! What will you do when you begin to grow and everyone in the land knows?"

"Not everyone in the land need know if she follows through with her original intention and goes on to Hallowshire," Sybilla murmured.

Alys sucked in an outraged gasp when Cecily nodded.

"That was my plan. I made a grave mistake entrusting my heart to Oliver. He is a notorious scoundrel and a liar. How could I ever be certain that he would be faithful to me, to our family? I would always wonder about the next Joan Barleg, the next woman at some feast. Where he was, what he was doing. It is very possible that he would resent me. He may feel as though I trapped him into marrying me."

"You're scared," Sybilla mused in an amazed tone. And then, quieter, "He's in love with you, Cee."

"I do doubt the capacity for that emotion exists in one such as him."

Alys shot to her feet and pointed a finger at Cecily. "That is the worst, most hateful thing I believe I have ever heard come out of a woman's mouth, and that is saying something as we both share a sister in Sybilla."

"Thank you, Alys," Sybilla quipped.

"You know what I am talking about, Sybilla," Alys snapped, and then brought her wrathful gaze back to Cecily.

"She's right, Cee," Sybilla said. "Oliver must be told."

"I already have a plan for it in mind," Cecily said. She would not reveal the details of it just yet. "But I will not act until I am safely at Hallowshire."

Sybilla seemed to be thinking very quickly. "Yes. There are things I must put to order first, any matter. Hallowshire is the best place for you right now in your condition." Her face turned to Alys. "You and Piers should go, as well. As soon as possible."

Alys glared at them both. "I can't believe the pair of you! I will be more than happy to return home, straightaway. I want no part of such treachery."

"I plan to leave at dawn tomorrow, with Father Perry," Cecily offered, ignoring Alys's dramatic proclamation.

"Yes, that should be soon enough. And I do doubt I need to tell you this, but I would not share your blessed news with any other save John Grey before you depart."

Cecily cocked an eyebrow at her older sister. "I will do my best not to shout from the battlements that Saint Cecily is carrying the child of the land's most notorious rake after a night at the Foxe Ring."

"Fair enough." Sybilla held out her hands. "Help me up, broodmares."

"That was mean, Sybilla," Alys chastised as she and Cecily pulled their sister to stand.

"Was it? Well, I'm certain I will have my comeuppance before the end of it all," Sybilla assured them. She looked to Cecily. "Congratulations, Cee. Surely your and Alys's children will be fast companions."

Alys seemed to remember the root of all the angst as she looked down at Cecily's midsection. Then she covered her face and began to cry.

Chapter 21

It was several hours before Cecily could bring herself to seek out John Grey. The confrontation with her sisters in Sybilla's room that morning had taken its toll on Cecily, and she retreated to her own chamber to find some courage and give her stomach a chance to calm its roiling. Vomiting on the man while she broke off their betrothal would only add insult to injury.

And she thought again of her decision to take herself and her unborn child to the abbey before contacting Oliver. Was it truly the right thing to do? Was Alys's outrage at Cecily keeping the pregnancy a secret for any length of time justified? Sybilla herself seemed to agree that the man needed to be told, but if Cecily was honest with herself, she knew the reason she would keep the secret was out of selfish fear.

She loved Oliver Bellecote. She loved him more deeply and more passionately than she could have ever imagined her heart capable. Even now, his absence from Fallstowe's walls was palpable to her in the way one keeps lifting an empty chalice to their lips, thirsting and wishing for wine and only sensing in the last moment that the cup had been emptied.

She loved him. And she was fairly certain that, should he find out she carried his child, he would insist on marrying her. He would use every low trick to convince her to do so. But then Cecily would never know if his affections and loyalty to her were true. And when he strayed from her bed, as surely he would, how much more heartbroken would she be? Cecily closed her eyes against those painful imaginings.

She would send word for him to come to her at Hallowshire. If he did so, only for her, because he wanted her, perhaps there was hope for them. But if he ignored her message, if he had already forsaken the memory of her in favor of his next conquest . . .

An abbey was no good place to raise a child, of course, but there was no reason why she should stay there after the baby was born. Cecily had already thought that once the child was old enough to travel, she would demand Sybilla take a tiny portion of Fallstowe's wealth and secure her and the baby a home abroad. In France, perhaps even Bordeaux, where there were likely still distant relatives to their mother. In France, there would be little chance of ever again laying eyes upon Oliver Bellecote.

Or John Grey.

Cecily paused in the stairwell leading to the great hall, her eyes easily finding the lone figure of the vicar sitting at one of the common tables, his back to her. His golden hair, shining and straight, was the brightest thing in the cavernous room. Like a beacon of light, drawing her to him. Cecily thought the analogy fitting. And she felt shame at sending that goodness away.

She took a deep breath and stepped off the bottom step and into the hall.

He turned his head at the small whispering sounds of her slippers on the stones, and immediately stood, his face lit with a smile so gentle that it crushed Cecily's heart.

"I'd wondered if I would have need to send Graves to wake you before supper."

She came to stand at the end of the long table, her fingers knotted together at her waist. "I'm sorry it took so long. I was . . . I wasn't feeling well."

"You're not ill again, are you?" His fine brow drew downward and he seemed to take stock of her appearance. "You do look a bit pale."

"No. No, I'm not ill." If only it were that simple! She indicated the spot on the bench next to him. "May I?"

"Please," he said, reaching for her elbow and seeing her settled before taking his seat once more. "You are troubled by something, then, I know it. I do hope that you're to share it with me now."

Cecily swallowed, nodded. "Indeed."

He reached for her hand, and although Cecily wanted to shirk away, pulling her hand out of his warm grasp, she did not. Instead, she looked down at their joined fingers and for a moment, wondered again at the wisdom of what she was about to do. Was she completely mad?

Yes, she said to herself. *I am completely, madly in love with a man. And that man is not the one who sits at my side.*

The idea gave her courage enough to look into his eyes at last.

"John," she said. "John, I bless the day you came into my life."

His gentle smile was back. "Well, that is very kind of you to say, Cecily. I thank you for such a deep compliment."

She shook her head. "No, don't thank me. Don't thank me, for you know not what I am about to say."

His smile faded a bit. "Oh? Say it then, so that I will know."

"I can't marry you, John."

He did not shout his surprise. Embarrassed anger did not redden his face. His forehead only crinkled a bit, as if he were mildly perplexed by what she'd said. Perhaps she had posed some sort of riddle to him.

"Why?"

Cecily licked her lips, swallowed again. "Because I'm pregnant."

John Grey's face went slack and he turned his face away from her toward the front of the hall. "Oh," he breathed. He pulled his hand away from Cecily's, and Cecily squeezed her eyes shut when he placed that hand over his mouth and chin, his elbow resting on the table. "What he said was true, then—you did make love. I thought perhaps Lord Bellecote was only—" He broke off and paused for a moment. "You let me believe it had not gone so far."

"I did." Her skin felt like ice now that his warmth was gone. He didn't speak again, and so Cecily offered, "I'm sorry, John. I'm so ashamed. I'm not worthy of y—"

He turned his face back to her suddenly and his words cut her off. "I don't care."

"I'm sorry?"

"I don't care that you are pregnant," he clarified, and although his expression still bore the heavy traces of a deep shock, his words were strong, his tone sincere. "I may not be as rich as some men—most men, actually—but I will give all I have to care for you and that babe. He or she will be like my own, and there need never be any mention of it. We'll marry more quickly than we had intended, and . . . well, babies are born early on in marriages quite often."

Cecily was stunned. "I . . . I can't let you do that, John. It wouldn't be fair to either of us."

"How would it not be fair?" he asked. "I want you to be my wife. That you would be bringing an extra, small person—a person made from your own flesh—into our lives, is no reason for me to discard you."

Cecily's throat choked with emotion. "It would be forever between us. You would resent me in time, perhaps the child, as well."

"You truly believe that of me?" he asked, the hurt clear on his face.

Cecily drew in a stuttering breath as she remembered John in the village, holding the newborn babe, and her eyes filled with tears. She shook her head. "No," she whispered. "Of course not. That was simply a lie I was telling myself."

"It's because you love him, isn't it?"

A tear escaped one eye and raced down her cheek. She nodded. "And it is also because I suspect that, deep in your heart, you were using our betrothal as an escape from your vows."

John turned sideways on the bench suddenly and grasped both of her shoulders. "That doesn't mean I don't care for you! That I would not put my whole heart into being a good husband to you, a good father to our children! You are smarter than this, Cecily! Oliver Bellecote obviously cares nothing for you—he abandoned you and the babe when he left Fallstowe!"

Oh, God, Cecily whispered to herself, *please give me the strength to see this whole thing through.*

"John, Lord Bellecote is . . . unaware of my condition at this time."

He continued to hold on to her shoulders for a moment, staring into her eyes as if he was having difficulty understanding her words.

"You don't want me, a man who is willing to marry you and would love your child, and yet the man you love, you deceive?" he asked carefully.

She opened her mouth to deny it, but she had no rebuttal for the way he'd worded the accusation.

"I don't deserve you, John, and you most certainly deserve a woman more noble of character than I. I am saving us all greater heartbreak."

"You don't believe that."

She nodded. "Yes, I do."

John released her then and his face went colder than she could have ever imagined possible. His light, his gentle smile was gone.

"Then you are a hypocrite and a fool."

She lifted her face to watch him as he stood abruptly. "Perhaps. I am very sorry, all the same."

"At least now no one shall mistake you for a saint, for surely you are one no more." It was as close to a sneer as Cecily could imagine John Grey capable.

"I never was a saint, John," she whispered.

One of his slender eyebrows flickered upward. "Obviously. How thoughtless of me to forget that you never solicited such wearisome feelings of respect and admiration from those around you. How dare they revere you so?"

Cecily frowned. "Everyone expected me to be perfect, all the time! I was never allowed any mistakes!"

"You've made up for it though, haven't you? You should keep your confessor quite busy in the future. I do hope he doesn't end up falling in love with you, too—perhaps once you've grown weary of playing the infamous woman and need to be rescued from your life again."

Cecily's breath caught in her throat. "You don't mean that."

"I do mean it." He looked down at her, his nostrils flaring, his lips set in a hard line. "Everyone is entitled to mistakes, Cecily. Everyone. It's only unseemly when you deliberately misstep at another's expense."

"John, you don't understand. I—"

"I understand perfectly," he interrupted. "For as much as you claim to be unlike your sisters, you are a grand combination of both: the recklessness of the younger with the sense of entitlement of the elder. You don't care who you crush as long as you get what you want."

Cecily gasped. "That's not true!"

"I will pray for you, Lady Cecily. As well as for your poor, bastard child." He gave a short bow and began walking away.

Cecily felt as though he had struck her. She stood, a wave of nervous dizziness washing over her. "John, please, wait!"

He did not slow, and in fact, Cecily thought she

heard his footfalls pounding up the steps in a run as he disappeared into the corridor leading away from the hall.

She stood alone in that grand stone room, her arms hanging limp at her sides. Tears slipped from her eyes like withered petals in a cold wind. He was right, of course. Everything he'd said was true. But there was no other recourse to her at this point than to carry on.

In a moment, she had composed herself and quit the hall, her head held high.

She needed to pack.

Sybilla knew it was him when the pounding shook her chamber door. He did not pause in his insistence to be admitted long enough for her to bid him enter, and so she crossed the floor and opened the door herself. He swept past her in a rush of air, and she caught the scent of him—incense and hay, beeswax and sunshine.

She closed the door quietly and then turned to face him, her back pressed against the wood, her hands stacked behind her.

"I'm sorry, John," she said quietly.

He stabbed a finger toward her, and she saw that his eyes glistened behind his rage. "This is your fault!"

She dropped her head in an incomplete nod. "I know. I've never before been so completely right and so completely wrong in the same instance."

"It was in being completely right that you were wrong!" he shouted inanely, and then scrubbed his hands through his hair. "*Dammit!* When you told me of her, I thought you must certainly be exaggerating—surely there could be no woman who would suit me so. No woman so beautiful in spirit and in appearance. No woman so charitable and yet struggling with the same questions I held up to myself! But you were *right!*"

"I'm sorry," Sybilla repeated quietly. "I knew that you would be perfect for each other. I knew it"— she brought a fist to her chest—"in my own heart. That's why I encouraged you to come to Fallstowe when the bishop introduced us and told me he was sending you to Hallowshire for your discernment. I wanted Cecily to be with someone who would truly understand her, appreciate her."

"I find that I don't understand her, though! How perfect for her could I be if she will not accept me even when I promise to honor both her and her child?"

"I can only assume that my sister no longer desires perfect. I wanted her to be safe. I had no idea that she and Oliver—"

"I knew!" John Grey shouted, his fury not abating in the least. Indeed, it seemed to grow with every word from his mouth.

Sybilla frowned. "What do you mean, you knew?"

"I knew something inappropriate had happened between Cecily and that scoundrel upon the second instance of our meeting. She confessed to me, although she did not reveal the very extent of their affair! I knew she was in danger of falling in love with him when I urged her back to Hallowshire with me!"

"Why didn't you tell me?" Sybilla demanded.

"Because it was none of your bloody business!"

Sybilla pressed her lips together. "I see."

"You see too much," John Grey accused. "You see too much that you have no business looking for. You are not God, Sybilla Foxe. You are a mortal woman. In taking on the role of supreme ruler, you have ruined my life, and quite possibly your sister's."

"I hope that's not true."

"It is true!" He stomped toward her suddenly and seized her upper arms. "Why would you do such a thing to me? Show me the very thing I had been seeking, my way out, only to then have it ripped away from me in a blink?" He shook her briefly. "Why?"

Sybilla let her eyes search his face, and she could feel the pain weeping out of him like spring water from stones. She understood his despair more than she could ever explain to him with words, so she brought her hands up, her palms cradling his face.

"I'm sorry, John."

He closed his eyes and dropped his forehead to hers. "Why?" he demanded in a harsh whisper.

"I'm sorry," she whispered again, and pressed her lips to the corner of his mouth. "You'll never know how sorry."

He turned his mouth to hers again and kissed her, almost hesitantly. His breathing was labored. His scent was hypnotizing, and Sybilla felt their mutual mourning for what might have been tangle together like an omen.

When he pulled away, Sybilla stroked the side of his face, searched his eyes with hers. "Forgive me, John. Please." She leaned up and kissed his mouth again briefly, firmly. "Forgive me."

He stared at her as she dropped her hands to his shoulders, pulling him closer.

"Close your eyes," he demanded. "They are too blue."

Sybilla understood. Cecily's eyes were brown.

And then she closed her eyes. Because in that moment she needed John Grey as much as he needed her. Perhaps she needed him more.

Sybilla was breathless when John Grey rolled away from her, and although she expected him to immediately depart from the taint of her bed, after only a moment he sighed and drew her to his side. She curled over him hesitantly, laid her head upon his chest, let her hand come to rest cautiously on his stomach.

It had been a long time since August, both figuratively and literally, and both Sybilla's body and heart ached. Even with August, she had not allowed this closeness after lovemaking. But there was no risk with John Grey. He did not love her. In fact, he probably was as close as a man of his character could come to hating her. They had a mutual interest in Cecily, and had given each other a tiny bit of comfort.

"What are you going to do now, Sybilla?"

She shook her head against his chest, hearing her hair rustle loud in her ear. "I was very wrong about a lot of things. Joan Barleg obviously knows nothing. It's quite possible that August burned all of our correspondence, and that is why Argo could not locate the letters. It seems something August would do. He was always very careful to destroy anything of import if he could not keep it directly under his hand."

John sighed. "So Joan Barleg was naught but another innocent casualty."

"I would not go so far as to call her innocent, yet. But I shall give her some money when she leaves."

John was quiet for a long time. "Oliver Bellecote needs to know that Cecily is not going to marry me. That she is going to Hallowshire."

"I know. He also needs to know about his child. Cecily says she will send word to him, but I know that she is very frightened of everything happening to her now." John Grey's warm skin felt so good under her palm, she could not help but smooth her hand over his stomach. It was as if she could feel the vibration of his aliveness into her bones. "Oliver is beyond furious with me. He would likely fire on a messenger from Fallstowe."

"Perhaps you should go yourself, then."

Sybilla chuckled. "Vicar, I am surprised you would knowingly send a child of God to her own certain death."

"You now claim to be a child of God?" John Grey snorted easily. "I'm not really a vicar, any matter. It's only a courtesy title."

"Allow me my little fantasy, hmm?" She smiled against his skin, and then went still. "He wouldn't fire on *you,* John."

He was quiet for several heartbeats. "Sybilla, you ask too much of me."

"I know." She said no more, only continued to marvel at the warmth of him beneath her hand.

"Why? Why me?" he asked at last.

"Because no matter how badly she has hurt you, you care what happens to her and her child." She turned her face up to look at him in the growing gloom of her bed. "Don't you?"

He was staring at the canopy. "Yes. God help me." He was quiet again, as if considering the idea, and Sybilla let him be. "But why would he come to Hallowshire to see Cecily? What if Cecily is correct in her summation of him as little more than a scoundrel and a liar? I happen to think that it's true, myself."

Sybilla thought for a moment. "If he refuses to come, well, we have lost naught for the attempt."

"Perhaps . . . perhaps she will change her mind about me then, given some time."

Sybilla thought there was little chance of that happening, but she kept her thoughts on the subject to herself.

"I'll go," he said at last. "But I will not tell him of the child. I can't. It's too much to ask of me."

Sybilla nodded against his chest again. "I accept that."

Then he was sliding away from her, off the edge of the bed. Sybilla pulled the covers over her bare breasts and watched him as he dressed quickly in his plain vicar's clothing and religious medallion. She felt her desire to be loved again rising along with her feelings of impending loneliness and responsibility, and she hoped he left straightaway.

He turned to her, glanced down the length of her body stretched beneath the thin covering and then back at her face.

"Did you make love to me to persuade me to do your bidding?"

No, Sybilla said to herself. *I made love to you because you are handsome and strong and good. Because you were sad, and I was sad, and I wanted to taste a little of your*

*peace. Because I was sorry for hurting you. Because I
knew you would be a good lover.*

"Yes."

John Grey nodded as he dropped his gaze to the
floor. Then he turned and strode toward the door.
Once there he unbolted the latch and paused, speaking over his shoulder.

"I'll do my best with Lord Bellecote, and send
word if there is anything you need to be informed
of. Afterward, I shall return briefly to Hallowshire
before going on to the bishop to resign my mission.
I don't know what I shall do with myself then. Perhaps we shall see each other again, Lady Sybilla."

"Perhaps we shall. Godspeed, Vicar."

He opened the door without returning the blessing, but Sybilla did hear his muffled "Pardon me"
as he departed, leaving the door standing open.

Alys swept into Sybilla's chamber, Graves at her
back. Sybilla closed her eyes and breathed a sigh of
dismay.

The youngest Foxe sister came to a sweeping halt
in the center of the floor, one hand on her hip, the
other pointing toward the door Graves was closing
decorously. Her eyes were wide and she stuttered in
her words for a moment.

"Was that . . . did you . . . " She paused, drew a
breath. "Sybilla, did you *sleep* with a *priest*?"

Sybilla sat up in bed with another great sigh and
took the robe Graves handed her before he turned
his back. Sybilla stood and covered herself, cinching the belt tightly while she walked to her table.

"Oh, shut up, Alys—it's only a courtesy title."

Chapter 22

Cecily leaned against a stable wall as she waited for Father Perry the next morning, her heart in her slippers. A single lantern cast a flickering circle of golden light at her feet as if in effort to keep the creeping darkness of predawn away, while her horse stood in the aisle patiently, quietly, Cecily's leather satchel strapped to its saddle.

Alys and Piers had left the previous afternoon, and Cecily had bid Sybilla a brief and stilted farewell last night. There was no one else to say good-bye to, and so when someone had knocked timidly on her chamber door this morning shortly after she'd awakened, Cecily had ignored it. She wanted no tea, no apple tart this morn. She only wanted to be gone. She was so tired, and yet anxious to the point of trembling.

She heard shuffling footsteps in the stable yard beyond the circle of light and so she stood aright, drawing a deep breath. A shadowy figure stepped into the main aisle.

"Good morrow, Lady Cecily."

"Joan?" Cecily said, not bothering to conceal the surprise in her tone. Her eyes went to the satchel over the blond woman's shoulder. "Good morrow. Are you only now taking your leave of Fallstowe? Forgive me—I thought you had already left."

Joan Barleg came to stand perhaps five paces from Cecily, an uneasy smile on her face. "I've kept myself hidden away, licking my wounds, you could say. But I think I'm ready to leave today. There's no reason at all for me to stay now, is there?"

Cecily swallowed. "I'm sorry. Of course."

"It's all right," Joan said lightly. "Your sister has given me a weighty purse for my humiliation. It's something, I suppose."

Cecily frowned. "Are you to return to your family?"

Joan shook her head. "I think not. Actually"— her eyes went to Cecily's horse—"I was rather hoping I could accompany you, Lady Cecily."

"Ah, well . . . " Cecily licked her lips and looked over Joan's shoulder to the darkened doorway. Where was Father Perry?

"You're going to Hallowshire, are you not?" Joan pressed, taking another step toward Cecily. "I don't mean to pry, but I saw the vicar leave last night. He seemed to be . . . in quite a rush. And, of course, everyone is talking."

She took a deep breath. It wasn't as if she needed to keep her estrangement from John Grey a secret, only the why of it. "Yes. It appears you are not the only woman at Fallstowe whose plans of matrimony fell apart."

Joan Barleg pulled a sympathetic frown, and then she fished a purse from inside her cloak and held it up. "I thought mayhap this might buy me a small reprieve at the abbey. It seems a good place to . . . think. I may even decide to take the veil myself."

"Hallowshire is a wonderful haven," Cecily admitted. "But, Joan, have you any desire for the religious life?"

"Not really," Joan admitted with a wry smile. "But what else is there for me? My family is not wealthy or well connected. I'm not exactly eligible. Oliver was . . . Oliver was my future, and now that future is gone."

Cecily winced. She did not want Oliver's old lover as company on the way to Hallowshire Abbey.

Joan continued as she tucked the purse away again. "It may be the only recourse left to me, unless I would go to a town somewhere and take a position in a household. But even then, I have not the skills to be of any use to a family of means. I could be little more than a scullery maid. At least at the abbey I would not feel that humiliation."

Cecily could see the logic behind the woman's reasoning, and she had to admit that, were she in Joan Barleg's slippers, the choice would hold some appeal. But even so, how could Cecily continue to keep her condition a secret should Joan decide to stay on at the abbey for any length of time?

"Perhaps you should return to your family first, though," Cecily began. "Discuss it with them. It is a weighty decision, and perhaps they have other plans for you."

Joan shook her head. "They don't care where I am as long as they don't have to feed me or pay my notes. Dare I return with coin, it would disappear into their coffers even before I could count it, and then they would likely only turn me out with nothing."

Cecily was dismayed. It seemed as though Joan Barleg's familial circumstances left much to be desired. After all the poor girl had been through, didn't she, too, deserve some peace?

"I do hope you'll grant me permission," Joan said with another hesitant smile. "I'd wager there would be many people aggrieved at the thought of Saint Cecily making such a long journey on her own."

"Oh, no—Father Perry is accompanying me," Cecily rushed to explain. "He should have been here a quarter hour ago, actually."

Joan's eyes widened. "Didn't you hear? There was an outbreak of sickness in one of the villages. Father Perry was summoned in the night. I would have thought that he'd sent word to you straightaway."

Cecily winced as she remembered the unanswered knock on her door. "I believe he did."

"Well," Joan sighed. "I suppose you can wait for his return if it better suits you." She looked at Cecily. "Or we can go now, just the two of us. You know the way, do you not?"

"I do." Cecily answered grudgingly, and looked at her horse and then the doorway again. She thought of facing Fallstowe in the light of another day, the empty places where Oliver had walked. The castle had turned into a sort of graveyard for Cecily, where she was haunted by the sham of her old life, her broken heart, her failures.

She looked back to Joan, so hopeful, so desperate, so sincere.

"Can you help me saddle a horse?"

Oliver began the tedious tasks of familiarizing himself with Bellemont's affairs straightaway after breakfast in the hall. Flanked by Argo and the head clerk at the lord's table, reams of accounts and thick ledgers littered the table like fallen bodies on a battlefield. But Oliver was not intimidated by the chaos. In fact, with his sword strapped to his side, he felt as if he had been waiting his entire life for this challenge. And he thought for the first time that not only was he competent to rule Bellemont, but would likely excel at it.

Already he had pointed out several instances where Bellemont had been overcharged for goods. Mostly ale and wine, but those were two products in which Oliver was well familiar with cost, and so he noticed right away the unwarranted inflation. Several landholders were in arrears in their dues, as well, and after careful consultation with the clerk, Oliver determined that addressing the overcharges and collecting the monies owed to Bellemont would not only increase the hold's financial accounts, but preserve them until the next harvest season.

Argo leaned back in his chair and stared openly at Oliver as if perplexed.

"What is it, Argo?" Oliver demanded, his gaze flicking away from the ledger he was perusing long enough to convey his irritation. "Have I a bogey on my nose?"

Argo shook his head. "No, my lord. Forgive me. It's nothing." He leaned toward the table once more and began gathering together a fallen tower of papers.

Now Oliver leaned back. "Tell me."

The steward stilled in his busied actions, but kept his gaze on the table before him. "I believe Bellemont is in very good hands. Perhaps even better than Lord August's, God receive his soul. I'm sure that means little to you, of course." He resumed his shuffling.

Oliver blinked and drew his head back. "Thank you for your confidence, Argo. I am rather surprised at some of the errors I've witnessed. I thought August more thorough. It's as if some things were deliberately neglected. Had this continued, Bellemont's coffers would have been emptied by Midsummer."

The clerk cleared his throat and Argo inclined his head slightly. "Lord August was preoccupied in the weeks prior to his death. I don't believe he was overly concerned for a lack of coin."

"Well, he should have been," Oliver said gruffly. "I'd like to know where he thought his funds would come from after everyone had robbed him blind and tarried on their dues."

The conversation was interrupted by a guard entering the hall. The man strode down the narrow side aisle and stopped in a bow before August.

"Lord Bellecote, Bellemont has a visitor."

Oliver's eyebrows raised and for one wild moment, he let himself fantasize that Cecily had come. "Oh? Who is it?"

"Vicar John Grey of Hallowshire Abbey."

Oliver's jaw tightened. *That fucking vicar.* "What does he want?"

"He said it was of a personal nature, my lord. We dared not press him."

"What? Why? It's your duty to find out the intentions of anyone seeking entry at the gates."

The man looked decidedly uncomfortable. "Well, because he's a priest, my lord."

"It's only a courtesy title!" Oliver shouted, and then flung up his hands. "Show him in. I'll find out myself!" He threw himself against the back of his chair, drumming his fingers on the armrest. "We'll continue this later, Argo."

"As you wish, my lord."

In only a moment, Oliver was alone in his hall, his eyes trained on the arched doorway set in the left wall.

What in hell could John Grey want? The self-proclaimed pious man had snubbed Oliver yesterday. It seemed more than a bit odd for him to make the journey from Fallstowe—riding through the night, no less—to only harangue him further for his shortcomings.

The vicar came through the doorway in a rush, but then slowed to a stop as his head turned and he seemed to see Oliver sitting alone at the table. The two men stared at each other for a moment. John Grey dropped his gaze to the floor, as if in prayer, and then made his way determinedly toward the table.

"Lord Bellecote," John Grey said as way of greeting. He did not bow.

"Vicar," Oliver said pointedly. "To what do I owe the

honor of this unexpected visit? Have you brought the wrath of God with you? Am I to be excommunicated for my supposed transgressions? Or has Sybilla Foxe consulted with her crystal ball regarding the message I sent to the king only this morn?"

"Unfortunately, I do not possess the authority for excommunication," the man quipped. "Your business with the king is your own. But my conscience has moved me despite my sinful will. I must do the right thing."

"The right thing, eh?" Oliver said, and slouched down in his chair, as if the entire scenario was of absolutely no interest to him. What he wanted to do was ask of Cecily. Why would the vicar leave her side so soon? "What do you want, Grey?"

"First, I must pose a question to you, and I do hope that you can put aside any animosity you feel toward me long enough to answer honestly, if indeed you are capable of honesty."

"You try my patience, Vicar," Oliver growled. "I don't owe you an answer to anything, honest or otherwise."

John Grey did not take the bait. "I must be certain."

"You can be *certain* that, should you not come out with whatever it is you want to say, I will *honestly* have you removed from my hall." He folded his hands across his midsection and stared at the man expectantly.

"Are you in love with Cecily Foxe?"

Oliver blinked. Of all the things he could have imagined the man to ask, this was the very last.

"What kind of a fucking question is that?" Oliver

demanded quietly. "You come all the way from Fallstowe to mock me?"

"I do not mock you. I need to know."

Oliver bolted to his feet and pointed toward the doorway. "Get out."

"Lord Bellecote—"

"Argo!" Oliver bellowed.

"Oliver, listen to me!" John Grey demanded. "I heard you admit as much the night Cecily and I became betrothed. I simply need to know if your profession of love was only a ruse stemming from your base desire of her, or in fact, sincere feeling."

"Why?" Oliver shouted. "So you can rub your triumph in my face? So that we can finish the brawl we started that night? Because, I assure you, I am not so surprised and dejected as I was when you struck me, and I will be happy to hand your arse to you."

"You deserved that blow, and well you know it. I had no fear of you then, and I have none now."

"Then you are a fool."

Do you love her?

"Of course I do!" Oliver hissed, and then with a startling blasphemy, he swept his arm across the table before him, sending reams of parchment and his own cup sailing to the floor. The vicar didn't flinch. "Have you come to humiliate me then? Foolish, drunken wastrel, Oliver Bellecote, pining for the aloof Saint Cecily, who, because she could not marry God outright, chose the next best thing to a fucking priest?"

"It's only a—"

"A courtesy title, *I know*," Oliver shouted. "For the

love of your sweet God, John, what the hell do you want from me? You have the woman I love, already!"

"Cecily loves *you*, Oliver," John said.

Oliver felt his teeth grind together. "You know, for a man of God, you are quite cruel. Cecily doesn't want me."

"No," John Grey said in a low voice, and shook his head. "No, it's me she doesn't want. She's broken it off with me, and has only this morning left for Hallowshire Abbey."

Oliver stilled, and felt remarkably like he had when John Grey had bloodied his mouth. "What?"

"It's true." John Grey had not moved from the spot he'd come to rest in upon arriving in the hall. It was as if his feet were rooted to the stones until he'd said what he had to say to Oliver. "Sybilla and I . . . discussed it, and we felt you should know."

"Of course. Sybilla must stick her noble nose into everything." Oliver fell back down in his chair, the thoughts in his head loud, disorganized. "Why would you tell me this? So that I could make a greater fool of myself by chasing her down? No, thank you. She doesn't want me. I'm not good enough for her."

"Is that why you think she made the choices she did? Me over you? Because she was too good for you?"

"Isn't she? Everyone seems to think so."

"She was protecting herself! How could she be sure that she was nothing more than another conquest to you, a novelty? She is not some worldly trollop who knows how to handle a casual affair of the heart, Oliver. And now she is throwing her life away because she cannot bring herself to marry a man she does not love, and the man she does love runs off like the shameful reprobate he is rumored to be!"

"She refused me. What makes you think she would have me now?" Oliver challenged him. "I am still the same man I was when I left Fallstowe. Why would she—this time—take my claims as sincere?"

John stared at him, his jaw working as if he had something distasteful clenched between his teeth. "You must try."

"Nonsense. Perfect nonsense. Why are you here, telling me this?"

John Grey seemed to swallow the unpalatable words he had been holding in. He lifted his chin. "Because Hallowshire is no place for her, especially in light of all that has transpired since you came to Fallstowe. I know it, and you know it. And because I do care for her. If you fail to change her mind, I still have hopes for my own suit. Regardless, she cannot stay at Hallowshire alone."

"Alone? Have the rest of the sisters deserted their station?" Oliver remarked snidely.

"It is no secret that I think your actions and behavior have been the stuff of the basest gutter dweller," John said calmly. "But if Cecily found the tiniest speck of value in your character, I can only pray that she was not blinded by loneliness and despair, and that you will sway her. Because if she stays, it is not only her life that will be ruined."

"What do you mean?"

"Go to Hallowshire, Bellecote. Pull yourself out of your sty of lecherous filth long enough to see that you have a rare second chance to grasp the kind of happiness mortal men only dream of. For once in your life, achieve something of value."

"Don't dare speak to me in that manner again," Oliver warned. "Not when it was you who was using Cecily in order to escape your own vows. I'm neither stupid nor blind. You don't know me, Vicar. Don't presume you know my interests."

"I don't give a damn for your interests. Only Cecily's. Go to Hallowshire."

"Get out of my hall."

"Go today, Bellecote."

Oliver had had enough. He reached across his body with his right hand and grasped the hilt of his sword, pulling it free with a sharp ringing gasp of metal and pointing it at John Grey.

Two pieces of curled parchment—obviously severed from a whole by the drawing of the blade—fluttered down to land on the bare table before Oliver.

Oliver frowned and immediately forgot about John Grey. What had been hidden away in the hilt? And how long had it been there? Oliver lowered the sword tip mindlessly to the floor as he reached out with his left hand and picked up one half of the page. He scanned it quickly, his heart tripping as the scrolled words seemed to jump out at him. He laid his sword on the table and then slid the two halves together on the wood, holding them flat with his palms and leaning over the split page, his eyes reading and rereading the decree.

"August, you fool," he whispered, and then looked up quickly, remembering the presence of the vicar.

But John Grey had quietly gone.

Oliver dropped his head, his thoughts wrestling with each other for order. He thought of the series of events that had played out since the night of the Candlemas feast. Every conversation with Sybilla, every plea from Joan Barleg. He thought of Argo's dismay that Oliver would send a missive to the king, as well as the conversation with the steward only moments ago.

Lord August was preoccupied in the weeks prior to his death. I don't believe he was overly concerned for a lack of coin.

He thought of the contents of the message he had sent to the king that very morning. Edward would have the letter in his hand by the morrow's evening.

Oliver's chest hurt.

Cecily had gone on to Hallowshire. She was not marrying John Grey, and according to the vicar himself, Cecily loved him. *Loved him.*

Oliver looked at the parchment again and realized that Cecily did not know of this. The king didn't know. No one knew, save Sybilla Foxe.

And perhaps Joan Barleg.

Oliver sheathed his sword with a rattling clang and then crumpled the parchments together in his hand before jumping down from the dais and striding quickly from the hall.

If he hurried, he could be at Fallstowe before nightfall, Hallowshire by morn.

Chapter 23

The sky was just turning white and butter yellow at the horizon as the unlikely pair of Cecily Foxe and Joan Barleg made their way over the hills and away from Fallstowe. It crossed Cecily's mind that perhaps the two women had more in common than either ever would have at one time guessed—they were both fleeing the memory of the same man.

Only Cecily would be left with a physical reminder of him for the rest of her life.

"Do you feel that it's God calling you to Hallowshire, Lady Cecily?" Joan asked musingly over the crunch of horses' hooves and the slip and jingle of tack.

"I used to," Cecily said.

"But not now?"

"No."

Joan was quiet for several moments. When she did speak, her words were hesitant, even if her tone conveyed extreme interest. "What happened between you and the vicar?"

Cecily turned her head to look at the woman, shocked at such a brazen and prying question.

"I'm sorry," Joan offered quickly. "You don't have to tell me, of course. I simply thought that since we shared the same destination . . . oh, never mind. It doesn't matter at this point," she ended rather bitterly. After a moment, she asked in a more sensible tone, "What sort of people take up with the abbey? Besides the sisters, of course. Am I to be an outcast should I not take the veil?"

"You shouldn't worry about that," Cecily said, happy that the young woman was no longer prying into her private life. "Although Hallowshire is indeed a home and workplace for the sisters, there are many laypeople in transient on any given day."

"Like who?" Joan pressed.

"Oh, anyone you can imagine really. Widows, orphans, travelers, monks. Even criminals."

Joan looked askance at her. "Criminals?"

Cecily nodded. "The abbey oft times grants religious asylum."

"Criminals," Joan repeated dully.

Cecily laughed. "Don't worry yourself overmuch, Lady Joan. The majority of residents who could carry that label are mostly wanted for things related to politics and money. No bloodthirsty brigand will invade your cell in the night. Although the sisters are free to accept who they would, they aren't foolish, and wouldn't invite an obviously dangerous person to live among them."

"Well, I suppose that's a good thing," Joan said, looking around at the countryside for a moment, and then suddenly back to Cecily. "Not even the king could come for someone there? Ever?"

"Not even the king," Cecily affirmed. "Ever."

"Perhaps Lady Sybilla should consider the religious life."

Cecily chuckled despite herself. "I do doubt that the sisters' rules would be to Sybilla's liking."

"She does prefer to run things herself," Joan said, and the bitterness was back in her voice.

"She does. She's quite good at it though, so I can't fault her."

"She wasn't very good at it with me though, was she?" Joan asked. She turned to look into Cecily's eyes. "Do you know the only reason she invited me to stay at Fallstowe was because she was convinced I killed August Bellecote? She thought to flatter me into confessing, I suppose."

Cecily's breath caught in her chest so that she could not answer Joan right away. She thought of Sybilla's confession of a mistake; she thought of Oliver's desperation to explain what had seemed to Cecily at the time to be a very clear-cut situation.

But had it been clear-cut at all?

"I prefer not to meddle in Sybilla's affairs." Cecily cocked her head thoughtfully and looked at Joan. "*Did* you kill him?"

Joan shook her head a moment before answering, but her eyes did not waver from Cecily's face. "No. She wanted Oliver to propose marriage so that I would stay at Fallstowe for her to interrogate. I thought he was sincere, at last. I thought *she* was sincere in her kindness. You didn't know? You didn't even suspect?"

Cecily had to look away. "No, I didn't know. I'm sorry, Joan. Sybilla is not often kind."

"It should not surprise me that you weren't

included in their deception. Saint Cecily would
never stoop to such depths, would you? Perfect,
in every way." Cecily wanted to snap at the
woman, but held her tongue when Joan gave a
deep sigh. "Look there, isn't that the Foxe Ring
ahead?"

Cecily had done her best to avoid casting her
eyes in the direction of the old ruin, hoping that
Joan too would ignore the place where this whole
terrible mess began.

"Yes," she tried to say lightly through gritted teeth.

"Would you mind very much if we rode through?"
Joan asked, her words almost a bit breathless. Perhaps wistful.

It was the last place on earth Cecily wanted to see
that morning, with the sun rising in a golden mist
now, soft and crisp with the light of a nearby spring.
The place she and Oliver had made love. Where
they had conceived the child Cecily now carried.
Where she had abandoned everything she had
built for a moment in Oliver Bellecote's arms, not
caring that it would crumble to dust. It was taking
the knife blade too close to her heart.

"Joan, I—"

"I'll only stay a moment," Joan begged. "Please?
Lady Cecily, it was the last place I was certain I
would be Oliver's wife."

And it was the first place where I imagined the same,
Cecily thought to herself.

The guilt was enough to prompt Cecily to pull
her horse in the direction of the standing stones
without a word. She could not trust herself to speak.
Every plodding step of her horse was like a blow,

the questions in her head circling and swooping down to snatch at her composure like carrion birds.

"Thank you," Joan said breathlessly, as she spurred her horse past Cecily to enter and then ride through the ring.

When she topped the rise, Cecily saw Joan Barleg dismounting at the entrance of the old keep.

Why was she getting down from her horse? And why on earth would she be going into the old keep? It was barely daylight now, and the inside of the ruin would be damp and dark and dangerous for the young, reckless woman, who obviously was experiencing a fit of melancholy.

"Joan," Cecily called out. "Joan, don't go in there! It's unsafe!"

The woman merely gave Cecily a wave before disappearing into the jagged, arched doorway, suddenly resembling a yawning mouth full of rotten and broken teeth.

Cecily shivered and looked around her, her feelings of unease growing. They were just stones. It was only an abandoned keep. If anything, she should feel more of the sadness she had experienced when approaching the ring, not the unreasonable fear that seemed to tiptoe toward her through the dewy grass, little whispers of breeze skimming the stones and breathing their song. . . .

One, two, me and you . . .

Cecily frowned at the memory of the childhood rhyme. She didn't want to think of her mother sitting beneath the old, long-dead tree just beyond the ring. She didn't want to think of her sisters, so carefree, dancing and singing, flowers in their arms.

Tre, four, forever more . . .

It was like suddenly recalling a sweet memory of someone who had just died, realizing fully for the first time that nothing will ever be the same as it was. Painful and sharp, it burst her stoic resolve like a blister until the pain of it ran fast and hot, and tears stung Cecily's eyes.

"Joan!" she called out, swiping at her eyes with the back of her hand. "Joan, it's time to go!"

Five, six, the stones do pick . . .

Where was that foolish girl? Nausea swept over Cecily, so violently that she was afraid to try to swallow.

"Joan!" Cecily said in a strangled shout.

The woman's short scream echoed darkly from within the stones of the ruin, and Cecily's breath caught in her chest as she envisioned the gaping stone pit that was the foundation of the old donjon.

"Joan, are you all right?"

The splintered branches of the gnarled old tree under which her mother had sat so many years ago clicked together in the cold wind like a dancing skeleton. Cecily stared at the empty doorway to the ruin. There was no sound from within. Had Joan Barleg fallen into the pit?

Cecily kicked her foot free from the stirrup and slid down from her horse awkwardly. Then she was running through the tall stones, like grim witnesses to an execution, toward the keep.

Seven, eight, 'tis my fate . . .

"I'm coming, Joan!"

She passed through the doorway into the gloomy interior, but instead of slowing to a halt as she'd intended, she was propelled forward by the hands that grasped her forearm, swinging her in a powerful arc toward the pit.

Nine, ten, now I ken.

"No!" Cecily shouted as she felt the wind pull at her hair, and then she screamed from the bottom of her lungs as she felt the blackness beneath her gain hold of her slippers and drag her through the damp air.

Cecily's eyelids fluttered and she gasped against the cold, wet slime that pressed against her face. She realized she must have blacked out the instant before her body had hit the floor of the dungeon. She turned her face away from the quilted filth encasing her, testing her neck gently, and spat and gasped for air.

And then she cried out in pain and grasped at her right bicep, slick with blood.

Although it would be impossible to tell by merely gazing into the pit from above, the floor of the stone-lined abyss was matressed by a thickness of leaves and mud and organic debris, perhaps three feet deep. Cecily couldn't know how far down she had fallen from her position on the ground, but she guessed it to be at least eight feet. Possibly ten. Falling from such a height had sunk her to the packed floor with quite an impact, dragging the softness of her upper arm against the shattered end of an old beam, but the muck had saved her life, certainly.

"Wasn't that *fun?*"

She heard a rustling overhead and peered through the gloom. As Joan Barleg lowered herself to sit at the edge of the pit, her legs dangling over the rim and her hands braced to either side of her knees, the horror of Cecily's reality smashed into her.

"I'd hoped you would break your neck," the blond woman said ruefully, rhythmically bouncing her heels against the stone foundation. Then a note of hope lilted her words. "Is it broken? Perhaps your back?"

"No," Cecily choked out. "I'm fine. Just cut my arm a bit on a piece of wood."

"Oh, come now—a woman of your delicate nature falling from, what do you think?" She peered over the edge curiously. "Ten feet? You'd had to have suffered some worse injury than a simple *scrape.*"

Cecily pushed herself up to sit on her hip. "Joan, why—"

"Perhaps you've lost your baby then," she said deliberately.

Cecily stared at the woman, still bouncing her heels, and her blood ran cold.

"Yes, I know about it. I guessed the morning after you came back from the abbey with John Grey, when I saw you from the window, retching in the weeds," Joan said bitterly. "Oliver was too dense to figure it out though, was he not? And everyone always thinks me the stupid one!"

"Is that why you . . . why you tried to kill me? Because . . . because I'm pregnant?" Cecily did not want to reveal anything more than she must.

"No, not really," Joan said dismissively. "Mainly it was because you had ruined everything for me, even before you and Oliver slept together."

She knew. Cecily's heart pounded fiercely in her chest.

"Joan, I—" Cecily broke off, her fear and confusion twisting her tongue and her reason. "What happened between Oliver and me—it was a mistake. A horrible, terrible mistake. He was so drunk and I was . . ."

"Feeling tarty?" Joan offered. "You know, I had no idea about the two of you actually for quite some time, although had I not been quite so trusting in your frigidity, I would have easily put the clues together." She paused, cocked her head a bit. "Frigidity is a real word, you know. Isn't that funny?"

Then Joan returned to her previous subject with a swiftness that was disturbing. "Oliver's bloodied knees, your reluctance to have him at Fallstowe, to care for him. The morning I found you locked in his chamber—did I interrupt the two of you having sex?"

"No," Cecily whispered, her face heating even while her body was beset by chills. "It was only once. Joan, I never intended to carry on with Oliver Bellecote—that's why I left Fallstowe for Hallowshire. I didn't want to hurt you."

Joan stared at Cecily for a moment, and then threw her head back and laughed. "You mean to tell me that you were giving up the man you loved so as not to hurt my feelings?"

"Not entirely, no," Cecily said. "I didn't trust him. Sybilla is not the only one with a questionable reputation."

"Ah, yes. Well, that does make a bit more sense, I suppose. Although it hardly matters. As I said, you would have ruined things for me one way or another."

"What are you talking about?" Cecily demanded.

Joan held up a finger and then scrambled to her feet, disappearing from the rim of the pit.

"Joan?" Cecily called out, and then she, too, struggled to stand. Her head swam and she held her arms away from her sides momentarily, fighting for equilibrium.

When her swaying had stilled, she gripped her right arm once more and then turned in a slow circle, surveying her captivity. Yes, the pit walls were at least ten feet tall. There was no mortar between the stones, no ridges that Cecily could see upon which her slippers might find purchase to climb out. She would try though, as soon as she had the opportunity.

Joan reappeared at the edge of the hole, a roll of parchments tied with a string in one fist. She worked at the knot while she talked.

"You were right not to trust him," Joan said, unrolling the pages and flipping down the corners, scanning them. "He is quite the scoundrel. You would have never stood for his behavior, although it didn't matter to me in the least."

"How could you say it didn't matter to you, and then you take your jealous rage out on me by trying to murder me?"

Joan looked down at Cecily over the pages for a moment, her eyebrows raised, and then back to the single sheet now in her hand. She cleared her throat.

"Let's see . . . la, la, la . . . unfortunate . . . yes, here we are. 'I know you say that Oliver is neither responsible nor settled enough to take a bride such as my sister, and that his behaviors will surely scandalize her, but I can assure you that Cecily is made of sterner stuff than most realize. Since you will not allow him to marry Joan Barleg, and since the idea of a betrothal between the two children was discussed on more than one occasion years ago, I must insist that we would be remiss in not exploring the option. Oliver is your heir, and Cecily is mine, for all intents and purposes. If something should happen to me, Fallstowe would be protected by their union.'"

Cecily stood in the wet filth of the pit, staring up at Joan Barleg, her lips slack.

Sybilla. Sybilla had been pressing August for a betrothal between her and Oliver?

Joan looked down at her. "Hmm, interesting. You truly had no idea."

Cecily shook her head.

"It doesn't matter, really." She gestured with the curled pages. "August adamantly refused the idea until he and your sister had come to other arrangements."

"What other arrangements?"

Joan smiled slyly and then tossed the pages into the pit, where they turned and wheeled like seabirds before fluttering to the ground. Cecily hurried about, scooping up the parchments quickly before the damp mass under her feet could contaminate them.

"Is this what my sister was looking for?" Cecily demanded. "These letters that you stole from August?"

"Sybilla was looking for something of August's, true. I was looking for the same thing. She never found it, and neither did I, although these letters did much to encourage my tenacity. And I don't think of what I did as stealing, so much as receiving payment. I'm still not quite certain what led Sybilla to suspect me. Certainly no one else did—poor, simple, stupid Joan Barleg, who is so slow as to not even have proper command of language. August would have rather taken his own life than allow Sybilla to discover that he'd used me like a whore when she broke it off with him and banned him from her bed."

"I'm certain he didn't force you," Cecily said bitterly. Her world had been turned upside down in the past hour.

Joan giggled girlishly and winked at Cecily. "Well, that's true."

Cecily's mind worked. "Were you hoping that he would then choose you? That August would marry you?"

Joan shook her head. "Of course not. I simply wanted him indebted to me. Especially after I discovered what he and your sister had planned. I wanted Oliver. *I wanted to be Oliver's wife.* I was owed that, by both of them. They both betrayed me. Sybilla betrayed me."

"You were going to blackmail him," Cecily guessed. "Instead, you simply killed him, didn't you? You killed August."

"No, I didn't. I've already told you that, and it is the truth. August was thrown from his horse. Some birds flew up out of their nest and caused his horse to start. It was very clear to me that he had broken his neck or his back or some other rather important part of his body. He couldn't really move."

"You were with him," Cecily realized.

"Yes. He didn't know that I followed him. But I didn't kill him."

Cecily tried to swallow. "You just left him to die."

Joan nodded. "As I will do with you."

"Why, Joan?" Cecily asked. "Why?"

"He was going to your sister when the accident happened; he was to let her have her way, offering up Oliver. It was to be a surprise." Joan smiled then in the gloom, her words increasing Cecily's chill. "Oliver was supposed to ride with his brother that day—August was going to tell him of his and Sybilla's plans to see the two of you wed. But tardy Oliver—he never met August that day to hear the joyous news. When I saw August thrown, I went to him right away. Once the extent of his injuries was clear, I realized then that the accident was the perfect opportunity for me. With August dead and completely out of my way, Oliver would turn to me in grief, honoring my faithfulness by making me his wife at last. I would never know the fear of poverty again, the shame of my poor family."

"But he wasn't going to marry you, any matter!" Cecily argued.

"You don't know that!" Joan screamed, losing grasp of her calm. Her fists were clenched by her hips. "Now it will never happen and it is *still* your fault!" She took several deep breaths, seemed to gain control of herself. "So, if I can never have what I have worked so tirelessly for, he will never have *you*—the only person I have ever seen him worship outside his equally stupid and pigheaded brother."

"Joan," Cecily tried, "help me out of here, and let us both go on to Hallowshire together. I sent Oliver away; obviously things . . . aren't going to work out between us."

Joan shook her head. "Bravo, Saint Cecily, but no. Sorry. I actually do know Oliver quite well, and if he should ever learn that you are carrying his child, he would kidnap you away from the abbey and have you wed to him before you could blink. He is very determined with getting his way. I cannot breathe on this earth knowing that the pair of you have each other, Bellemont, *and* Fallstowe."

"What are you talking about, Joan?" Cecily demanded. "Fallstowe is Sybilla's."

Joan stared at her thoughtfully. "I wanted to be like you, at one time. I wanted to be sweet and meek and charitable. Perhaps Oliver would have loved me like he loved you. But I was so wrong. You are no different from me after all. At least he never took me drunk, on the ground." She began to turn away.

"Wait!" Cecily shouted. "Where are you going?"

Joan paused and turned back slowly, a small smile on her face. "I already told you—I'm going to Hallowshire. I have heard they will grant anyone asylum, even criminals. And no one can reach them, not even the king. Ever."

"Don't leave me here, Joan," Cecily begged.

"Thank you for the horses," Joan said with a smile, and then she turned away completely and disappeared from the rim of the pit.

"Joan!" Cecily screamed, her breath clouding in the gray cold. *"Joan!"*

In a moment, Cecily heard the muffled hoofbeats of the horses fading into the morning.

And then she heard nothing at all.

Chapter 24

Oliver rode as fast as he dared to Fallstowe, and still it was late afternoon when his horse galloped loudly onto the drawbridge. The gates were still open and the guards clearly recognized him. They did not stop him as he entered the bailey, although had they known what was on his mind as he rode through the gates, they would have likely shot him dead.

He was so furious, he thought he might strike Sybilla Foxe when he laid eyes upon her. And he was humiliated, too. Had no one thought he was worthy to know? Not even his own brother?

Were you worthy to know, then? An annoying voice challenged him from inside his head. He ignored it. He *was* furious, and his rage would find an outlet.

He swung down from his mount in front of the great hall doors before his horse had pulled to a complete stop. His boots hit the dirt with a satisfying stomp and he threw the reins across the saddle as a young boy came from the stables toward his horse.

Oliver was nearly to the steps when he saw the figure of Father Perry skimming around the side of the keep, one hand helping him along, his gray head bent. The normally spry old priest seemed unsteady on his feet, and although Oliver wanted nothing more than to storm through the doors without so much as a word to the holy man, Father Perry raised his head just then and signaled to Oliver.

"Thanks be to God that you're here!" Father Perry rasped. "And just in time."

"I'm sorry, but I'm in a terrible hurry, Father. Please excuse me," Oliver said brusquely.

"You've come for Lady Cecily, haven't you?" Father Perry called out, and then Oliver did stop.

The old man had paused and leaned against the stones. He looked dreadful.

"I have. But it was my understanding that— Father, are you all right?"

The old man squeezed his eyes shut. "I think I took some bad wine last night before bed, and I must warn Lady Sybilla, as it came from her own stores. I can't risk Lady Cecily taking it. I'm just not going as quickly as I would like."

"Let me help you," Oliver said with a frown, and went to the priest to take his arm. He helped the old man up the steps. "Father, I was led to believe that Lady Cecily had left for Hallowshire."

The old man stopped to look up at Oliver through his wheezing. "Who told you?"

"The vi—John Grey," Oliver corrected himself.

Father Perry closed his eyes and raised his face to the sky. "That man surely is a saint." Then he looked back to Oliver. "She was to leave this morn—I was to accompany her."

"She never went?" Oliver said quietly, his stomach

suddenly leaping amongst his guts like deer over
a log.

Father Perry gave him a weak but knowing smile.
"I'm still here, aren't I? I'm certain she is quite put
out with me, although, of course, she will never
admit it. And I do hope that after she sees you, she
will forget the whole thing immediately."

Oliver looked up the sheer, gray walls of Fallstowe, and suddenly all thoughts of Sybilla Foxe, of
his brother, and the scheming the two had orches-
trated ceased to matter. Somewhere within, Cecily
waited. Waited for him. He didn't know what he
would say to her, but he would find the words somehow. He must. This time, she must believe him.

Oliver smiled at the aged priest. "Let us go in
together then, and take our punishment."

Father Perry's watery blue eyes carried a dim
spark of mirth. "And may God have mercy on us
both."

Oliver grinned. "Amen."

The shadows were creeping long once more
across the ruined skeleton of the old keep, and the
pit that was Cecily's prison grew darker still. She sat
against the seam of rock and ground, covered in
filth and blood, shivering, clutching Sybilla's letters
between her drawn-up knees and her chest beneath her cloak.

No one knew she was here. No one would know
until it was too late.

She had scoured every rough and craggy surface
of the circular pit for hours, seeking escape. She

had found only a single handhold, the width and
depth of three fingers, at the very limits of her outstretched arm. There were no crumbling stone
steps, as there were on the first level of the ruin, no
holes where old wooden supports had rotted away.
Just a circle of very well-constructed stone, as long
as eternity, and as high as heaven itself.

The bleeding had mostly stopped, leaving her
torn sleeve and the flank of her bodice sticky wet.
What was not tinged a terrible brown color was
soaked in the wet compost of the dungeon floor.
Her skirts and cloak were wet to her knees. Her
back was damp, her chest, from her exertions. She
was so cold now, and would be colder still once
night was fully upon the stones.

She had read Sybilla's letters to August Bellecote
over and over, straining her eyes in the gloom, and
then running her fingers over each word when the
light had grown impossibly dim, as if she could in
that way reach out to her sister. She had prayed
aloud until her throat was raw, and then she had
prayed silently, her lips moving, her heart moving,
but her words for God's ears alone.

What a vain fool she had been! She had used
Oliver Bellecote, she realized that now. She had
used him out of fear of who she was, what she was
slated to become. She had used him to defy the
persona of Saint Cecily, and her moment of reckless sin had grown into something not damning
and shameful as she had once thought, but bigger
than herself and involving her whole heart.

She loved him now, just as he was. Perhaps she had
loved him even since he had jokingly refused her at

the Candlemas feast, but in her fear and pride, she had run. Cecily Foxe with such a scoundrel as Oliver Bellecote? No! Cecily needed a man completely above reproach. He would never make a mistake or a wrong decision. He would have no human feelings or desires. He would be pure and righteous and godly above all else.

And then when that ideal man had seemingly been placed at her hand, she had too late realized that John Grey wasn't at all what she wanted. She wanted someone irreverent, someone who would bring joy and laughter and color into her life. Who knew she wasn't a saint and did not care. Who loved her passionately, her heart, her body.

She had wanted Oliver Bellecote all along.

And now she had committed the gravest sin against him in sending him away ignorant of the fact that they had created a child together. She had stolen that which was not hers to steal, a gift given to them both. She had prayed for an answer that night at the Foxe Ring, and shortly thereafter Oliver Bellecote had literally fallen at her feet. At every turn, she had asked for guidance, and when faced with the clear answer, she had childishly turned away.

She was very cold now, and sleepy. Perhaps the next time her eyes closed, they would never again open. And the idea scared her, not that she would die, but that there were so many things left unsaid, undone.

She let her knees fall to the side within her cloak and then fell forward onto one hand, dragging her legs beneath her. Stacking her palms atop one another in the wet dirt, she lowered her forehead to her hands to whisper a prayer into the cold, black ground.

"My God, my God," she rasped. "Please forgive me. Should I die this night, receive me and this innocent child, and judge this babe not on its mother's deceit and cowardice. I ask that you bless Sybilla; be with Alys and Piers and their child—bless them in all their days."

Cecily swallowed. "Please bless Oliver Bellecote richly. I love him, and I realize now that it was I who was not worthy of the gift of him all along. Thank you for bringing him into my life. Guide him to be the man that he can be, and bring him happiness and love through you. Should it be your will that I die, please heal any wounds that I have caused in him, and bring him peace."

She paused, thinking hard about her next request.

"And I ask that you forgive me for what I am about to do, if it is an affront to you."

Cecily stayed in that position, on her knees with her forehead to the ground. She was so tired, it seemed too much of an effort to move. So she simply turned her head and laid her cheek against her hands, staring into the black until the darkness seemed to swirl with shimmering color. Tears leaked silently from her eyes, sliding over the bridge of her nose, into her hairline, the shell of her ear.

"Sybilla," she whispered. *"One, two, me and you . . ."*

Chapter 25

It was as if they had been waiting for Oliver.

Sybilla Foxe stood in the square stone entry just inside the doors, her decrepit old shadow, Graves, at her shoulder.

"Oliver," she said in what sounded like a relieved sigh.

He stepped into the entry fully, letting the guards take Father Perry's arms and help him past the threshold.

"Where is she, Sybilla?"

"Didn't John tell you? She left for— Father Perry! What are you doing here?"

The old priest was half dragged in behind Oliver. "My lady, you must not drink any of the wine you sent to the croft last eve—I do vow that it has made me very ill. I could not so much as pull myself from my pallet this morn."

"What wine?" Sybilla demanded. "I sent no wine."

"Where is Cecily, Sybilla?" Oliver repeated. "I do have great want to speak with you about some very interesting discoveries I have made, but before that you must give me your word."

"Oliver, she—"

"You will give me your word that Cecily is free to marry me," Oliver spoke over her. "As soon as can be arranged."

If Sybilla was surprised at the demand, she hid it well. "Of course. But, Oliver, Cecily is not here." She looked to the priest. "Father, who brought you the wine?"

"Lady Cecily cannot be allowed to partake of it," the old priest wheezed. "I fear that—"

"Who brought it?" Sybilla all but shouted.

Oliver stepped between Father Perry and Sybilla. "What do you mean, she's not here?"

"I didn't see who left it," Father Perry admitted in a curious tone. "There was a knock on my door late in the eve and the jug was leaning against the stoop."

"Sybilla!" Oliver shouted.

"I knew I was right," Sybilla breathed to no one in particular, and then Oliver saw the Foxe matriarch's chest rise and fall with a deep breath. She looked at him then, her icy blue gaze seeming to bore into his skull.

"Cecily left Fallstowe before dawn. I assumed with Father Perry, as the stable master noted two mounts missing from their stalls."

"Who else would she have left with?" Oliver asked.

"Joan Barleg is also gone. Her room has been emptied, save for this." She held up the long finger of crystal Joan had coveted so. She spoke over her shoulder. "Graves?"

"Madam?"

"Have Octavian saddled, as well as a fresh mount for Lord Bellecote. Call to arms a score of soldiers with torches prepared to search in the night. We will come to the stables to join with them in moments." As the old steward turned away to do his mistress's bidding, Sybilla Foxe looked to the guards still supporting the priest. "Take Father Perry to a room and arrange for his care from the kitchen. Also, go to the croft and search for the jug he drank from. Bring it to Cook so that she might ascertain the poison used and concoct a remedy."

The guards began to help Father Perry toward the stairs leading to the upper floors, but the old man was resisting. "Lady Sybilla, what do you—"

"Go and rest, Father. Pray if you can." She turned to Oliver. "If Joan Barleg is with her, Cecily is in great danger, Oliver. We must try to track them, to Hallowshire or wherever Joan has led her."

"Sybilla, Joan is not going to kill Cecily. Perhaps she was privy to some information that you and August wished to keep secret, but she was in my bed the morning August was found. You don't know for certain that she had *anything* to do with his death!"

"I *do* know it for certain," Sybilla argued.

"How could you possibly?" Oliver asked in exasperation.

Sybilla held up the crystal again. "Because she dreamed of it every night."

Oliver was silenced. He swallowed. Sybilla continued.

"This was no pretty bauble I gifted Joan with. It is a powerful dream crystal, from deep within Fallstowe's lands. I broke off a shard and kept the mother rock for myself, giving me the opportunity to see firsthand through Joan Barleg's eyes August's twisted body, his tears, his pain. *His last hour on earth.*"

Her voice was breaking, and so she paused. "August was to leave for Fallstowe in the early afternoon, after he had met with you. It would have been no great trick for Joan Barleg to have followed him, and then after his death, be safely returned to Bellemont before you were sober enough to realize she had not been with you the entire night."

Had Joan begun the evening festivities with him? Now that Oliver tried to recall, he found that the details were fuzzy. He didn't remember.

Sybilla continued. "Joan knows you are in love with Cecily. And if you have found what I suspect you have, only think upon the benefit for Joan Barleg had she married you, and you will understand my concern and my haste."

Oliver's heart grew so cold, it felt like a block of ice in his chest. "August was dead, and I was his heir."

Sybilla continued quietly. "I was certain Joan was in possession of letters that I wrote to August, detailing my suggestion that you and Cecily should wed."

Oliver's breath caught in his throat, causing his words to come out as a croak. "What?"

Sybilla nodded. "Yes. You were never consulted because, frankly, August refused in no uncertain terms. I think the idea of it was why Joan would never leave your side while you recovered at Fallstowe. And then you ended up actually falling in love with Cecily any matter."

Oliver felt a sheen of sweat blanket his neck as he recalled every minute instance in Joan's company while they had been at Fallstowe, every word of every exchange.

"My God, we ruined her plans but good, did we not?"

Sybilla nodded. "But in Joan's mind, it is all Cecily's fault. Joan even dreamed of the morning we found the two of you at the old ruin—I could see clearly the edge of the pit where you were lying, just inside the door. It was eating at Joan, even in her sleep."

"Sybilla, did Joan cause August's death?" He knew his voice sounded pleading, but he didn't care.

She shook her head. "I don't know, Oliver. I simply don't know."

Oliver nodded and then swallowed hard. "Let's go, then. Quickly, while there is still some daylight."

The daylight didn't last long. No more than an hour after they had departed Fallstowe, the land was blanketed in indigo. Two mounted soldiers flanked Oliver and Sybilla as they traveled the worn road northwest, in the direction of Hallowshire.

There had been no sign. The women had left Fallstowe more than twelve hours ago, and there was no way to discern their passing from the scores of other travelers' marks on the packed dirt. It was assumed that neither woman would stray from the road, and unless there was sign to the contrary, they could do nothing more than follow in the wake of the eighteen soldiers who rode ahead at top speed.

"I do love her, you know," Oliver said abruptly. "She is not simply another dalliance to me."

Sybilla nodded. "I know."

"I will never forsake her, should she have me. I vow this to you now."

"I know," Sybilla repeated. "Oliver, you are more like your brother than you realize. It is widely known that you have been little more than a popinjay for much of your life, but I can't help but think now that it was through August's own fault. He never required anything of you." Sybilla was quiet for a moment. "Someone very dear to me once said she had never been responsible for anything, because she'd never had anything to be responsible for."

"That's very wise, I suppose," Oliver ceded.

"It is. And I believe it is the case with you. What care should you have for marriage when it would not benefit you? When you had scores of women throwing themselves at you, plenty of money, and no title to defend?"

"You make it sound as though I was rather useless."

"Weren't you?"

"Yes. I suppose I was." Oliver looked to his right, over the black hills. His jaw clenched, his teeth aching. "I was never jealous of him. I only admired him greatly. And I . . . I miss him, very much."

"So do I," Sybilla said quietly. "And I'm sorry that"—her words broke off in a soft gasp. Sybilla pulled abruptly on the reins of her horse.

Oliver and the pair of soldiers also stopped. "What is it, Sybilla?"

She held up a palm with an annoyed frown. "Shh!"

She seemed to be listening for something, and so Oliver, too, raised his chin, quieted his breathing in the still night.

They were in the middle of blackness, nothing around them but rolling land.

Sybilla closed her eyes, the shadows of her eyelashes lengthening and flickering over her pale cheeks in the glow of torchlight. Then suddenly, her eyes opened, and she looked to the guards.

"Where are we?" she demanded.

"Two hours yet from Hallowshire, milady," a soldier supplied immediately.

Sybilla turned Octavian in a tight circle. "She's not there. It's too far away still. Oliver," she said distractedly, "Cecily is calling to me. But I can't— Oh my God," she gasped. She turned her frightened gaze to him for only an instant, and then back to the soldier. "The old ruin."

"The ruin?" Oliver asked incredulously. "Sybilla, why would Joan lead Cecily there, on Foxe lands? It makes no sense—it's practically under your nose!"

A soldier cleared his throat and said, "A half hour hard ride, milady, that way." He pointed a quilted arm over Oliver's head, across rolling hills with no visible trail to the southeast.

"Joan wasn't thinking of you when she dreamed of the Foxe Ring, Oliver," Sybilla said. "She was planning Cecily's death."

"Are you certain?" Oliver asked.

"If I am wrong, then we are too late and Cecily is already dead," Sybilla said with grim certainty.

Oliver wheeled his horse around with a shout and both the man and the beast leapt into the desolate darkness.

Cecily felt the reverberations under her face, but she could not force her eyes to open. Her body was frozen numb, still curled over her midsection on the ground of the pit. At least she thought as much. She couldn't feel her legs. She had the odd sensation of being on a rocking ship, her equilibrium tossed about as if on great, high waves.

"Cecily!"

The word was faint and broken, so that Cecily could not be certain that she had heard it at all, or that, if she had, the voice had not come from inside her own head.

"Cecily!"

It was louder that time. Closer. But she could still not call out a response strong enough to be heard. Whoever was searching for her would move on.

"Quickly, bring the torches! *Cecily!* Are you here?"

Oliver?

She heard a crashing thud, and then hands were grasping her, lifting her painfully, turning her.

"Cecily! Dear God!"

It *was* Oliver. Oliver. Oliver . . .

"Sybilla, she's soaking wet! I can't wake her!" She felt a pinch on her cheek. It rather hurt. "Cecily, please open your eyes!"

Cecily felt her eyelids strain to pull apart from each other.

"We're in hell, Oliver," she whispered. She could not see the details of his face—the torchlight above the rim of the pit was too distant beyond his silhouette.

"Hell? No," he said emphatically, and leaned his lips near her ear. "Cecily, no—it's not hell."

"Must be," she breathed. "I'm dead, and you and Sybilla are here."

He was still for a beat of time, and then he laughed, drawing her to him fully, rocking her, his face in her hair.

In a moment, the torchlight sloshed into the pit, stinging Cecily's eyes. She was wrenched from Oliver's arms and Sybilla spoke to her in her typical terse fashion.

"Cecily, where are you injured?"

"My arm," she said, so happy to see her sister's pale frowning face. "Fell onto a beam." She closed her eyes again, because she simply could not keep them open. The dizziness was upon her again. She felt her clothing being shuffled and rearranged, and then heard the distinct sound of her sleeve being torn open. Sybilla did not gasp, which was a good sign, in Cecily's mind.

"It's stopped bleeding," Sybilla said. "But I would cinch a belt over it before we move her."

"She will ride with me," Oliver announced.

"No," Sybilla said. "Your own arm is perhaps still too weak. She might fall."

"She will not fall. My arm will hold her." His words were so firm, so sure, so sweet to Cecily's ears.

To Cecily's deepest surprise, Sybilla relented. "Fine. We'll use the ropes and blankets to raise her."

In moments, Cecily was jostled into a sling and began the rocking ascent from the ground of the stone dungeon that Joan Barleg thought to make her crypt. Cecily felt the grateful tears leaking from her eyes. When she was at face level with Sybilla, Cecily called out her sister's name.

"Wait!" Sybilla's face was before her eyes in a blink. "What is it? Pain?"

Cecily looked into her sister's eyes. "I called you."

Tears welled in Sybilla's pale blue eyes and her lips thinned for only an instant. "I know," she whispered. She drew a palm over Cecily's hair, leaned forward, and kissed her forehead. "I heard you."

"Joan Barleg . . ." she began.

"She did this to you."

Cecily nodded. "She went on to Hallowshire, for asylum. What if . . . ?"

"Don't worry about Joan Barleg, Cecily," Sybilla said firmly. "She will never hurt you or anyone else again." Sybilla stepped back. "Carry on," she said to the soldiers.

Then Cecily was moving up once more, into the ruin, but out of despair.

Oliver mounted his horse with great effort in deference to his trembling legs, seating himself carefully to the rearmost of the saddle. The soldiers bundled Cecily onto his lap, securing the ends of her sling around his back. She was lost to unconsciousness again, and Oliver tried to still his pounding heart as he told himself it was only an exhausted slumber.

It would be all right now. It had to be.

Out of the corner of his eye, he saw Sybilla Foxe mount her own horse and then walk the beast to stand facing the opposite direction of Oliver's.

"She'll not die, Oliver," Sybilla said quietly and with a slight smile. "I daresay you were much worse for your initial encounter with the Foxe Ring than Cecily is now. Take her on to Fallstowe, and have Graves assist you with whatever care Cecily requires until I return. I should be no later than morning."

Oliver snorted and pulled Cecily's slight frame to his chest. "Like that old badger would ever take an order from me."

"He will," Sybilla said lightly. "Tell him . . . tell him that I've gone to camp again."

"What?" Oliver said with a frown. "What does that mean? What camp? Where are you going?"

"Graves will understand, and at those words, he will heed your every request."

"Sybilla, are you going on to Hallowshire after Joan? They'll never let you in!" Oliver argued. "If she has begged asylum, the sisters won't let you near Joan."

"I don't expect it to be the sisters who admit me," Sybilla said. "You need only take care of Cecily. I shall be back as quickly as I can."

And then she was gone, riding deeper into the night, with no guard at her side this time. Oliver watched her until her shadow was gone from the fringes of torchlight, and he wondered for a moment what she would do.

But then Sybilla Foxe was gone from his mind and his attention was once more completely focused on Cecily.

"Upon your word, Lord Bellecote," one of the soldiers said respectfully.

Oliver kicked at his horse lightly and began carrying Cecily back to Fallstowe.

John Grey met her in a small cell, his face drawn and worried, the questions hanging in the air between them like wet, dripping linens.

"Where is she, John?" Sybilla asked straightaway.

"Cecily?" he asked, his frown deepening. "She's not here. I thought mayhap she would come, but it was only Joan Barleg."

"I know where Cecily is," Sybilla said. "It is Joan Barleg whom I seek."

John looked at Sybilla for a long moment. "I can't give her over to you, Sybilla. She said that you might one day come for her, spouting mad accusations. She seemed very frightened of you."

"Frightened she should be. Where is she?"

John shook his head. "No. It is against the rule of the abbey."

"Joan Barleg poisoned Father Perry. I don't know at this moment whether he still lives. She then lured Cecily to the Foxe Ring and threw her into the pit of the old keep. Joan left her to die, just as she did August Bellecote."

John Grey's face went quickly white. "Cecily . . . ?"

"She lives, and will recover quite well. Oliver has taken her home to Fallstowe, and so I must do what

I have come here for quickly that I too might return and see to her care."

"He came for her," John said.

She nodded. "He did. Whatever you said to him had the desired effect. Well done, Vicar."

He did not smile at her. "It wasn't all what I said, I think. He actually drew his sword on me, to run me through. Did he tell you that?"

"No," Sybilla said.

"He drew his sword, and with the blade came a parchment of some sort. Lord Bellecote read it, and then damned his brother. He also mentioned something prior to that about a message he had only recently sent to the king. He seemed to imply that the subject matter was aught with which you might find offense."

Sybilla's stomach drew in on itself so that she thought it might have disappeared altogether from her body.

Oliver had pledged his support to Edward, against her.

And now Sybilla was away from Fallstowe.

"Then I truly have no time, John. Where is she?"

"I cannot be party to this," he said sadly. "I am to return to the bishop on the morrow, to commit to my vows."

Sybilla rushed to him, putting her nose directly beneath his.

"Then I would suggest that you leave this night instead, after you tell me where Joan Barleg is," she growled. "I have been most sympathetic of you thus far, *Vicar,* but I will do what I came here to do, and you will either show me the way or *I will destroy you.* Don't force my hand, John."

"You don't frighten me, Sybilla," John said quietly.

"No?" she asked in a light whisper, still a scant inch from his face. She felt her palms tingling, her blood bubbling in her wrists.

John Grey looked into Sybilla's eyes and then a curious frown creased his brow. "She is only across the corridor," he said in a low voice. "But please, don't go to her until I've left."

"Then you should go right now," Sybilla emphasized. "*Now,* John."

John Grey swerved around Sybilla, picking up a small satchel on his way across the chamber floor. Sybilla turned to watch him as he went out the door, leaving it swinging wide behind him. He did not look back.

Sybilla could see the closed door across the narrow corridor. She stared at it for several moments, the bells tolling Compline ringing around her, quickening her pulse. Sybilla walked to the doorway, stepped across the corridor, and stood before the door. She did not bother to look for any witnesses lurking about this wing of the abbey. She didn't care.

She held her right palm over the door latch but did not touch it. A moment later, she heard the faint whisper of the bolt on the other side of the door slip free. Sybilla let her hand fall away. The door began to swing open very, very slowly.

A single candle lit the impoverished cell, on a table beneath the window where Joan Barleg sat, her back to the room. Before her on the wooden surface was the contents of the purse Sybilla had given the girl before she'd left Fallstowe. Joan was scraping each individual coin into a separate pile, counting carefully.

Cecily's leather satchel rested against the table leg in a puddle, the dull twinkle of her prayer beads peeking out from under the flap like a tongue.

Sybilla stepped inside the chamber on silent feet, bringing the colder air of the corridor with her. The little breeze batted at the candle flame and Joan Barleg looked over her shoulder with an annoyed frown. When she saw Sybilla, she spun on her stool with a small gasp, her eyes wide, her mouth turned down.

"Hello, Joan," Sybilla whispered.

"No," she cried. "How did you get in? You . . . you shouldn't be here!" She stood and tried to back away as Sybilla began walking slowly toward her. The stacks of coin toppled with merry jingles. "What's wrong with you? Get away from me!" Joan screamed. "Get away! *Get away! Get awa—*"

The cell door slammed closed.

Chapter 26

Cecily slept all night and into the next evening. Oliver nearly worried himself to his own grave, hovering over her, examining the color of her skin, counting her respirations. It mattered not that Sybilla said Cecily would be fine, nor Cook, nor Graves, nor Father Perry, who had since fully recovered after a long night and day in the garderobe. Oliver would not take her recovery for granted until she opened her eyes for longer than a moment, and until they could speak to each other at length.

And so he was not expecting her soft "Oliver" from the shadows as he sat before the blazing hearth in her room on the second night.

He leapt to her side, his eyes searching her face. "Cecily, how are you feeling?"

"I'm feeling . . . I don't quite know. Tired, I suppose, although I can't see how that is possible since I'm abed now. How long have I been here?"

"Since we arrived last night," Oliver confirmed. "How is your arm?"

"It feels much better," she confirmed. "A bit sore,

but not nearly as bad as before." She paused and looked into his eyes. She did not smile. "Thank you for coming for me."

"Cecily, I . . . I love you and I want you to be my wife," he blurted. He had meant to give her a well-rehearsed, romantic speech, and then lay out practically all the reasons why she should marry him. But when she had spoken to him, looked at him so intently with only the two of them in the room, the flowery phrases and logical reasons had fled his mind completely.

"Do you believe me?" he asked.

"If you say that you love me, then I believe you. I am through not trusting you, Oliver. I do trust you. And, yes, I will marry you."

He stared at her. "Are you joking?"

She smiled then and chuckled. "No."

Oliver swallowed. "I know I am not worthy of you, Cecily, but I vow that I will spend the rest of my life—"

"Stop," she interrupted quietly. "You are more than worthy of me, Oliver. I am sorry if it was I who ever made you think differently. How did you know to come for me?"

"John Grey paid me a visit," he said, and Cecily winced. "He told me that you broke it off with him and why. It was the most wonderful news I've ever had in my life, and I must confess that I did not quite believe him at first. I left Bellemont immediately."

Her smile remained, but Oliver detected a note of sadness in it now. "I'm sorry I didn't tell you before."

"I wouldn't have gone, had you," he insisted.

"That is why I didn't tell you," she said with a wry

grin. Then she grew still again. "I'm glad you are happy about the baby."

Oliver frowned. "What baby?"

Cecily gave a huff of a laugh. "What baby! Only the most wonderful news you've ever had in your life? The reason you came for me?"

"Cecily, I came back because John Grey told me you broke it off with him—that you were in love with me," he said slowly. And then, more emphatically as her eyes widened and her mouth rounded into an O, *"What baby?"*

"You came back just for me?" she asked in disbelief.

"Of course I did! What in the bloody hell are you talking about, and whose baby?"

Cecily's brown eyes glistened. "Your baby, Oliver. Our baby."

He had been bent over her on the bed, but at her words, he placed his hands on the mattress and leaned hard, his head hanging down for a moment.

Our baby . . .

He looked up at her. "You're pregnant?"

She nodded slightly, her eyes wide. "I thought you knew. I thought that's why you came."

"You weren't going to tell me?" he demanded harshly.

"I was going to send a message to you from Hallowshire. I decided in the ruin that I no longer cared if that was the only reason you wanted me, I only knew that I could not live without you."

His anger fizzled like a candle flame in a downpour. "How could you have ever doubted my love for you?"

"It wasn't you I doubted. It was me. I didn't know who I was, Oliver. I do now."

"Who is that, then?" he asked.

"I am . . . your woman," she said simply. "I have been since . . . well, perhaps since I was born."

Oliver nodded. He understood.

And then he leaned toward her slowly, his mouth hovering over hers. "I have wanted to do this for weeks." And then he kissed her.

A sharp rap on the door drew him away from her mouth and then Sybilla Foxe's cool voice threw ice on Oliver's fire.

"Cee, you're awake. How are you feeling, darling?" She came to stand next to Oliver, and he noted the sheaf of parchment in her hands.

"Better, Sybilla. Thank you."

Oliver stood aright and turned on the blue-eyed woman. "Why didn't you tell me about the baby?"

"Oh, good—you know."

Oliver growled and stepped toward Sybilla. "I should throttle you!"

"Oliver, no," Cecily called out weakly from behind him. "It was not Sybilla's place to tell you. She did me a great honor by maintaining her silence. Put no blame on her."

Oliver knew Cecily was right, but his jaw still clenched nonetheless.

Sybilla Foxe gave him a smirk, with one raised eyebrow. "Thank you, Cee. And while we are on the topic of throttling each other, why did you not tell me exactly what was in the message you sent to the king some days ago? Hmm?"

Some of the fight went out of him then. "I was angry. Very angry, Sybilla."

"What did you tell him, Oliver?" Sybilla asked, almost gently. "I must know, you understand."

He nodded. "I pledged him my support in a siege against Fallstowe. I told him that you were prepared to resist."

"Oliver, you didn't!" Cecily gasped.

He turned and walked to the bedside, perching his hip there and taking Cecily's hand in both of his. "I'm sorry, Sybilla. If only you would have told me . . . if I would have known—"

"That you were vowing to hand over a vast fortune to Edward? Perhaps die in a siege for the privilege of it?"

Cecily turned her head on the pillow. "What is she talking about, Oliver?"

He reached into his tunic and brought out the two halves of the parchment, looked down at them ruefully.

Sybilla crossed the room and held out her hand. "I believe those belong to me."

"Would one of you please tell me what is going on?" Cecily demanded in a strident voice.

Sybilla took the pieces Oliver handed to her and then she, too, perched on the side of the bed, near Cecily's feet. Oliver turned to face her. Sybilla looked down at the now three parts of parchment in her hands, her face sad and pale, for a long moment. She looked nothing at all like the Sybilla Foxe Oliver had grown accustomed to, nothing at all like the sketches in August's book. This Sybilla was . . . different.

She at last raised her eyes to Oliver and Cecily.

"It is time for my confession."

* * *

A knot formed in Cecily's stomach, despite the fact that she was still more than a bit dazed at the euphoria surrounding her. Oliver was at her side, clasping her hand, and she was going to marry him. He had come back for her, and only her, and wanted to marry her without any knowledge of the child she carried.

But Sybilla's tone, her posture, her sad face, struck fear in Cecily. Sybilla was never bothered, never anxious.

"As you know, Cee, August and I entertained a very brief physical affair, last year at the winter feast. And I say with no pride that he was in love with me. He wanted to marry me. I have never professed an interest in matrimony, preferring instead to remain autonomous, even against the Crown, until I could secure safe positions for both you and Alys."

"Wait," Cecily interjected. "You said 'until.' What do you mean? That you would have married Oliver's brother had I left for Hallowshire right away?"

Sybilla ignored the questions. "I was unsure of your commitment to Hallowshire. Although you did a fine job of hiding it, I could sense your discontent with your future, Cecily. And so I suggested to August that we revisit the idea of a betrothal between you and Oliver."

"Why though?" Oliver asked, this time. "What good would that have done you?"

"If the king eventually executed me, you would have been the next in line for Fallstowe, Oliver," Sybilla said matter-of-factly, and it made Cecily's stomach turn. Cecily brought a hand to her mouth to still the tremble of her lips.

"But why me?" Oliver insisted. "It makes no sense, Sybilla. I was little more than a ne'er-do-well. Why would you entrust Fallstowe to me?"

"Because you were August's brother, Bellemont is a legitimate and valued holding, in accord with the Crown. Edward would be hard-pressed to take it from you, even though he would likely fine you outrageously. And because, with Cecily as your wife, Fallstowe would always be her home, a place Alys and her family could come to, as well. The king wants *me* now, you see. I have committed grave insubordination against him, and he would see me punished whether he reaps Fallstowe as a result or nay."

"You had more faith in me than my own brother," Oliver said, and Cecily clearly heard the dejected tone of his words.

"August and I were very much alike," Sybilla said with a sad smile. "He would never send someone else to perform a task he felt he could do better."

Cecily frowned, the knot in her stomach tightening, but she said nothing to interrupt Sybilla as she continued. She took her hand away from her mouth in order that it could join the one already in Oliver's grasp.

"After August refused a betrothal between the pair of you in no uncertain terms, and Alys was safely married to Piers and you seemed unsure regarding Hallowshire, Cee, I knew that I had to make a decision, else we could all lose Fallstowe forever."

"Sybilla," Cecily whispered. "What did you do?"

"I compromised."

Cecily knew what her sister had done, without seeing the proof. "You never compromise."

"I know," she said ruefully. "And there is a reason why, which will become clear in a moment. I shouldn't have, that is for certain. I sent a letter to the bishop." She dropped her eyes to her lap, to the parchments she was shuffling over and over.

"John Grey's bishop?" Oliver guessed, and when Sybilla nodded, Cecily felt her eyes go wide.

"John himself came to collect quite a large sum of money. After I met him and learned how unsure he was of his own role, I increased my donation to the bishop, with a request that John Grey be sent to Hallowshire temporarily. I asked him to return to Fallstowe specifically for you, Cee. I thought he would either hasten your departure to Hallowshire, or beg for your hand. Which he did."

"John Grey was your compromise?" Cecily asked, dumbfounded. "You thought to orchestrate my removal from Fallstowe, one way or the other?"

"Yes," Sybilla admitted. "But that was not the reason John Grey had originally come to Fallstowe."

Oliver chimed in then, his face a study of concentration. "He came to claim a large sum for the bishop," he prompted.

"Yes," Sybilla said lightly, looking down at the pages again for only a moment before looking back at Oliver. "He went to Bellemont, as well, of course. And when John Grey returned the payment to the bishop"—she looked into Cecily's eyes—"August and I were married by proxy."

The knot in Cecily's stomach snapped, and her breath huffed out of her as if escaping.

Sybilla was married. To August Bellecote.

She had been married to him when he died.

"How long?" Cecily croaked. "How long before—?"

"One day," Sybilla supplied. "I assume August was on his way to Fallstowe because he had received his copy of this." She held up the severed proclamation. "His plan was to have Oliver accompany him, and then the three of us would work out the details." She looked to Oliver. "He was to come to Fallstowe, negotiate a treaty with the king, and turn over the running of Bellemont to you."

"That's not all, Sybilla," Cecily said, and squeezed Oliver's hand. "Joan Barleg told me that August had relented—he was to agree to your suggestion that Oliver and I wed. It was to be a surprise."

Cecily heard Oliver swallow. "But I never met him that day. His death was my fault."

A wistful smile touched the corners of Sybilla's mouth before she turned to Oliver with a stern look. "No, you mustn't think that August died because of you. His death was not even Joan Barleg's fault, although her leaving him alone as she did, knowing he would die . . . it was unforgivable."

"Soulless scavenger," Cecily hissed. "I had no idea the type of woman she truly was."

"You always want to think the best of everyone, Cecily," Oliver said gently, and then grinned. "Save for me, of course."

Cecily gave him a rueful smile, then she grew solemn once more as she looked to Sybilla. "You are Oliver's sister-in-law. You are August's *wife*."

Sybilla looked across the room toward the blazing hearth and shook her head sadly. "No, I was never really his wife. Perhaps I am his widow, though. But the only people alive who know that are in this room now, save for the bishop. And he would never volunteer the information for fear of punishment from the king as well as a heavy tax on the coin I paid him."

"I'm so sorry, Sybilla," Cecily whispered, feeling tears sting her eyes. A thousand images swirled in her mind, of what life could have been like for Sybilla and August, had he lived. She could not help but think that Sybilla might have at last been happy.

Sybilla turned back to them suddenly. "You will be married right away."

Oliver nodded. "Yes. As soon as it can be arranged."

"Father Perry has recovered. I am sure he would be honored to perform the ceremony in Fallstowe's chapel, both of which I know are dear to you, Cee. Tonight, I think."

"Tonight?" Cecily gasped, and looked to Oliver.

The corners of his mouth were turned down as he seemed to think, then he nodded. "Yes, tonight is fine. I have nothing else pressing to do." He tossed a wink to Cecily.

"But, Alys and Piers aren't here! And I have no gown to wear! And—"

"There is no time for those things," Sybilla interjected gently. "Edward will send soldiers to Fallstowe now. They are likely already en route. You must be married and away from Fallstowe when they arrive. You have a family to think of now, both of you."

Oliver held out a palm, indicating the room in general. "I fail to see how the pair of us leaving Fallstowe will put us out of the king's reach. Once he finds out that you and August married, and that I have—through his death—inherited Fallstowe, it will be no burdensome task to find me."

"I will not leave you, Sybilla!" Cecily argued.

"You will leave me," Sybilla said firmly. "For the sake of your child growing up with a father, you most certainly will. And there is nothing for the king to find out."

Oliver laughed harshly. "Nothing for him to find out?" he challenged.

Sybilla's gaze went between Cecily's and Oliver's faces. "I love you both. I will love your child. And I will do everything that I can to protect all of you." She stood and walked swiftly across the room toward the hearth.

Cecily felt her eyebrows draw down hard. "Sybilla!"

She tossed the parchments onto the blaze.

"No!" Oliver shouted, and his hand ripped from Cecily's as he leapt across the room.

But he was too late. The parchment curled and melted into the wicked flames.

"You stupid woman!" Oliver shouted. "You have just burned whatever protection I could offer you!"

"It doesn't matter, Oliver," Sybilla said mildly, turning toward him. "The real truth—not those words on parchment—will come out. And when it does, there is no protection to be had for me. But the three of you, and Alys and Piers and their child, you will all be safe now."

"Sybilla, you're frightening me," Cecily said.

"Don't be afraid," Sybilla said to her, and gave her a rare, encouraging smile. "Everything is as it should be. Mother warned me of this. I did not enter into it ignorantly."

"Warned you of what?" Cecily demanded. "Sybilla, you must tell me—"

"I'll send a maid up to help you dress," Sybilla interrupted, and she walked to the door. "We shall join Father Perry in the chapel in . . . let's say two hours." She opened the door, but paused to look at them both. "I am very happy for you. Truly. And I know that August would be, as well."

Then she was gone.

Cecily and Oliver stared at each other for several moments, and Cecily knew that the shock on Oliver's face must be reflected in her own.

She began to cry then, and Oliver flew to her side, gathering her close.

"Be not sad for Sybilla, my love," he whispered into her hair. "She is doing as she pleases, what she feels is right, as she always does. And this time, I am inclined to trust her."

Cecily pulled away to look up at him. "Are you sure, Oliver?"

"Sure that I want to marry you?" he asked incredulously. "My darling, I have never been more sure of anything in my life."

"But, is this the right way?" she pressed.

He nodded briefly and then flashed her a smile. "I think it might be the only way."

Cecily drew a deep breath. "All right, then." She nodded. "All right."

"Ho there," he said gently, and placed a finger under her chin so that she would look at him. "We're getting married. *Tonight.*"

And then Cecily caught her breath. Whatever happened tomorrow, she would be Oliver's wife.

She began to cry again, but this time, she was smiling.

Chapter 27

The next pair of hours seemed like a very swift dream for Cecily. A maid had appeared in her room only moments after Sybilla left, bearing a beautiful rose gown that Cecily had never seen Sybilla wear. There was an ornate crispinette and veil, and matching slippers, as well. Oliver excused himself reluctantly as the maid assisted Cecily in a hurried toilette, brushing and scenting her hair before twisting it into a long rope of individual spirals. The bandages on her upper arm barely fit into the slim sleeve of the ivory underdress, but the pressure felt good to Cecily, and the wide sleeves of the gown proper hid any bulkiness.

Oliver returned from his own preparations just in time to take her elbow and lead her from her small chamber. He had wet his hair and discarded his tunic, stained with her blood. He would marry her in his billowing white shirt, and slim black hose. His eyes were merry now, his grin quick and infectious, and the pair of them actually hid their smiles of excitement behind their hands as they made their way from the keep and across the bailey to the chapel.

Cecily tried not to notice the scores of soldiers grimly and hurriedly crisscrossing the dirt beneath red torchlight, and Oliver did not mention them at all.

They stepped into the dark entry of the chapel, the smell of incense like a welcoming perfume to Cecily, and she breathed deep as her eyes welled again.

Father Perry beamed through his pale skin and tired-looking eyes. Cecily knelt at Sybilla's side, flashing Graves a smile, and the three remained silent as Father Perry ushered Oliver away. In moments, Oliver was kneeling at her side. He nudged her with an elbow and then gestured over his shoulder. Cecily rose and entered into that dark closet, ready to purge her soul of her doubts and fears before committing to Oliver before God.

Cecily could not help but notice that neither her sister nor Fallstowe's dignified steward partook of the penitential sacrament.

Then the four of them, Cecily, Oliver, Sybilla, and Graves, were standing before Father Perry and the altar.

Cecily and Oliver knelt, they prayed, they repeated their vows, promising their love and fidelity to each other and their maker. They shared the Host, and then a kiss.

And just like that, Saint Cecily became Lady Bellecote.

Father Perry embraced her first, with a kiss on her temple and a special whispered blessing in her ear.

Old Graves bowed over her hand and brushed his dry lips across her skin. "Has there ever been a more beautiful bride?" he asked rhetorically.

To which Oliver answered, "No, you old crab, there has not." Then he and Graves shared a clasping of hands.

Sybilla turned Cecily into her own arms and embraced her tightly. "Congratulations, Cee," she said. "I know you will be very happy."

"Thank you, Sybilla. For everything," she emphasized, and then pulled away. "I know we must be off first thing in the morn, but—"

"No," Sybilla interjected, and her eyes went to Oliver, too, as he came to stand at Cecily's side, his arm going around her waist possessively. "No. You must go now."

"Now?" Cecily squeaked.

"I'm not certain Cecily should be astride so soon after her fall and now that she is carrying our child," Oliver said.

"I've provided a conveyance and team," Sybilla said matter-of-factly. "Cecily, your personal things are already inside, as well as some food and drink for the journey. I'm sorry, Oliver, but your mount will have to be left behind. I can spare no man to drive you."

"Sybilla, aren't you being a little rash?" Oliver queried. "Surely we can wait until the morning, when my own mount is rested. I can tether him to—"

"You must go now," Sybilla insisted. "Please."

Cecily looked up to Oliver, prepared to fight if he said they must.

Her husband stared at her sister. "All right, Sybilla," he said quietly.

And then they were out of the chapel, where the carriage Sybilla had promised was waiting just outside the doors.

Sybilla embraced her again before Oliver helped her inside and closed the half door. Cecily placed her palms on the door and leaned out, the heavy drapes brushing her face.

"You will send word to Bellemont, won't you?" she begged. "I shan't be able to stand the thought of you here alone, not knowing what is happening."

"I will," Sybilla promised. "And I hope that I will see you again soon."

Cecily frowned as Oliver embraced her sister. "Do send word. If there is anything I can do, I will do it. I owe you so much, Sybilla."

"Just take care of them," Sybilla said, and pulled away. "Take care of them both, and drive as fast as you dare."

Oliver nodded with a grim look and then he leaned in the window to press a kiss on Cecily's mouth. "Give a rap if the ride is too rough."

The carriage rocked as Oliver took his seat above, and then Cecily swayed as the conveyance lurched forward. She leaned further out the window, waving to Sybilla as the carriage rattled into the barbican.

Sybilla raised her hand, standing with Graves in the midst of a storm of soldiers.

And then her sister was gone from Cecily's sight, the carriage wheels clattering over the drawbridge that had barely had time to lower before Oliver drove over it at full speed, away from Fallstowe. The drawbridge began rising again immediately.

The scores of torches on the battlements high above gave the illusion that Fallstowe was afire.

Sybilla let her hand drop to her side as the carriage carrying Cecily vanished into the black throat of the barbican.

She had fulfilled her promise. Her sisters were safely away, and happy.

Her general approached her, and Sybilla wasted no more time dwelling on the melancholy of her singularness.

"How far?" she asked of the soldier.

"An hour, at least, milady."

"How many?"

"It was difficult to estimate in the dark and from such a distance," the general said. "More than three hundred, certainly. Perhaps even twice that."

"Ready the men for a siege," Sybilla instructed. "Put out the torches once everyone is accounted for at their stations. Let them think they're catching us unawares."

"Should we open fire on them when they draw near enough?" the general asked.

"No. Wait," Sybilla said. "Let us fully know their intentions. Should they make a push in the end, or should you see the great war machines, send for me, and we shall plan our next move."

The general bowed, and then was off quickly about his grim duties.

Ever at her side, Graves asked, "What shall I do, Madam?"

Sybilla gave a great sigh. Who knew if she would be alive in two hours?

"You shall accompany me to the great hall and pour us both a very large drink, Graves."

Chapter 28

It was very early in the morning, and yet not quite dawn, when Oliver carried Cecily into his chamber at Bellemont—the poor angel was exhausted, having been unable to close her eyes the whole of the bumping, harried ride. But as tired as she was, her eyes were bright with curiosity as she looked around the room that had once belonged to August.

He thought perhaps their child would be born in this room, and the thought caused his heart to skip clumsily.

Argo and two servants followed them into the chamber, carrying one of Cecily's satchels and a tray of food and drink.

"Is there anything else you require of me, my lord?" Argo asked as the servants deposited their burdens and swept out of the room, yawning and rubbing at their eyes. Argo himself looked mussed, and Oliver was certain that he had been roused from his bed at word that a lone carriage was demanding entry to Bellemont.

"Send a pair of soldiers to roost some distance away from Fallstowe. Have them keep watch over the goings on there, and instruct one to report back to me this evening. Send a fresh man in his place when you see that he has returned."

He set Cecily on her feet and she turned away, her cheeks pale, as she swirled her cloak over August's favorite armchair and then began to dismantle her headpiece and veil.

"As you wish, my lord," Argo said with a shallow bow.

"And make sure they understand that they are not to engage or draw attention in any way—from anyone. Fallstowe will be vigilant and if they are discovered, they will likely be killed."

"I understand," Argo assured Oliver. "Good . . . er, morning my lord, Lady Bellecote."

The door was still closing when Cecily whirled around, a gentle smile on her face. "Oliver, I am Lady Bellecote."

He crossed the room to wrap his arms about her middle and she laughed as she smoothed her hands up his chest. "You certainly are. Are you happy?"

Cecily nodded. "Happier than I've ever been. I can hardly wait to see my new home."

"It will be my deepest honor to accompany you," Oliver said, and then dropped a kiss on her nose. "Bellemont cannot boast of a dangerous, superstitious old ruin, but we do have a waterfall that is quite lovely."

"You do?" she asked, delight clear in her face. "That sounds much more to my liking. Is it far?"

He took the hand not of her injured arm and led

her to the window. With only slight effort, the pane gave way with a rusty sounding creak and the cold, crisp air blew their hair back as it dashed into the room to play. His arm cleaved the black beyond the window frame as he pointed to the west.

"See you the outlines of those two hills?" She nodded, peering into the dark. "In that valley lies a deep lake, fed by that waterfall. August and I would swim there when we were boys."

"Will you take me there?" she asked, a smile in her voice.

"I'll take you anywhere you wish, wife," he whispered near her ear.

The wind threw a rogue tendril of her hair across her mouth, and Oliver brought up his hand to scrape it away before cupping her cheek in his hand and kissing her gently.

"How about bed?" she murmured against his lips.

Oliver stilled and drew away. "Cecily, your arm—"

She actually laughed. "The first time we made love, *your* arm was *broken,* but you performed well enough to get a child on me."

Oliver felt his face heat. "Well, it's not everyday you meet such a ravishing beauty in the midst of a crumbling pile of rocks, is it? But, speaking of our baby . . . "

"It's fine, Oliver," Cecily assured him quietly, and she reached up with one hand to run her fingers through the hair over his ear. "It will be fine. You can be gentle, can't you?"

Oliver felt his desire for her burst into flame like an oil lamp thrown into old hay. The cold breeze through the window, belying the heat of his passion, only fanned his want of her. "Oh, I daresay I can be very gentle."

He pulled her to him fully and kissed her while the wind caressed them both, stinging their skin, whispering of nature's own tempest, unseen but very real. A whicker of noise drew Oliver's attention, and his eyes opened to look for the source of the sound.

Over Cecily's shoulder, on the wide table, sat August's bound journal. The wind was fanning the pages so that Sybilla Foxe seemed to dance with joyful abandon across the pages. Another stiff gust of air, and the heavy chalice above it toppled, sending the cup of Fallstowe coins spilling onto the book, stopping the dance. Oliver felt a chill on the back of his neck.

"What is it?" Cecily asked worriedly, drawing her head back.

"Nothing," Oliver said, bringing his eyes back to her face and giving her a smile. He drew away slightly to close the window. "Just things blowing about. Do you need help changing?"

She gave him a sly smile. "I don't think so." And then she walked behind the tall dressing screen.

Oliver began unlacing his shirt, and strolled to the table. He let his fingers fall onto the open book. The coins had spilled over one of the blank pages— there was no haunting sketch to taint the moment.

All the same, Oliver gently pushed the coins onto the table with a shower of muffled clinks and then closed the book.

"Sorry, old chap," he whispered, and tapped the book twice with his forefinger.

He turned then, and noticed Cecily's satchel still sitting on the floor by the chair. He walked toward it, chuckling. "I think you've forgotten something, my dear," he said as he swiped up the bag and turned toward the screen.

"I didn't forget anything," Cecily said, stepping from behind the cover, completely nude.

The satchel fell from Oliver's hand and landed on the rug with a thud.

Cecily felt a delicious, warm spiral of desire in her stomach at the way Oliver was looking at her, but when he continued to stare after several moments, she huffed and put her hands on her hips.

He shook his head suddenly. "Sorry—did you say something?"

"No," she said with a smile. "But here I stand, clothed in only my skin, and you've not even removed your boots! Shall I dress again?"

"No! No, no, no!" Oliver rushed, lifting his leg and fighting with the top of his boot while he hopped toward her on one foot. "Only a moment, they practically fall off by themselves, I swear. *Aaagh!*"

Cecily brought her hands to her mouth and laughed as he fell over beyond the end of the bed.

"I'm all right," he called out, and Cecily laughed harder at the struggling sounds she heard. "Nothing broken this time!"

In a blink, he appeared standing again, and this time Cecily doubled over, her hands at her stomach— he was completely nude.

But when he came to stand before her and

wrapped his arms around her middle, his hot skin searing her cold flesh, the laughter stopped. She looked up into his eyes.

"I love you, Oliver," she said solemnly. "You're . . . you're . . ."

"What?" he whispered on a smile. "What am I?"

"Perfect," she finished. "Perfect, in every way."

He kissed her slowly, gently. "And you, my lady are . . ."

She wrapped one hand around the back of his neck, but had to be satisfied with her injured arm lying atop his. "What?" she challenged in a husky whisper, pressing her breasts into his bare chest, drawing her foot up the rear of his calf.

Oliver growled, and then picked her up and took her to the bed, where he lay her down gently and covered her body with his. Cecily gasped as his mouth explored her breasts, her navel, her hips, thighs. "You are . . . you are . . ."

"Never mind," she whispered, and he brought his mouth back to hers, kissing her while he explored her body with his hands. Her flesh was on fire, her body ached for him.

When he had taken her in the Foxe Ring, their coupling had been frantic, violent, passionate to the point of fear. But now, lying in his bed, Cecily felt an even more frightening depth of desire for him. Passion that meant giving her whole self over to him completely, forever. Until eternity had passed away.

He was true to his word, and took her gently, his deliberateness causing her to cry out. He slowly, incrementally increased his pace, rocking her into the mattress until she panted his name.

And then her time was come, and tears ran into her hairline as the universe brightened around her, the sun rising in that moment through the windowpane.

He was only a heartbeat behind her, giving a strangled cry, holding himself so still, and she looked upon his face, enchanted by the glory of him. Her husband.

He disentangled himself gently and lay down at her side, panting, pulling her close, covering her face in kisses.

She giggled and kissed him back. "I'm cold," she complained.

"Already playing the harping wife, are you?" He reached behind him and pulled the coverlet over them both, the cold, stiff embroidery bringing a little extra chill at first, and Cecily snuggled into Oliver's chest.

"Perhaps I will be a harping wife," she said on a happy sigh. "Isn't that a delightful notion? I vow it's better than being a saint." She paused and looked up at him with a warning glare. "Oliver, if you call me a saint in this moment, I vow I will strike you."

He shook his head with a chuckle. "I wouldn't dare." He stroked her face with the back of his fingers. "You, Lady Bellecote, are a perfect scoundrel."

Please turn the page for an exciting sneak peek
of Heather Grothaus's next historical romance,
coming soon from Kensington Publishing!

With one step, it would all be over.

Sybilla Foxe swayed with the stiff breeze that shoved its way between the battlements where she stood more than one hundred feet above the ground.

Beneath her, six hundred of King Edward's finest were readying to make war against her, their torches and balefires blooming in the night, the creaking of wooden beams and the clanging of metal wafting up to her as discordant notes from a demonic orchestra. The conductor of the affair had only just arrived in an ornate carriage, driven to the fore of the company and rocking to a stop. As of yet, no one had emerged.

To either side of Sybilla—indeed, around the whole of the castle's impressive topmost perimeter—Fallstowe's soldiers crouched behind the protective stone merlons of the castle's tallest turret, their own torches snuffed. They were one with the shadows cast by the bone white moon, round and glaring down on them. . . .

Save for Sybilla, who stood in an embrasure, her arms outstretched so that her palms held her fast within the teeth of the battlement. She knew that her silhouette would be visible to anyone with a keen eye who looked in just the right spot. The wind came again, pushing her, buffeting her so that Sybilla's spine bowed, her palms scraped against the stone. She was like the mainsail of a ship filled with a sea-borne tempest, her rigging straining where it was lashed to landlocked Fallstowe. Her hair blew forward around both sides of her face, catching in the seam of her mouth. If she but loosed her stays, the wind would rip her away from the turret into the night, wildly, silently, without remorse.

Sybilla closed her eyes and tilted her face up. Now she was the carved figurehead on the bow of the ship, so free and fearless. She could feel the grit beneath her slippers rolling as her feet slid almost imperceptibly nearer the abyss.

With one step, it could all be over. . . .

"Madam?"

The wind relented, and Sybilla sagged back between the merlons. Disappointment prickled along her jaw, causing her chin to tremble, her eyes to sting. She forced her reluctant arms to fold, stepping backward and down from the battlement and onto a mantlet, the large wooden shield ready to be put into service at a moment's notice. Sybilla turned calmly to face her most faithful friend—Fallstowe's aged steward—properly.

"Yes, Graves?"

In that instant, the air before Sybilla's face went white hot and flames flashed before her eyes with a blinding whoosh. A solid-sounding thunk echoed in the soles of her feet and both Sybilla and Graves looked down at the flaming arrow stuck in the thick wood of the mantlet, a handsbreadth before her right foot. A parchment was tied to its shaft.

Sybilla looked up at Fallstowe's steward in the same instant that he too raised his eyes.

"Shall I fetch that for you?"

Sybilla forced herself to swallow. She had been closer to death than she'd realized.

Without waiting for her answer, Graves reached out one long, thin arm and jerked the now sputtering missile free before snapping the shaft in half and tossing the glowing ash of the fletching to the stones. The only sounds atop the turret were the wind, the barely discernable rustle of armor covering the backs of impatient soldiers, and the scratching of Graves's fingernails against stiff parchment.

Sybilla could scarcely hear them above the blood pounding in her ears.

At last Graves handed the missive to her. Sybilla held the curled ends in her hands, turning the page more toward the bright moonlight. The page was covered with thin, scrawling characters, indecipherable in the night, but the ornate preface as well as the thick, heavy seal under her thumb were clear enough that Sybilla understood without reading the royal proclamation.

Edward I had come for her. The king meant to take Fallstowe, this night.

As if she had not already ascertained that fact by

the six hundred armed men arriving by moonlight to camp beyond her moat.

She sighed and dropped the missive to her side in one hand. "Thank you, Oliver," she muttered. Certainly Edward would have come for her eventually, but the king had no doubt been prompted to act by the message recently sent by Sybilla's newly acquired brother-in-law, Oliver Bellecote.

Sybilla hoped her younger sister, Cecily, was enjoying her wedding night more than she was.

Only a handful of months ago, the king himself had warned the youngest of the Foxe sisters, Alys, at his own court. Alys was now safely ensconced at bucolic Gillwick, with her husband, Piers.

It will come down to you, Sybilla. She heard the phrase in her mind, spoken to her so many times by her mother. She could still picture Amicia vividly, lying in the bed that was now Sybilla's, her useless right side both bolstered and half hidden by pillows.

And it will end with you.

Sybilla wondered who the king had sent to lead the siege against her, and she called to mind the ornate carriage she'd seen arrive below. She turned her face toward the battlements again, just as another flaming arrow whooshed over the crenellation and sunk into the wood at her feet.

Sybilla gasped this time, and she felt her brows draw together as she saw another parchment tied to this arrow's staff. She was becoming slightly irritated with this particular method of correspondence. The murmur of soldiers' armor was more insistent this time, and Sybilla knew they were anxious to act.

"My lady?" Her general rose from his position, obviously waiting for her to give the signal to return fire. His drawing hand hung at his hip, the exposed fingers in his glove catching the ivory moonlight as they clenched and unfurled.

"Hold, Wigmund," Sybilla cautioned.

"It nearly struck you," the knight argued. "'Tis obvious the thieves are aware of your presence—they think to avoid a fight should they fell you in advance."

"I know your men are eager. You will likely gain the battle you crave before the dawn has stepped both feet onto the earth." Sybilla looked back down at the arrow. "But I am as yet untouched. Hold."

"Madam?" Graves asked solicitously.

"I'll get it," Sybilla said, hitching her skirts up slightly into the crease of her hips in order to crouch down on the massive wooden shield. She untied the parchment, leaving the flames to flicker their little light while she unfurled the message and held it near the dying flame.

Shall we negotiate?
JG

Sybilla looked to the battlements instinctively, although from her crouched position she could see nothing but sky. Negotiate? She could see no points on which either side were willing or able to concede. The only knowledge that might save Sybilla and that the king couldn't know was aught which she had sworn to her mother while Amicia lay dying that she would never, ever tell.

Fallstowe might be taken, the Foxe family would be no more, Amicia's name would be synonymous with deception and scandal, but the greatest secret of all would be buried in a grave.

Most likely Sybilla's.

As if to emphasize the inevitability of her fate, another arrow lofted over the battlements, this time pinning the hem of Sybilla's gown to the wooden platform.

The roar of armor shook the night as soldiers rose like a black wave to the battlements, even as Wigmund bellowed "Place!" and was answered by the echoes of his lieutenants around the whole of Fallstowe Castle. The air trembled with a whiny reverberation, the audible tautness of hundreds of bowstrings.

Graves cleared his throat. "Won't you come away from the edge now, Madam?"

But instead of fear, Sybilla began to feel the familiar rumblings of anger. *"I said hold!"* Sybilla shouted up at Wigmund. "Hold your men!"

The general glared at her, but relayed the command. He did not order the men to stand down, and Sybilla had not expected him to. Sybilla knew they would only be pushed so far, with or without her word.

Still, once they fired on soldiers of the king, their fates were sealed.

Sybilla tossed the earlier plea for negotiations aside and, without unpinning the still-flaming arrow from her gown, removed the latest message.

Last chance.
JG

"That pompous ass," Sybilla growled, her fury spreading like thick ice on a deep lake. "Wigmund," she called out calmly as she jerked the extinguished arrow free from the wood.

"My lady?"

"Bring your bow. Wrap and dip a fletching—I want to be certain it is seen."

Sybilla turned the dead arrow in her hand, using her other hand to place the most recent missive on the flat shield. With the coaled end of the arrow she scratched a short, crude message, and then tossed her makeshift writing utensil aside.

When she looked up, Fallstowe's general stood above her, his longbow in one hand and a single arrow in the other, its end bulbous and dripping with pitch.

Sybilla stood in one swift motion, still anchored to the wooden shield by the flickering arrow, the parchment crumpled in her hand. She seized the projectile Wigmund offered and then glanced at the general out of the corner of her eye as she tied her message to the arrow.

"I haven't the strength to draw a longbow, good sir; I shall have the one across your back."

If the general was surprised that Fallstowe's lady intended to send the message herself, he hid it well, ducking his head to remove his shorter weapon and holding it toward Sybilla. Before she took it, she bent at the waist and yanked the flaming arrow from her hem, quickly touching it to the primed fletching in her hand. Then she grabbed the bow and turned to the battlements once more.

"I shall be the only one to fire," she advised her

general, and was satisfied as the command to hold made its way around the turret and away into the night.

Sybilla stepped into the embrasure and knocked her arrow, the bubbling pitch hissing, the heat from the flames rising up to warm her face. She knew she had only seconds before she was spotted. She quickly raised her elbows and lowered her weapon until she had sighted in on her target.

The carriage. A lone archer stood with his back leaned against the ornate conveyance, bow in one hand, arms crossed over his chest, as he conversed casually with another soldier. He paid Fallstowe no mind.

She drew the bow, her muscles quivering with effort. The flesh of the first two fingers of her right hand felt cut to the bone by the bowstring with no archer's glove to protect her. Her shoulders, chest strained, but she no longer felt like stepping off the ledge into oblivion. In fact, she felt rather better.

Below, the archer's face turned upward, and she heard his faint shout of surprised alarm.

One more fight then, for posterity's sake.

Sybilla felt her lips curve into a smile, then she let her arrow fly.

Books by Bestselling Author
Fern Michaels

___	**The Jury**	0-8217-7878-1	$6.99US/$9.99CAN
___	**Sweet Revenge**	0-8217-7879-X	$6.99US/$9.99CAN
___	**Lethal Justice**	0-8217-7880-3	$6.99US/$9.99CAN
___	**Free Fall**	0-8217-7881-1	$6.99US/$9.99CAN
___	**Fool Me Once**	0-8217-8071-9	$7.99US/$10.99CAN
___	**Vegas Rich**	0-8217-8112-X	$7.99US/$10.99CAN
___	**Hide and Seek**	1-4201-0184-6	$6.99US/$9.99CAN
___	**Hokus Pokus**	1-4201-0185-4	$6.99US/$9.99CAN
___	**Fast Track**	1-4201-0186-2	$6.99US/$9.99CAN
___	**Collateral Damage**	1-4201-0187-0	$6.99US/$9.99CAN
___	**Final Justice**	1-4201-0188-9	$6.99US/$9.99CAN
___	**Up Close and Personal**	0-8217-7956-7	$7.99US/$9.99CAN
___	**Under the Radar**	1-4201-0683-X	$6.99US/$9.99CAN
___	**Razor Sharp**	1-4201-0684-8	$7.99US/$10.99CAN
___	**Yesterday**	1-4201-1494-8	$5.99US/$6.99CAN
___	**Vanishing Act**	1-4201-0685-6	$7.99US/$10.99CAN
___	**Sara's Song**	1-4201-1493-X	$5.99US/$6.99CAN
___	**Deadly Deals**	1-4201-0686-4	$7.99US/$10.99CAN
___	**Game Over**	1-4201-0687-2	$7.99US/$10.99CAN
___	**Sins of Omission**	1-4201-1153-1	$7.99US/$10.99CAN
___	**Sins of the Flesh**	1-4201-1154-X	$7.99US/$10.99CAN
___	**Cross Roads**	1-4201-1192-2	$7.99US/$10.99CAN

Available Wherever Books Are Sold!
Check out our website at **www.kensingtonbooks.com**